Contents

The Last Frontier

The Sword of Cartimandua Series
Book 8
By
Griff Hosker

The Last Frontier

Published by Sword Books Ltd 2014
Copyright © Griff Hosker Second Edition

A CIP catalogue record for this title is available from the British Library.

Dedication

To all the people who have supported me so much. Thanks to Rich and Alison, Pam, Steve and Gordon. You make writing the books much easier!

Part One
Troubled Times

Chapter 1

Livius Lucullus Sallustius peered over the stern of the swiftly moving trireme. The Pillars of Hercules, through which they had passed the previous day, were now just a thin grey smudge on the distant horizon. At first, Lucius had taken to standing by the stern to look on Britannia and then latterly Aquitania, the scenes of many battles recently fought by the scarred young man. He glanced down at his disfigured legs; the result of torture by his brother Decius, Lucius knew that he would never be able to run again as he once had or even walk with any dignity but at least he had ended his family's disgrace with the death of his brother in the estuary in Aquitania. The damage to his legs had been a small price to pay for the honour which he had regained.

He noticed that the rollers which had pounded them all the way from Eboracum had now changed to gently rolling, inconsequential waves which barely disturbed the increasingly blue sea. They were in the waters owned, ruled and controlled by the mighty Roman Empire, they had moved away from the precipitous edge of the world to the very centre of its existence. The Pillars of Hercules seemed to mark the boundary between barbarity and danger to civilisation and security.

During the voyage, the crew had assiduously avoided him. Apart from pleasantries from the Praetorian Centurion, Titus Aculeo, sent to fetch him by the Emperor, he had lived in a silent and undisturbed world. Part of the silence was the fear that they carried a frumentari, one of Trajan's feared secret police. They were not to know that it had been a disguise to enable Livius and his companions to capture his brother and regain the gold stolen from Eboracum by them. He had not minded the silence for it gave him the chance to think and to weigh up his future. It allowed him to reflect on his military career and life thus far. He had spent too long in the service of Emperor's like Vespasian and Trajan to even consider a quiet retirement. He knew he had the money to do so and he knew where he would choose to spend the quiet, peaceful days of reflection, Morbium, where he could be close to those he loved the most, Gaius' family and the retired members of the exclusive club which had fought in Marcus' Horse. That was in his future. His present would be determined by his interview with Emperor Trajan and his acolyte Hadrian. Having been summoned to Rome, he had speculated upon its purpose, as the Centurion had said, it was for a reward, not a punishment. He had also implied, in their first brief conversation, that another task was required of him but what could he do for Rome with his crippled legs and damaged body?

Ostia made Eboracum look like a fishing port. The smell from the busy gateway to Rome assaulted his senses even before they could make out the buildings. The produce of the world seemed to be sucked into the port and then sent on the cobbled Roads to feed the greatest city in the world. Livius felt himself shrinking back against the rail. If Ostia was this powerful then how much more so would Rome be?

The Praetorian had his servant bring Livius' belongings from the hold and gestured for him to head for the gangway. In truth, Livius would have preferred to stay on board the trireme which had been his home for so many weeks rather than entering a world of which he knew nothing. The oppressive heat of the city and the smells emanating from the busy port of Ostia felt like an invisible barrier preventing him from stepping on to the gangplank which was the ship's umbilical cord. The Praetorian was eager to be rid of his charge and he took Livius' arm to propel him down the gangplank. As soon as his feet touched the stones of the wharf he felt unsteady as though he were standing on the pitching deck of a ship in a storm and not the solid stones of a road.

Titus Aculeo laughed at Livius' drunk act, "It always gets you when you step ashore. Don't worry Decurion, it doesn't last."

He took him by the arm and steered the Briton towards the imposing stone structure guarded by the soldiers of the Imperial Guard. The sentries immediately recognised the Praetorian and, from the looks on their faces and the speed of their salute, Livius surmised that the Praetorian was feared.

"You have two horses ready for us." It was not a request, it was a command and the sentries responded immediately.

"Yes, Centurion. We'll just get them."

Once mounted Livius felt less nervous. This was his territory, on the back of a horse. Although he felt guilty it was good to be above the human detritus which ebbed and flowed like a living sewer. He found that the smell of the horse was preferable to the smell of his fellow men. Around him was a sea not of saltwater but all manner of humanity, ebbing and flowing in a human tide.

The Praetorian noticed him as he wrinkled his nose. "This must be your first time in Italy. If you think this is bad then wait until we reach Rome then you will see and smell far worse things than this." He looked down disdainfully, as his horse nudged a cripple into the gutter, "It is no wonder that the Emperor lives on a hill above the maddening crowd."

"I am not used to towns. I am a cavalryman and more used to sleeping under the stars where it might be cold, especially in Britannia, but at least it is healthy. This smell does not bode well for health."

"You are right there Decurion. We have the plague galloping through the city every couple of years." He shrugged philosophically, "Gets rid of the weak and the rest, who remain, are stronger."

Livius glanced over at the callous soldier. Perhaps he was right. Livius and his men had taken many men's lives, what was the difference if they were taken by the Allfather? The road to Rome was a crowded heaving mass but the Praetorian's uniform and his free use of his vine staff ensured that their passage was as swift as it was possible to be. Once they had entered the Porta Ostiensis, the massive gate in the walls of Rome, then the wheeled traffic ceased as they were not permitted to use the roads during the hours of daylight. The thoroughfares were still thronged as the busy bees that made up Rome's population scurried about eagerly looking for a profit but at least there were no wagons or chariots to contend with.

"Where are you taking me Praetorian?"

As soon as the words were out of his mouth Livius regretted them as they sounded like he was issuing an order and Livius was intimidated by the huge Centurion with the icy eyes and arms rippling with knotted muscles. The steely glare he received in reply told him that he had been correct and the snarled answer ensured that he would not open his mouth again. "You have the honour of lodgings in the Castra Praetoria and you would think well to watch how you use the term Praetorian Not all my colleagues are as kind and thoughtful as I." Even as he was speaking the words the huge Centurion was slashing down on the head of an unfortunate traveller who had mistakenly stumbled against the warrior's mount.

Livius deemed it wiser to hold his tongue and refrain from any further irrelevant questions as they negotiated the capital of the Roman Empire. He glanced up as they passed the Palatine Hill and marvelled at the palace which adorned its crest. As he did so he shivered a little for when he did visit that edifice it would be to meet with the Emperor and Emperors, even one held in such high esteem as Trajan, could be precocious and unpredictable. Many visitors had arrived at the palace expected advancement only to have their remains end up in the Tiber.

The Praetorian camp was outside the walls of Rome on the northeastern side of the city but as it had control of its own gate this was not a problem. Livius was admitted with a cursory glance due to the towering presence of the Praetorian. He was pointed in the direction of the Principia, the camp office. "Present yourself at the Principia my role has finished. I have finished my stint as a baby sitter!" He started to turn away but then reined in his horse; he leaned close to Livius, speaking quietly for only the young Explorate to hear. "A word of advice Decurion. You seem like a decent sort. "He leaned forward and lowered his voice even further so that only Livius could hear. "Beware your tongue. Use your ears wisely and do not trust every smiling face. Rome is filled with those who appear as a friend. These are not your comrades be careful whom you trust." Nodding, as though to confirm his words, he rode away leaving Livius even more worried than he had been.

The optio behind the desk had been expecting him. He was a young officer with an arrogant air about him; he looked to Livius like a young nobleman on his way up through the ranks. He would probably end up commanding some auxiliaries on the frontier with no experience of war of any kind. Livius suddenly wondered why he had been expected and then he remembered the signal station at Ostia. Although it had taken them half a day to negotiate the road from the busy port the signal had been sent as soon as it had been sighted and the message would have reached Rome within an hour. The Empire was mighty indeed.

"Ah, Decurion. "The nasally voice grated on Livius' ears and oozed condescension, "You were to have been housed here in the camp, but as the Emperor is still in the East it has been decided that you will stay in an inn we have located for you. It is half a mile out of Rome on this road. It is the one with the sign of the black grapes. You will stay there until sent for." He threw over a small bag of coins. "This should be sufficient for your needs." He looked up, a cold look upon his face. "Do not return for more. There will be none forthcoming. You have one visit to this well so husband your finances accordingly."

From the sly look on the optio's face, Livius surmised that the optio had taken more than he had given as his cut; not that it bothered Livius. Around his waist was the belt which contained enough gold to keep him comfortable, it never left his body. Nodding his thanks he took the paltry bag of coins and mounted his horse once more. As he left by the camp's, Porta Decumana he noticed that the looks he received were very suspicious. He absentmindedly patted his hidden money belt in which were also secreted his letter from the Emperor and the frumentari pass. No-one had asked for their return and he was certain he would need them again. Having once suffered the horror of the Emperor's gaol he would be as prepared as it was possible to be.

When he reached the inn he was pleasantly surprised. He had expected his accommodation to be basic at best but the Praetorian optio has not risked the ire of an Emperor. Livius might look like a nobody but the fact that the Emperor had sent someone to the edge of the world had made the optio a little more circumspect. The innkeeper greeted Livius like a long lost son. The Decurion was in no doubt why; he would be expecting more business and a healthy return on accommodation provided for a guest of the Praetorians. The horse would be looked after like Pegasus, he was assured. Once Livius had found his room he decided that Rome was worthy of closer inspection and he would return to the capitol and explore its streets. The Explorate in Livius meant that he always tried to prepare for any contingency. If he had to leave Rome in a hurry then he wanted to know the quickest and the safest way.

Walking back along the road towards the city walls he reflected that the Emperor could return to Rome and the west in days or in months but whichever it was Livius felt that he had to find his way around the city and he began to examine the city with the eye of an Explorate. He decided to use another gate and avoid the inspection of the Praetorians. He headed for the Porta Esquilina which he knew from the landlord was further south but much busier than the one close to the Praetorian camp. He soon found out just how busy this gate was as its route was from the east and the road did not have to cross the Tiber and the bridges there. The wagons and carts were backed up down the road as they waited to enter the gates at dusk. Livius approached the gate confidently and the two sentries nodded to him as he walked through. Once inside he turned and looked at the others trying to gain admittance. They were all being searched and questioned. Why had they let him through so easily? He quickly discovered the reason; his sword and clothes identified him as a soldier; he was openly wearing a sword. Perversely that would guarantee minimum inspection as they were looking for any visitor intent on wrongdoing and hiding both their intentions and their weapons. He stored the information. When he returned to Britannia he would use that idea with his Explorates, new skills and techniques would make his spies even more effective than they were.

The cobbles began to hurt his injured legs but he gritted his teeth and persevered. He had exercised as much as possible on the ship and his legs were now stronger than when he left Eboracum but the cobbles and the jarring caused spasms of pain to shoot up his legs. If he was to become fully fit again then he needed to build up his muscles and his strength even further. Heading due west he saw the mighty buildings and temples on the Capitoline Hill begin to spread out and dominate the skyline looming above his head like something dropped there by the gods.

He had heard that the Forum was always a good place to start a visit to the Eternal City and, avoiding the newer Trajanic Forum he headed for Caesar's Forum. He was intrigued by the legend of Caesar and wanted to see where the great man had been struck down. It would also afford him the opportunity of visiting the Senate. Although not as powerful as it had once been, it was still an important body and one which every Emperor tried to rule and control.

After negotiating the crowded streets filled with people who seemed anxious to get somewhere finally, he reached Caesar's Forum, famed throughout the civilised world, he was surprised by its compact nature. The usual opportunists, who inhabited every city in the world, thronged around selling herbal remedies, get rich quick schemes, sexual favours or just tried to steal the purses of the unwary. Livius was far too accomplished a spy and scout to be caught out and every sense tingled. As he was jostled he felt the hand trying to creep beneath his jerkin. His own hand snapped out to grasp the arm which he twisted in one fluid motion. The high pitched yelp emerged from a young boy whose terrified face peered up at Livius.

"Please don't hurt me, sir!"

Livius saw the boy's eyes flick to the column of vigiles on the other side of the forum. "Well son if you do try to steal then you should expect to be punished," he pulled out his razor-sharp pugeo with his left hand. "What I should do is slice off a couple of your fingers and mark your forehead so that everyone will know you are a thief." The point of the pugeo pricked the centre of the boy's forehead drawing a tiny droplet of blood.

The boy's face filled with terror and tears welled in his wide eyes. "No sir. Please, sir! It is my first time! I have never stolen before! I promise I'll never do it again!"

"Now you are adding lying to your crimes perhaps your tongue would be better being fed to a dog!" The boy was squirming and weeping with terror.

"Now then Livius surely you aren't going to hurt the boy when he actually failed to relieve you of your purse?"

Livius recognised the voice immediately. "Julius!"

He turned, still holding on to the boy's wrist, to see his old Decurion Princeps, Julius Demetrius, now Senator of Rome. The years had been kind to the old warrior and yet he showed his age. There was a paunch there which was missing in Marcus Maximunius and Gaius Aurelius, the other officers left from Marcus' Horse. The hair was whiter and showed signs of thinning. But the face was still as honest as always and the smile was genuine. "I think, before you break his arm, we should deal with this urchin." He turned to the boy and held his arm. "Now then boy what is your name?"

A small crowd of people had gathered around them and the boy could see that he would not be able to escape. He relaxed his arm and Livius let go of his vice-like grip. The boy rubbed his arm. "Furax sir."

"Ah the magpie and the thief," Julius liked the irony of the name, "well you are well named. Do you have parents?"

The boy shook his head. "Not living sir."

"And where do you live?"

The boy vaguely gestured off to the north. "Near to the Lupanar sir."

Julius nodded and patted the boy's head. Livius looked at him curiously. "The Lupanar?"

"The red-light district Livius where the prostitutes are to be found." He turned back to Furax. He held out a coin. "I will give you this coin. Wait over there and when I call you, come back and there will be more. Do you understand?" Nodding the boy moved to the wall of the Temple of Peace which afforded some shade from the blazing sun.

Livius shook his head sadly. "You'll never see that coin again Julius."

"I wouldn't be too sure Livius. Some of these boys barely steal enough to feed themselves. Many end up selling themselves in the Lupanar, sexual favours for the young rich Romans, in exchange for a little food." He took him by the arm and led him to the wine seller who had an awning which gave shelter from the sun's rays. Julius pointed at the wine he wanted and then paid for the two beakers. "Before I find out why you are here in Rome let us have a toast to Marcus' Horse."

They both toasted each other and Livius swallowed the whole beaker. "Marcus' Horse no longer exists Julius. It was disbanded when the numbers fell."

"I know. I follow events in Britannia as best I can. I know that you and the remnants of the ala did well in the last rebellion." He paused to sip at his wine and watch Livius' face for a reaction. "The one led by your brother and Fainch's daughter." Livius' face and body stiffened at the memory and the disgrace and he nodded. "Where have you been since then? That was a couple of years ago. Since then I have heard nothing of you or our men. I heard that the Ninth had a problem in the land of the Selgovae but other than that…"

Livius ordered two more beakers and then told Julius of the events of the past year culminating in the death of Decius. "And when I reached Eboracum I was summoned by the Emperor to Rome to be rewarded."

Julius suddenly became serious. "I see and the Emperor is not here. Where are you staying? In the palace?"

Livius shook his head. "I was supposed to be staying in the Praetorian barracks but the Praetorian Optio had found accommodation for me at an inn."

Julius pulled Livius to one side, his eyes darting from side to side. "You must come and stay with me. I like this not. The Emperor is not a well man and there are senators in Rome just waiting to take power. Someone who is important to the Emperor could be considered a threat."

"I am just a Decurion Julius. I am not important." Livius thought that Julius was overreacting. He was not a threat to anyone anymore; he was a crippled old soldier.

"Do not deceive yourself. You are important to someone." He snapped his fingers and Furax, who had appeared to be asleep raced over and stood with eager palm outstretched.

"Sir?"

He turned to Livius. "What is the name of the inn?"

"It is the sign of the Grapes, just past the Castra Praetoria."

Julius looked at the boy. "Do you know where it is?" The boy nodded his head eagerly. Julius gave him five coins. "Here is more money than you would see in a week. Go to the inn and tell the innkeeper that you are this officer's servant and you are going to look after his horse. Tell him that he is staying in Rome with a relative. You will collect his belongings from his room and put them in the stable with the horse. You can sleep there tonight and tomorrow bring the horse and the belongings to my home." He looked curiously at the young boy who had overcome his terror and now looked quite confident. "Do you know where I live?" The boy shook his head, "Casa Demetrius?"

"Oh yes, sir. It is the largest house in the Viminal."

"Good boy. Then tomorrow you can bring the horse and his belongings to my house where I will reward you with another five coins."

The boy's face lit up. "Oh yes sir!"

"Off you go then." They watched the urchin dance his way through the crowds and Julius led Livius towards the Viminal.

"Well, that is ten coins, my horse and my traps that we will never see again." Julius shook his head, a smile on his face. The boy would return, he knew that. The smile suddenly left his face and Livius was suddenly aware that Julius was gripping his arm and looked nervous. "What is it, Julius. This isn't like you?"

9

"Keep your hand on your sword for these are dangerous times. You were watched in the Forum. I saw at least two men, and they are still following us." Livius looked quickly around, annoyed that he had missed them. "You won't be able to see them but they are professionals. Someone is very interested in you young man and I shall do all in my power to protect you."

By the time they were in the bath in Julius' magnificent house, Livius was exhausted. His legs were hurting and he felt hungry. His last meal had been aboard the trireme and it was now becoming dark. At least it was cooler now. He felt his face and it seemed to be on fire. Julius looked over and saw the distress on his face as the pain in his legs suddenly coursed through his body. The Senator waved to the servants to dismiss them. "We will send for them when we are ready for a massage. And fear not Livius I have ordered food for us but we eat later in the city because of the heat."

"Do not worry about me, Julius. I am an old soldier remember. As an Explorate I sometimes went days without eating. Will your wife be joining us?"

Julius' face darkened. "She died last year. The doctors said it was something she ate but..."

"But you think otherwise. Why?"

"You are as quick as ever Livius. Yes, I think she was poisoned but I think it was intended for me. As I told you politics in Rome is a dangerous business. I am too honest for many and cannot be bought. In Rome, you buy your support and achieve what you may. I do not play that game." He saw Livius look behind him. "I have sent my men out to discourage those who followed you." He shrugged, "they may be replaced and if so it will tell us just how important they think you are."

Livius climbed out of the hot bath and plunged himself into the ice pool. He took a towel and lay on one of the marble slabs looking up at the corrugated concrete ceiling. "That's better. I cannot think when I am hot. Why do you think I was followed, Julius?"

"Have you heard of someone called Senator Lucius Quietus?"

"I can't say I have. I met someone called Hadrian and someone else called Attianus when I was sent on my mission but they are the only Romans I have met. Apart from the two Praetorians, of course."

"Ah, then you have it all. Attianus is a mentor to Hadrian who is Trajan's right-hand man." He paused and then confided, "In my view a good man and a sound leader. Then you have Lucius Quietus who is the Emperor's left-hand man if you will." He smiled at his own joke. The left hand was always considered suspicious, indeed sinister. "Hadrian and Quietus hate each other. "If the Emperor's life were to come to an early end, and from the reports I have, he is a little unwell at the moment, then these two would engage in a power struggle. It could even mean war."

"But where do I come in? Surely I am not important."

"I would not have thought so until you told me your story. Let us look at it. You met Hadrian but not Quietus. You successfully killed an enemy of the state. You recovered a vast amount of gold. Added to which your name may well be known to Quietus as one of the Frumentarii. "

"But that was just a cover!"

"Lucius does not know that. He will have bribed the clerk and discovered that you received the letter from Trajan himself. As you told me, your mission was only known to the Governor of Britannia, who by the way was murdered last year, Hadrian and the Emperor. As far as Senator Lucius Quietus is concerned you are the most dangerous man in Rome now that Hadrian is with the Emperor in the east."

"Suddenly being a scout behind the enemy lines doesn't seem such a bad place to be."

Chapter 2

Livius felt refreshed when he awoke in the cool bedroom of Julius' magnificent house. He opened his eyes to a brightly painted mural depicting Roman auxiliaries fighting barbarians. Livius smiled as he stood and stretched. His former commander's heart was, like his, with Marcus' Horse and the bonds they had formed which continued long after the events were but a memory. He found fresh clothes at the foot of his bed and noticed that they were more senatorial than utilitarian. Julius had been kind enough to ignore the rough dress which Livius had worn the previous day.

As he dressed he realised that at one time he too would have worn the finest clothes and disdained those who did not. The days of life at his uncle's court now seemed a lifetime away and he had become accustomed to dressing for action. His time in the ala had changed him irrevocably. Feeling somewhat awkward in his clean bright clothes he made his way to the dining room wondering what action he might actually have now. He hoped that Julius was exaggerating the danger he was really in but, as he wandered down beautifully intricate mosaic lined corridors, he realised that the stakes that this Quietus was playing for were so high that any obstacle, no matter how insignificant, would have to be removed. He was just such an obstacle; a miniscule object but one which would have to be eliminated.

Julius was already eating when Livius entered. "I hope you don't mind but I started…"

Livius dismissed the apology with a wave of his hand. "I am just grateful that you have given me sanctuary."

As Livius began to take fruits and cheeses Julius looked at his young friend. The years had filled out the callow youth who had so nearly lost his life on the cross. The intrigues and plots of his uncle and brother had almost taken an innocent life. He was now an assured and confident leader of men. Over the years Julius had received reports of the heroics of Livius and the others in the ala. He sadly reflected that most of those he knew, Marcus, Decius, Gaelwyn and Macro were now dead but their memory lived on and as long as the deeds of Livius and his men continued, so would that memory. "I sent a servant to inform the Praetorians of your new lodgings. When that boy reappears…"

"If he reappears."

"I think you misjudge him Livius. He will return and not just because he has five more coins coming. There are many such orphans living in Rome. The fact that he lives near the Lupanar tells me much.

He was probably the liaison between a customer and a whore. Who knows, the father may even have been a soldier on leave. How many times did our men pay for a prostitute and then never think of any consequences?"

"We normally got nowhere near civilisation if memory serves."

Julius laughed. "I am amazed that you call some of the places we visited civilisation but I wonder how many offspring of the ala are now eking out a living on the frontier? So do not judge Furax too harshly. Who knows, he may come of good stock."

When they had finished eating Livius stood and stretched. "Well, Julius, what is the plan?"

"Plan?"

"Yes, what will we do now and," he added ominously, "and in the future. From what you said last night, and, by the way, thank you for giving me the nightmares of knives and poisons in the night."

"I am sorry Livius but I had to let you know the danger you were in. When I took over from my father I had to learn that there was little honour in the Senate. I was used to dealing with barbarians who seemed like paragons of virtue when compared with the Senate." He led Livius out into a quadrangle lined with fragrant olive and lemon trees surrounding a tinkling fountain in the centre. "We will sit here it is cool and calming. I find I can think here." They reclined on the couches placed there. "Let us look at your problem. Here you are safe. When you need to leave the house, I will send two of my servants to accompany and safeguard you." Livius looked up sceptically. "Oh do not worry about my men. I employ ex-soldiers who have retired but do not wish to take up a ploughshare. You will be safe. I have sent a letter to Hadrian informing him of your arrival. He knows me and, I believe trusts me. He will advise the Emperor. As they are only in Cilicia then the letter should reach him by next week. Until then you rest," he nodded at Livius' damaged legs, "and I will get my masseur to work on your legs. Soon you will be as fit as you ever were."

They were disturbed by a sudden noise from the entrance of the house. Livius looked in concern at Julius who shook his head. "My doormen can stop any who wish to do you harm."

They heard shouts of, "Stop!" and heard the sound of caligae pounding down the mosaic corridors. Suddenly Furax burst into the room with the doormen in hot attendance.

"Sorry, Dominus. We tried to stop him. He said some nonsense about working for you."

Smiling Julius held up his hand. "Thank you, Cato, but in a way, he does sort of work for me. You may leave us." Furax's body was heaving with exertion and emotion. Julius noticed that the boy's face was bleeding. His face hardening he asked, "Did my men do this?"

"No dominus. It was at the inn."

"The innkeeper?" Furax shook his head, his whole body convulsed with sobs and shock.

Livius came over. "Let him have a drink Julius and sit and compose himself. I think there is more here than meets the eye."

Julius nodded and brought over a beaker of wine which he heavily watered. "Drink this boy and, when you are ready then you can tell us your story."

They watched as the boy swallowed the whole beaker and then he looked from one face to the other. He gave deep sigh and then launched into his explanation. "I did as you asked. The innkeeper was suspicious at first but when he found I only wished to sleep in the stable he allowed me to do so. I groomed your horse, had the food I had bought and then I slept. I was awoken in the night by the sounds of men fighting and people shouting and screaming. When I looked out of the stable I could see that there were armed men and they were questioning the innkeeper. There were bleeding bodies on the floor. I saw him point at the stables and then they killed him. As soon as I saw them come towards the stables then I knew that they sought me." His tearful face turned towards Livius. "I am sorry sir. I thought only of myself. I left your belongings in the stable with your horse and I ran."

Livius went over and put his arms around the boy's shoulders. "The horse was not mine and there was nothing of value in the inn." He looked over and nodded at Julius. "You were the only thing of value and you escaped. Continue."

"They tried to get hold of me but I kicked them and bit them. One of them tried to stab me with his dagger," he held his hand up to his injured face, "they did this."

Julius noticed, for the first time, the wound. He called for a servant. "Clean up this boy's wound and tell Cato to be on his guard. We may be in danger. Carry on Furax."

"There is little more to tell sir. I ran through the streets. I wanted to come here straight away, to tell you, but I knew that the gates would be closed and…" he paused, almost afraid to continue.

"Carry on Furax. Remember what I said yesterday, the truth cannot hurt you," Livius' words seemed to reassure the terrified boy.

"I think that they were soldiers sir. The ones who killed the innkeeper and tried to get me, I mean they didn't have helmets or shields but they had gladii and pugeos and their caligae, well sir I have seen enough soldiers at the Lupanar to know those when I see them."

14

They both smiled and nodded at the boy to continue. "Well sir I hid near to the Esquilina gate and when they opened it I came in with a party of merchants and then, well sir, I am here."

The two ex-soldiers looked at each other. Livius smiled approvingly at Furax. "You have done well and you will stay with us where you will be safe." Livius smiled at the look of relief on the boy's face. "Go with Atticus here, he is a Greek and the best doctor I know. He will tend to your wound and feed you." The bald physician took Furax by the elbow and led him from the room. "He is a good and kind man Livius, he will heal the boy both inside and out. Our little thief did well."

Livius looked at the door which had seemed so safe and secure and now seemed so dangerous. "I have put you in enough danger, Julius. And now I have endangered the life of a child. I will leave and go back to Britannia."

Julius dismissed the concept with an irritated wave of his hand. "You will do no such thing. Firstly, you are a friend and a comrade; we did not fight together side by side for me to desert you at the first sign of trouble. Secondly, they will look for ships to Britannia. Quietus must think you are more important than you actually are and thirdly this is bigger than you Livius. This concerns the Emperor and the safety of the Empire. If Quietus wins then my life would be forfeit anyway. He likes me not. No Livius Britannia is not a safe haven for you at the moment. Here, although there is danger, is safer for you, and the boy."

Livius studied the mural on the wall before him. It was a battle scene. "So, we have something of a dilemma then." Now that it was a military problem Livius' mind began to work more effectively. "If they are soldiers then I assume they are Praetorians." Suddenly the words of the Praetorian Centurion came back to him. "It is not all of the Praetorians. I think it is a group of them; I met one Praetorian who warned me of the danger I might be in."

Julius jumped up. "You are right and that makes sense. Quietus would have bought some of them. He would only need a century or two and he is a rich man; he could easily afford them. The question is where next? This is not a fortress and we certainly couldn't hold it against a century of Praetorians. I will send another message to Hadrian. He needs to know of the treachery and intrigue here. He will inform the Emperor. The message will take time to reach him which means that we need to hide out for at least two more weeks." He led Livius to his study where he took out a wax tablet.

"If that is intercepted won't it alert Quietus?"

"Hadrian and I use a code. Rome is not a safe place and wise men use discretion. We will go to Surrentum. I have just purchased a villa there although I have never visited it. It will take Quietus some time to discover where we have gone. The Emperor has a villa at Capreae just across the bay and that might prove useful to us all." He added enigmatically.

"Isn't that where Tiberius lived, where he ran the Empire?"

"It is. Not far from Neapolis. "

"But won't they be able to follow us there?"

"That is the beauty of the plan. We will go by sea and, hopefully, Quietus will assume we have gone to Britannia. Remember the boy merely told the innkeeper that you had sent him and you were staying with a relative. He will discover it is me but by then we will have left. We need to move quickly. Cato!"

By the time that Cato had completed his master's instructions, it was noon and the streets were emptying as people fled the heat of the day. One of Julius' men had already left to secure a ship at Ostia while Cato had organised the horses and guards. Julius had made it clear that they did not wish to attract attention and his men had begun to head for the port singly and in pairs to wait along the route and provide protection. "The problem is Livius you and the boy. The Praetorians will be looking for you." He had smiled when he addressed Furax and Livius. "We will dress you like women, with a veil and you will be carried in a closed carriage carried by two slaves."

"Women! We'll never carry it off. If they look inside…"

"If they look inside they will see a mother and daughter whose heads are covered in cloth and whose faces are hidden behind a veil. If you hide your hands and lower your eyes when they look inside they will see what they expect to see. Once on the ship, you can revert to being yourselves." He looked intently at Livius. "It is the only way to get you and the boy out of the city" Reluctantly Livius agreed.

By the time Julius, his slaves and the carriage along with Atticus and Cato were walking towards the Porta Ostiensis, the roads had emptied of all but the most desperate to make a journey. The problem that created was that they were the only group travelling through the gate at that time of day. The interest of the sentries was piqued. However, once they saw the Imperial Purple of the Senator they allowed them through, without bothering to look inside. Julius knew, however, that they would be remembered and if the Praetorian traitors asked the vigiles about them, they would be identified. All that mattered was that they reach the port before their pursuers. Julius hoped that they would have at least a day, for once at sea, it would be harder to follow them; the Mare Nostrum was big and ships could hide in many places. The ex-Decurion Princeps was beginning to enjoy the action although he knew that the stakes for which they were playing were high. He also realised that for the first time since leaving Britannia his actions would have far-reaching consequences. He was alive once more; he was no longer the crippled ex-soldier looking at retirement.

As they travelled down the main road to the port, they picked up the guards sent ahead by Julius. Although they remained at a discreet distance, they surrounded the cargo and reached the port safely.

When they reached the port it was obvious that there were observers all around. Although the port had its normal quota of idlers these idlers looked like ex-soldiers and were appraising everyone just a little too closely. Cato was approached by his messenger who spoke quietly into the old legionary's ear. After a moment or two, he returned to Julius. "It is the liburnian over there sir. '*The Swan*'." He gestured to a small two-masted craft at the end of the quay. "Antoninus said that you would pay the fee. It seemed easier sir rather than him negotiating." He added apologetically.

Julius put his arm around Cato's shoulder. "Do not apologise you have done well." He looked around at the people he had brought with him. "As much as I would like to take all of these men with us I fear it would attract too much attention. Go with Antoninus and Atticus and take our guests onboard. I will follow. Then you can send half the men back to the domus and have the other half come aboard singly and quietly."

The hardest part was negotiating the gangplank on to the ship and Livius feared that they would be plunged into the stinking foetid water of the busy harbour. Julius' men were up to the task for they carried the carriage successfully up the narrow plank and they found themselves on board the ship. The curtains were opened on the seaward side and Cato's gnarled face appeared grinning. "If you two ladies would like to slip out on this side you can go below decks and change into more suitable attire."

By the time the carriage had been returned to the land, Julius and half of his men were aboard. Julius went, with Antoninus to speak with the captain. The captain was ancient. He had but one tooth in his mouth and barely a hair on his head which resembled a dried fig left in the sun too long. He was barely taller than Furax but the hugely muscled arms belied his size.

"Captain...?"

"Hercules." He shrugged apologetically as Julius appraised him," my parents had grand ideas for me and thought I would be bigger than I actually turned out to be. Your man here said you needed passage. Where to?"

Julius drew him to one side away from his crew. "Firstly, do you trust your crew?"

Hercules looked around. "Some of them as for others...? Why do you ask?"

Julius looked closely at him. "I judge you to be an honest man and as such I will deal with you honestly. We are being pursued by people who wish my two friends harm. They are also working against the interests of the Emperor." Hercules shrugged as though that was not his problem. "All of this is nothing to you I know but it means that your ship might come to harm and as an honest man myself I could not accept that. I would like to buy your ship."

Hercules showed surprise for the first time. "Buy my ship? That seems a little excessive for a voyage. Where are we sailing to? The edge of the world?"

Julius looked grimly at the man. "I have been to the edge of the world my friend and it is not as dangerous as the waters into which we may sail." The old man looked with new respect at the paunchy senator who had looked so soft when he boarded the ship. "No the voyage is not long but I, we, may need the ship again and if it is mine to command then..." he could see the indecision on Hercules' face. "When I have finished with your vessel then I will give it back to you as a gift."

The sceptical look which appeared on the old captain's face told Julius much. "Why?"

"An honest question and you deserve an honest answer. I am rich but the value of my passengers to me is greater than any gold. One hundred gold aurei is the price I will pay you."

Hercules gasped. The amount was more than the old ship was worth, in fact, the Senator could have bought a small fleet of 'Swans' for that. "That is a princely sum."

"My friends are worth it."

The captain spat on his hand and held it out. Julius did the same and they shook hands. "The tide is right for the next few hours. Are all your men aboard?" Julius glanced around and nodded. "Then we had better slip it looks as though your pursuers are here." He pointed over to where eight Praetorians had galloped up to the vigiles at the Custom House. They would not know which ship they were on but it would not take them long to find out.

"Then let us go." Hercules gave him a quizzical look. "Ah, the course. Our destination is Surrentum but could you sail towards the Pillars of Hercules until dark?"

"You wish them to think we are travelling west and not south. Aye, that will not be a problem." He turned and began to roar orders, a huge voice from such a small body. "Cast off forrard, hoist the foresail. Come on you lubbers, the tide is waiting."

Leaving Hercules to his business Julius descended to speak with Livius. They had crossed their own Rubicon; there would be no going back now.

By the time Livius had changed into male attire once more the ship was far enough out of Ostia for him to come up on the deck. Furax joined them, as excited as any that he was at sea. Hercules, leaning easily on the tiller grinned. "Ah, the ladies! Looking a little better now than when you arrived."

Julius introduced him. "This is my friend Livius and this, my friend, is Hercules our captain."

Livius took a step back to view him better. "I thought he would have been bigger."

Hercules grinned, "I've not been well. Now if you gentlemen would keep out of my way, go forrard, then I will steer this ship and we will try to confuse our friends." He gestured to the horizon where they could make out a small sail. "I think we are being followed."

Julius and Livius walked along the gently pitching deck with Cato and Furax in attendance. "It looks like we have been tumbled."

"Yes, Livius but the plan is still a good one. Once it is dark then the captain will turn south and sail south until dawn then we will head east and by noon we will be in my villa. Already two of my men are riding along the Via Appia and the Via Popilia to prepare the villa for us. They have weapons with them. Once at the villa we will have more security."

Their first sight of Surrentum took away Livius' breath. All that he saw was a wall of stone rising; it seemed, to the heavens. It seemed so high that it was impossible for anyone to ascend the heights, certainly not from the sea. Julius pointed to the island they had passed to the south. "That is Capreae and the reason we are here. The Emperor keeps ships there and it is where Hadrian will come when he returns from the east. It is but a short boat ride from my villa and the villa, as you can see is safe enough."

"How in the Allfather's name will we get up there?"

"There is a path up the cliff but halfway along I believe that there is a tunnel which takes us to the heart of my villa. It is one of the reasons I bought this property. Its previous owner liked to have a safe way in and out and, in the present political climate, I thought it judicious to do the same."

There was a small harbour in which a few fishing boats bobbed up and down; their fishing was a nocturnal activity and, as Livius plucked the sweaty cloth from his body, he could understand why. The heat was overpowering and the humidity seemed to suck the energy from their bodies much as the wind was plucked from their sails as they edged closer to the jetty.

Julius turned to Hercules. "I think we will be safe for a few days should you wish to take on supplies. And well done, you did well to lose our follower." The Captain had obviously evaded others before for as soon as it was dark he had turned north and then east and finally south so that he turned a full circle around the boat that was trying to catch them.

The old man nodded, accepting the praise, which he knew he had deserved. "I will do that but I noticed a beach just down the coast. I think I will check the old girl's bottom. That way I can be close enough to return quickly to pick you up. If we have to leave in a hurry then I want to be able to outrun those who follow." He pointed to the skiff which they towed. "I will leave two men here. If you need me send them and I can be here within half a day. Once her hull is clean I will return."

Julius clasped his arm. "Thank you, Hercules."

As they watched the ship head south Livius turned to Julius. "You are a trusting soul. What is to stop him from leaving with your gold and your ship?"

"Nothing!" He turned to begin to walk up the cliff path.

Livius followed him. "Nothing? Do you think he will return?"

Julius looked paternally at Livius. "I think old friend that your experiences with your brother and Morwenna have coloured your judgement. Learn to see into people and judge them. As I did with Furax and as I now do with Hercules. There are those that you can trust and those who will deceive you. You need to learn the skills to decide which is which."

Chapter 3

Radha was nervous as she awaited the boat which would take her across the short stretch of water to Manavia, home of the Witch Queen, Morwenna. The confident young Queen of the Votadini had left her husband, Lugubelenus, consolidating their land following their eviction of the Roman Army from the territory north of the Stanegate. The Ninth Legion had been all but destroyed in their short campaign and his wife Radha had been instrumental in that success. Buoyed by their victory, revered and honoured by husband, warriors and people alike, Radha had planned this quest, this pilgrimage to visit Morwenna, the High Priestess of the Mother cult, even while she was helping to destroy the vaunted Ninth legion. Morwenna had almost destroyed the Roman stranglehold in the North and Radha was anxious to tap into the mystical power which the infamous witch possessed. Morwenna's mother, Fainch, was still a legend north of the land ruled by Rome and her defiant death after the battle of Mons Graupius was still spoken of in hushed terms around the fires in the long nights of winter. Radha had some powers but she had persuaded her husband that she needed to seek the advice of such a powerful adversary of Rome and increase her magic to finally eradicate all traces of Roman rule. Travelling discreetly with a handful of bodyguards and attendants she had made it to the west coast of Britannia undetected by the fragmented Roman patrols. The worst wait had been for the contact who had secured their boat journey to Manavia and now Radha could see the red sail looming large on the horizon. She almost giggled in anticipation; soon she would meet the most powerful woman in Britannia a woman who had outlived many partners both warriors and fellow witches. Radha felt the tingle of excitement course through her veins as she fantasised about the meeting. Her life would be changing again.

Morwenna was no longer the lithe and slender beauty who had enchanted warrior kings and Roman leaders but she was a still a stunning beauty. Her hair was devoid of grey, her eyes had no lines, her skin was perfection and her green eyes still glowed with the hidden power of the priestess. Her daughters had reached womanhood the previous year and the three of them had now become the Queen's acolytes replacing Maban and Anchorat both of whom had succumbed to the coughing sickness during the dark winter. The daughters were just younger versions of their mother and their green eyes glistened and sparkled with both power and insight. It was said that no-one could withstand the combined stare of the four women. Your soul would be laid bare, it was said, and your thoughts revealed to this most powerful quartet of witches.

Morwenna was delighted that Radha had asked permission to be granted an audience. Despite her mystical power Morwenna no longer controlled vast armies as she had once done. Her domain was no longer the land of the Brigantes but was the tiny island of Manavia and her army was a bodyguard of a hundred dedicated warriors. The success of the Votadini had emboldened her. For the first time since Agricola had destroyed the Pictish armies, the native population of Britannia had had a victory over the Romans and Morwenna knew that the time was ripe for another rebellion. Her spies in Morbium and Eboracum had told her that the Brigantes were becoming disenchanted with the rule of the Romans. The security they had enjoyed was now threatened as the Imperial forces were withdrawn for wars far in the East. The incursions of the Votadini and Selgovae had made the land around the Dunum a war zone. The visit of Radha had been created by the Mother of that Morwenna was certain.

Macro and Marcus were not sure how to feel now that they were working with Metellus, Rufius and Cassius once more. During the ill-fated campaign against the Votadini, they had achieved a certain status and independence which had now disappeared. They were once again the junior members of the team. Had they but known it they were considered as equals by the older members of the remnants of the Explorates but they were young and took offence at the slightest comment. It had been left to Metellus, older, wiser Metellus to reassure the two young scouts that they were valued. Cassius had arranged for the three of them to scout ahead so that he could talk to them more privately.

The land through which they were riding was familiar. The Prefect at Eboracum had not known how to use them now that the Ninth had been disbanded. There was, as yet, no other legion in the north and yet he felt it would be dishonourable to rid himself of the five mouths which needed feeding and he had not thrown them on the scrapheap. He had compromised and sent them to the land of lakes to evaluate the status of the frontier. There had been reports of unrest amongst the Brigantes, not around Morbium, but further west and the scouts were there to gauge the mood of a people who had never been truly content since the rule of Queen Cartimandua.

"You two acquitted yourselves well with the Ninth. I hear you were standard-bearers?"

They both glanced at Metellus to see if it was mocking them or meant the question as a slur. His face was as open and honest as ever and they took his words at face value. "It was not for long but yes. The two of us defended the eagle during the last attack of the Votadini," Marcus spoke with a passion. "It showed us the value of such emblems. We would have died happily and died proudly defending the eagle."

"Better to have done as you did my young friends and defended the eagle and yourselves and return safely from a disastrous war. A lost eagle would not have been worth your lives."

Macro said quietly, "I think it would."

Metellus peered at Macro who now had a body almost as big as his father had had. The boy was now a man. "Well let us just say that there would have been many of us who would have regretted the death of two such valued scouts."

Marcus again looked to see if there was an insult in the face but there was not. "You think we are valuable?"

Metellus laughed an easy booming laugh which echoed around the fellside. "There is not a pair of scouts who are held in higher esteem made all the more laudable by the fact that you are yet young and do not know the esteem in which you are held. None of the Explorates, living or dead was your superior. Some were your equals and some, like Rufius, is still an equal, but never doubt that you are valued."

"We are Rufius' equal?" Rufius was the ideal to which both boys aspired.

"Oh he can do one or two things better than you but you have shown qualities, especially when fighting the Votadini, that he has not had the chance to show."

The two of them pondered that. Although they looked up to all the Explorates, it had been Rufius who had been their role model in every way. It had hurt them when he had been chosen to go with Livius and Metellus leaving them in Britannia. At the time they had resented the fact that their youth had kept them in the province. The glory they had found compensated somewhat, but they were still envious of the adventures which their three colleagues had had. They were now in limbo; their present mission was nothing more than a means to rid the fort of an unwanted reminder of the disaster which had befallen the Ninth.

Metellus could gauge the mood of people easily and he sensed the gloomy mood of the two young men. "Come on or Cassius will be frying my balls for your rations and believe me that is a meal which would neither fill nor satisfy a pair of lusty young lads like you. Let us split up and meet two miles up the valley. If we have found no sign then we will hunt our supper."

Whooping with delight the two young men split left and right. Metellus smiled to himself. All the training Livius had put in with all the Explorates had borne fruit. Each man knew his role and, more importantly, the roles of others without the need for command. Metellus rode along the main trail looking for any sign of warriors or those who were not going about their rightful business. He noticed that he was following the trail of horses. That in itself was unusual. Mules or wagons were normally used by farmers and merchants; they could transport more than horses. It could be a legitimate party of travellers but Metellus moved slowly and carefully as he did not wish to miss anything. His sharp eyes picked out a small piece of cloth caught on the thorns of a bramble bush. It was coloured and showed more than one dye. That made it a higher status piece of cloth than that used by a farmer. He slipped it into his pouch. When he found the remains of the campfire he stopped and scouted all the way around. He found footprints from shoes, not caligae, which indicated that the party had not been Roman. The footprints varied in size from those of a child or woman to those of heavy set men, probably warriors. The fact that intrigued him the most was the lack of human dung. He found piles of soil which showed where it had been buried but not on the surface. That was the most revealing evidence of all. Warriors, farmers and merchants would just shit some way away from their camp but these piles were within sight of the fire but behind bushes. That meant women, allied to the horses, the cloth and the feet all suggested high-status women. As he mounted his horse to meet up with Marcus and Macro he began to run through the various scenarios which would result in high-status women and warriors travelling westwards in the land of the lakes.

The boys were waiting for him at the head of the valley. They were both grinning from ear to ear. "What is it then? Have you discovered some enemy warriors? Their trail? You have at least found some weapons?" They shook their heads grinning less broadly. "Don't tell me you have merely shot a couple of hares for supper and are feeling proud of yourselves?"

Their mouths opened. Marcus was the first to speak. "How did you know? We hid them behind the rocks."

"I know and so did the swarm of flies which are buzzing around the bloody stones."

24

They glanced back and then Macro said, "How did you know it was hares? It could have been a deer."

Metellus peered around the barren hillside. "If it was a deer then it would have to be tiny and so far away from its natural habitat that it would have been scared to death by your bows, besides which it wouldn't have fitted behind the rock." Reaching into his pouch he took out the piece of cloth. "Ever seen this before?"

They both examined it and then looked at each other, nodding as they did so. "Votadini weave. We saw many of the bodyguards of the king wearing such cloth."

Metellus looked back over his shoulder towards the campsite and then down at the trail. "A large party of warriors and high-status women came down the trail sometime in the past few days. Now you fought against the Votadini. Why would such a party travel west?" They both looked at each other and then in panic at Metellus who shook his head, "It was a rhetorical question. I wasn't expecting an answer. Let us check the trail ahead and see which way they went when they reached the col."

Once they reached the head of the valley they could clearly see the trail heading south-west. "They are going towards the coast Metellus."

"Which means?"

"Which means they are going to get a boat."

"Excellent Marcus; Now Macro where could they be going in a boat from this coast?"

"Ireland?"

"Could be but the first patrol we had, took place when we were pursuing Morwenna and Aodh and they were heading for Manavia. Equally, it could be Mona but both those are not good places for us because it means the Votadini may be allying themselves with the Druids and that cannot be good."

"Couldn't they be allying themselves with the Irish?"

"They could Marcus but in that case, they would catch a boat from further north, in the land of the Selgovae. It is a shorter crossing and has less risk of running into our patrols. Did you not tell us that the Selgovae and Votadini fought together?"

"They did."

"No, if they risked crossing Roman land, no matter how heavily armed they were they would be heading for the Druids. Come, we return to Cassius and get those hares cooked before they are completely covered in fly shit. A good hunter would have gutted them straight away and the flies would have followed the offal."

Shamefaced the boys retrieved their catch and as they rode along Metellus could hear the hares being skinned and cleaned as they hastened back to meet the rest of the patrol. He smiled to himself. The boys were no longer feeling sorry for themselves. Things were back to normal.

When they met up with their comrades they shared their intelligence. Cassius set the two youngsters to cooking their hares while he and Metellus discussed their options with Rufius. "This reminds me of when we chased Morwenna."

"And me Metellus. Do you think we could catch this elusive prey before they board a ship?"

Metellus considered, reaching down to take a handful of soil from the trail. "Difficult to say. I suspect not, the tracks did not look fresh and even if they were a day old that would put them at the coast." He stood and stretched. "And there are the warriors. I estimated that the party was at least twelve strong, more if they used scouts and outriders away from the main group. We are but five…"

Cassius nodded his thoughts were in tune with Metellus. "However, Metellus we don't know who it is and that might be important."

The two youngsters had joined them and the hares were cooking on the fire hidden in the rocky dell. "I think we can make some assumptions. The party is too small to be a warband and they are heading for either Manavia or Mona which suggests a Druidic connection. We know that there are women amongst the party which would make sense as it is the cult of the Mother which prevails there. I think someone close to the female side of the royal family is travelling west."

Marcus jumped up. "That Queen, Cassius, Radha. She used magic didn't she?"

Cassius thumped his fist into his other palm. "By the Allfather you are right and she led the warriors to attack the Ninth. I remember thinking how much she reminded me of Morwenna. I now believe you are right Metellus. We will return tomorrow to Eboracum and report to the Prefect. We are guessing a little but then that is what we do. These are dire occurrences. The Votadini almost destroyed the Ninth. With the Red Witch on their side…"

In Eboracum, the Prefect was ploughing his way through the myriad of reports from his units spread across the northern half of Britannia. They all pointed to one thing, general unrest. The Stanegate was in a high state of tension. He had sent messengers to the Governor urging him to request a legion to replace the Ninth. So far it had not even merited a reply to say he had received the request. He was forced to use his depleted auxiliaries to plug the gaps and to fortify every fort, no matter what the condition. . He leaned back and stretched. The only good news was the arrival of an under-strength ala of Pannonians. They had been requested when Marcus' Horse had been disbanded some years earlier but troubles in Lower Germania had delayed their departure. They were not up to full strength having only three hundred troopers and one Decurion but they were, at least, some cavalry and, as such, able to cover and control larger areas of Britannia. It also afforded him a solution to the problem of the Explorates of the Ninth. Three of them could be promoted as Decurions into the new ala and, with their local knowledge, could help with the recruitment of new troopers. He walked to the window of the Praesidium. It was a shame that the old commander of the Explorates, Livius Sallustius had been so badly wounded otherwise he would have made a perfect Decurion Princeps. He watched as the Decurion of the Pannonians rode out of the gate. He knew he ought to promote Aelius Spartianus to Decurion but there was something about the man he disliked and distrusted. There was no urgency in promoting anyone as the ala needed building up with new recruits. Once his Explorates were returned he would throw the dice and see which way they fell. He just hoped that the province would not erupt before the ala was trained and the legion replaced.

Aelius Spartianus felt the gaze of the Prefect as he rode out of the gate. He shivered in the early morning chill. He had hoped, after the rigours of Germania, for a posting to a warmer clime. He had hoped that he and his men would be posted to Syria to join Trajan in his troubled subjugation of that people but it was not to be. Here they were at the very last frontier, the edge of the world. He consoled himself that, at long last, he was almost Decurion Princeps with all its attendant benefits. He was a man who did not see his future on the back of a horse. Once he had made his money and found the patronage he wished, he would begin to milk the cow that was the Roman bureaucratic machine. He had known enough corrupt officials to know that, with power, one could make money and retire comfortably rather than with a pathetic plot of land. His ultimate aim was to be made a Camp Prefect. In order to do so, he needed to be promoted sooner rather than later. The recent deaths in Germania had been fortuitous. Some of his men thought too fortuitous, especially as at least one of Aelius' rivals had been struck from behind by a stray javelin during a recent skirmish.

Aelius kicked his horse on once he was free of the confines of the fort. He was a good rider. He was the son of a Pannonian trooper and had been born in a fort in Batavia. As such he had learned to ride at an early age and the men of his father's turma had spoiled the boy but trained him well. It had been inevitable that he would follow in his father's footsteps and he had had a meteoric rise to Decurion at an early age. He was still only twenty-seven and had been the youngest Decurion in the ala. His good looks and easy charm made him a magnet for every pretty girl in the fort. There were many young Spartiani running around Germania but Aelius had no intentions of tying himself down. When he took a woman it would be because of the money and power it brought.

Although he knew the Perfect expected him to be in the fort raising and training new troopers he had decided to get the lie of the land first and find out as much as he could about the land around Eboracum. It was likely that this would be his base and he had learned long ago that the more intelligence one had the more one could control their own destiny and he knew his destiny was for greatness. The Allfather had not caused him to be born just to have him end his days the same rank as his father.

Chapter 4

Julius had never visited his new villa before this sudden, unexpected trip had been forced upon them. It had been purchased on his behalf by an agent but he had had a description of it. The reality exceeded every word he had heard. It was perched atop a cliff which was at least two hundred paces above the sea. The city wall was just fifty paces away with a busy thriving market hidden by the solid walls. The grounds were extensive and had a high wall which could be defended by a determined garrison but its beauty was in its secret escape to the sea. With just one gate in and the secret passage out, it was as safe a location as he was likely to find. He smiled grimly to himself. Although he had never seen it, he expected that the villa of Tiberius, perched high on nearby Capreae was the only villa more secure.

Cato returned from his inspection and nodded his satisfaction. "With the men we have, we could defend this place against anyone who tried to gain entrance. And that includes Praetorians!"

"I do not think that it will be Praetorians who will follow us here Cato. In Rome, it is where they would expect to operate. Here? Unless the Emperor returns to Capreae then they would have no reason to visit us. No, I think that my young friend here is safe for a while." Livius looked up and felt Julius' gaze upon him. "However, they will discover where we have fled and then I think we will need to be more vigilant and look for the knife in the night. Before then, Livius, we will have made your legs stronger and prepared our defences. Hopefully, we will see the Emperor before that day arrives."

Hadrian received Julius' letter sooner than the senator had anticipated. He wasted no time in seeking out his mentor, Emperor Trajan. As he made his way through the corridors of the villa in Selinus he hoped that the Imperial party would depart for Rome sooner rather than later. Turning the corner, he found himself face to face with Pompeia Plotina the Emperor's devoted wife and companion. Denied children of their own the couple regarded Hadrian as their heir.

He bobbed his head, "Divinity."

The sensible and pragmatic Pompeia waved away the flattery and she took his arm; her face showing the emotion she felt as her husband prepared to join his ancestors. "He is worse Hadrian. I fear he will not last the night."

Hadrian had feared this outcome. The normally robust Emperor had succumbed to this terrifying disease which had everyone, even the Greek doctors, perplexed. Whilst his face and body were emaciated his legs had swollen out of all proportion. No amount of leeches and poultices had any effect. He leaned in to speak quietly to the Empress. "I have had news from Rome, Lucius Quietus is flexing his muscles and beginning to use the Praetorians."

"It is as the Emperor and I feared. The Praetorians can be unpredictable and if they took control of Rome then it would be harder for you to gain control. Go to him Hadrian, and apprise him of the parlous situation. I need to make preparations of my own." The hand she placed on his arm confirmed her affection for the young man. She and her husband regarded Hadrian as the son they never had and the Empress would do all in her power to ensure his succession.

The Emperor's tired eyes looked out from a gaunt, haggard skull. "From the look on your face my son I see that you do not bring me good news."

"No Divinity. I have had news from Senator Julius Demetrius that Lucius Quietus has tried to kill Livius Sallustius."

The Emperor looked confused. "Livius Sallustius? Who is…"

"The Explorate we sent to Aquitania to recover your gold and kill the traitor."

"Ah yes I remember, a most resourceful young man but why should the Senator be interested in him? He is not important."

"No Divinity but if you recall you sent a Praetorian to bring him to Rome. We had a role for him. It shows that the Praetorians have been infiltrated. Apparently, Quietus has seduced some of them with gold. They would have told the Senator that you wanted to see him and, by eliminating him they would weaken you. "

The aged Emperor smiled wryly, "Weaker than this?"

Hadrian spread his arms. "We need to return to Rome as soon as possible."

The Emperor shook his head, "I will not be in a condition to travel for a while, if ever. No, my son. Take a fast ship and a century of Praetorians; Praetorians that you can trust. Go to my villa on Capreae. From there you can send messages to those that we trust and eliminate Lucius."

"And you, divinity?"

"I will rest here." He looked earnestly at Hadrian. "And ensure that you succeed me. It is important that you continue our work."

Hadrian took a deep breath. "You have always valued my honesty?" The Emperor nodded and waved a weak hand to signify that he should continue. "Mesopotamia is not defensible. Neither is Armenia. They are both draining the lifeblood of the Empire. We leave Mesopotamia and allow Parthia to rule Armenia for us. That way we still have all the benefits of a trade link without the draining of Roman blood. The Parthians will have enough to contend with controlling the wild peoples of those regions and we will not have to keep such a large army there." The Emperor closed his eyes and when he opened them he nodded, albeit sadly. "We then build a new frontier in Britannia. There is little point trying to conquer the barren land in the north. Better that we build a wall and encourage trade. We will do as we have in Germania. The Empire is big enough. Alexander's Empire did not last a generation after his death. The Divine Augustus was a wise man but you, Divinity, are wiser and the Empire has never been as big as it is now. There may be a time in the future when we expand north and east again but…"

In a weak tired voice, Trajan murmured, "You are right. Make it so and now I will sleep."

By the time Hadrian had informed the Empress of the conversation, his Praetorians were ready and the boat prepared. "You may leave the Emperor in my hands my son. May the gods watch over you." She leaned up to kiss him on the cheek. "You will be Emperor, you may rely on that."

Livius and Julius were taking their daily walk down the path from the city to the beach. Cato and two armed men followed them. It had become a daily routine as recommended by Atticus. Furax had insisted on accompanying them and darted along the path picking up lizards, stones, in fact, anything which piqued his interest. Livius was glad that Julius had persuaded him to spare the boy and bring him with them. It was as though he was having a childhood for the first time. Although Cato and the guards were gruff with the street urchin it was obvious that they were fond of him and Julius had heard them practising with wooden swords after dinner. He smiled ruefully to himself; would that his childhood had been filled with such affection. All he remembered was his bullying brother and a father who was so distant that he appeared to have no affection for his young sensitive son. Once at the sea Livius would exercise his crippled legs in the salty seawater. The Greek doctor had assured him that it would heal them quicker and make them stronger. He was being proved correct.

"Well, Julius Atticus is right. The walk hurt me at first but now, after ten days, I feel much stronger."

"Good and very timely."

31

Livius shot a look at his friend. "You have heard something?"

"Yes, it appears that the man who arranged the sale of this villa disappeared two days ago. I received a message today that his body was found in the Tiber. I think we can assume that they know where we are. I have ordered Hercules to moor '*The Swan*' below the cliff should we need to make a hasty departure." He laughed. "He seemed inordinately pleased that they had cleaned all of the slimy weed from its bottom. He seemed somewhat disappointed that I was not more excited!"

"And still no news from Hadrian?"

"I would not have expected a response so swiftly. You of all people should understand the vagaries of the sea. Cato and his men are prepared. There will be two men at the gate each night and two more in the entrance. I believed it will be during the night they will make their attempt. During the day they would attract too much attention from the town."

Livius mentally agreed. Since his arrival, Julius had gone out of his way to make friends and spread his largesse amongst the townspeople. He had feted the senior citizens of Surrentum and the senior officers of the vigiles; any incursion would be greeted with aggression from the citizens of Surrentum. Surrentum had not had such patronage since the days of Augustus and they were keen to maintain the benefits.

Livius found himself hoping that he could stay, here, in this most beautiful part of Italy. It was no surprise that first Augustus and then Tiberius had chosen this as a summer retreat. Although still hot, the cool sea breeze made the climate far more palatable. The blue ocean was a marked contrast from the grey chill seas around Britannia. The purples, greens, oranges and yellows of the olives, lemons, oranges and bougainvillaea made the lands of Britannia seem drab and dour by comparison. His body had responded well to the excellent food, exercise and the sun's rays. His skin, at first reddened by the sun, had now bronzed making him look more like a Roman. He also enjoyed the company of Furax. It was as though he had never been a thief on the streets of the Lupanar. He was intelligent and interested in all that he saw. Atticus in particular took great delight in imparting knowledge to the sponge that was the young boy's brain. Once again Livius wondered at the Allfather's machinations which had caused the boy to try to steal from Livius and brought Julius to them both. He knew that but for that hand of fate, he would now be lying gutted in an inn in Rome.

Lucius Quietus was not a happy senator. His confederates, the three senators and the Praetorian Prefect had already felt the sharp edge of his tongue and the lash of his words. The insignificant creature that was

Livius Lucullus Sallustius had grown out of all proportion into a giant Hydra which seemed capable of destroying them! The fact that he had been secreted away by one of Hadrian's staunchest allies had created the idea that he was somehow pivotal in the rise of Hadrian which would culminate in his becoming Emperor. Lucius had no intention of letting that happen. Were it not for the wasteful war on the east, the ulcer that was Parthia, then the Emperor would have been in Rome and the powerful senator in a better position to consolidate his power.

"How stands the guard?"

The Praetorian Prefect shuffled uneasily from foot to foot, like a naughty boy in front of a schoolmaster. "We have five hundred on whom we can count, they are totally loyal and there are another thousand who will watch and wait to see what happens. As for the rest…"

Lucius exploded with rage. "What of the monies I have put your way? Has that been wasted? Did you not use it as I told you to buy the senior officers?"

"We did. But some who were bought were taken by the Emperor to the east and others have had a change of mind."

"Well change it back then!" He softened slightly. "It is certain that they are now in Surrentum?"

"Yes before he died the agent confirmed that Julius Demetrius had bought a villa on the cliffs overlooking Surrentum."

"And have you hired the mercenaries who will rid us of this troublesome pair?"

"I have fifty thugs hired from the Lupanar and they are making their way there even as we speak. By tomorrow night the threat will be eliminated."

"Good. Then we can prepare Rome. Have your men watch the names I gave you last week. They are the supporters of Hadrian and must be the first to die when we are certain that your killers have succeeded this time." The last words were spat out, almost as a threat.

The Prefect coughed and then interjected, "His mentor Attianus, he has disappeared. He cannot be found."

"Another loose end. Fortunately, he is an old man and should not pose a problem. But find him! And quickly."

The following morning was unusual in that Livius saw two clouds. He wondered if this was an omen. Cato came along the sea wall to speak to him. "The master would like to see you at the dock."

Livius peered over the sea wall and saw that '*The Swan*' was tied to the jetty and there was activity. He wondered what had occurred. As

33

he cautiously made his way through the villa he crossed the small garden Atticus used to teach Furax. Furax saw him and shouted, "Livius! Is something happening? Can I come with you?" The haste with which Livius was crossing through showed the bright young boy that something was amiss.

Livius saw the minute shake of the Greek's head and smiled. Obviously, this was a mathematics session and he knew how Furax hated that. "I will not be long and I promise to keep you informed." He saw the shoulders slump and remembered when he too had tried to get out of learning Latin in his uncle's home. How glad he was that he had been forced to endure what he had deemed a punishment. Perhaps Furax would view his mathematics lessons in the same light when he was older.

Julius was engaged in a serious-looking conversation with Hercules when he arrived, slightly out of breath at the dock. When he emerged from the cool of the passage into the heat of the day it was like walking into a wall of lava. The smoking top of Vesuvius across the bay was a constant reminder of the parlous and precarious nature of their existence on this little piece of paradise.

"Ah, Livius. Good of you to be so quick. Hercules here tells me that he saw an Imperial Trireme pull into Capreae last night."

"The Emperor?"

"Could be. Equally, it could be Praetorians."

Livius peered across the water to the saddle-backed island. "There is only one way to find out Julius. Let us go and make a visit."

Hercules stroked his beard with a gnarled hand. "If they are Praetorians we can't outrun them. They have oars on their ship and the wind is as light as a woman's touch today."

"So it is out of the question?"

"Possibly not. Hercules, just near the Sirens you said there was a rock called Tiberius' Leap and that you could see the villa from it?"

"Aye." Livius looked puzzled and Hercules pointed to the island. "You see those three rocks? Well, they are supposed to be the sirens who called Ulysses to the rocks." Looking back at Julius he said. "Yes, you can see the villa, or part of it at any rate. How does that help you?"

"If we sail there and anchor at the nearest rock to the island then we will be seen from the villa. I can wear my senatorial robes. If it is the Emperor then he will contact us. The winds do blow towards south from here do they not?"

"Aye you generally have a northerly at this time of year but how does that help us?"

34

"The Trireme is anchored on the north side of the island. We would have a head start if they pursued us and the wind would help being at our backs. Now that you have taken the weed from the ship '*The Swan*' should fly should she not?"

Hercules puffed himself up, "Oh she'll fly all right, like a true swan!"

"Without raining on your idea Julius, if it is the Praetorians then they will pursue us as we pass their mooring. They will see us."

"Good point and convinces me that we are right. If they pursue us we will know that they are the enemy and we will sail straight to Britannia, for we still have the … what do you call it Hercules, the weather gauge?." He shrugged at the shocked look on Hercules' face.

"That means leaving Furax here alone."

"Not alone Livius for he will have Atticus and with us gone he should be much safer. Come let us go. Time is wasting."

The voyage across the bay seemed to take an age as they were in the lee of the mountains and Vesuvius. It seemed to add exponentially to the tension. It was taking forever to get to their destination but when they reached it their end might be imminent. The Trireme looked menacing, its beak facing to sea, ready for a swift departure or was it to head off intruders such as '*The Swan*'? Livius could feel the tension from all on board; From Hercules with his hand grasped tightly around the tiller, through Cato who was nervously slipping his sword in and out of his scabbard through to Julius who was trying to affect indifference by pretending to watch Vesuvius but his drumming fingers belied his calm. Livius felt he was the calmest of them all for no matter what the outcome it would mark an end to the uncertainty. It might also lead possibly to his death if it were their enemies. If it was not then it was a solution to their problem. Either way, he was looking forward to the anchorage beneath the deadly drop.

Once they were halfway across the bay their speed increased as the wind caught their sails. Suddenly one of the lookouts shouted something to Hercules. Julius and Livius didn't catch the man's heavily accented words and they looked at Hercules for a translation. "He said there is activity on the trireme. They have seen us." They watched as flags were suddenly raised from the Imperial ship. "That'll be a signal to the shore."

"About?"

Hercules shrugged. "Could be getting the crew back on board to chase us, could be a message to say they have seen us or," he added ominously, "it could be signalling a ship from the south side of the island to cut us off."

Livius look accusingly at Julius. "Which was not one of the possibilities we considered eh Julius?"

"Don't listen to him Livius. I have come to learn that Hercules regards the bottle as half empty when in fact it is half full."

Hercules spat contemptuously over the side. "If I had a bottle now it would be totally empty because I would drain it." Their laughter eased the tension and it was with some relief that they slipped around the headland and headed for the Sirens.

As they edged their way gingerly around the cape under reduced sail every eye was on the stretch of water beyond the Sirens. A collective sigh of relief was breathed when they saw an empty sea. "Lower the sail!" As the sail was lowered Hercules pushed the tiller hard over. "Drop anchor!" As the anchor was dropped Hercules signalled his first mate to stand by with an axe. If they needed to leave quickly he would lose the anchor and the rope.

The stone anchor dropped through the bluey-green sea. Livius was amazed that he could see it clearly on the bottom some forty feet below. The seas around Britannia were so murky and grey that it would have been impossible to see. He turned to see that Julius was staring intently at the tip of the building which loomed some three hundred feet above their heads. "That is some drop, Julius."

"Emperor Tiberius thought himself a scientist and had his guards throw slaves from the top to see the effect. Me I just think he was a cruel bastard."

"And now we wait."

"And now we wait. Hopefully it will not be too long."

"For good or ill you mean? There is no happy medium with this wait. Either we end in a cell or a palace. Life in Rome is a little more precarious than on the battlefield Julius. There at least you control some of your own destiny. Here we are at the whim of the gods."

The air was still and the pennant on the masthead hung limp and slack. "We couldn't move now even if we wanted to," observed Hercules morosely.

"Half empty again Hercules."

"I've told you before just give me the bottle and I will empty it."

Their banter was ended by the masthead lookout who yelled. "Ships coming around the headland!"

Suddenly, propelled by banks of oars two small galleys hurtled around the headland. They were so small and swift that Hercules knew they could never escape in time and he shook his head at the first mate. Their fate was no longer in their own hands. One of them stopped across their bows whilst the other their stern. "I'm with Hercules on this one Julius. Definitely half empty."

A voice from the boat at the stern called up. "You are invited to the villa gentlemen please join us."

Shrugging Livius and Julius nodded their farewells to Hercules and began to climb aboard the galley. The officer in command, a marine optio shouted out cheerfully, "Come along Captain. You too are invited!"

Mentally cursing his decision to join this ill-advised venture Hercules climbed down to join the other prisoners. "Look after her Gaius!"

The optio smiled a joyless smile. "Do not worry captain. My companion will remain with your ship until a decision has been made about your fate."

Chapter 5

The harbour was dominated by the huge Imperial Trireme but there were still many other ships hidden in the harbour. They could now see that the guard boats, like the one in which they were interned, had been hidden by the huge ship which seemed to fill the entrance to the harbour. A century of Praetorian Guards awaited them along the jetty with a small covered cart. The marine optio grinned cruelly at them as they were led off by the Praetorian Centurion. He took them to the cart and said, "Get in! You get a ride to the palace." The captain waited until the other two had mounted and made to follow. "No old man. You wait here. We just wanted to make sure you didn't try to slip away in the night."

Hercules sniffed his indignation but wisely remained silent. This was, potentially, the base of all their enemies. "Take care, Hercules."

"You too master."

Their mule was led and Livius faced Julius in the cart as the column began to plod its way up the steep and twisted track which led to Tiberius' palace. "I half expected Lucius Quietus to be waiting for us at the dock, gloating."

"No Livius. He would wait in the cool of the palace to add to our discomfort." He glanced across the water to the hazy cliffs of Surrentum. "I hope Atticus and Furax are safe. Perhaps I should have left Cato with them?"

"I do not think that old soldier would have traded his role as a bodyguard to that of a babysitter. I am sure that the two of them have enough wits to survive. Do not forget Furax survived on the street."

"True but then his only danger comprised whores, murderers and thieves. A traitorous senator is a totally different proposition, far more dangerous."

The journey up the steep slope seemed to take forever and Livius was glad that he did not have to walk it as his legs were not quite ready for such a stern test. The villa, when they reached it, had all the appearance of a fortress with small towers, ditches and heavily armed sentries. Should anyone have been foolish enough to try to assault the refuge they would have needed an enormous force. A different Centurion greeted them and gestured for them to follow him. Julius noticed that their guards were all fully armed and that they were surrounded completely as they made their way from the searing heat of the hill into the cool of the atrium. The Centurion halted and turned to them. "Wait here."

Leaving four men to guard them he left. A few moments later he returned and took the guards with him. Livius looked at Julius. "What does this mean?"

"I am not sure. Perhaps no witnesses to our end. Don't forget Tiberius' Leap. We may yet get to swim! Keep your wits about you my young friend and look for a way out."

"I wouldn't do that my old friend or you would miss an excellent dinner." Hadrian's voice preceded him into the room in which they waited. "And good to see you too, Livius Sallustius. The Emperor's thanks for a job well done last year." Livius had expected to die and now he was being greeted by the Emperor's right-hand man. He couldn't quite take it in. "Come let us bathe and then eat. We can talk more privately there."

Once they were in the bath and the sweat and dirt of the day began to ooze from their bodies Hadrian ordered his servants and slaves to leave. "I am sorry about the pretence but I am afraid that your message has made me suspect my own guards. I brought with me those that I can trust but there are some on the island whom I suspect are in the pay of our friend, the treacherous Quietus. Now I am sure, young Decurion, that you have questions. The senator and I know and understand each other well but you, well..."

Embarrassed at being the focus of attention and being in the presence of such an august personage he was not sure where to start and then he remembered Marcus Maximunius and his advice. '*Just say what you believe and all will be well.*' "All I need to know sir is what you want of me? My friend here seems to think you have a role for me in Britannia."

Hadrian roared with laughter. "Excellent! An honest question from an honest man. How refreshing and how so unlike Rome. Are there many like you in Britannia?"

Julius answered for him. "Many, sir. I know for I was honoured to serve with them."

"Good, then I shall have to visit this island which terrifies so many of our leaders. The land at the edge of the world! To get to business then. The Emperor is not a well man but he still has plans for Britannia. He intended to build a solid frontier in the north of the country; across the land in which you and the senator did such fine work for the Empire. We need someone we can trust. Someone who can watch everyone including the Governor." Livius and Julius exchanged looks of amazement- he was being asked to spy on the Governor! "This is not that we do not trust the Governor but we need a non-political eye. We also know that you know and understand the people. There is unrest there and your views would be most useful. Could you perform that function?"

"Well yes but, if I am to be completely honest, wouldn't the Governor be suspicious of an old crippled soldier wandering around the country?"

Excellent! Intelligent too. You are quite right. No, we have another role for you. We have sent over some Pannonian Horsemen. I believe you were in Marcus' Horse which had been Pannonian?" Livius and Julius nodded. "It is under strength and we would have you bring it up to strength and do what you did before and patrol the North of Britannia."

"But sir my legs. I am not as mobile as I was."

"Livius you are getting better and remember the Decurion Princeps does not have to ride as much as a Decurion." Julius knew his young friend could do the job easily, he was made for it; a born leader and a natural spy.

"Besides the role would be short term. Once you have brought the ala up to strength then you would be promoted to Prefect. As that means you would need to be a member of the equestrian order I have provided the papers. You are now an equestrian citizen of Rome."

Julius raised his beaker. "I would say welcome Livius but this particular club is more disreputable than a Selgovae slave raider's party!"

"As I do not understand that then I assume that it is a Britannic reference."

"Yes, sir it is."

"What are your plans now then sir?"

"I merely came here to put in place certain actions which may become necessary in the foreseeable future. Sorry to be so cryptic but the less you know the less I can be hurt." Julius waved a dismissive hand while Livius still ruminated on his sudden elevation to the Roman aristocracy. "I intend to return to Cilicia and the Emperor. Things are still undecided in the East." He looked carefully at Julius. Are you staying or should I say hiding nearby?"

"I have a villa on the cliffs at Surrentum. Not far from the old villa of Augustus."

"And people are used to seeing your visitors come and go?"

Intrigued Julius leaned forward. "Yes but why?"

"I was going to sail into Ostia and send my messenger to, well deliver my message, but that would mean the whole world would know my business. If I land at your villa then I can send my messenger by a more, shall we say discreet means."

"Certainly."

Livius' mind was working as sharply as ever. "We have a passage from the sea, away from prying eyes. No-one would know that you were there."

"Good."

"There is one worry though. We believe that Lucius has sent killers to eliminate my young friend and me. The villa may not be the safest place."

"Worry not. I have a hundred trained men here. That is sufficient bodyguard."

Livius continued his train of thought, "And if we took '*The Swan*' then there would be even less interest than an Imperial Trireme as the old ship puts in and out all the time."

Hadrian slapped Livius on the back. "I can see that we made a wise choice. We will leave after we have eaten. That will give your captain time to bring his ship around and moor it behind my trireme so that my Praetorians can board unseen."

By the time they had been taken to the port, it was becoming dark. '*The Swan*' was bobbing in the slight swell, a little lower in the waterline than before, Livius noticed. They were about to board the galley which would transport them when Hadrian's sharp eyes picked out a fast messenger boat hurtling towards them. He raised his hand to prevent his bodyguard from hurling their spears in its direction. "Rest easy. This boat I know." An Imperial messenger leapt from the boat some paces from the shore and waded as quickly as he could manage to hand Hadrian a sealed packet.

"From the Empress," he lowered his voice, "Divinity." Livius and Julius were the only others who heard the message and shared a glance.

Hadrian appeared as though he had been told it was time for dinner. "I will read this on your boat." To the messenger, he said, "Get some food and tend the boat. Rest if you can. I will return with a message before midnight."

Hercules looked uncomfortable when Hadrian boarded. He was not used to such high company. He had been relieved that he was still alive but unhappy at the eighty men crammed below his decks. Julius just said, "Back to the villa and moor in the usual place."

They left Hadrian to open and read his missive in the privacy of the lee deck where no-one could see, hear or read. When it was read he tore it into pieces and dropped the pieces overboard. He came over to them, still in a very calm and measured frame of mind. "I trust you will keep this to yourselves."

"Of course, div... sir."

Hadrian smiled. "You are both wise choices." He gestured for them to come close. "Decurion all my instructions will come through the Senator. And yours will go through him. You will need a code. You Explorates are good at that sort of thing aren't you?" Livius nodded. "The letters will ostensibly be an exchange between old friends. Livius," his eyes bored into those of the Briton. "I need to know everything! No matter how trivial it appears. Do I make myself clear?"

"Sir."

"Good and now let us get ashore however briefly while I make my plans which are now even more critical."

Leaving just ten Praetorians to guard the ship, they began to wend their way up through the passage. The light was just dipping below the horizon and a pink glow seemed to spread like fire across the water from the isle they had just left. The still air was warm enough to make them shiver as they ascended the stone steps up to the clifftop villa. Julius ensured that he was the first through the doorway into the villa. His men had been told to guard all the entrances to the sanctuary and Julius did not want the new Emperor to die because his men thought he was an intruder.

Gaius greeted them when they arrived, looking in surprise as the column of Praetorians began to spread through the building efficiently setting up a perimeter. Livius looked on in amusement as ten of the Praetorians began to remove their armour and don civilian clothes. Swiftly moving with Julius to the senator's office Hadrian began to ask questions and give commands. "Senator, have you any horses?"

"Yes, about eight."

"Good that will have to do." Turning to his Centurion he said, "Make sure the entrance is clear of any observation."

Julius held up his hand, "If I might suggest sir that my man Cato scouts. He will attract less attention than a heavily armed Praetorian."

"Good thinking. Yes, that will do. Centurion, I believe there is one entrance. Put six men there and then have the rest line the perimeter wall but keep out of sight. Now, Julius, I need to write some messages. Do you have a clerk?"

"I have Atticus, a Greek doctor who teaches."

"Can he be trusted?"

"He can."

"Then the three of us will write some letters." He turned to a Praetorian. "We do not want to be disturbed."

As they disappeared into the office Livius was left wondering what he ought to do. Furax had heard the commotion and came running from his room. His young face was shocked into a grimace of terror when the

Praetorian blades were pointed in his direction. "He is harmless, at least to others. He lives here."

The Centurion slid his blade back into its scabbard with a sharp ring. "He nearly died here running around like that."

"What is it Livius?"

"Nothing to worry you Furax. Let us say that we are safer now than we were. Now try to keep out of the way. These are not like Cato and the lads, these are very serious soldiers."

Just then Cato entered and looked around for Julius. When he didn't see him he came to Livius. "Sir there is a gang of men surrounding the villa. They are all armed."

The Centurion caught the tail end of the conversation and strode up to Cato. "You report to me!"

Cato had been a legionary in the twentieth who had fought in Britannia. As with all ordinary legionaries, he resented the elite and arrogant Praetorians and he turned to face the huge centurion. "I was a proper soldier and fought in real wars. I am not some poncy overdressed Praetorian and I do not take orders from you."

Stepping between them Livius took charge. "Well spotted Cato. Well, Centurion, I think it would be a good idea to let this little band in and, as we outnumber them, surround them and finish them off in the grounds. I don't think your master would want any left on the road to ambush the messengers eh?"

The Centurion stepped back and nodded to Livius. He did not know who Livius was but Hadrian appeared to respect his views and, on reflection, the plan was a good one. "You were an officer weren't you?" Livius nodded. "It shows; more intelligence and honour than a legionary grunt." He almost spat the last word at Cato. "Good plan. Keep your men close to the house. My lads will kill anyone who is not in a Praetorian uniform."

Livius could see anger infusing Cato's face as the Praetorians left the building. "Guard the inside of the house, Cato. These Praetorians may not be as good as they think they are and we do not want any getting through the perimeter and into the villa. I will join you." He turned to Furax, handing him his dagger. "You stay with me and guard my back." The young boy seemed to grow several unciae with the responsibility but Livius wanted him safe and the safest place would be behind him. There was an oppressive silence and then suddenly the sounds of blade on blade and then grunts and moans could be heard drifting in from outside. It was bizarre for Livius. He had seen many battles and skirmishes; he had participated in many but this was the first time he had heard one. It was maddening to hear and not know what was going on. There were at least fifty Praetorians outside, he felt sure they must be able to despatch whoever Quietus had sent against them.

Suddenly a Praetorian fell backwards through the door his neck a new grinning mouth pumping arterial blood. Cato and two of his men stepped up to face whoever came through the door but were bowled back to the rear wall as five men hurtled through the door; they were all well armed with swords and axes. Two of them had small shields and Livius, with a sickening realisation, saw that they were gladiators. The Praetorians were soldiers for show, these were warriors for hire and they were good. Picking up a stool for his left hand Livius stepped forward to face the two men who were heading for the study. One of them hacked down at Livius' left side and he thrust the stool in the direction of the blow while stabbing forward with his own blade. The stool took the blow but shattered leaving Livius defenceless. His speculative stab had caught his opponent on the knee and he was able to fend off the second axe strike. Out of the corner of his eye, he could see Cato and his two companions being beaten back by the gladiators. This was the sort of scenario which was made for the mercenaries; there was no order, it was a confined space and they were incredibly well trained. It was only a matter of time before the handful of Julius' men fell. The wounded swordsman came at Livius in an angry attack forcing him back. Livius tripped over the broken remains of the stool. It first saved his life as the sword scythed above his head but then almost killed him as the axeman sliced down on the recumbent, helpless decurion. Even as he lay there, knowing that he would not survive Livius chose honour and stabbed upwards at the swordsman. He would despatch at least one of his enemies. The blade entered the unprotected groin and there was a sudden rush of blood and entrails as one mercenary cried a noisy death. Livius could not move his sword which was embedded in the dying man and he braced himself for the blow from the axe. He looked up at the scarred and grinning face of the gladiator realising this would be his last sight in this life. He watched as the axe began its downwards arc and then watched as the look of exultation turned to a look of horror as the pugeo entered his ribs. Livius took his chance and rolled to the side. The blade delayed enough to miss Livius, thudded into the dead swordsman. Livius grabbed the dagger still embedded in the side of the wounded gladiator and in one fluid motion slit his throat.

The guard from the study had joined Cato and the surviving guard to finish off the three remaining gladiators. Seeing no other enemies Livius retrieved his sword and then turned to Furax who was heaving as sobs rippled through his body. Livius put an arm around the distraught boy. "That was bravely done Furax. I owe you my life and, "he pointed to the doorway where Hadrian stood with Julius, "that of an Emperor."

The Praetorian Centurion burst in and surveyed the scene. Cato spat a gob of blood at one of the dead gladiators. "Not bad for legionary grunts eh Centurion?"

To his credit, the Praetorian took his medicine and nodded his thanks to the old legionary. He turned to Hadrian. "The rest are all dead. They were gladiators. We managed to find out who sent them. It was Lucius Quietus. "

Hadrian's face did not show any emotion. "He has just signed his own death warrant. Centurion, get rid of the bodies over the cliff and have the messengers mounted and readied for their mission." He paused. "What is the butcher's bill?"

"We lost fifteen men."

Cato glanced around, "Four."

"They will be added to the price our traitorous friends will pay."

It was just before dawn when the villa was back to a semblance of normalcy. The eight riders and two foot messengers heading for Rome had been sent off in twos and threes over a period of an hour to maximise the chance of success. The Praetorians had begun to load *'The Swan'* with the bodies of their dead for burial on Capreae, and Cato and his men had cleaned as much of the blood and gore from the once beautiful villa as they could.

Livius was summoned into the study with Julius and Hadrian. "I owe you much, both of you and I will repay the debt. You at least deserve to know what will happen now and, after tonight, I know that of all men in Rome, you two are to be trusted with my life. "I have sent messages to Attianus and the Prefect of the Guard ordering them to arrest and imprison the traitors." He saw the look of doubt on Julius' face. "The Prefect I can trust. The Centurion found a traitor on the island and extracted the names of the traitors in the Guard. I will return to the Empress and secure the East. Senator, I will charge you with returning to Rome to aid my guardian. As you know I have informed him of your role in all of this. That only leaves us with you, Decurion, and your role. " he handed him a pouch. "In this are written instructions for the Governor of Britannia to give you command of the Pannonian Ala and to afford you all the help you require," he smiled ruefully, "He may not be happy for I know that many governors make a healthy profit from selling such promotion however he will follow my instructions. You still have your letter identifying you as frumentari?" Livius nodded. "Good then do not hesitate to use it. I have also given you permission to rename the ala as the First Sallustian Ala of Pannonians.

It is a small thing but as you discovered with Marcus' Horse and Indus with Indus' Horse it makes a unit have a sense of identity. I think it goes some way to repay you and your family for the deeds you have performed for Rome. I will borrow your ship to return to Capreae and then it can drop the Senator off in Rome and," he looked questioningly at Julius, "take you to Eboracum." Julius nodded. "It seems the safest way. I will be coming to Britannia as soon as the East is secure. I need to know from you the best route for the defence we discussed. I want to know all the potential dangers both human and physical. Are you up to it?"

"Yes, Emperor." He hesitated.

"Is there a problem?"

"If I am in the north with the ala then how will I know what the Governor is up to? The Senator will tell you that many Governors prefer the comfortable life in the south of the province to the hardships and rigours of the North. I want to do as you wish but I am struggling to see how I can garner the information you want and need."

"You were right about this man Julius, he thinks. The fact that the Governor is not in the North is valuable information but more than that is the information you send me about the state of the Province."

Smiling with relief Livius nodded, "That I can do."

"Good." He came over and gave Livius the soldier's clasp. "I am glad that the Emperor and myself made such a wise choice. If all Britons are as you then Rome's frontier is safe for a thousand years."

46

Part Two
The poisoned tongue

Chapter 6

Morwenna had made Manavia her own little kingdom. Those who aspired to join the priests and priestesses of Mona no longer went to that holy isle, now under the watchful gaze of the Twentieth Augusta, but instead travelled to the secure island sanctuary of Manavia. The former tormentors of the island, the Irish, were in awe of the Red Witch's power and now acted as the island's guardians, their pirate ships no longer preying but now protecting. Warriors also travelled from all over Britannia and Ireland to join the bodyguard of the Mother. This elite group of warriors had begun with Aodh, the Queen's consort, and had grown over the years. Part of it was the glory of fighting for the famed queen who had bested the Romans so many times and who had almost defeated them outside Eboracum but also because there was a belief that her witchcraft imbued warriors with even greater skills. Others sent tribute to ensure that the power of the Mother was not directed against them.

With her three daughters, Morwenna ruled the island benevolently. An astute leader she knew that she needed the base as a refuge, a rock protecting her from the rapacious Romans. Perhaps one day the Classis Britannica might decide to take an interest and put an end to her security but as long as they had the pirates of the Mare Germania to contend with she was safe. She had watched with increasing joy as the Votadini and the Selgovae had destroyed the vaunted Ninth and so nearly claimed the eagle. Although not of her doing she took pleasure in knowing that the enemy of her revered mother, Fainch, had been humiliated and scattered to the winds. It confirmed the power of the Mother, for Morwenna had heard of the influence of Radha who seemed like a younger version of herself from the reports sent to her by her priestesses. However, she was sceptical and would need to view the warrior queen before passing judgement; others had claimed powers that were fictitious. Had Radha not risked the perilous journey across Roman Britannia and the sea voyage she had considered visiting the court of the Votadini herself. This suited her plans far more for it showed that she held the young queen in her thrall.

The Red Witch had stage-managed the arrival of Radha into her presence. The dais was in the open beneath a canopy of mistletoe, elder

47

and laurel. Fragrant bunches of rosemary and thyme were interspersed amongst the wood making the rustic structure look more regal. Her three daughters, Brynna, Caronwyn and Eilwen were arrayed before her, on the lower level, looking as though the Mother had sculpted models of the queen and made each one slightly different. They had all had their naming ceremonies when their bleeding began and they became women. Morwenna was already deciding on the mates for her daughters for that was an important decision and she knew from experience that if one did not choose wisely then mistakes could occur. She remembered her liaison with the Roman, Macro, which had resulted in an unwanted son. She had hoped he would have died before now but the next time he crossed her path he would die and that reminder of one of her few mistakes would be eradicated. The four women were dressed almost identically, the pure white shift adorned with nothing more than mistletoe and their coronets were the same, rosemary and mistletoe intertwined. They wore no jewellery but their lips were reddened with cochineal, making a striking image against their pale white skin and pure white dresses. Around her stood a line of warriors each one with a bare tattooed torso, a shining helm and a long sword; their bracelets and amulets a sign that they were all warriors who had killed many enemies.

Radha was already in awe of the Queen before she arrived but, when she entered the wooden hall lit by torches, she suddenly felt like a poor relative in comparison to the vision in white which greeted her. She was glad that she had left her bodyguard outside. They looked like thugs and ruffians compared with the magnificent body of men arrayed before her but it was the presence of the queen and her daughters which most impressed the young Votadini Queen. They seem to glow and pulse-like ethereal and magical beings. The red hair of the queen was reflected, but not duplicated, in her daughters making the shimmering quartet look like a rich jewel which sparkled and showed a different facet with every glance. She suddenly realised that she did not know how to behave in the presence of the Queen who was also the High Priestess of her cult. She prostrated herself on the floor before the dais and her two companions followed suit.

There was silence in the hall. The only sound which could be heard was the slight crackle and hiss from the torches. When Morwenna finally spoke, her mellifluous voice seemed to enchant, not only Radha and her companions but every warrior in the Hall. "Welcome Radha, Queen of the Votadini. Your fame and renown have reached us with the news of your great success against the Roman invader."

Suddenly, from the throats of her three daughters, an ululation erupted which made the warriors and the three visitors jump with fright. Morwenna stood and spread out her arms. "Come and embrace me." Morwenna came down the steps slowly, almost as though she was floating. Radha too approached the witch as though in a dream. She felt nervous tension tingling through her body. She did not know what to do. She was but a young queen and, hitherto, had had little to do with other queens. The slight smile playing on Morwenna's lips made her more comfortable and the two women wrapped their arms around each other. The perfumes and aromas emanating from Morwenna appeared magical and Radha was aware of the smell of horses and travel which oozed from her, it seemed to Radha to be redolent of a farmyard. Morwenna leaned back slightly to view Radha's face. "And now the kiss of friendship." When their lips met it was more than a chaste politic gesture, for Radha felt the passion in the red lips of the Red Witch and felt the vibrant body pressing close to hers. When Morwenna's tongue touched her lips she suddenly felt like pushing away but Morwenna's whispered words reassured her. "You are now one of the sisters; you can now join us in our ceremonies and celebrations do not be afraid." Suddenly relieved Radha returned the passion and she wondered why she had not embraced the idea before.

It seemed like an age before they broke and yet it was but a heartbeat. "Send away your ladies," she turned to her guards, "Luarch. I will not need close protection, surround the hall and let no-one enter. I need to have close congress with our new sister."

When the hall had emptied Morwenna took Radha's hand and led her to the fire before which was laid an enormous wolf skin. Her daughters followed, hand in hand. "You will be tired after your journey and I will not hinder your rest. We need to talk and then my daughters will take you to your quarters. Tonight will be the opportunity for a deeper discussion." The husky voice left Radha in no doubt that the evening would be a new experience for her. As they lay on the wolf skin Brynna began to comb Radha's hair, Eilwen washed her feet while the third daughter, Caronwyn rubbed exotic smelling oils into her hands.

"You and your warrior king did well to defeat the Romans. How stand you and the Selgovae to finally rid our land of the Romans?"

Radha's voice was bitter as she spoke. "Speak not of the Selgovae. The worthless curs deserted us at the end. Not a Roman would have escaped and we would have captured the eagle had they stood. My husband will destroy them."

Morwenna silenced the queen with a kiss. "Be calm my sister. We do not become angry but we use anger to our own advantage. Impress upon your husband that we need the Selgovae and their warriors." Radha's face showed the signs of anger once more. Morwenna placed a slender finger upon her lips. "Calm and peace. I will find a way to bring an end to their king and then we will find a new leader to lead them. Your husband should invite the King of the Selgovae and the other allies to a meeting, a conclave to drive the Romans from this land, and, there, the man you hate will die."

Mollified Radha lay back and relaxed. "How will he die? He has bodyguards."

"You are a sister and we will teach you the ways. There are potions and poisons which will give you a power of which you have only dreamt." She took Radha's face in her hands. "The Mother told me you were coming. You are the stone which begins the avalanche but we need to manage the avalanche. We only wish for the Romans to be destroyed not the peoples of Britannia which is why we must preserve the Selgovae people and not destroy our warriors in futile wars of revenge against one another."

Radha did not know if it was the fire, the words or the wonderful perfumes in the room but she found herself realising that Morwenna was right. "Do you think we can defeat the Romans?"

"Now that you have destroyed their legion I have no doubt. The Brigante are ready to rise and the three tribes can sweep all before. All we need is to plan carefully and choose our battles well. With the new power, you shall have your armies will be even stronger. Now you are tired and we have much to do. Brynna will take you to your rooms. There are fresh clothes there. After we have supped and are refreshed we will all retire to my quarters to continue what we have started."

The Prefect looked up at Cassius. "How sure are you of this?"

Cassius had spent an hour explaining what they had discovered in the land of the lakes. The alliance between the Votadini and Morwenna would be a disaster if true. The Prefect was a worried man. With barely three cohorts of auxiliary infantry and a depleted ala of cavalry, the northern part of Britannia was more vulnerable than it had been for a generation. All of his pleas and requests to Rome had resulted in nothing. He desperately hoped that Cassius was wrong. "The party which went to Manavia was definitely high-status Votadini and it was a substantial number. It is likely to have been the queen or someone similar and we know from the last battle that their women are as formidable as their men. In addition, the Brigante are not as cooperative as they were. The defeat of the Ninth has made them realise that they could be attacked at any time and, I am afraid to say, that the once invincible legions are not so invincible. They can no longer be relied upon to be our allies"

The Prefect stood. "Well, at least we have some cavalry now. You will not be the only mounted force in Eboracum." Cassius looked quizzically at the Prefect. "An ala of Pannonians, under-strength, of course, but recruiting, arrived a few weeks ago, just after your patrol began. Rest your men for a few days and then ride up to the land of the Votadini see what you can discover. I think your Explorates are still needed."

Cassius left the Praetorium and headed for the vicus. The rest of the patrol had made The Saddle as their place to meet and drink when not on patrol. It had been set up by one of their former troopers, Gaius Metellus Corsus, known to his comrades as Horse because of his size. He had lost an arm fighting against Morwenna and Decius Lucullus which meant he retired early. He had enough money to build a roundhouse and begin brewing beer. The saddle which adorned the doorway was his own from his days with Marcus' Horse. It was now five years since he had expanded his premises to provide a couple of rooms and food. His girth had increased along with his profits but his old comrades found it a safe and secure place in which to unwind. When Cassius entered there were only his four friends and Horse. Horse brought him a beaker of black ale and asked, "Want any food?"

"What is on today?"

He grinned and nodded at Macro, "You eat well today Macro's lad here brought in a young suckling boar. I have a nice stew."

"That will do for me then. Well, lads, we have a few days' rest and then it is up to Votadini country again."

Metellus and Rufius quickly glanced at the two boys who both studied their beer as though it might move of its own volition. "You two lads alright with that?"

Marcus looked at Rufius, they were almost the same size now and the three of them could be taken for brothers. "It won't be easy, passing the place where so many of our friends and comrades died but yes. We are Explorates and we go where we are ordered."

Macro nodded his agreement and drank heartily from his beaker. Rufius put his arm around Marcus. "Our comrades are there too, Marcus. In fact, we have left comrades from Deva to Mons Graupius. It is not a bad thing to see where they fell. It is good for it rekindles the memories of those warriors who fell."

Horse had returned with Cassius' stew and overheard the conversation. He winked at Metellus. "You see it's like this my old son. When I go over to Mamucium for supplies and I see where all me mates fell and I lost me arm, I remember and after all, there's no harm in it is there?"

The three older troopers groaned at the awful joke while Marcus and Macro grinned and blushed. "I've got to hand it to you Horse. Like your stews you are tasteless." Metellus quipped back.

Again, they all groaned and Horse sniffed as he left. "Well, I don't know. I thought it was harmless enough."

Cassius tucked into his stew, which, despite Metellus' jokes, was excellent. The others just enjoyed the relaxation of not being on a horse and drinking without worrying about danger and death lurking around the corner. The adrenalin rush of being on patrol had to be tempered with rest and that is what they were enjoying. Before Cassius could tell them all the news that the Prefect had told him the door was hurled open and Decurion Aelius Spartianus stood there with five of his cronies.

"What have we here? Is it a barbarian band of thugs? Oh no, it's worse, it is Explorates." He turned and grinned at his sycophantic troopers who dutifully laughed. Cassius saw the young Explorates' hands go to their swords and he and Metellus shook their heads and were relieved when they were sheathed. "Anyway real soldiers are here now so make way for your betters and fuck off."

Cassius continued eating and Metellus and Rufius merely looked bored at the blowhard's words. Marcus and Macro were becoming increasingly angry at the insults they felt they should not be taking.

"Are you deaf as well as dirty? I told you to leave."

Cassius finished his stew and pushed the dish away. He stood and faced the Decurion. He was a good head taller. "Now listen, son. We have just had a hard patrol and we are enjoying a drink in our favourite drinking hole. There are many more in the vicus. Stop behaving like a newly promoted optio and leave yourself."

The sound of five swords being drawn made Marcus and Macro look nervously at Metellus but he grinned and shook his head.

"That sounds like a threat, a threat to a superior officer. Severe punishments will be involved." Aelius Spartianus normally got his way by physical threats but he could also bully with rank.

"Officer I sincerely doubt, and superior? That I definitely question. Well, I am a decurion as is my comrade over there, Metellus, and as I have been a decurion for eight years I think I outrank you, sonny. But I don't like to throw my rank about." He looked pointedly at Aelius. "I leave that for dick heads that haven't learned yet how to behave like an officer in front of their men and are still wet behind their ears."

The next few moments were a blur of action. Aelius and his men advanced on the Explorates, trying to draw their swords as they did so. Cassius punched Aelius in the stomach; Metellus cracked two of the others' heads together while Rufius, Marcus and Macro had the others disarmed in the blink of an eye. Finally, Horse appeared in the doorway behind them all with an enormous cudgel in his hand.

"Now who is causing upset in my inn?"

Aelius pulled himself to his feet, glaring at them all in turn. "You will pay for this! Fucking barbarians."

"Speaking of paying, you have damaged my property so pay up. Four denari."

"Fuck off you cripple!"

In answer, Horse swung his cudgel to crack into the knee of the Pannonian Decurion. "I could just call the vigiles." He looked innocently at Cassius. "Wasn't their leader in Marcus' Horse too?"

"I believe he was. If I were you, Decurion, I would pay my friend here and then try to get out with whatever dignity you have left before we really get angry."

The four denari were hurled at Horse and the troopers lurched their way out avoiding bumping into Horse and his deadly cudgel. Shutting the door behind them Horse pocketed the money. "Well, that's your food paid for. More ale lads?" As they nodded their assent he left.

"Who the hell are they?"

Cassius smiled as he drank some of his ale. "That, my friends, is the new ala in town, The Pannonians!"

"But Marcus' Horse was the Pannonian ala!"

"Yes, Macro but there is more than one ala of Pannonians. I have no idea what this one is called. I hope the other officers are better than that thug or they won't last a week out here."

Rufius stood. "I think I'll take a little turn around the fort and see what I can discover." It was no surprise to Cassius when Marcus and Macro offered to join him.

"Be careful. Let's not piss too many of them off. We may need them yet."

When they were alone Metellus moved next to Cassius. "What else did the Prefect say?"

"Oh that he still hasn't replaced the Ninth and these few cavalry are the only reinforcements we are likely to get. Apparently, they are hoping to recruit and get the ala up to full strength."

"I hope they have a good Decurion Princeps. If that one is a measure of their competency then they are in trouble."

"The problem is Metellus that we served in the best ala with the best leaders and the best men. But it wasn't always that way. There were bad buggers along the way. Gaius was flogged once by Julius' dad and he was innocent. No, a good ala doesn't just happen. Someone has to care and make it a good ala."

"We could always go back as Decurions. Make something of it."

"Could you give up the independence of the Explorates? Could you go back to the discipline? The duties? The army?"

"The thing is Cassius I am not sure that we can continue doing this. When we had thirty of us we could cover large areas, we could work as a team to make sure we missed nothing. It took us five weeks to find one track on the last patrol. If we had had all the Explorates we would have found that in a week. We are too few to be effective."

Before Cassius could reply Rufius and the other two returned. "Well, the good news is they only arrived last week and the bad news is that that thug is the only decurion. He is in charge."

Metellus looked at Cassius. "Well, that has decided me. I am not going to join that ala with him as my leader."

Macro looked intrigued. "Join the?"

"Yes Macro, they are recruiting for that under-strength ala. Cassius and I were thinking about joining as Decurions but if he is Decurion Princeps then there is no way we would serve with him."

Macro and Marcus looked crestfallen. It was the dream of both of them to follow their father into the cavalry. Marcus was desperate to wield the Sword of Cartimandua, still languishing in the family farm and awaiting its next call to duty. He wondered if he should go against the others and join as a trooper? He was just old enough. One look at his friends convinced him, his father had taught him to be loyal and he would be loyal to this band of brothers.

Rufius drank off his beaker of ale. "I just wish Livius was back. He would have an answer to this."

At that moment '*The Swan*' was just entering the estuary of the Ouse. Hercules had found the voyage challenging especially as he had had to persuade his crew to pass through the Pillars of Hercules. It took all of Livius' persuasive powers and a pouch of silver to convince them. Livius had been surprised by the speed of their voyage. It was far faster than the reverse journey in the bireme had been. The winds had been favourable and Hercules was right, with the weed off her bottom, she fairly flew.

Hercules had explained the reason. "Galleys are reliable. You can always row but sailing is faster because the boat is lighter and the wind is more powerful than men. It doesn't need food!"

Now as they edged their way up the estuary Hercules pointed out the deficiencies. "Now this won't be easy as the river twists and turns and will get narrower but we'll manage. I tell you what though Livius, I wouldn't like to sail these waters too often. They look dark and dangerous give me the blue Mare Nostrum any day."

"On that, I agree with you. I'll just go below and gather my gear."

When they had reached Ostia, Julius had insisted upon providing Livius with not only the codes for their letters but money and equipment. As he had said, "I served in the ala and know the value of a good suit of armour. I have the best and Cato can have it back here before the tide turns." The armour had proved to be a magnificent cuirass; not fancy but immensely strong, a good cavalry helmet with excellent protection, a shield with extra metal protection and a spatha which was almost as magnificent as the Sword of Cartimandua. "This was my father's sword and I know he would like it taken into battle. I have no sons, wear it as my heir."

Furax, of course, had wanted to join Livius and Julius had to be very firm at the end. "You can go when you are no longer a child and have learned all the lessons given to you by Atticus." That had silenced him and Julius and Livius had said their emotional farewells.

When Livius returned to the stern even Hercules was impressed. Clad in his armour he looked every uncia the leader he was. "It looks, Livius, as though I'll be in Eboracum for a week or so. The Master wanted me to bring some trade goods back to distract attention from you; make it look as though you were just a passenger who paid for a voyage. It also means it you need a message going back I will still be here. If you need me you know where I am. Do you know of any good inns?"

"The best one I know is **The Saddle** in the vicus. An old comrade of mine is the landlord, you'll get on well, and, by the way, he's called Horse. Just use my name."

Wondering at the name he said, "I will and I hope the gods are with you."

It was closing towards dusk as the old ship edged its way in to the quayside of Eboracum. Although the port sometimes received strange nautical visitors, the particular lines and rigging caused more than a few stares from the idlers who frequented the waterways. It was the sort of attention which Livius did not require and he went below to return with a cloak. He tucked his helmet under his arm and then shook hands with

Hercules. "I'll report to the Prefect and send for my belongings when I can."

Hercules nodded edging the ship to gently touch the stone quay. "Tie her off."

Winking at Hercules he said, "Thank you for the voyage Captain. It has been most illuminating."

Once down the gangplank, he merged quickly with the throng of people who attempted to get to the ship; there were those who wanted employment to offload the ship, others required passage whilst there were a handful of stranded sailors who wished to go to sea again. Hercules chuckled to himself. He might have sailed halfway around the world to the very edge of the Empire but sailors and ports never changed. "Back off there. We have no cargo and we don't need any sailors. When I do need any help, I'll ask."

Julius and Livius had not been sure where the Governor might be. Marcus Appius Bradua had been recently sent by Emperor Trajan to Britannia but the new Emperor Hadrian had not been happy about his Governor. If Livius found him at Eboracum then it would mean he was a worthy Governor who was addressing the problems of the unrest. If he were in Londinium or somewhere in the safe hinterland then Julius and Livius were of the opinion he was not worth his salt. As he strode towards the gate he placed his helmet on his head and self-consciously tapped the pouch at his waist. The sentries came to attention when they saw his approach.

"Sir. Please state your business."

As it was getting close to dusk and the closing of the gates the sentries were even more vigilant than during the hours of daylight. "Decurion Princeps Livius Sallustius of the First Sallustian ala of Pannonians. Is the Governor in residence?"

"No sir, he is in Aquae Sulis."

"Very well then my business is with the Prefect."

"He is in the Praetorium sir."

One of the sentries looked as though he was going to question the stranger's right to enter when the other sentry suddenly recognised Livius. "Sir weren't you with Marcus' Horse and then the Explorates?"

"Yes, I was a soldier."

The man grinned and turned to his companion. "I would have had my bollocks on a Brigante spear if it wasn't for this man and his men. Good to have you back sir."

Smiling at the memory Livius strode towards the office, "Thank you soldier and I hope you have kept your balls safe ever since."

"Oh yes sir!"

The Prefect looked up when he heard his visitor announced. When Livius entered he sat back in his seat. "I don't believe I have heard of your ala Decurion Princeps."

"That is because it doesn't exist yet. I come from the Emperor Hadrian."

The Prefect went pale and almost fell off his chair. Livius cursed himself. They had left Rome so swiftly that they had outrun the news of the change of Emperor. "Emperor Trajan?"

"Died, natural causes," he added quickly. It was an amusing feeling to be completely in the know. The ordinary people, even the leaders, just heard the major events, but he knew the story behind the major events and had even had a hand in them.

Relieved, the Prefect gestured for Livius to take a seat. "Good, good. How may I help you then?"

"I have been commissioned to take charge of the Pannonian Ala based here and build up their strength. My orders are then to scout the northern lands."

"You will need the Allfather's help then for the north is becoming more of a problem. My Explorates brought me news of Selgovae travelling across the land of the lakes to visit with the Druids on Manavia."

Livius smiled to himself. The Prefect had been appointed after Livius departure two years ago for Aquitania; he did not know that he was the leader of the Explorates. "That gives me even more urgency to train my men."

The Prefect leaned forward. "I fear you will have trouble from the only officer, Spartianus. He expected to be given command. Between you and me he is an unpleasant customer." He stood and poured them both a beaker of wine. "He is not what I would call an officer. He and some of his men limped back into the fort today injured after a brawl in the vicus. I think they had been throwing their weight around as usual. I would have reprimanded the man but they are the only cavalry I have. And they are under strength."

Livius nodded and took out his orders. "Here are my orders from the Emperor."

"You have met the new Emperor?" Livius smiled and inclined his head. The Prefect waved away the papers. "No, you don't need to show them to me."

"I insist Prefect. I want them to be quite clear." As he pushed them over he made sure that his frumentari credentials were also visible on the table. He did not want to be a bully but he needed the complete cooperation of the fat man across the table and he knew he had to employ any means that were possible.

"That is satisfactory. Now as to your quarters…"

Livius stood and returned the letters to the pouch. He waved away the implied offer from the Prefect. "Tonight, I will stay in the vicus and I would appreciate it if you did not mention my arrival to the Decurion."

"Of course, of course."

"Once I take command, I will be moving the ala out of Eboracum and station them further north. They need to learn that they are a fighting force and not a garrison. I will expect supplies for my new recruits. You do not need to worry about horses I will deal with that but I will be sending all bills to you. I assume you have a clerk who will deal with that?"

The Prefect suddenly realised that his income would be halved. Had the order come from Decurion Spartianus he would have ignored it but he could not ignore an order from the Emperor and delivered by a frumentari. "Of course."

"I will let you know where the ala will be based as soon as I do. I expect you will let Governor Bradua know the news I bring?"

Livius was in no doubt that the Prefect would waste no time in passing on all the information he had given from his role through to the death of Trajan. "Of course, of course."

Chapter 7

The gates had closed by the time Livius was finished but, as the Prefect had accompanied him to the gate, he had no difficulty in getting out. He decided he would stay at The Saddle. He knew he would get a good room and he enjoyed the food. As he approached the building, he could hear a lot of noise from inside. The door was ajar and, pulling his cloak over his lower face he took off his helmet and slipped inside. He was unnoticed, for all were intent on an arm-wrestling contest between Hercules and Macro. There were half a dozen sailors, the Explorates and four or five other drinkers. Livius smiled to himself as he watched the old man and young warrior struggling. It was not obvious who would win.

"Come on Macro, he's an old man!" Marcus' strident voice rang out and Livius smiled at the filthy look Hercules threw his way. He caught Horse's eye and shook his head. Horse tapped his nose; he would not give Livius away. Livius saw him disappear into the kitchen.

"Put your weight behind it!" Rufius' comment did not help Macro who glared at his idol.

Both men were sweating heavily. Livius was confident that the younger, fitter, Macro would win but would he begin to doubt himself and then the ancient Hercules would snatch it at the death? Horse appeared with a beaker of ale.

"A room for the night?"

"Certainly. You are waiting for the outcome no doubt decurion?"

"Yes, Horse. I know both men and believe me Macro will win but not easily. How long has it been going on?"

"Long enough for the boys to have five beakers each."

"Ah. Is there money involved?"

"You know the lads, of course, but not enough to cause a fight."

"That's what I hoped."

Both men were now desperately seeking an honourable way out of the encounter. Livius provided it. He threw the contents of the beaker over the two men's locked arms. As soon as he did they both broke and turned to tear apart the man who had broken the rules. As soon as they saw him they both shouted, "Livius!" and then looked at each other.

"You know him?"

"I just brought him halfway around the world! And you?"

"I grew up with him and his comrades."

"So a draw I think." Livius judged.

59

Everyone burst out laughing and slapped each other on the back. Hercules and Macro embraced each other, both praising the other's skill. By the time they had settled down, there was a silence and they all looked expectantly at Livius. "Horse. I appear to have spilt my drink!"

His beaker refilled they made a space for him and he sat in the middle. He held his beaker up and said, "I give you a toast, the new Emperor Hadrian and the finest ala in the Roman Empire, the First Sallustian ala of Pannonians."

Everyone cheered Hadrian and then there was an embarrassed silence. Marcus spoke for them all when he said, "Surely you mean Macro's Horse."

Hercules sat chuckling to himself and Macro stared at him. What did the old man know that he did not? "My new command, I am Decurion Princeps of the new Pannonian ala. I am looking for decurions. I wonder where I can find some." There was a roar and Livius was surrounded by his colleagues who were slapping him on the back. "Is this any way to treat your new senior officer?"

Horse brought in more drinks and Livius, with the aid of a beaming Hercules, told them of Livius' exploits over the past months. "Hobnobbing with the Emperor! I can see how mundane our lives have been."

"No Metellus. The interlude with the Emperor merely showed me how much I missed those comrades who fought with me against impossible odds and, gentlemen," his voice became more serious, "I think those odds became longer."

They relaxed into a conversation about the events of the past couple of years, Rufius and Metellus chipping in about the adventure in Aquitania and Cassius giving them accounts of the heroic stand of the Ninth. Metellus could see Macro and Marcus itching to ask a question but in such august company felt intimidated.

"Before our two young comrades and eagle bearers burst I will ask the question which is on their lips and in their heart. Livius are you looking for volunteers?"

Livius hid his smile behind his beaker as the two young men blushed and fidgeted with their ale. "I am looking for some decurions, say three to start with? How about it would you three like to rejoin the auxilia?"

The pause was so brief that it really didn't exist at all. "We thought you would never ask," voiced Cassius. "The problem is that piece of shit who is the only decurion."

"Don't worry about him. Before you joined Marcus' Horse we had characters like that. He will either change or go."

In a wee small voice, Marcus ventured, "And us? Can we volunteer?"

"I don't think I can offer you the post of Decurion yet."

Metellus burst out laughing spraying Hercules with his ale. "Waste of good beer," was all the old man said as he wiped away the suds.

"Sorry."

"No, we just want to join," Macro added eagerly.

Livius turned to Cassius, winking. "You have seen these lads more than I have. What are their skills?"

"They are both excellent trackers and superb archers."

"Good but that means they should stay with the Explorates really. I would hate to deprive the new legion of two such superb scouts."

"Macro is the best swordsman I have seen since his father and the only men better with horses are Marcus and Cato." Livius drank some of his ale and sat back in his seat. Macro and Marcus were on the edge of their seats.

Metellus shook his head, "Come on Livius fun is fun but these lads will burst soon."

"It needs thought Metellus, a new ala doesn't just happen. I am building something new. Marcus' Horse grew out of a great ala. We have not that luxury." He put his ale down and leaned forward. "Here it is lads. I would like you, Marcus, to be the horse master. You will be a trooper at first but once you are fully trained and all things being equal I will promote you to sergeant. How does that sound?"

Macro slapped him on the back and an embarrassed Marcus nodded his acceptance. "Macro yours is a more difficult role. I want you to be a weapons trainer like your father and like Marcus you will have to start as a trooper, however, I suspect that some of the members of the ala may need some convincing so that part will not be announced." He looked around at the circle. "That will be our secret." They all nodded. "Marcus I want you to go to Cato tonight and arrange to purchase two hundred horses from the stud. Return by noon tomorrow with the best horses which the sergeant possesses. I doubt they will all be ready but then again we have no new troopers yet but it is good to be prepared. The rest of you come to the fortress tomorrow afternoon and go to the Prefect saying you wish to join. We must do all of this properly. Do you understand? There is more at stake here than the creation of a new ala. The security of the frontier is the prize for which we are fighting." Livius smiled as Marcus left almost as soon as he had finished his sentence. Keen was an understatement.

Livius took Hercules to one side. "This may be the last time we meet, old friend, for I know that Julius will keep his word and give you back '*The Swan*'. I would like to thank you for all that you did for both Julius and me. Were it not for you this venture would have ended before it began."

"For myself, I thank the gods each day for the moment you and the Senator walked into Ostia docks. My life had become dull and now… for one thing I had never met an Emperor before and now I am on nodding terms with one. As for my ship; whenever you or the Senator need me, for whatever purpose I will be there. It has been an honour to serve with you. "He leaned forward and spoke quietly, his good arm waving around the room. "You learn much about a man by what his friends say. Before you entered the inn tonight the only conversation concerned you and the praise would have made you blush. These men would follow you to the jaws of Hades and beyond. You cannot buy such loyalty. I knew the measure of you before they spoke to me, this merely confirmed it. As your men would say, May the Allfather be with you."

"And with you and, may you always have a wind at your back."

Horse gave Livius a good breakfast and then had his slave burnish his armour until it shone. When Livius protested Horse waved them away. "I want to see the little prick when you stand before him and tell him you are his commander."

"I am not sure I am the man I once was Horse. My legs were badly injured."

Horse laughed. "Look at me with one arm and it doesn't stop me. Besides didn't I hear that Ulpius Felix, the finest warrior in the ala only had one eye? What are a couple of gimpy legs? Besides I have seen you move sir and they don't appear to slow you up."

"You may be right Horse. Thank you for your hospitality. How much do I owe you?"

"Owe me? Nothing. You are a comrade."

"And I am a comrade who wishes to come again and not receive charity. Besides I am sure you didn't charge the decurions and the lads enough. Here." He tossed a gold aureus on the table.

"This is far too much."

"It was a payment from the new Emperor. Let us just say I am spreading his generosity."

"In that case sir… thank you!"

The sentries at the gate were expecting Livius and they snapped to attention. He had arrived early enough to have ensured that none of his new ala was up and about. He intended to start as he would go on. He nodded to the sentry. "Prefect in?"

"Yes, Decurion. He said to go straight in." He leaned over and said shyly. "Good to have you back sir. I fought with you against... against." his voice trailed off.

"My brother."

"Yes sir. I didn't like to say. I know what families can be."

"Well in my case I killed him so there is no disgrace now."

The sentry looked seriously at Livius. "None of the lads ever thought there was any disgrace sir. You can't help your family can you?"

The Prefect looked up and clasped Livius' arm. He was pleased, now that he had had time to reflect, that the new Emperor had sent this man to his fort. It boded well. The reputation of Marcus' Horse and all its men and officers was still spoken of around campfires and feasts. If this new ala could only be half as good as their predecessor then the barbarian incursions might be halted. "How are you going to play it then?"

"Straight sir, or," he grinned impishly, "as straight as someone who was an Explorate for a few years can manage."

The Prefect smiled, "Go on you intrigue me."

"Today you will receive four volunteers, technically five, but I have sent one to acquire some horses so we will need to enter his name in the books. Three of them are Decurions; you know, them Cassius, Metellus and Rufius."

"Damn good men. I shall miss them as Explorates."

"I think Prefect that many of the things they did as Explorates will have rubbed off. I think they will be better officers because of that. Have you uniforms for them?"

"I think so. We had spares left over from when Marcus' Horse was operating out of Morbium."

"Good. I intend to send for the Decurion and arrange an inspection. Once they are all here and my new decurions have arrived then we shall leave your fortress and build a camp." He looked knowingly at the Prefect. "I daresay that the Quartermaster will be glad that he no longer has the mouths to feed and the hay to find."

"I think I can safely say that he will buy you drinks the next time you visit."

"As soon as I have built the new camp, I will let you know and you can begin to send my supplies."

"How long will it take you to train them up?"

"I haven't got any untrained recruits but I will spread the word around the Dunum. The people there still hold us in high esteem and the land to the south of the Dunum is good horse country. I hope to make up the numbers quickly. It will take us a couple of months to get up to speed but I intend to pick the best forty-five men and give them to my three decurions. The sooner we make our presence felt the better."

The Prefect breathed an audible sigh of relief. "That has taken a load off my mind I can tell you. I was dreading a long training period and no cavalry patrols."

"I intend to train the turmae and get them on patrol as soon as I can. From what my decurions tell me we have danger heading our way and I fear that Morwenna has been spinning her webs once more. All we need is that sly bitch stirring up the tribes with her enchantments."

"You knew her I believe?"

"Aye. She suckered us all in, especially Decurion Macro but she will not fool us again. Right sir. With your permission, I will use one of your sentries…"

"Go ahead."

Livius left the office and gestured to the sentry. "Would you be so good as to fetch Decurion Aelius Spartianus to the Prefect's office?"

"Should I tell him why sir?"

Livius smiled, "No let us not spoil the surprise eh?"

Grinning, the sentry saluted, "No sir!" The Decurion had made himself totally unpopular with the entire garrison and the sentry could not wait until he received his comeuppance.

Livius put his helmet on and made sure his armour and sword were correct. From what Cassius had said this was a young arrogant officer and worse still, a bully. Livius would need to use all his skills with this one. The memory of his brother helped him. He had been mercilessly bullied by his sibling for years but when he had defeated him, not once but twice it gave Livius the confidence to face all bullies knowing that he could defeat them.

The sentry returned, a huge grin on his face, "He's coming sir but he is not a happy trooper!" He leaned conspiratorially into Livius. "He thinks it is the Prefect and started mouthing off about jumped up fat little nobodies ordering him around!"

"Thank you….?"

"Gratius Galba sir."

"Thank you Gratius I will not forget you."

Livius leaned back into the shadow of the roof and watched as Aelius Spartianus stormed over. He was a small dark-haired man with a full beard and moustache although the thinness suggested he had only grown it recently, probably to make himself look older. He was not a tall man and he was not muscled and it was no surprise that Cassius had bested him so easily. He had made the mistake of not coming in full uniform and he had neither helmet nor vine staff. His uniform looked as though he had slept in it. Marcus, Gaius and Julius had always impressed on the young decurions that you made sure you wore your best when meeting a senior officer but, of course, Spartianus only thought he was meeting the 'fat little nobody' and not his superior.

When he mounted the steps the sentry held his spear across the door. "Damn it! He sent for me! Am I to wait outside like a naughty boy? I am the Decurion Princeps of the Second wing of Pannonians and I will not be kept waiting by a has-been." He had shouted loudly to make sure that the Prefect would hear him and he lounged against the doorway an arrogant grin on his face.

Livius timed his entrance to perfection. He stepped out and, as luck would have it, the sun came out and glistened on his burnished cuirass. The effect was as though he had appeared in a magician's puff of smoke. "The Prefect did not send for you sonny. I did and I am the Decurion Princeps of the First Sallustian ala of Pannonians."

To do him justice Spartianus tried to bluster for a moment or two. "So, who are you? I have never heard of the Sallustian ala."

"Perhaps that is because until yesterday it was the Second wing of Pannonians but Emperor Hadrian has decided to give it to me and rename it after my uncle, in his honour."

It was as though someone had punched him in the solar plexus. "Emperor Hadrian but, I thought that Emperor Trajan still…"

"Which should tell you decurion," Livius emphasised the last word, "that I know considerably more than you. Now close your mouth before a horse falls in it and then get your men on parade with full equipment and this time make sure you are properly dressed. Tell them we are leaving Eboracum to go to our new quarters."

Scipius Porcius had left his office to observe the end game of this encounter. Aelius glared at him, then the sentry and began to move off. "How about a salute Decurion or will I have to show you how it is done?" The salute was ragged and the enmity glared out from his angry eyes.

The sentry murmured, to no one in particular, "Definitely not a happy little trooper."

The ala arrived a little less promptly than Livius would have expected. It did not worry him as he had plenty of time. He intended to leave Eboracum mid-afternoon and make the ala build a camp as dusk was descending. He had chosen his site already in his mind but he would keep that privileged piece of information to himself. He allowed them to shuffle into vague lines and then stepped down from the steps of the Principia. The sentries were all eagerly anticipating the impact that Livius would have. Most of the Batavians in the fort knew him formerly from the time he had been a Decurion in the auxiliary and latterly as an Explorate. Everyone looked up to him and admired him for what he had done. The Pannonians knew nothing about their new commander. He walked down the lines examining each horse and each trooper. Spartianus sat in front of them, feeling proud of himself. He knew that they were a smart ala.

"I am Decurion Princeps Livius Lucullus Sallustius and I am your new Decurion Princeps. We do not, as yet, have a Prefect. The numbers do not merit one but we will and when we do I hope that you do not embarrass me as you must be embarrassing your decurion. I served with Marcus' Horse." He let the words sink in. "That is right. The finest ala which ever served in the Roman Army." He glared at them, daring any to gainsay him. "The only thing you have in common is that you are Pannonians and there the resemblance ends." He stared at Spartianus. "Yesterday some of you went into the vicus and tried to pick a fight." He shrugged. "It happens but unfortunately for you, your men lost. You are now a new ala. You are the First Sallustian Wing of Pannonians." He noticed that they looked at each other in surprise, obviously, Spartianus had not told them." The New Emperor of Rome, the Divine Hadrian, has granted my family that honour for the service we have done." The bemused looks told Livius that the troopers of the ala were less confident in the veracity of their former decurion. "We will be in the field for the foreseeable future. We will have to patrol the whole of Northern Britannia because I can tell you all that trouble is coming and the only thing in its way will be us so prepare yourself to be between a rock and hard place."

Livius had caught out of the corner of his eye his three decurions and Macro arriving. He had given them enough time to get their new uniforms and don them. He only hoped that Marcus had reached Cato and had a horse for him or the whole show would appear pathetic. "We will be recruiting but until that time you will have to perform as one ala."

Spartianus could not restrain himself. "How can we do that with only two officers?"

"How can we do that with only two officers sir?"

"Sorry, sir."

"You should know that I have not been idle and I have three decurions who served with Marcus Horse, let me introduce Decurion Cassius Nautius. Decurion Metellus Scribonious and Decurion Rufius Lividius and finally weapons trainer, Decius Macro Culleo son of the great Macro, the greatest warrior in any ala in the Roman Empire."

The silence was resounding. Everyone had heard of Macro and to see his son standing alongside the other heroes of Marcus' Horse was intimidating beyond belief. Spartianus slumped in his saddle. He had hoped to foist his own cronies upon the new commander and drive him from his command. The four men who had bested him yesterday stood before him and glared pointedly at the decurion. Livius allowed the silence to hang, like a sword of Damocles above the ala. When he broke the silence he was pleased that some of the men actually jumped. "I now have four decurions and there are two hundred and fifty of us. Each turma will be fifty in number until I have seen who amongst you are worthy of promotion. You have enjoyed a pleasant time in Eboracum. That pleasant time has ended."

He heard the clatter of hooves as Marcus rode in with a string of five of the finest horses ever seen. Livius resisted the temptation to look around and continued. "We are now leaving Eboracum. Whatever you have forgotten stays here. This is the day when the First Sallustian makes its reputation. You will not let me down!"

The last word was roared out as Marcus rode in front of Livius with the most magnificent black stallion anyone had ever seen. Livius mounted as though he had ridden the horse forever. He murmured under his breath to Marcus, "What is his name?"

"Thunder."

"Thank you and well done Marcus, he is magnificent!" He turned to his ala and unsheathed his sword. "Today is the first chapter in the book which is the annals of the First Sallustian Wing of Pannonians."

The men had been caught up in the rhetoric and, apart from Spartianus and his cronies, roared out an answer. Livius turned to Marcus and winked, "So far, so good!"

Chapter 8

By the time Livius finally rested the ala, all the men, apart from the Explorates, were exhausted. They had ridden fifty miles and were some thirty miles northeast of Cataractonium in the lee of the hills which rolled away to the sea. Livius himself was feeling the effects of trying to control a fierce horse and ride such a long way. He suddenly remembered that it was over three years since he had ridden such a tiring distance. He was pleased that the men and Spartianus looked even worse. His five companions looked as fresh as daisies.

Spartianus rode next to him. "Where is the fort?"

Livius looked at him as though he had asked where the Tiber was. "Fort?"

"Where we will be sleeping tonight."

"Tonight, Decurion Spartianus, we will be building our own camp and tomorrow it will become a fort."

The look on Spartianus' face was priceless. He had never had to build a camp. In Batavia, they had operated out of existing forts as they had at Eboracum. Marcus' Horse had been used to building a camp each night as they had advanced north with Agricola. Livius could not help giving a knowing nod and then murmuring. "Welcome to the future, Decurion! And get used to it. For now, you will earn your pay."

The site which Livius had chosen was a good one. He had first seen it when he was a young decurion leading his men after Caledonii raiders; it had stayed in his memory. There was a small knoll with natural banks leading down to a stream. The vale leading to Morbium stretched away west and behind them were the steep hills leading to the sea. The men had obviously never erected a camp before and he smiled as his three Decurions chivvied and chased their men. Marcus and Macro were able to help the troopers and soon became firm favourites of every trooper they encountered because of their good humour, hard work and knowledge. They disappeared as the troopers began to erect their tents. Livius gestured to his three trusted confederates.

"Well?"

"There are some keen lads who have potential but it is obvious that they have not been led. They have been bullied. They wouldn't know how to wipe their arse if someone didn't tell them."

"Eloquently put Cassius."

"Speak as I find sir."

"Any officer material?"

Metellus nodded, "A couple sir. The thing is Spartianus has got his cronies ruling the roost. The men are scared shitless of them."

Livius nodded, it matched his assessment. "Tomorrow we rearrange the turmae. Put his cronies in your turmae and mine. Let's isolate the bastard."

They watched as the last tent was erected and the men fell into heaps around them. "Look at that sir, no horse lines and no kitchens."

"I know Cassius. You go and organise the horse lines. Metellus organise the kitchens and Rufius pick out ten men and take a patrol around the area. Send Spartianus to me." Livius almost heard the collective groan as exhausted men were dragged to their feet.

A murderous Spartianus approached. "You sent for me sir." He almost spat out the 'sir'.

"Are you pleased with the ala?"

"The lads have never done this before."

"What they have never had to march fifty miles and build a camp? Then I am afraid your officers, may the Allfather protect them, did you no favours. This is how the Roman Army survives, why it has been so successful over so many years. They march, build a camp and then fight. If we had to fight right now I wouldn't give you two denarii for our chances. We will be here for a short time but get used to this Decurion, this is the future."

He called Metellus over. "Make sure you have three fire pits going."

Metellus looked dubiously at the dusk which was making it hard to see a hand before a face. "Are you sure Macro and Marcus will deliver? It is getting dark very quickly."

"Do you trust Macro and Marcus?"

"With my life!"

"Then trust them to get supper," he leaned over conspiratorially, "even a couple of hares would seem like a feast." Metellus nodded, a grin spreading across his face. How could he have doubted the young lads?

By the time all the tasks were finished the men were lurching like drunkards. They looked accusingly at the two fire pits blazing merrily away; hatred in their hearts for this martinet who had disturbed their tranquil lives living in the relative luxury of a garrison town with alehouses a stone's throw away. He strode into the light of the fires. "Well done men. Tomorrow we begin our training. Some of you will be building a gyrus, some will be making the walls of our fort higher and the better warriors amongst you will be bringing the first of our mounts."

Someone, Livius thought one of Spartianus' cronies yelled out, "We're fucking starving!"

Cassius made to go and find the voice but Livius restrained him. "You have rations do you not? Then eat porridge and dried meat."

There was a sudden murmuring which began to grow. The three decurion's hands went to their swords but Livius said quietly, "Faith boys, faith." Suddenly every trooper turned as they heard the galloping of horses. "You see what happens when you are slipshod and do not set guards?"

It was a relief to all two hundred and fifty terrified faces when the grinning pair of Marcus and Macro rode in and threw down two buck deer and four hares. "Luckily gentlemen, you have two of the finest hunters in Britannia in the ala. Now, do we have a cook?" There was silence. "I am sorry I expressed myself badly, do we have someone who can cook and would like to be a cook?"

Livius peered around and saw a hand appear from the exhausted mass of troopers. A man stepped forward. Livius looked quizzically at him. "Septimus Porcus sir." The man was squat and as round, as he was tall.

"Can you cook?"

"A little bit."

A voice from the back shouted, "He is really good sir he makes the shit they serve as rations actually edible!"

"High praise indeed. Right, Septimus tonight is your chance. Pick four men to help you to skin and prepare the animals."

Marcus spoke up. "Found some bilberries sir, not as good as juniper but they might help."

"Any use Cook?"

Septimus grinned, "Oh yes sir and I saw some wild garlic a ways back, can I send a couple of lads for it?"

"You are the cook. "He went to his saddle and returned with a flask and a lemon. "You can use these too. The lemon is from Rome as is the olive oil. Use them well Cook and tomorrow you may be a sergeant."

Septimus roared, "Yes sir!" and Livius knew he had converted at least five of his troopers.

Aelius Spartianus deigned to share the Decurion's tent with his three new brother officers. Instead, he joined the small cabal of followers. There were seven of them and they had all attached themselves to the young officer early on in their military career. They were the bullies who forced any dissenting voice in the ala to be silent. They were the ones who chose the easy duties and they were the ones who took money from the men to avoid beatings. Each one of them hoped for advancement both professionally and financially and, indeed, had already shared in the profits from the money Spartianus had obtained through his various frauds.

They spoke quietly in the tent. The Fist was a de facto second in command for Aelius. He had his nickname because of the enormous hams at the end of each arm. A powerful thug of a man he had once almost beaten a recruit to death had he not been stopped by the old Decurion Princeps. His punishment had been a flogging which had proved unfortunate for the Decurion Princeps who had suffered a Roman javelin to the back in the next frenetic skirmish. The Fist had spoken with many of the other troopers whilst they were working. "I don't think we will be getting as much cooperation from the boys now. They aren't exactly queuing up to make trouble for us but they think the new leader and the decurions will make their life a little easier."

"I think that you will have to persuade them otherwise."

Wolf was named for his oversized canines which, added to the hirsute nature of his body, meant he looked like a wolf; his enemies added, behind his back of course, that he smelled like a wolf too. "Not quite as easy as you might think boss. They all heard about the kicking we got in that inn the other night."

Aelius rounded on his hairy companion. "We did not get a kicking. They took us by surprise that is all."

"Tonight's little stunt has won over some of the boys though. You know the ones who never look beyond the next meal." The Fist was an intelligent thug and had observed the effect the evening meal had had on men whose rations were dull at best. If the two young hunters continued to supply such food then the men would side with Sallustius.

Aelius waved away the idea as though it was a gnat. "Once he has the men building walls and training, they will soon tire of a little game. We need to keep our eyes and ears open. Watch for an opportunity to sow the seeds of discord. This man is watching us as are his little band of spies but they will make a mistake and when they do we need to be in a position to take advantage."

They nodded their agreement and then fell into an exhausted sleep. A figure silently rose from the environs of the tent and walked over to the officer on guard. Walking away from the troopers who were on duty Rufius reported what had transpired to Livius. "It is as I suspected then. They are trying to undermine us."

Rufius took out his pugeo, "We could end this dissension tonight."

Livius smiled and put the dagger back in the scabbard. "I can see that I will have to whittle away some of your Explorates tendencies. No there are more ways to skin a cat. I have some ideas which I will put in place on the morn. Get some sleep Rufius, you have done well."

The next morning saw an aching camp awake. The men had not ridden so far nor done so much work for a long time. Septimus had been up early cooking up the bones of last night's feast and adding wild thyme, wild garlic and some sausage he had acquired. The hot meal in the early, chill hours raised the men's spirits and Livius called him over. "Well done Septimus. You are as good as your word and I appreciate the gesture of rising early to feed the men."

Septimus shrugged, "It didn't take much sir and I know how men like a hot meal if they can get one."

"None the less it shows me the mettle of a man. You are now Cook with the rank of sergeant and the accompanying pay."

"Thank you, sir!"

"No, thank you, sergeant, you are right, a man with a full stomach works and fights better."

"If I might be able to start on a bread oven today sir? Men work better with fresh bread and the smell makes them feel better."

"Good idea. Take as many men as you need." Livius next called over the decurions. The last to arrive reluctantly was Aelius and he stood apart from the other three. Macro and Marcus were unsure of their role; they were, ostensibly, troopers but they knew that Livius had other plans for them. He saw their indecision and with a half-smile gestured for them to join them. Spartianus spat on the ground as they approached. Macro's hand went to his sword but the glare he received from Cassius made him back off.

"We have much to do today. Cassius, I want you to take Macro and Marcus and forty troopers. You can build the gyrus over there." He pointed to a flattened area in a dell a hundred paces from the fort. Metellus you can take twenty troopers and build the enclosure for the horses next to it. That will leave Rufius, Aelius and me with the rest of the troopers to finish the building of the fort. Questions?"

Spartianus spat his question out, "I thought you said last night that you wanted some men to bring in the horses?"

Livius walked over to him. "I realise you have become used to running things around here Decurion but I am your superior officer and I will have a sir from you or you will be flogged. Do you understand?"

The Decurion's face flushed but he grunted a," Sir!"

"Now we will be sending for the spare horses Decurion but not today. I need to find out from all of you who the most able men are and we will use them to fetch the new mounts."

72

The sharp eyes of Spartianus glinted at the news. His men would all be recommended and, hopefully, he would be able to make the most of the opportunity. He did not know yet how he could manipulate the situation but if the new leader wanted the best then his men would infiltrate that particular elite group.

Marcus raised his arm, "Sir?"

"Yes, Marcus?"

"Do you want Macro and me to go hunting again sir?"

"Good idea. Help Cassius this morning and then go hunting this afternoon. Take the Cook with you."

"Sir!"

"Right off you go. Metellus and Cassius choose your men and we will have whoever is left." Rufius remained with Livius as Spartianus sulked off to find The Fist and the others. "Tonight Rufius I want to reorganise the ala. I want those seven men split into seven of the eight turmae."

Rufius looked confused. "But we only have five decurions."

"At the moment we do but I have a mind to give Macro, and Marcus one temporarily, along with the cook and his men. Hopefully, we will discover a potential decurion who will shine in the next few days. Besides one of us can command a couple of turmae eh?"

Rufius grinned, "Never stopped us before sir."

Livius and Metellus stripped down to their tunics and joined in with the troopers as they toiled away making the ditch deeper and the ramparts higher. The troopers looked at them as though they had the moon madness, at first, never having seen an officer working. Aelius looked on them in disdain and just barked orders until Livius walked over to him. "Decurion if your commanding officer can work then the least you can do is to join him eh?"

Unable to refuse such a command, however pleasantly couched, the truculent decurion had no choice but to comply. He was seething with anger, for his seven cronies had been selected for the other work parties and he was left isolated amongst troopers who were beginning to lose their fear of this man. Aelius worked along with the others but with less effort and less energy. It did not go unnoticed by both the officers and the troopers. Rather than having a negative effect, it seemed to inspire the men so that they worked even harder, determined to show their new commanding officer that they not all cast in the same mould as Aelius Spartianus. They worked so well that Metellus was able to begin the construction of the Principia. The men could live in their tents but if there was one wooden building then it would give a sense of permanency.

The troopers were just tidying away the rubbish which they had accumulated and making the fort look more military when Septimus rode in with Macro and Marcus. They had a packhorse with them and the men roared their cheers when they saw it was a male boar, an enormous tusker. They halted next to Livius. "Good hunting I see Septimus."

Marcus slipped off his horse. "We remembered the woods not far from here where Gaelwyn took us hunting. We knew there were some big buggers there but we never expected to find one as big as this."

"Did it put up much of a fight?"

Marcus and Macro shook their heads modestly. "Put up a fight? I thought it would gore one of the troopers sir. It took five arrows, a javelin and had to be finished by young Macro using his sword! I have never seen the like," Septimus was happy to sing their praises even if Spartianus had a face like soured milk. "We also found some greens and some more hares. It will vary the diet. I suppose that I had best be off and start to prepare this beast." Septimus had a grin on his face as wide as a river estuary, this was a way of life he actually enjoyed.

Livius smiled. At least one of the troopers was doing something he liked. The gyrus builders and the corral builders arrived simultaneously. Cassius saluted, he was sweaty and grimy but the smile on his face told Livius that he had had a good day. "All finished sir. We can begin training tomorrow."

"Excellent." To the ala as a whole Livius raised his voice. "You have done well and tomorrow we can begin to make this ala the finest in Britannia." The reaction was all that he had hoped for, with the exception of eight or ten the whole of the ala shouted a tired, but heartfelt cheer.

Livius watched as Spartianus sloped off with his seven acolytes. He gestured for his decurions to follow him to the partly built Principia. "Well?"

"Some good lads here sir. Some lazy bastards but they are without malice."

"Cassius is right but those seven who follow Spartianus, well, the only way to describe them is, evil. I am not certain but I am sure the one they called The Fist knocked around a couple of the lads when we weren't watching. They are sly"

"Yeah, and I am sure that the one called Wolf tried to sabotage the corral luckily some of the good lads happened to notice the damage and repaired it."

"Right Cassius well when we make up the roster I will have The Fist in my turma and you take this Wolf. Divide the rest between

Metellus and Rufius. You may have more of his men but the dangerous ones will be separated."

That night Spartianus again held conference with his confederates. "Things went too well today."

The Fist looked apologetically at the floor. "We tried but those Decurions have eyes like hawks and seemed to be watching only us."

Aelius could not help but agree. They had been outwitted by the Decurion Princeps and handled piecemeal. "Tomorrow we can begin to disrupt their plans for tomorrow we will be in our turmae and training in the gyrus. You can show them your power." The Fist inclined his head. He was a powerful fighter and had never been bested in any of the contests in which he had participated. In combat, he was like a ferocious, rabid dog and every trooper feared being paired with the mighty warrior who treated every training bout as a real battle. "We must make the men fear us again. The hunted meals will soon pale; especially if they begin to suffer injuries and wounds in training. By the time he has us on patrol he will be ready to leave and return to the Explorates from whence he came."

Wolf look across at his leader. "You know where he was before he was an Explorate don't you?"

Aelius did not like being kept in the dark but he did not know the Decurion Princeps' origins. "No. What did you discover Wolf?"

"He served with Marcus' Horse and has just returned from a mission for Emperor Trajan where he journeyed to Gaul, retrieved gold stolen by traitors and killed his brother. This is not a man to underestimate."

Aelius dismissed the praise with a wave of his hand. "Pah! I have seen him move, he has wounds on his legs. When the time comes The Fist will take him and I will assume command of this ala."

His men looked doubtful but so far their leader had delivered all that he had promised and they were willing to stay with him just a little longer.

Livius stood in the middle of the gyrus. Five targets, man-sized dummies stood in a line along the middle of the open training area. The ala was gathered in five ranks before Livius and his decurions. "Today we will see what you are like in the saddle and in combat. This morning will be spent on horseback, the afternoon in combat. The best fifty riders, after this morning's session, will go with my horse master to pick up our herd." They all looked at each other wondering which of the decurions would be the horse master. Aelius imperceptibly nodded to his cronies. This might be an opportunity to score points over the hated

Decurion Princeps. Livius raised his hand and Marcus galloped, full tilt into the gyrus. The Decurion Princeps could see the joyful look on Aelius' face. Marcus did not pause but galloped the full length of the gyrus shooting five arrows into five dummies, wheeling and then returning to slice off the top part of each dummy's false head.

"Now some of you may be looking at Trooper Marcus Aurelius, son of Gaius Aurelius, and thinking he might be a little young to be a master of horse. And you may be right so I will make this promise. If any of you can repeat the trooper's actions then you will become the Sergeant Horse Master of the ala."

There was a silence as they all looked at each other. One lone, hidden voice yelled out, "We do not use bows in this ala."

Livius smiled, "You mean you did not use bows in this ala but you will. Three of your decurions are almost as good as young Marcus and Trooper Culleo is his equal. They will train you so that you too become as proficient as they."

A subdued ala spent the rest of the morning learning to ride with their knees whilst throwing javelins at the targets. At first, their performance was abysmal but gradually they improved. Exhausted they rested at noon, grateful for the hot soup and bread which Septimus had produced. He and his team had spent the previous afternoon building a bread oven and as the smell of baking bread permeated the air Livius knew he had made a good appointment.

He approached Cassius and Marcus. "Any candidates?"

They looked at each other and Marcus deferred to Cassius. "There are about thirty outstanding horsemen. Surprisingly enough two of Spartianus' cronies are amongst them."

"Good, then this is the First Turma. Rufius, it is yours to command. They will be the archers we use. Marcus and Rufius take the turma and go to Cato. Return with the mounts."

Marcus looked at the darkening sky. "And if it is too late?"

"Then I am sure you will enjoy Cato's hospitality." Grinning Rufius and Marcus left to collect their men. They had counted on a night at the villa of Marcus and Cato.

The afternoon was a dull and dismal affair. The weather had changed to become overcast and threatened rain. The men were weary after three days which had tested their fitness and they had been found to be lacking. As they lined up on the gyrus they were all armed with their rudius, a wooden sword and their small training buckler. Livius knew that the wooden rudius could strike as painful a blow as an edged weapon. The Fist and the remaining men of Spartianus' club were standing together, eagerly awaiting the opportunity to inflict punishment on some hapless trooper. Aelius was also grinning confidently. He might not be the best horseman nor the hardest working trooper, but he could fight, not always fairly but normally successfully. With Rufius away, Livius was left with just four Decurions which suited his plan perfectly.

He stood before them. "You have worked hard men and we are all pleased with you. This afternoon however we begin the real work. I know you can ride but can you fight? Pair yourselves off with someone of equal stature." No-one wanted to be paired off with neither The Fist nor any of his cronies and there was a rush to find someone less aggressive. Soon there were just nine men left, the five Spartiani and four unlucky troopers who looked decidedly unhappy. Metellus went over to pair off the four troopers and The Fist was left with an evil grin on his face. He had counted on the fact that no-one would wish to fight him and he would be left with a decurion and he would inflict crippling punishment. Livius too had counted on that fact. "As an incentive, men, the most successful amongst you will be appointed weapon trainer for the ala." The Fist looked over at Spartianus and punched his buckler with his wooden sword. "Now it would be unfair to pair one of you with a decurion but fortunately Trooper Culleo has just returned from his hunting expedition and I am sure that he will pair off with you trooper. The rest of you, begin!"

Soon there was a clack and crash of wood on wood and the occasional cry as someone received a blow. As each contest finished Cassius moved the successful combatants to one side of the gyrus. Metellus was not sure if Livius and Macro had planned it that way but as the last combat ended he emerged with wooden rudius and buckler. Although he had grown over the years he was not yet fully grown and The Fist towered over him. The difference was that Macro had not an ounce of fat on him. He was lean and well-muscled. He trained every day, lifting weights and honing his skills; The Fist was big but there was more fat and flab than muscle. He grinned at the young trooper and then murmured, "Well there is no fucker to protect you here and I will give you a world of pain." Macro looked at him, his steely eyes despising someone who would deliberately hurt a comrade. It hardened his resolve to defeat the ala bully.

Livius began to wonder had he made the right decision. Cassius had assured him that no-one could defeat Macro but the evil-looking trooper looked like he could chew him up and spit him out. Macro looked calm with a half-grin playing on his lips. He glanced over at Livius and raised the rudius in salute.

The Last Frontier

The two men warily moved around the circle made by the winners and the losers now combined to enjoy this exhibition; bets and wagers were already being exchanged. Suddenly The Fist dived in pummelling a flurry of blows at Macro and his buckler; all were easily deflected by the sword and skill of Macro. The Fist looked a little disconcerted. That combination of blows had normally ended other similar contests for him. He tried it again and once more Macro calmly defeated every attack. Macro noticed, with some satisfaction, the sweat on The Fist's top lip and forehead. He could see that the exertions were making the unfit bully breathe heavily. The third attack was despatched with as much ease as the first two. Macro knew that he was fitter than the older man; he also knew that he was a better swordsman. He had been taught that the best will always win. The Fist looked around in desperation, catching the eye of his superior, Aelius, the look pleaded for help. He launched into another attack trying to beat back the young, accomplished warrior. Suddenly a rock was rolled from the crowd and Macro's foot turned on it and he fell. In an instant The Fist hacked down, deliberately, at Macro's knee; there was a crack and everyone could see that the boy was injured. There was a roar of anger from the crowd and Cassius raced forward to end the contest. Livius shook his head. Metellus and Rufius appeared on either side of Aelius Spartianus for it was obvious to the officers who had thrown the rock.

Macro was at a severe disadvantage; movement had been his secret weapon and now he found himself to be struggling to keep pace with an opponent who knew he was going to win. He had no option, he had to go for the win or the man who would be the weapon trainer, the same rank as his father, would be a cheat and a bully. He watched as The Fist glanced around to his mentor to nod. Macro seized his chance; he charged in, his wooden rudius a blur of blows. He struck The Fist's shield and then his sword and then his knee. As his opponent favoured one side Macro went in the other and hit the rudius into The Fist's stomach with such force that the breath left his heaving, sweating body. As he stood like a fish out of water, trying to gulp in air Macro smashed his rudius ruthlessly on the side of the warrior's head, rendering him unconscious. He fell like a tree chopped by an axe and lay in a heap. The capsarii strolled in to see if he was still alive. They did not seem bothered either way.

There was a sudden roar of 'Macro!' and every trooper raced to pat Macro on the back. As they flooded past them Metellus and Rufius punched their fists into the ribs of Aelius Spartianus. Metellus leaned down, "Big mistake, decurion, for Macro is one of our own. Watch your back for you now have Explorates as your enemies and we leave corpses behind."

Livius called over the capsarius, "See to the sergeant."

Even as he lay in agony Macro heard Livius' words. "Sergeant?"

"I think you have earned it." Turning to the ala Livius raised his arms for silence. "The weapon trainer, Sergeant Culleo will receive medical treatment and then begin training. Until then the decurions will take you through your paces." He nodded to Cassius and Metellus who then turned to Spartianus to give him his instructions.

Septimus came over with a beaker. The capsarius was finishing off bandaging the injured leg when Septimus proffered the drink. "Here Sergeant, drink this."

Macro looked at it suspiciously. "What is it?"

"Poison of course." He shook his head impatiently. "A mixture of soup, herbs and something my mother swore by. It will do you good." The capsarius glared at Septimus. "Don't worry I am not trying to do you out of a job but this man gets us the best game around. It is in all our interests to keep him healthy eh?" Grinning he slapped the capsarius on the back and then wandered cheerfully back to his kitchen.

Livius smiled. The ala was becoming a team. All he now needed was to give them some steel and then find another two hundred and fifty to make up the numbers. Creating the bond was one thing but finding men who could ride and fight was another. The wars around the frontier had taken the best men and the progress of Rome was marked by their trail of graves. Livius would need to search far and wide to find the men he needed.

Chapter 9

As the capsarius tended to Macro, Livius spoke to his senior decurions, "Not the way I would have wanted it to play the scenario out but Macro is now a hero and Spartianus and his cronies are becoming more isolated."

Rufius looked around at the body of Aelius being helped to his tent by his diminishing group of friends, "Let me finish it tonight sir. A blade in the night and that sly bastard is history."

Metellus smiled and put his arm around Rufius. "Think of the bigger picture my friend. Livius is right. We gain more by this than the death of Spartianus would achieve. He would be a martyr and his friends would gain support. This way they will be watching for the blow in the night and the sudden death of a conspirator. The Decurion Princeps can now make Macro his weapon trainer without having to fight every thug in the ala."

Rufius looked at Metellus and nodded. Livius said, "Keep an eye on both Macro and on that shower. I do not trust them and I don't want one of them taking revenge on the lad. Tomorrow we begin our patrols."

By the time Marcus and Rufius returned with the string of horses Macro, bandaged and limping, had the men training. He was trying to get them to be able to ride in echelon and throw their javelins at the same time. Although enthusiastic they were not very effective. The absence of The Fist, still being looked after by the capsarius and Wolf, away with Marcus, meant that there was a lighter atmosphere. Spartianus' remaining men had been closely watched by Cassius and Metellus and had not had the opportunity to create any more mischief.

Cassius pointed northeast. "It looks like we have our horses. Now we just need men."

"The problem is, Cassius, that we have too few men we can rely on and trust. Septimus and his cooks are good examples of what we can achieve when we have reliable men."

"There are about six or seven who I have been watching and I think they are our kind of men."

"Do you trust them?"

Cassius considered a poor decision could be disastrous for the future of the fledgeling ala. "Yes sir. I think that they can be trusted."

"Very well then bring them to me after I have spoken with Marcus. We will put them to work and see if they can be given the responsibility on a temporary basis."

Cassius peered at the whinnying line of horses. "Livius we only sent fifty men with Marcus, didn't we?"

"I believe so."

"I think that there are more than fifty there."

Livius could now see the civilian clothes amongst those of the auxiliaries. "I wonder what that pair have been up to." They could now see that the old sergeant from Marcus' Horse, Cato, was with them. Cato had been responsible for setting up the stud which produced the horses for the old ala. After they had retired Marcus Maximunius and the sergeant had built up their farm to produce the finest mounts in Britannia. Cato was now over sixty years old but he looked as fit as ever. It had been said that he preferred the company of horses to men and, certainly, Livius had never seen anyone who could communicate with horses like Cato.

Marcus and Rufius reined in their horses with Cato; the two decurions were grinning from ear to ear and looking very pleased with themselves. "Well then report. Or do you intend to keep us all waiting?" Livius nodded to Cato. "Welcome Sergeant Cato. I hope this pair hasn't made you ride all this way for nothing."

Cato dismounted and came to clasp Livius' arm. "No, Decurion Princeps, I just invited myself. I wanted to see how you were going to look after my fine horses and," he winked, "to make sure I would be paid."

"Ah, I can see that you are now a good businessman. I can guarantee you will be paid and paid promptly or there will be a clerk in Eboracum minus his balls. Cassius, take the sergeant to inspect the stables." The two old friends wandered off and Livius put his hands on his hips to look up at the two young men. "Well? Are you going to sit there grinning or are you going to report?"

Marcus gestured with his hand to Rufius who smiled and began. "After Marcus had told Cato that we needed horses the word began to go around that Marcus' Horse was reforming. Men and boys began turning up at Gaius' farm and Cato's stables. The two of them culled the ones who were too old, too young or infirm and the rest," he waved his hand behind him, "are here."

Livius looked at the fifty volunteers who sat astride their horses in the easy manner which suggested they knew their way around a mount. "And the horses?"

"We have brought a hundred. That means there are fifty remounts. The sergeant will have broken another hundred by next week."

"You have done well." He went closer to them, "Macro did well yesterday, he defeated The Fist but, thanks to Spartianus he now has an injured leg." He saw the look of anger flash across Marcus' face, his sibling honour touched. "He is fine and I have announced that he is to be made up to the rank of sergeant. Wait a few days Marcus and I will confirm your promotion as well."

"Don't worry about that sir. That isn't important but Spartianus is. What are we going to do about him and his troublemakers?"

"Cassius has half a dozen men we can trust. I will put them to work watching the bad eggs."

"We have ten good men as well sir. I have been watching them and I think they can be trusted." Rufius was a good judge of men as well as horses.

"Good then bring them to me when you have delivered the horses." He addressed the recruits. "Welcome to the ala. When you have looked after your horses report to the kitchen where Septimus will feed you." Turning, Livius shouted, "Septimus wave so that they know where to come." Septimus waved a ladle in the air. "Carry on."

While the men were eating their meal, the recruits admiring the uniforms they would soon don, the officers and Cato ate in the Principia. Livius had spoken to the fifteen chosen men an hour before. He had told them that they were chosen men and had been identified as such by the decurions. He was pleased that they all had seemed proud of their selection. He told them that when the new rosters were complete each would be in a turma with the role of assisting the decurion. He honestly told them that some amongst them would be promoted but it was not certain. Livius did not want to go down the Spartianus' route of bribery and coercion. He did leave them with the role of making sure that there were no more accidents and sabotage. Without naming perpetrators, he knew that they had worked out which men they should watch. Now as he sat eating with all of his decurions he felt more comfortable knowing that there were twenty men watching the six potential threats.

"So Cato, what do you think of the stabling?"

The old horse whisperer thought for a moment. "Is this your camp for some time?"

"At least until the spring."

"Then I would put roofs on the stables. We get deep snow here in the winter and the last thing you need will be horses down with the colic."

"Thank you, Cato."

"I'll get on to that this afternoon, sir. "

"Thank you, Marcus."

"Uniforms and payments for the sergeant are the next items of business." Cassius noticed that, for the first time Aelius Spartianus took an interest, his ears pricking and his furtive eyes bright with curiosity. "I will take a couple of men down to Eboracum to chivvy along the Prefect. He is a good man but, like all quartermasters, a little prone to hang on to his supplies." They all laughed, the exception being a sour-faced Spartianus. "When we have finished here Sergeant Culleo can continue with the training of the men. Metellus you and Rufius can begin to process and train the new men. Aelius can assist Sergeant Culleo." The last order did not please Spartianus who stored the implied insult up with the others to be paid back at some future date. "Cassius if you remain behind we can finish off the work on the new turmae." If Aelius' face was angry before it was apoplectic when he heard that particular snippet of news; he had worked to get his cronies in his own turma and he was not going to see them split up. Livius had noticed the infusion of anger. "Is there a problem decurion?"

"Well sir," Spartianus struggled to sound calm even though inside he was seething, "it seems to me a little unnecessary to change the turmae around. The men are used to working in their own turma, they have team spirit. This would just cause upset for no good reason." Cassius almost laughed when he heard the words 'team spirit' coming from Aelius' mouth, he had no concept of the term!

"Thank you for your sound comments Aelius," the use of the first name was intended as an olive branch which the decurion could take or reject, "but there are, as you can see from the kitchen area, many new and inexperienced men. The last thing we need is for them to be in turmae without any experienced troopers. No, we will spread the inexperience and the experience and one more thing. We need to identify potential decurions, keep your eyes open for those with the required skills." The scowl on the face of Spartianus told Livius that the olive branch had been cast aside.

Cassius and Livius sat with the rosters moving names and numbers around. The original ala members were entered in the books already but the new men were just numbers. "I will need to inveigle a clerk from the Prefect. This bookwork is too demanding to take away a decurion who should be doing other things."

Cassius grinned, "Thank you for that sir. I prefer the action to the writing."

"And we will need a quartermaster for, when I return, we should have uniforms and weapons for all of the men."

"I think I have someone who might do well. How about Spartianus? Is he finished?"

"No Cassius I am sure that he has more mischief to come but we now have more eyes upon him and now I need to embroil you in the Emperor's work." He rose and went to the door to make sure that no one was around. "Before I begin I want to tell you that you can refuse my request and I will not think any the less of you, for the work involved, is dangerous."

Cassius smiled, "More dangerous than being an Explorate behind enemy lines? Then I am your man sir."

"Seriously Cassius the work is of the greatest importance to the Empire."

"Then seriously sir, thank you for the honour and I accept the role unreservedly."

"Good then you must not involve anyone else in this, not Rufius, not Metellus, no-one. Is that clear?" Cassius nodded. "It is not that I do not trust them but the fewer involved in this the safer it will be for all of us. I need to involve someone else in case anything happens to me." Cassius looked startled; the Decurion Princeps was definitely serious. "I have to send intelligence reports to Julius Demetrius in Rome but they will be in code. I need to give you the code so that if a message arrives for me whilst I am away you can decode it and if something occurs whilst I am away which is important you can send it to the Senator."

"What sort of intelligence?"

Livius decided not to mention the Emperor's suspicions about the Governor but instead focus on their role. "The Senator and the Emperor need to know what the state of the frontier is therefore we will tell them the truth about the situation."

Cassius leaned back relieved, "Thank the Allfather for that. For a moment I thought we were to spy on Romans."

"No Cassius, just the enemies of Rome. Now the code is a simple substitution code."

"How do you mean sir?"

"Let me show you." He took a wax tablet and a stylus. He wrote out the first few letters of the alphabet and then a series of others above.

A B C D E F G H I K L M N O P Q R S T V X Y Z
T H E S V O R D F C A I M N B G K L P Q X Y Z

Cassius peered at it. "The Sword of Cartimandua. Simple."

"Yes, easy for any who fought in the ala to remember and to know. You just have to remember not to put down repeat letters" He smoothed out the code from the tablet. "We do not write it down and keep it anywhere." He tapped his head. "We keep it here. Just write it on a wax tablet if you are decoding, although, Cassius, I hope that does not occur for it will mean something has happened to me and I should like to be around to see this ala achieve the success of our other endeavour."

The significance of the meeting was not wasted on Cassius. "You can rely on me sir and, like you, I hope I never need to use it."

"Good, then I will leave you in charge while I go to Eboracum. I will take two of the trusted troopers. I hope I won't be leaving you short-handed?"

"We'll manage sir."

As Livius rode out in the late afternoon with two proud troopers, all three of them fully armed with javelins, bow, arrow and shield, Decurion Aelius Spartianus gathered his men around the cot of The Fist who was beginning to recover from his wounds. "The Decurion Princeps is making life more difficult for us. He needs to go. This is a perfect opportunity. He will be away from his precious decurions."

His men looked uneasily at each other. Bullying, stealing and minor acts of sabotage was one thing but if this went awry it could lead to crucifixion. The Fist raised himself on one elbow. "Are you sure sir? I mean I think I will need a few more days to recover."

"Thank you, my friend, but others," he looked around meaningfully at the rest of his coterie," will have to take up the challenge."

Wolf shrugged, "I think I have had enough of this army anyway." The rest stared at him. Only Aelius nodded. "It is obvious, isn't it? Whoever does this will have to desert. If the Decurion Princeps is eliminated here they will know who did it so the best way is now while he is on the road to Eboracum."

"You may not have to desert. If you leave tonight then you can get rid of him and the troopers and be back by morning. We can cover for you."

"I'll need a couple of others then. I can't take three of them on my own."

The decurion glared at the other five men who looked at the ground. Eventually, two of them Quintus and Sulla stepped forward. "Good and you will be rewarded. If you leave whilst we are eating then no one will miss you. I will engage the guards in conversation so that you can get the horses. Do not ride until you are out of sight of the camp. Tomorrow, when you return just bring your mounts back to the corral and, if anyone asks, you tell them you were exercising them." He clasped each arm in turn. "I will not forget this."

Wolf looked at him his eyes narrowing, "if we fail and live then we will not return. We, or at least I, will desert. This ala is not the one I joined. If I cannot have it the way it was then it is the forests and brigandry for me."

Spartianus inclined his head, "Your choice but if you succeed then believe me this ala will return to the way it was."

Livius and the two troopers made good time to reach the military road which traversed the province taking men and supplies from the safety of the fortress to the dangerous frontier. The two troopers were both behaving as Livius expected, watching all around for although this was Roman territory there were brigands and bandits who preyed on lonely travellers. Livius wondered whether he ought to build a road linking the fort with the road but then dismissed the idea. The fort was only a temporary measure to help bond his men. Next year they would begin to head north and he needed a solid stone fort for that. Morbium or Luguvalium seemed ideal. It was a pleasant ride heading south with the sun slowly dipping to the west. Livius said over his shoulder, "We'll be too late to make the barracks tonight. We'll stay at The Saddle." He heard a chuckle. "Do you know it?"

"Perhaps not us, sir, but we hear that Decurion Spartianus visited there and didn't like it."

There was a pause and the second trooper said, "So it should suit us." Livius chose to pretend that he had not heard the comment but it confirmed his view of his Decurion and the bulk of the men. They were good soldiers, just badly led.

Further up the road Wolf and his two associates had ridden hard across the open country. The wide vale was no hindrance to desperate men and in fact, the copses and hedgerows had helped them to hide from view. Wolf knew what he sought; Roman engineers cleared the land to the side of the road for ten paces on either side. This made ambush difficult. If it were night time then it would not be a problem but at this time of year, it was light until late and Wolf knew that he had no chance of intercepting the Decurion Princeps before he reached the safety of Eboracum. He also knew that at least one of the troopers had to die in the initial attack to give the three killers the edge they needed. Wolf had chosen where the road crossed one of the rivers. The bridge was narrow and the victims would have nowhere to go once they were attacked. Sulla had one skill which none of the others possessed; he was the best man with a slingshot that Wolf had ever seen. He would wait at the southern end of the bridge. With luck he could take out two of them and then Quintus and Wolf could emerge from their concealment on the north side and finish the survivor.

"Now remember Sulla you have to get at least one of them and hopefully two. When you have thrown two stones then, if they are still alive you can retreat, but I hope that they will have turned and Quintus and I will finish the job." Sulla tied his horse below the bridge so that it was not visible from the road and the bridge. Quintus and Wolf hid behind the hedgerow of elder and hawthorn some thirty paces from the road, on the northern side. All they had to do now was to wait and their victims would present themselves.

Livius had dropped back to ride between his two companions. "How long have you two been in the ala?"

"I joined last year sir."

"So you are a Briton then?"

Yes, sir, Marcus Scribonious, my father was an Atrebate, and he had served with the auxilia before I did."

"And you, son?"

"Antoninus Quintus, sir from Batavia. I joined just before we were posted over here."

"Were you happy about that?"

"Not really, sir."

There was the kind of pause which tells the listener that the speaker has more to say. "Come on Antoninus out with it. I hope that in the short time I have commanded you, you have seen that I respect honesty."

"Yes sir. The thing is I wasn't happy. The ala wasn't what I thought it was going to be. There are some men in the ala, well sir they are little better than thieves, but since you came it has been better sir. And sir, I am not flattering you, I am not that kind of trooper. I mean it."

"Thank you for your honesty and I hope that your faith in me is justified." They were approaching the bridge and Livius felt uneasy. His Explorates nose had given him a sixth sense. "Hear that?"

"Hear what sir?"

"That magpie." When they were silent they heard the unmistakeable strident call of the magpie.

Scribonious spoke up. "My gran hated magpies; she called them maggot pies, the birds of death."

"And that they are but they also make that noise when they are disturbed. It may just be a fox nearby or a hawk but let us take no chances. Which do you prefer bow or spear?"

"Spear," said the Atrebate.

"Javelin," said the Batavian.

"Right load up and be prepared. Single file, Marcus, take the rear, Antoninus, a horse's length behind me." They nudged their horses forward, every sense on the alert. Livius had just stepped on to the bridge when his horse smelled Sulla's mount and whinnied. The ala horse heard and replied. "Ambush!"

Instinctively Livius' hand brought up his shield and he heard the sharp crack as the lead missile pinged off the metal rim. There was a whoosh above his head and Marcus' arrow buried itself in the chest of the traitor. Wolf and his henchman galloped from their place of concealment. Wolf swung his sword at Marcus' unprotected back. It cracked against something hard; the trooper had slung his shield beneath his cloak to enable him to shoot. It saved his life but the blow was so hard that he crashed from his horse on to the stone parapet. Scribonious turned in the saddle and threw his spear in an attempt to hit at least one of the attackers. Wolf was wily and ducked but the missile caught a little of his helmet and flew at Quintus. The spear struck his leg and he screamed.

Wolf could see that they had failed. It was not two on two it was two against him for his companion was injured. Wheeling his horse he grabbed his companion's reins and galloped up the road. By the time Livius and Scribonious had turned, their ambushers were out of sight. "See who Marcus killed and I will tend to him."

Marcus was stunned and winded; the Decurion Princeps checked for any sign of blood but could find none. He took off the trooper's helmet but there did not appear to be any damage to his skull. He knew with head wounds that you had to be careful. The boy needed waking and fast. . Livius turned him on his side and then poured water from his flask over his face. He began to come to. "What happened, sir?

"One of the ambushers hit you and knocked you off your horse but I don't think there is any serious damage."

They both heard the clatter of hooves as the Batavian brought over Sulla's body on the back of the horse. "It's Sulla sir." He paused, "one of the Decurion's men."

"And the one that got me, sir, that was Wolf."

"The other one sir, the one I speared it might have been Quintus another of that group."

Their silence was eloquent. "Before you start adding two and two and making five. While these three may be associates of Decurion Spartianus it does not follow that he knew anything of this attempt on my life. For that I am sorry. Your lives were put in danger but I think it was me they were after. The question is why? Are you fit enough to ride?"

Marcus smiled wanly. "If I don't need to wear my helmet then yes sir."

"Good. You ride next to me and Antoninus bring up the rear with Sulla."

It was just becoming dark when they reined up outside The Saddle. Horse came out and glanced at the body on the horse. He sniffed. "I can see that you have started as you mean to go on eh Decurion Princeps." Over his shoulder, he shouted. "Make up two rooms, get some food on the table and Niagh come and take these horses and the body to the stables."

Niagh was an old fat man who came out scratching his bald pate, "Did you say body master?"

"Yes and take it off the horse, if it stiffens in the night we'll never get the bugger straight." He caught sight of the face as Niagh flopped it over his shoulder. "That's one of them that Cassius and the lads had to deal with." He grinned up at Livius, one less bad apple then eh sir?"

Far to the north Wolf had decided that they were not being pursued and he removed the javelin and applied a tourniquet. "You are lucky. If this hadn't hit my helmet you would have bled to death."

The pale Quintus gritted his teeth as the pain kicked in, flooding in waves. "Where to then boss?" He was now totally reliant on the goodwill of Wolf. If he was left on his own he knew that he would die."

"South is no good. He will have the garrison alerted. North is no good; we'll run up against the ala. It will have to be west, maybe get a boat to Ireland or join the barbarians. Either way, we have finished with the army, at least finished fighting for it. We are now free agents and you know Quintus, I am glad. I just wish The Fist was with us."

Chapter 10

Radha had never had an experience such as the one she had been enjoying for last month on Manavia. She and her ladies had been the privileged guests of Morwenna and her daughters. They had each become initiated into the cult of the mother and taught many of the spells, incantations and potions which would give them power over others as well as improving themselves. They all now understood their own bodies and minds and how to get the most out of them. Radha and her companions had been taught the language of love and how to enchant and please men with their body. Radha could not believe the liberation of finding out that she was in control of the man and not the other way around. She had been taught from a young age that women were there to serve and please men. They had practised, nightly, the many acts which Radha would satisfy Lugubelenus and make him totally dependent upon her when she finally returned north. She now understood that the love of a woman was as important as the love of a man. She felt different as she looked in the polished shield Morwenna had left in her room. The food and the exercise had honed and shaped her body so that she looked twice as beautiful as when she had arrived. Morwenna had shown her how to use lemons and herbs to make her hair silky. She had taught Radha and her women how to make lotions which strengthened their nails and polished their skin. When Radha had examined Morwenna's naked body close up she had been amazed for it look like the body of a young woman, not a middle-aged woman approaching forty. After only a month Radha could see the effects.

Her bodyguards too had benefited. Morwenna's mercenaries and bodyguard had taught them how to fight outside of the shield wall; how to use two weapons and their bodies and how to build up their muscles so that they were all more powerful warriors than when they had left the land of the Votadini. They too had taken Morwenna's potions and four of them selected to service Morwenna's daughters. They were flattered that the Queen wanted her daughters impregnating by men such as they. They would have been disappointed to know that they were selected after the Queen discovered that each of the warriors was the only boy in a gaggle of girls. If the offspring were a male it would be sacrificed to the Mother; Morwenna had no need of male offspring in her land women ruled.

That was the other gift Radha took with her; the knowledge that women could rule. She had always felt instinctively that it was true and to be fair to her husband, the King of the Votadini, he had indulged her and allowed her to jointly make decisions. Now she saw that she had the power to do and to use the wives of other rulers to increase her power. Morwenna had told her of the sisters and how they were throughout the country. They had no sign that others could see but Radha was taught how to recognise a sister and, more importantly, how to convert a woman to become a sister. As Morwenna had said, "It is the one area the Romans do not understand. To them, women are virgins to work in their temples, or whores or mothers. Their job is determined by a man. We are priestesses, we too use sex for our own ends and pleasure and we are mothers. The difference is we choose what we are at any moment in time and the Romans will never defeat that idea."

Radha was delighted when Morwenna offered to come with her to her husband's court. "We will leave my daughters here so that they may continue to blossom, grow and become better witches. We will take some of my warriors and join your husband. We have to travel through the land of the Selgovae and this may be an opportunity to meet this king, Aindreas, who so offended you."

Radha had been amazed at how much she had changed. "When I first came here I could not mention that man's name without wanted to strangle him but now, Mother, after studying with you I understand my power and know that this man is in my power."

They sailed northwards, five ships with over two hundred warriors, from Manavia. They made a powerful looking force. They sailed north of Luguvalium to avoid the Romans there and landed on the north bank of the estuary. Radha wanted to send a messenger to the king to tell him of her arrival. Morwenna counselled discretion. "If you tell him you have landed he will come to meet you will he not?"

"Probably."

"Which creates two problems we would not meet with Aindreas King of the Selgovae and we need to meet him first and find out the best way to eliminate him and secondly your husband might run across the Romans and we want no warning of our war until we launch it. No, sister, this is the best plan of action; travel north to the Selgovae and thence to your husband." She had looked around at the countryside. "It is many years since I lived here. It was before the time of my daughters."

"You lived close to my country? I wish I had known we would have become acquainted sooner."

"But in those days the Votadini tribe was ruled by weaklings who allowed Rome to push the frontier north and they settled for payments and baths. It made them weak. This way is better, for your husband and yourself have destroyed a Roman army and the tribes will flock to your banner."

Two weeks after they had avoided death at the hands of their commanding officer, Wolf and Quintus were half-starved and exhausted. They had eaten one of the horses after five days and were now reduced to chewing on the maggoty flesh still clinging to its remains. They took it in turns to walk, knowing that their survival depended upon each other and their one surviving mount. The fine weather had helped as had the fact that they were travelling through a land with many lakes and rivers but neither man had the skills or the equipment to fend for themselves. Had Sulla been with them they would have had hunted hare but they were both lean and haggard after many days heading for safety. They had only a vague notion of where they were. They had crossed the spine of the country about the time they had eaten their first lame horse and they knew they were going the right way by the sun which occasionally peeped out from behind the overcast clouds. Wolf had a feeling that they were close to the sea for he heard the gulls and could smell the sea some way to the west.

The river which barred their way was gentle but wide. The rest of the rivers they had crossed had been fordable but they would have to swim this one. "I think," pondered Wolf, "that this is the end of Roman territory. Once across we will be in the land of the barbarians. Let us get rid of some of these symbols of Rome." Their shields had long gone as had their last spear thrown after a deer which took the weapon deep into the forests. They kept their armour and sword and threw the rest into the river. Holding on to the horse's saddle they floated on either side as the weary mount kicked its way across. Once on the other side, they slumped to the ground, partly out of weariness but also out of relief. Wolf held on to the reins but closed his eyes, basking in the warm sunlight. They were free and they had escaped

Suddenly Wolf felt steel at his throat. "Be careful Romans for your lives are now in my hands. My lady wishes to speak with you otherwise I would have sliced you into so many body parts a legion could not have put them together."

Wolf opened his eyes and looked up at a circle of heavily armed men. All of them had naked tattooed torsos and each wore many combat bracelets and amulets. A wonderfully enchanting voice which seemed to sing in Wolf's ears spoke. "Let them rise, Idwal. I do not think they can escape us. They look to be starving and exhausted."

When Wolf and Quintus rose they saw that they were surrounded by a heavily armed warband. What was unusual was the number of women accompanying it but more than that both men were mesmerized by the beauty of the women especially the two in the white dresses, one with flame-red hair and the other with hair the colour of night.

"We watched you discard your Roman helmets and that, alone, has saved your lives. My men here would dearly love to have two Romans upon which to vent their anger. So answer my questions truthfully or you will be handed over. Who are you, where are you going and where have you come from?"

Quintus nodded to Wolf who spoke. "We are deserters from the Roman Army. We tried to kill an officer but failed and we have fled north to seek sanctuary beyond Rome's grasping, greedy fingers." He added the last part as he thought it would ingratiate them into their captor's favours.

"So failed killers. I think, Idwal, that you and your men can enjoy some sport for there is no reason to keep them alive."

The grin on the barbarian's face told Wolf that they would enjoy hurting the two deserters but something in the woman's voice and eyes told him that he could still save their lives. "Oh, mighty Queen we can be of service to you for we know of those in our ala who would work with you and betray the Romans."

"Traitors? Hardly a commendation for trust."

Wolf sensed that he could offer her some crumbs of information which might result in a safer future. "We were sent to kill the officer because my leader, one of the officers, wished him dead. He would rather lead against the Romans than take orders from this Roman."

Morwenna ran the man's words through her complicated and subtle mind. If there were traitors in the Roman army then they could be used. She remembered Luigsech telling her how her own mother, Fainch, had used the weakness of some of the officers to infiltrate their forts and she too had become the partner of the Decurion Macro to do the same. It was worth keeping them alive until she had investigated their use. "For the time being then you shall live." Wolf saw the disappointment on Idwal's face. When Wolf got the chance he would end the barbarian's life before he lost his. "You are our prisoners but we will not bother to tie you up for if you try to escape I will allow Idwal to finish you both off. Now we have wasted enough time. Let us ride."

Livius was pleased with the progress of the ala. Once the young men of the north heard that Marcus' Horse was reforming, then recruits flooded in. There was little use in Cassius and Livius explaining that this was not the famed ala, they could see the warriors whose exploits had filled their fires at night. The fact that Macro's son and the son of Gaius, the wielder of the Sword of Cartimandua, were in the ala was enough for most men. Their uniforms and horses made them feel part of the ala and Livius had had to send to Cato for more mounts and the Prefect for more uniforms. They had four hundred and fifty men and all had received some training. Antoninus and Marcus had been temporarily made into decurions, a quartermaster appointed and Marcus promoted to sergeant. The only cloud on the horizon was the desertions. There had been no sign of Quintus and Wolf.

Livius was in the office checking the new rosters and ensuring that the new men were all correctly allocated. One advantage of the desertions was that there were only four bad apples plus the Decurion left in the ala. Cassius came in with the reports from the decurions.

"Cassius, did you believe Spartianus?"

Cassius sat opposite and looked Livius in the eye. "Not for one moment but, like you, I knew we could never prove it."

"Could I have handled it any differently?"

"Not without losing the fairness we know is one of your characteristics. I suspect old Ulpius would have gutted him as soon as he returned but that was in the old days. I think Spartianus is a viper but at least he is not under a rock, we can see him and the others."

"The rest have better behaved since I returned haven't they?"

"They are scared, even The Fist is wary. The men respect you and they hate the thought that someone tried to kill you. The five of them move in each other's shadows, for that is their only safety. But I do not think Spartianus has finished but for the moment he is marginalised."

"Right. Let's get down to basics. I would like to leave for Morbium tomorrow. If we leave Marcus and Macro here to continue to train up the new boys how many trained men will we have?"

"If Septimus takes charge of turma eight then we will have two hundred and ninety-three men and officers. That will leave the two lads with one hundred and fifty-eight." He whistled. "A lot of men for two young lads to command."

"You think they can't handle it?"

"No they can but, at their age, I wouldn't have liked the responsibility."

"I suppose that is the difference, they do. Hopefully, we can promote another five or six men and then we will be fully staffed. Right let's get them all in here and we will tell them of the plans."

The small Principia was quite crowded by the time they were all assembled. "I'll try to be brief. Tomorrow we take out turmae one to eight up to Morbium. Septimus will be in charge of Turma eight as the two sergeants are going to stay here and train the rest of the men. When they are all trained, you have one week, gentlemen, then you will dismantle the fort, you can leave the gyrus and the corral they may be useful in the future. Any questions."

Marcus and Macro grinned at each other as all the other decurions smiled; the exception was Aelius Spartianus. "You cannot be serious sir, you are leaving these boys to manage one hundred and fifty men."

There was an uncomfortable silence as the others looked at the ground. The only person who did not trust the two sergeants was Aelius and he was now totally isolated amongst the officers. "Decurion when I appoint a man as decurion or even sergeant then that means I have complete faith in that man. Let us leave it at that."

Spartianus heard the insult and stormed out. "Septimus looked confused; Metellus said, "He is the only officer the Decurion Princeps did not appoint."

As Livius led the ala out the next morning, he was inordinately proud. The men looked magnificent, many wearing their new uniforms behind their dragon-headed standard, a remnant from their time on the steppes. He was even more proud as he saw that the two sergeants had their men already training, Macro in the gyrus and Marcus in the corral. The sour look on the face of Spartianus told him that he had not forgotten the insult. The two carts which followed contained all the spare uniforms and equipment. Septimus had left two of his men to cook for the trainees but Livius was sure that they would eat better than the rest of the ala as Marcus and Macro would make sure their charges had the finest of food.

The journey to Morbium was a short one, just over an hour. In an emergency, he could have his spare troopers there in less than thirty minutes. As he approached the fort he hoped that he would not need to use his Imperial letter; he hoped the Batavians stationed there might be some of the ones he had fought alongside all those years ago.

The sharp-eyed sentries had seen their approach and the Camp Prefect rode out to meet them. Livius was disappointed; he did not recognise the man. He was a typical Batavian, squat and almost as round as he was tall. His face showed the signs of many combats. Livius halted his horse. "Decurion Princeps Livius Lucullus Sallustius with the First Sallustian Wing of Pannonians."

The Prefect leaned forward, "Are you the same Livius Sallustius who served with Marcus' Horse and fought in the battle just north of here all those years ago?"

"Yes, sir I am."

"Then I am glad to meet you. I was a centurion the day your lads made that magnificent charge and routed those bollock eating barbarians! Welcome. What can I do for you and what looks like almost a full ala?"

"Emperor Hadrian wants to re-establish control of the frontier with a more flexible force. With your permission, we will rebuild our old fort."

"Be my guest."

Livius turned to Cassius. "Take the men to the old camp and rebuild it. It shouldn't take long, the ditches are still there and all they need are the palisades. I want a word with the Camp Prefect." Cassius saluted and trotted off to begin a task which a year ago would have been impossible but now would be completed in a very short time.

"I would like a favour, er…"

"Prefect Marius Arvina."

"Thank you Marius. I don't want to waste my men guarding our camp when they can be better served patrolling the frontier."

"I agree and my men will have shorter patrols if you are stationed here. I assume you are suggesting that my men sentry your fort whilst you are on patrol?" Livius nodded, relieved that the Prefect thought the same as he. "It will also help to make our two forces closer." He looked meaningfully north to where the famous battle had taken place. "It helped last time."

"It certainly did."

"When you are settled in, come over to my quarters for a drink and you can fill me in on this new Emperor. I only heard about him yesterday."

"I will, Marius, and thank you." He kicked his horse on and was pleased to see that the horse lines were already up and two of the walls almost finished. The men weren't tired having only ridden fifteen miles or so and they set to with gusto.

Metellus came over. "The lads are all working hard. Well, all apart from our own particular brand of bad apples."

"He's a fool you know Metellus. He is not making friends with the men and he alienates all of you every time he opens his mouth or walks into a room."

"I still believe that an Explorate knife in the night would work."

"Much as the idea appeals we are different now, we are regulars. I am afraid we now play by the rules, this is not Aquitania."

Three days after Livius had left them in charge, Macro and Marcus paraded the men. They had worked extremely hard and the two sergeants knew that their men were as well trained as the rest of the ala and yet they were reluctant to rejoin them. They had enjoyed their independence. They had used humour and praise to bring the best out of their raw recruits. The fact that the two of them were superb horsemen and really effective with any weapon helped for the men knew they were being trained by someone who could actually do it. After supper, the two sergeants had been prevailed upon to tell them of the battles with the Ninth. They told the story but minimised their own role in the heroics. Most, however, had heard the legend of the two young boys who had saved the eagle and they nodded knowingly to each other.

"Well Marcus, we ought to rejoin the Decurion Princeps."

"I know Macro but one more day wouldn't hurt."

"You are right, besides which we have to dismantle the camp. We'll have one last day of training, rise early, and we can be at Morbium by noon."

"Excellent plan."

Before they could begin to enjoy their training one of their sentries, placed on a knoll a mile away from the camp came galloping up. "Sergeant. Riders approaching."

"Barbarians or Romans?"

"Roman sir, regular cavalry I think with a carriage."

"Thanks, trooper, well done. Rejoin your turma. Shit! A carriage and regular cavalry sound official. "

"Probably the Prefect coming to check in on us and to see if we needed all the uniforms he sent."

"Better make a good impression. Let's put them in two columns and parade."

By the time the column was in sight of the camp, the two sergeants had their one hundred and fifty men in perfectly straight lines. The Decurion who rode in at the head of the thirty regular cavalry looked around for an officer. He looked puzzled and rode over to the two young men. "Where are the officers?"

"Sir, we were left by Decurion Princeps Livius Lucullus Sallustius to complete the training of these hundred and fifty recruits."

"We had just finished when you arrived."

"And you are?"

"Sergeant Marcus Aurelius and Sergeant Macro Culleo."

"Well you don't look old to be sergeant to me, however," he leaned forward, "this is the Governor of Britannia, Marcus Appius Bradua and he is here to visit with this Decurion Princeps of yours. He was hoping to have a comfortable fort to sleep in but instead he has this, a ramshackle camp."

"Sir that's not fair, we were about to dismantle it and join the Decurion Princeps at Morbium."

The Decurion shook his head, "Better think on your feet lads or you will be up shit creek without a paddle."

Marcus Bradua hated Britannia. Emperor Trajan had appointed him following his stint as consul in Rome. Of all the postings he had to get, he was unlucky enough to get the one at the coldest place in the Empire. He hated the food, he hated the people and he loathed the fact that he could not grow his lemons and olives. How could the people live without fresh lemons and olives plucked from a tree outside your villa? And now, to make matters worse, he had heard that the new Emperor was going to visit Britannia and he required a detailed report from the Governor outlining the security issues. Bradua had never been further north than Aqua Sulis in all the time he had been in the province. When he had reached Eboracum he had heard of this new ala created by the Emperor. His interest was piqued and he had foregone the dubious pleasures of Eboracum to ride north. As he stepped from the carriage he thought someone was playing a huge joke on him. There were but one hundred and fifty very young troopers and two boys, or equally young men, in front of them. He turned to speak with the Decurion as he did so Macro said out of the corner of his mouth to his quicker thinking brother, "You need to come up with a plan."

"I'm thinking, I'm thinking."

"My Decurion tells me that I have wasted my time and your commander is no longer here. Do you expect me to sleep in a tent?"

"No Governor, as we were about to explain to the Decurion that Sergeant Marco Culleo and fifty of the men will escort you to Morbium which is a much more comfortable, stone-built camp and I will dismantle the camp here and follow you to our new posting later this afternoon."

The Decurion smiled and shook his head. He could begin to see why these two had been left in charge. They had wits and used them."

"How far is it, this Morbium?"

"An hour at carriage speed. sir."

Bradua looked at the camp, looked at the threatening sky and nodded. "Very well then. Decurion let us go."

Macro winked at Marcus who shouted, "Turmae nine and ten, form up behind the Governor's carriage in fours."

The Decurion was impressed with the speed with which the order was carried out. As he rode next to Marcus he murmured, "Nicely done son, nicely done."

Chapter 11

The unhappy Governor sat once more in his carriage. His friends in Rome had told him of the rise in power and influence of Julius Demetrius who had, until recently, been an obscure senator with a dubious background in the auxilia. Bradua's associate, Lucius Quietus, had been one of the first victims of Hadrian's mentor, Attianus and Demetrius' consolidation of power. He had no doubt that the imprisoned senator would be found guilty of some misdemeanour or other against the state. The problem was, where did that leave Marcus Bradua? The Emperor was still in the east and there was a power vacuum in Rome. Attianus was an old man and Julius Demetrius had come from nowhere so fast that he could not have enough of a power base to take control. And where was Marcus Bradua? Stuck on this forsaken frozen frontier where barbarians still raided to take slaves and mutilate men. It was one reason he had insisted on a full turma of Roman cavalry. The Prefect of the Twentieth Augusta had been loath to lose his elite cavalry but when the Governor ordered the Prefect had jumped. As soon as he had inspected this flea hole in the north he would scurry back to Eboracum, write his report and send it on the first boat back to Rome. When he was in the comfort of his villa at Aqua Sulis he might be able to think and plan his way out of his dilemma.

He peered out of the carriage. The land was just rolling hills, the trees were dull and uniform and, so far, he had not seen a single person, not even on the road. If this were Italy there would be a line of travellers, merchants, entrepreneurs, businessmen even farmers using the fine facilities which Rome had provided. Perhaps it was a measure of the nature of this part of the world. The Prefect in Eboracum had told him how tenuous the hold they had on the north was. Since the demise of the Ninth the tiny line of forts which held back the barbarian horde on the Stanegate, the thin line of defence, had been manned by auxiliaries; a stop-gap measure at best. He was also intrigued at the promotion of this Decurion Princeps. From what he had gleaned, from a close-mouthed Prefect, the appointment and the renaming of the ala had come from the Emperor himself on his first day as Emperor. How the young man had managed to get from Selinus to Britannia in the time he did was a mystery. It also begged the question, who was this young man and what power did he hold over the Emperor? He leaned his head out of the carriage window and summoned over the Decurion.

"How long have you served in Britannia Decurion?"

"Twenty years Governor."

"Did you know of an officer called Julius Demetrius?"

The Decurion smiled, "Oh yes sir. He was a good commander, he led Marcus' Horse. They were almost as good an ala as regulars."

"What happened to them?" The Governor was curious about their present status.

"I believe that they were disbanded because they lost so many men in the Brigante rising a few years ago. A great shame. We miss them. The North was a lot safer when they patrolled. Still politics."

The Governor looked up sharply, "Politics? Explain." This was an area in which he was an expert.

The Decurion realised that he had said too much and he tried to ease his way out of the situation, "Well sir I just think that some people high up were worried about their success and power especially as the Decurion Princeps was a Briton. A man who had been related to the last King of Britannia and he was thought to be a potential danger."

"I think I remember the name. He and his brother grew up in Rome I believe. Sallustius or something. Uncle executed when he was Governor of Britannia, ostensibly for naming a lance after himself." He waved away the Decurion and returned to his ruminations. So that explained why the Governor of the time and Bradua was in no doubt that it had been the Governor, had decided to use the opportunity to get rid of a potential rebel and magnet for the malcontents of the southern half of the land. He suddenly thought that he should have asked the Decurion what had happened to the young man. He would save that question until after supper; if they were capable of providing supper in this cold and empty land.

Marcus was at the rear of the column ensuring that there were no stragglers when he noticed, for the first time a civilian riding a very scruffy looking mule and struggling to keep up with the column. There were large panniers on the back of the mule, obviously containing his traps but it was the man's appearance which intrigued Marcus. He had not a hair on his head which accentuated his long pointed nose. He looked like a bag of bones covered in grey flesh and he appeared to be as unhappy as it was possible for a man to be. Marcus smiled at him and he attempted to smile back. The mule was doing its best to go backwards rather than forwards. Marcus rode behind the mule and gave it a slap with the flat of his sword. The blow to the rump made the mule turn around to try to spit at the perpetrator, but also made it move a little faster.

"Hello."

"Hello sir, thank you for that. The mule does not appear to like me."

"Oh I am not a sir, just a sergeant, temporarily. And you are?"

"Julius Longinus the new clerk for the First Sallustian Wing of the Pannonians. A bit of a mouthful if you ask me."

Marcus smiled. "You are probably right, never thought about it. I think that you are in the right place, sort of. We are the ala you seek. Why didn't you stay at the camp?"

"I was attached to the Governor and I didn't want to get stuck in the middle of nowhere with the wrong outfit."

"I see," Marcus appraised the man. He looked to be over forty which made him ancient in Marcus' eyes. The man's fingers were stained with a multitude of different hues with what appeared to be ink. It made it look as though he was tattooed. "Can you ride?"

Longinus looked perplexed, "I thought that was what I was doing?"

"No, you are sitting on the back of a mule. I mean can you ride a horse?"

"Is it easier than this?"

"Much."

"Then yes I can."

Marcus whistled and then shouted, "Trooper bring a spare horse here, a docile one if possible." One of the young recruits handed his string of remounts to a colleague and trotted back with one he carefully selected. He was a keen recruit and obeyed the command to the letter. Marcus dismounted and grabbed the mule's reins. It seemed to know that this was the man who had struck him and he snorted and squirmed. Marcus rapped him sharply on the nose. "Settle down or you will be supper tonight. I am in a mood for mule meat." To the clerk, he said, "Right sir, jump off that beast and mount the horse. Trooper, dismount and give him a hand."

The grinning trooper hopped down and cradled his hands to help the clerk up on to the much higher back of the horse. "There you go sir, up you jump." Marcus and the trooper had to contain themselves at the clerk's attempt to jump but once on the mount, he seemed happier.

"Right trooper, take the mule and lead him. That better sir?"

The man was actually smiling. "This is much better and much higher. I can actually see the land. Oh, and I am Julius, not sir."

"I am Marcus and it will be good to have someone help with the lists and the other duties, we are warriors, not writers. Cassius, the adjutant, is getting really piss... er unhappy with writing and checking lists."

"Is he the other sergeant then?"

"Oh no, he is second in command, one of the senior Decurions."

"And you call him Cassius?"

Marcus grinned. "He's known me since I was a bairn and I think Uncle Cassius would not do the trick eh? Besides we are like one big family. You'll like it well all apart from," realising he needed to be more discreet he sighed. "I daresay you will make your own judgements."

Longinus looked around. "This is a beautiful country; do you know it well?"

Marcus laughed. "I was born just up the road, not far from that fort."

The clerk then plied the sergeant with questions which were answered and elaborated on with enthusiasm.

"Fort ahead sir. We will be there in no time." The Governor snorted; at least the young sergeant had been accurate about the time it took to travel through this dreary and decidedly cold land.

The Prefect groaned to himself when he saw the column of Roman cavalry escorting the carriage. It could mean only one thing, dignitaries and that meant he would lose his quarters as his was the only room suitable for guests. It also meant inspections the depletion of his supplies for visitors rarely brought any with them. At least the cavalry ala had brought their own and even supplemented their diet with some fine game. He looked north. The whole ala was out once more as they had been each day since they arrived. The Decurion Princeps certainly kept them active. He noticed a column of Pannonians behind the carriage. He realised that they must be the recruits Livius had promised. He turned to the optio on duty. "When the recruits arrive, direct them to their fort and tell them that the rest of their ala is on patrol."

The cavalry lined up on each side of the fort as the carriage crossed the bridge and halted at the gate. The Prefect opened the door of the carriage. "Marcus Arvina Camp Prefect of…"

"Save the introductions for when I am warm with food and drink inside me. Drive on."

Leaving an open-mouthed Prefect in the gateway the Governor rode on. The Decurion trotted up. "Our Governor likes his comfort and he has been travelling. Makes him a little short-tempered. Where can I put my men and horses up sir?"

Marcus remembered his manners, "Sorry Decurion I am just… Er, why don't you join the auxiliary cavalry over there, the First Sallustian Wing of Pannonians." He pointed in the distance. "Follow the recruits. They have stables and feed for your horses and then you had better join me to help entertain the Governor. You know what they say, misery likes company."

"Sir," the Decurion had been looking forward to finding out a little more about this ala of which he had heard nothing before.

It was good to be riding in this land again. Livius never felt threatened. He knew of the dangers but felt that the land was an ally, not an enemy. The potential danger came from those who were raiding and they did not know the land as well as he. He had had the ala operating in pairs of turmae as he wanted the new officers and men to gain from the experience of Metellus, Rufius and Cassius. As soon as Macro and Marcus arrived he would have even more potential.

His men were resting on the crest of a low line of hills overlooking the Tinea and Votadini country. His sentries were alert for he had impressed upon them their precarious position. He chewed on his dried venison and thought about the last letter he had had from Julius. It told of the arrest of Lucius and his conspirators which was a relief to the Decurion Princeps. He had worried that the powerful traitor might have enough friends to turn the tables on Hadrian and Julius and complete a coup themselves. Perhaps they had chosen the right Praetorians. Hadrian would have to spend some time in the east which meant his arrival in Britannia would be delayed. That suited Livius in many ways. He had yet to find where to build the *limes* which the Emperor wanted. He hoped that by the next spring he and his men would have surveyed all the suitable places and he would have a better idea. All of that depended upon the frontier being quiet. Rufius had reported disturbing events further north; kings had been invited to a conclave at the court of the King of the Votadini. It had been planned for their midwinter festival, the festival of Yule. Although it was some months off he would need to send that intelligence to Rome and then he could begin to think how he would gather information on the Governor.

He glanced over to his companion decurion for the day; Decurion Aelius Spartianus sat alone, morosely munching on his rations. He had made no attempt to engage in conversation with anyone, neither officer nor men. It was as though he wanted to be alone. He was like a sulky child who was forbidden to play with their favourite toy. All of Livius' attempts had resulted in a snapped, almost insolent, reply and, whilst Livius could have disciplined him for the comments it was not in his nature to do so. He had now taken to returning the silence. He knew it was not just him, for his other decurions had reported the same cold attitude to comradeship.

One of his sentries called him over. "Sir, there's some movement about a mile upstream."

Livius mounted his horse and rode over to the escarpment lookout point. "You have good eyes trooper for I can see.... ah yes, now I can see what you mean."

There was a primitive wooden bridge just upstream from their position. It afforded him the opportunity of viewing the column of riders who crossed. As the bridge could only support a few riders at a time it meant that their numbers could be accurately ascertained. "Count them trooper and we'll compare numbers afterwards."

There were clearly armed warriors and from their accoutrements, they were high status. There were too many to be the same group identified by Cassius but Livius could see some females. He assumed they were females for they had long hair, were slender and wore no weapons. Suddenly a shaft of light broke from behind some clouds and shone upon flowing red hair. The memory of the red witch was forever etched in Livius' mind. "Morwenna," he murmured.

"Sir?"

"Nothing trooper." The last of the column had clattered over the bridge and Livius turned to the trooper. "How many did you make it son?"

"Over two hundred and twenty, sir."

"That tallies with mine. Go and tell the decurion to mount up the turmae and join me here." As the trooper trotted off Livius ran the information through the machine that was his brain. He could have been wrong. If some priestess of the Votadini had gone to Manavia, it might well mean that Morwenna had elected to return with them. Certainly, they were heavily armed men and Livius remembered the Irish Morwenna had used the last time. Where was she going? He was sorely tempted to follow them but across the river was Votadini country and he and his ala were in no position to face a Votadini army still cock a hoop over their recent victory. Lugubelenus had made it quite clear that the Romans should stay in their land. Technically Livius was in Votadini territory for the king had said to stay south of the forts which began with Coriosopitum on the Stanegate. As Spartianus and the other troopers arrived he reached his decision. They would ride to the bridge and see if they could gain any clues about the mysterious column.

"We are going down to that bridge decurion. A column has just crossed over and I would like to know who they are."

"Isn't that Votadini country sir," the 'sir' was always tagged on as a deliberate afterthought. Livius was used to the implied insult and knew that the decurion was merely paying lip service to him. "Isn't that dangerous?"

Livius laughed and the unexpected noise made their mounts start. "In this land, Aelius, getting up in a morning can be dangerous. Yes, it is a risk but a managed risk and it is important that we know who they are. I think I saw Morwenna the Red Witch amongst them and if so then it does not bode well for the province."

"The Red Witch?"

"Yes from Mona. Part of the Druidic cult."

"I thought they were wiped out and all their holy places destroyed?"

"That is what Rome was told but they still live and they still cause trouble. Their new base is Manavia which is beyond Roman control. Believe me, she is a dangerous woman."

Livius waved them forward and they made their way down the escarpment, every uncia of them ready for danger. Even Spartianus had understood the danger in which they were and he joined with his troopers to constantly scan their surroundings. When they reached the bridge Livius detailed six troopers to watch the northern bank. He sent another west and Aelius and his turma east. He took the remaining troopers with him. "You are going to learn today how to scout. I was an Explorate," he saw the sudden glances the men shot at each other and smiled, the Explorates were known to be the most dangerous men in the Roman army, they had an interesting if short life. "We learned how to sift evidence and come to conclusions. That is what we are going to do. Dismount and spread out in a line. We are going to backtrack up the trail."

The trail the column had taken had come down a little-used path from the west. It was just wide enough for a horse. The hawthorn and blackthorn extended over the path and Livius knew, from his experience, that some of the guards would have ridden off the path. "You are looking for anything, hoof prints, footprints, cloth, broken branches and, most importantly anything which shouldn't be here."

The men shouted out when they discovered things and Livius halted the line until he had investigated. He was very patient with his men for he knew that he did not want them to feel foolish. He had learned, as someone who had developed into a skilful scout, that the most insignificant object could tell much. He heard to his right, close to the edge of the path, a conversation which made him halt. "Don't be daft he doesn't want anything like that. It is nothing; it doesn't tell us anything."

"Stop!" He wandered over. "What is nothing?"

An older trooper was standing grinning at a young blushing recruit. "It is Atticus here sir he's found some mistletoe and some rosemary. He must want to kiss someone." He laughed at the young trooper's embarrassment.

"Well done Atticus. That is the best find so far."

The other trooper stood open-mouthed. "What sir?"

"Trooper, when did you last see mistletoe up here and, even stranger rosemary?"

"Well never sir but they are just plants."

Patiently Livius explained, aware that others were listening, "And they didn't get here themselves did they. They were brought here. Who do you know who uses and wears mistletoe and rosemary?"

"Never seen anyone, well apart from the old woman in the village, the one who used to made herbal remedies."

Livius could see the others making the connection but the older soldier was struggling to understand. "That old woman was probably an old priestess from the cult of the Mother, on Mona. She was probably a witch, which means…"

"Which means that there are probably druids or witches from Mona up here." He grinned. "That's good that sir."

The others laughed and Livius smiled, "Well thank you trooper, compliments are always welcome. Now let us return for we have found enough to confirm my suspicions."

Marcus Bradua was less than happy that there was no private bathhouse for him at the fort. He hated sharing with the plebeians but he was forced to do so as otherwise, it meant he would have to spend even longer in this desolate hole at the backside of civilisation. He and the decurion shared the facilities with the Prefect. "This ala which is stationed here. Who gave them their orders Prefect? It certainly wasn't me!"

The Prefect had shrugged his shoulders, he knew, but he wasn't going to tell the Governor more than he had to. He suspected that high politics were at stake and he knew enough to know that Camp Prefects were dispensable. Better to plead ignorance than become embroiled in a conspiracy even if the Emperor was at the heart of it.

"Who is the commander then?" asked the Governor.

"Livius Lucullus Sallustius."

"I have heard that name recently," mused Bradua.

"Yes sir. It was when we were travelling here. I mentioned his name; he was in Marcus' Horse."

The significance of that fact hit the Governor like a shock of cold water. There was a plot here and he would need to untangle it. "Where is he now?"

"They are on patrol to the north of here gathering intelligence."

Marcus Bradua regained his composure, "Good, for I have been charged by the Emperor with sending a report on the state of the province. If the Decurion Princeps has done his job then that should help my report."

The two soldiers exchanged looks. Both knew what that meant, any credit would not go to the man who gathered the intelligence but the one who reported it. Politicians were the same the world over.

Livius and the decurions made sure that all the horses had been fed and watered before they saw to themselves. Livius heard the clatter of hooves as Macro brought in the last of the recruits. When he heard the sound Marcus came from his tent to join them. "You have done well. I didn't expect you for a couple of days. Are they all trained up then?"

The two sergeants looked at each other sheepishly. Marcus spoke up. "We would have returned tomorrow but the Governor turned up unexpectedly." He added quickly, "But they are trained up sir!"

Livius flicked a glance at Cassius who smiled a wry smile. "What did he want?"

Macro shrugged noncommittally, "Well he was a little pissed off that no-one above the rank of sergeant was there to greet him but when he saw the tent he would have to sleep in he became even less happy. He was going to burst a blood vessel when Marcus suggested escorting him here."

Marcus looked at the ground in an embarrassed manner. "Well done. And we now have the whole ala together."

Marcus suddenly remembered something. "Er, sir. We have a clerk."

Cassius roared, "Thank the Allfather for that, at last, my prayers have been answered!"

"His name is Julius Longinus and he came with the Governor's party."

"Where is he now?"

"I left him in the Principia with the books."

Marcus led the way with Cassius and Livius in tow. When they entered the cluttered office they found Julius with inky fingers tut-tutting away. "Decurion Princeps Sallustius, this is the new ala clerk, Julius Longinus. "

Ignoring Livius the clerk pointed a sharp ink-stained finger accusingly at Cassius. "And I bet that you are this Cassius who has had a pet hen scratching away in the books."

"Hen? I don't have a hen."

"Surely this is not your writing, dear me, dear me. Well, I can see why they sent for me and I will have my work cut out here." He turned to Livius smiling, "Pleased to meet you, sir. Your sergeant, a very pleasant young man has been singing your praises." He glanced pointedly at Cassius, "But I expect you can actually write so that it can be read."

Marcus and Livius burst out laughing as a red-faced Cassius slammed the door shut. "Nice to have you here Julius but Cassius did his best. To be fair to him I would rather he could handle a sword than be a scribe."

"Decurion Princeps, I couldn't agree more!"

Chapter 12

"Don't take it to heart Cassius, he was just having a little fun at your expense."

"I know sir but I did my best!" Cassius sat on his cot and then saw the funny side. "A hen indeed. It seems that we are becoming a proper ala now sir; clerk, Quartermaster, recruits and horses."

"Aye but the Governor. What does he want?"

"Information."

"This is the first time that he has left the south since he took charge. No, I think there is something else afoot. We found more evidence of Morwenna today."

"Morwenna?"

"Yes, she has crossed into Votadini territory with a heavy escort and what looked like Votadini women."

"Will you tell the Governor?"

"I will have to but I will write my report for the Senator now. Send a despatch rider to Eboracum whilst I am at supper."

"You are going to send it before you speak with the Governor?"

"I will send another one when I have the gauge of the man. The Morwenna news is vital and Julius will know its import. Here help me with this uniform. I have to look my best tonight."

Marcus Arvina had struggled to find any wine which could be presented to the Governor. Normally the only visitors to this lonely but, vital fort were army personnel and they would drink horse's urine if it contained alcohol. He was lucky in that Marcus had brought with him a freshly killed boar and the Prefect had gratefully accepted half. He had already learned of Septimus' skill with a cleaver and had managed to acquire his services. The wine, poor as it was, would have to suffice. He would have to learn that once you left the south then delicacies such as snails and stuffed dormice were in short supply. The brief conversation he had had with the Cavalry Decurion had given him an insight into the man who had had Governorship thrust upon him. Marcus was also worried about Livius, for some of the sharp questions thrust at him Marcus Bradua had led him to believe that the Decurion Princeps was in danger of becoming a victim to politics.

The Camp Prefect breathed a sigh of relief when Livius arrived promptly, walking over from the auxiliary's camp with the Roman decurions. They had had an immediate rapport as they discussed campaigns in which they had both served. Gaius Saturninus took an immediate liking to this level headed officer who, although his superior, spoke to him easily like an old friend. Indeed had the fourth member of their quartet not turned up it would have been a very pleasant evening for the three veterans of the wars in Britannia. As it was the evening took a nosedive when the grumpy, unhappy little man shuffled in.

"Is your hypocaust not working Prefect?"

Livius and Gaius suppressed a smile as the Camp Prefect said, quite simply, "We do not have a hypocaust Governor. It was not deemed necessary."

Marcus Bradua looked appalled. "But what do you do in winter? I believe it snows up here."

"It does and we, well, we just freeze."

"Why on earth the Emperor wants to hang on to this part of the Empire is beyond me. No olives, no lemons, the next thing you will be expecting me to believe that that there are neither dormice nor snails to whet our appetite."

"Actually Governor, there won't be. We only get the basic supplies here on the frontier." Livius actually watched the Governor pale. "Fortunately thanks to the sergeant who escorted you we have some fine venison cooked by the ala's cook."

"Then we are in for a treat Governor." Livius' comments were halted by the entrance of the steaming plate of casseroled venison. The smell was aromatic and heady with herbs and fruits. Even the Governor forced a thin smile.

Septimus had served one of the trooper's favourites for dessert a rich steamed pudding. He had used the last of the lemons given to him by Livius and the fact was not lost on the Governor. "Well, surprisingly, that was a good meal. A little basic but satisfactory and the smell of lemons made me feel quite homesick. You have a good cook there Decurion Princeps, hang on to him."

"I will don't you worry."

After Gaius had finished his wine he asked, "Where did you find him then Livius? Eboracum?"

"No on the back of a horse. He was an ordinary trooper. I asked for a volunteer to cook for us and… well that is all there is to it."

"Hm. You seem to do things your own unique way Decurion Princeps." Marcus Arvina detected something sinister beneath the statement. He just hoped that Livius had his wits about him. "For one thing how did you manage to get the ala named after you?"

"The Emperor made the decision, not me. It is after my uncle really sir. He was one of your predecessors, a Governor."

"Executed for treason wasn't he?"

The only sign that Livius had reacted to the baiting was the tight grip with which he held his beaker. "Yes and then he was found to be innocent. I think the Emperor felt that this was in some way a redressing of the dishonour."

"Emperor Trajan or Emperor Hadrian?"

Livius had the measure of the man now. "The Emperor Hadrian."

"Did someone tell me that he appointed you personally, that he actually met with you, a lowly decurion?"

Livius ignored the insult for he could see the quicksand before him. He couldn't say that Hadrian and he had met in Italy for he, officially, had never left the side of the dying Emperor. "Yes, I did have the honour of meeting with the Emperor who personally asked me to make sure that the frontier was safe until he can make a visit."

Marcus Bradua looked up sharply. There was more to this young man than met the eye. "So you will control the whole frontier? My, you must think highly of yourself."

"No Governor. The auxiliaries, who are stationed here, will control the frontier as they have done since before the time of Julius Agricola. The presence of my ala merely means that we can patrol more territory and react to incursions a little more quickly. The Decurion will tell you that is the best role for auxiliary cavalry."

"Which is why, my friend, that I prefer the regular cavalry. Your line of work is far too dangerous."

Marcus Bradua tried a different tack. "Didn't I hear that you had led the Explorates?"

Livius smiled, "Yes Governor. They were exciting times."

Gaius was now in his cups and enjoying the conversation, "Now they really are mad buggers. Operating behind enemy lines, wearing civilian clothes and no armour; you wouldn't catch me I can tell you."

"You are right Gaius. Out of my command of thirty, there are but six of us left alive and the ones who remain are here in this ala."

"Six out of thirty, Phew! I was right the odds on survival are slim."

"Which begs the question, how did you and your five fellows manage it? Very convenient I think."

Marcus Arvina could hold himself no longer. "Governor, I think that the Decurion Princeps' reputation is beyond reproach. He has done nothing which is dishonourable."

Bradua shouted and slapped the table, "I will be the judge of that." He looked slyly at Livius. "Perhaps I should send to Rome for a frumentari eh. See what they can unearth about you and your murky past. I believe they are good at getting answers."

Gaius and Marcus both paled and moved away from the table slightly. Livius was being threatened with the Roman secret service and yet he appeared like calmness personified. He looked over at the Governor, almost telling him, that he had his measure. He slowly reached into the pouch which was hung around his waist and removed a document and he carefully placed it in front of the bemused Governor, the Imperial seal uppermost. "You don't need to send to Rome, Governor, we have a frumentari here, in fact, there are another two within shouting distance and yes," he added with a threat in his voice, "we do know how to get answers; from all kinds of people"

Marcus Bradua scrutinised the document desperate to find if it was a forgery. He began to pale visibly as he understood just how much power this lowly Decurion Princeps possessed. He handed it back, carefully folded, and then began to slowly rise. "Well it has been a long day and I need to…"

Livius gently restrained him. "Before you go, Governor, I understand from my sergeant that you are compiling a report on the state of Britannia and its security. Well as of today and my last patrol I can report that the Red Witch of Mona, the Queen of the Brigantes in exile, Morwenna has joined forces with the Votadini and is heading north to meet with them." Marcus and Gaius slumped in their seats; they too knew the import of the message. The Governor patently did not, looking bemused at the report, and Livius continued. "She led the last rising of the Brigante when she almost captured Eboracum and came within a whisker of defeating the Ninth. The Votadini actually did finish off the Ninth and many of my Explorates as well therefore if they do actually combine then we are in trouble. In fact, the whole of Britannia is in trouble."

"Er thank you Decurion Princeps. Excellent intelligence." He gave a weak smile, "No rest for the wicked then. I will have to write the report before I retire for the night."

When they heard his door slam shut Gaius and Marcus both burst out laughing. "Where did you get such a good forgery?" Gaius examined the document still lying on the table.

Livius looked him straight in the eye, "It isn't a forgery. I am a frumentari although it is not a line of work I enjoy."

Marcus Arvina poured them all a beaker of wine, "Allfather I will walk carefully around you from now on."

"I am still the same man I was, Marcus."

"I cannot believe you took all that crap from him when you had such power in your hands."

Livius shook his head. "It is a secret Gaius. I was appointed by Emperor Trajan and had it confirmed by Emperor Hadrian but I do not like to use the power. I just wanted our Governor to realise that the soldiers of the north were not to be insulted."

"I like you, Livius, but trust me I will never get the wrong side of you. By the way, are there really other frumentarii with you?"

"Yes, Gaius but before you ask I will not divulge their names and I hope that you will keep my secret."

Marcus Arvina leaned over and said very seriously, "I think I can guarantee that we will take that secret to our graves but I will also say that I will sleep easier in my bed now knowing what a resourceful officer we have here on the frontier."

"And I will thoroughly enjoy the journey back to Aqua Sulis watching a Governor who will be petrified of a knock on his door in the night and squirming at the memory of his gaffes tonight!"

As the royal party crossed the Tinus, Morwenna halted the column. She turned to Radha. "You saw the Romans."

"Yes, my husband will be angry when he finds out that they have left the Stanegate."

"I can see, little one, that you are forgetting the lessons I taught you. Peace and calm. We use this to our advantage. This is not a problem, it is a solution. What do you think that patrol will report to their officers?"

"That they saw a column heading..."

"Heading where?"

"Why to the land of the Votadini of course."

"Whereas we are heading for Aindreas and the court of the Selgovae. If you can misdirect your enemy then you are winning. We also now know where they are patrolling. I will leave Gwynfor and ten men. Who knows they may pick up a prisoner or two."

The guards took up a position on the bluff close to the bridge and Morwenna led the depleted column north-west towards the land of the Selgovae. "Will your husband have called the conclave?"

"Of course, Mother. It is a tradition in these parts that we celebrate the midwinter festival. People expect to drink and eat well. If my husband is providing the food and drink then I can guarantee that every king and petty chief will turn up for a free feast."

"I wonder which of my people will come."

"Your people mother? The Druids?"

"No, I am Queen of the Brigante through my father." She laughed. "That son I had with the half-witted soldier is probably the heir to the throne if he did but know it."

"Have you never seen him then?"

"Not since I dumped him on that simple-minded Ailis when he was but a child. There is a lesson to you Radha; unless the male child is to be a king and therefore of some use do not waste time wet nursing them. A sacrifice to the mother is much more profitable."

Radha had much to learn and she was not convinced that she could ever kill a child of hers but then a few months ago she would never have believed that she could love a woman more than a man and that she would have been initiated in the most secret of mysteries and ceremonies. She knew she was changing but how far was the journey she had begun?

The scouts from Aindreas' main camp spotted them as they meandered along the upper Tinus. The scout who saw them had been at the fateful battle when the Selgovae so ignominiously fled the field. Since then there had been border raids and blood feuds but he recognised the Queen, Radha and, although there were Votadini warriors with them, the vast bulk of them were not and that gave him pause. He turned to his companion. "Ride to the King and tell him that the Queen of the Votadini approaches with a party of armed men and ask him what I should do."

As he settled in to the simple task of watching the huge party pick their way up the twisting banks and through thickets he wondered if this was the start or the end of a war. He had not enjoyed running away at the last battle, for his honour said that he should stay with his comrades but the king had made that fateful decision. It was even more galling that the Votadini won. As he chewed on the liquorice root he wondered if his king had gambled on the Votadini losing. He would not put it past his wily king. He did not like Aindreas but he was a loyal Selgovae. This might be an ultimatum but why send his beautiful wife into harm's way? He remembered that the King of the Votadini had used that ploy before to draw the Romans into a trap. When his companion returned he would backtrack and make sure that this was not a trap. He wondered about the red-haired beauty with them. There was something familiar about her but Garoc could not quite bring it to mind.

His companion galloped up an hour later. "I found the king and his men out hunting. He is quite near, close to the valley of the hawthorn. He has asked me to watch them while he speaks with you."

Garoc knew that the king valued his opinion even though there was mutual dislike. As one of the older warriors, he had chosen to scout, mainly because it kept him away from court and close to the land that he loved. Aindreas greeted him like a brother. "Well done Garoc, greatest of scouts. Now tell me what you saw and, more importantly, what it means."

Garoc ignored the obvious false flattery. "The Queen Radha is there with a small party of retainers, no more than twenty but there is a large party of heavily armed men who are not Votadini. They appear to be guarding a red-haired woman, beautiful and familiar."

Aindreas became excited. "This redhead was she wearing a simple white shift and were her eyes a wonderful green."

"Aye."

"Then it is Morwenna the Red Witch!"

"That is her, now I remember. I was younger when I first beheld her but she was a beauty."

"That makes it interesting. What is your assessment? Speak freely for I need honesty."

As he spoke, the irony stuck in Garoc's throat. His king was the most mendacious of men and as straight as the upper Tinea but he was his king. "It is probably a peace envoy, however, King Lugubelenus is a devious man and he may be putting his wife in harm's way to achieve some strategic victory. I will, with your permission, backtrack and see if there is an army waiting to envelop us."

"Good and I will go to greet the Queen and her entourage." He turned to one of his bodyguards. "Go and tell the Steward to prepare rooms and quarters for a large number of guest and bid the warriors of my house to arm themselves," he paused, "just in case."

Despite his misgivings, Aindreas was confident that this was a peaceful embassy. The presence of Morwenna confirmed that in his eyes. She had been the catalyst for the last rebellion which had so nearly succeeded. Lugubelenus had not wanted a war but he had been drawn into one by the incompetent Romans. They could not count on incompetence too often. Agricola had been an example of a good Roman leader who had almost managed to conquer the whole of the island. The king knew his land, especially this area around his hunting grounds and he waited patiently for the visitors to arrive. Radha had had her scouts out too and was not surprised by the appearance of the king.

"Welcome Radha Queen of the Votadini and to you Morwenna, Queen of the Brigantes."

Morwenna nodded, "You recognised me then?"

"Who would not recognise the most beautiful Queen who defied the Romans for so long? If you would like to follow me my camp is but a little way through the forest." He hesitated, "You were coming to see me were you not? What other reason could you have for wandering through Selgovae land?"

"It is my fault oh king," Morwenna's silky voice began to enchant all those who heard her. It was both mellifluous and magical. "I wished to see the land of the Selgovae again, having seen it when I was much younger. It is only a slight deviation from our intended route."

"Your destination is not my home then?"

"No mighty king; I have been summoned to the conclave that the King of The Votadini is holding over the Yule festival and, as all the other important kings and queens will be there, I wanted to be part of it."

Aindreas pulled his horse up sharply. "A conclave? Of all the kings and queens? All the chiefs? Why was I not invited?"

Radha rode next to him. "It may have been that my husband thought you may not have wished to come. You did part badly the last time you met did you not?"

Aindreas regained his composure. "Things are done, and said, in the heat of battle which are regretted by all parties. I certainly hold no grudge against the King of the Votadini."

Morwenna touched his arm and he felt his whole body tingle. "I am sure you will be welcome there. In fact," she turned to Radha, "I will stand surety that there will be no trouble and both you and your retainers will be safe from harm."

Radha humbly bowed her head, "I am yours to command in all things." The king was so flattered he did not see the sly smile exchanged between the two powerful women.

Garoc rode up and shook his head. He took his place at the head of the column. Aindreas smiled to himself. This was not a trap and it was peaceful. He would be able to use the meeting to his advantage; a widower, he was sure he could woo this most powerful queen and then Lugubelenus would see the cruel side of the Selgovae king.

His people were both intrigued and joyous that the two queens were visiting. Since Aindreas' wife had died the kingdom had been a male-dominated country and the wives of the nobles looked forward to seeing and speaking with these two famous warrior queens. The camp was partly made of stone and stood surrounded on three sides by water, atop a rocky knoll. The ramparts were wooden but the main hall was made of stone and timber. They halted before the gatehouse. "Your warriors will have to camp outside the walls I am afraid. We do not have room for them within."

Radha's men began to bristle and become agitated but Morwenna nodded imperceptibly to her acolyte and Radha spoke to her bodyguards. "If the Queen is happy with this then so am I. Besides," she added, looking directly at Aindreas, "if anything happened to me, then not a Selgovae would be left alive, would they?"

Aindreas took the point although the Queen would be as safe within these walls as in her own. They rode through the gate and the bodyguards headed for the field set aside for them. As they approached the hall they could see many of the noblest Selgovae waiting to greet them. Most prominent was a handsome young man, broad of shoulders with long red hair and a fine beard and moustache. His upper body was bare and rippled with muscles. At his side hung a mighty war axe which appeared to have all the weight of a bracelet, it was carried so easily.

Morwenna leaned over to the king. "Who is the fine-looking man on the steps? Is he your brother?"

Flattered, the king murmured, "No majesty, he is my son Tole; the finest warrior amongst the Selgovae. I am immensely proud of him."

"As you should be, as any father would be. I would deem it an honour to sit next to him tonight."

"Your wish is granted."

Morwenna rode next to Radha as Aindreas trotted up to the hall to announce them. Quietly Morwenna said, "I can see now that the Mother has planned all things. The boy becomes our tool and you shall soon have your revenge on the king."

In an excited voice filled with the emotion of the memory of those who died because of the faithless king, Radha asked, "When?"

Calmly Morwenna turned to her and said, "Why tonight of course, in his own rooms with not an enemy warrior in sight."

117

Chapter 13

With little time to prepare, the Steward had had to make do with whatever came to hand. He evicted three of the king's bodyguards from the two rooms adjacent to the King's. The two queens were thus adequately accommodated. He gave up his own room for their female attendants as he and his wife had a room in the main hall and then he turned his attention to the food. As the king had been hunting, there was plenty of meat but the queens would want something more refined and sophisticated after the meal. The cook was a plain man who did not know other than to serve hearty and filling meals, delicacy he didn't do. It was the steward's wife who found the solution. "There are many berries in season, mix them with some whipped cream, some honey and a little toasted oatmeal and just put them in wee bowls. They will love it." The Steward kissed her and then inclined his head, "Aye you big soft lump I'll make it for you but mark ye I'll be wanting a shift just like yon queen that the men canna take their eyes off. I won't be as bonny but I'll do."

He kissed her again. "Aye, ye'll more than do for me, bonnie lass." Relieved that the sudden influx of guests and dignitaries had been dealt with, he next began to house the guards and bodyguards. There was no room in the main hall and so King's Aindreas' bodyguards would sleep behind the main door of the hall preventing any attack during the night. Although the Votadini came in peace the Steward was taking no chances. It also had the advantage of holding the two queens inside the hall, not exactly hostages but surety for the good behaviour of their men. The extra men were given the materials to build themselves a shelter abutting the ramparts. He dusted his hands off as he went back into the kitchen to taste the feast that was being prepared.

Radha sought out Morwenna as soon as she could. "Tonight? Have you a plan?"

"Of course. I'll flatter the young Tole and persuade him that he would like to visit me after the house has gone to bed. You will ingratiate yourself with the Steward and his wife. Make them like you, "she smiled genuinely, "it will not be hard for you have the face and the personality that people naturally like. When you go to bed make a little noise so that I will have to come in to see you. I will slip along to the king's room and place a potion in the drink he keeps by his bed."

"How do you know that?"

"I checked before we came into these rooms. One of the servants was putting an amphora and beaker there." She smiled knowingly. "Many men, especially of a certain age, do the same thing."

"How do you know that he will not be abed before us?"

"That part is easy. We will steer the conversation to the potential of an alliance between the Selgovae and the Votadini and how easy and glorious it will be to defeat the Romans. He and his entourage will sit up half the night plotting and the only two who will not be suspected will be us two for I will be abed with the Prince of the Selgovae and you will have spent the evening, being as friendly as can be, offering an alliance. Besides which the potion I intend to use will make it look as though his heart has stopped. It is the belladonna which I will use."

The king was so pleased with the feast that he ordered the whole of the assembly to toast the wonderful organisation of his Steward who had managed all in such a short space of time. Tole was totally mesmerized by the beautiful Morwenna and hung on to her every word. Her mellifluous words and heady perfume intoxicating him as much as the ale he supped. When Radha offered the alliance to the assembled body she thought that their work would be done for them and the king would die on his feet in a surfeit of joy so great was the effusive nature of his reaction. She and the steward's wife took to swapping recipes and ideas for dresses, which allowed the king and the Steward to begin to plot and plan how they would defeat the Romans. The polite conversations with the women could now be replaced by more manly talk of arms and strategy, logistics and battles.

With all the attention on Radha and the king, Morwenna went to work on the gullible young warrior. Morwenna had dressed simply but used her potions, perfumes and charms to enchant the warrior prince who had spent the last six years perfecting the art of becoming a warrior. He had never met a woman like Morwenna; the rough and tumbles and furtive sexual encounters had been with milking maids and servants. His meeting with the Red Witch would open not only his eyes but also his mind to the wiles and ways of older women. Morwenna was the consummate sexual predator and Tole stood no chance of resisting her, even had he wished to. She leaned on an elbow, her green eyes like pools in the forest into which Tole fell. She ran the back of a tapered fingernail down his hairline to gently remove a stray lock of his red hair. "Our hair is almost the same colour young prince, perhaps it is a sign."

"Oh no my Queen for yours is lustrous and flows like the Tinea on a spring morning mine is rough and uncontrolled. Like my heart which beats like a wild stallion galloping over the hills."

"Your honeyed tongue is trying to woo me, young prince."

"My tongue is doing what my heart wishes it to do." By now the warrior was so aroused that he was almost becoming embarrassed and was grateful for the table which covered his legs.

Morwenna slipped her hand between his legs, hidden by the groaning table of dishes and beakers; it was unobserved by any in the hall. She said quietly, in a husky voice, which further aroused Tole, "And not just your heart." She leaned in and whispered in his ear, her darting tongue just touching the lobe, "shall we go to your chamber?"

No-one saw Morwenna and Tole slip away until the king saw the empty chairs and realised that his son had done what he had intended to attempt later in the feast. He was, at first, a little discomfited and put out but he knew that with the wine and aqua vitae he had consumed he would not have done the queen justice, and he smiled philosophically. It would be a conquest by proxy and in his time the old king had bedded many a high born lady. He would enjoy the night with his peers and relive the memories of past wars and battles.

Radha had kept her wits about her and watched as the two lovers stole away. Turning to the wife of the Steward she said, "I am tired, it has been a long and exhilarating day, I should like to go to my room. Which one is it?"

"I will show you." Bowing to the king, the two ladies left the main hall and Radha was shown to her room. The wife of the Steward and the Steward were staying on the opposite side of the settlement and she hurried to get to her much-needed bed anxious to be asleep before a drunken, and, no doubt, the amorous husband left the king for their marital bed.

Radha waited a suitable amount of time for the older woman to wend her way across the camp and then she gave a sudden shout. She waited a few moments and then went to open her door. Keeping watch on the bedroom of Morwenna and Tole, she watched Morwenna slip into the king's chamber, as she did so she said, "What is it Radha? Nightmares?" and disappeared to slip the poison into the beaker and amphora of wine.

Radha carried on the deception by answering, "Nothing my lady. I was just frightened by a shadow."

Morwenna closed the door of the chamber and said loudly so that Tole would hear and be flattered, "Sleep well. I fear I will get little sleep tonight."

As Radha closed the door she smiled as she imagined Tole hearing those words. Young men were the same the whole world over. The meeting with Morwenna had merely revealed to her the power women had over men. On the journey north, she had reflected on all the actions of the men in her life, including her father and she saw that they could be so easily controlled by powerful women. Her father, Tam, would still do anything his daughter wanted, all she had to do was flutter her eyes and cuddle in to him and he would comply with any request.

When Aindreas retired, escorted by two of his chamberlains, he was a little unsteady on his feet but not drunk. The two men ensured that the room was safe; one of them poured wine from the jug he carried, into the beaker by the bed. When they were satisfied that the king was safe they said goodnight and then one lay outside the door whilst the other slept behind the door. No-one could enter and do the king harm without risking the wrath of the two bodyguards. While many kings felt safe in their own fortress Aindreas trusted no-one. He applied his own standards to everyone else. Just as he would stab a brother in the back so he worried that his son might do the same to him. He settled in to the bed and turned to sleep. He had thought that he had drunk more but perhaps it was the excitement of Radha's announcement which had intoxicated him. He knew that he needed more drink to sleep comfortably and not be disturbed by his limbs, which increasingly ached, the older he became. He took a good swallow from the beaker and felt the liquid warm his old body. It felt very comfortable and he drained the beaker. He would sleep well on this auspicious night. Inside his body, the drug, carefully concocted by Morwenna seeped swiftly through his veins and made its insidious way through his body. It was not a quick drug but it was effective and, coursing through his body, it made its inevitable way to his heart. The pain he received made him sit bolt upright in bed and clutch as his chest. He shouted and the chamberlain behind the door leapt to his feet.

"My king, what is it?"

The other chamberlain entered sword in hand and looked at his companion. The king's eyes were wide open and he groaned, "My heart!" rolled over and died.

The two guards spun around as Morwenna and Tole appeared in the doorway. Tole waved away the sword. "What is it?"

"Your father, mighty King Aindreas of the Selgovae, is dead, sire."

"How?" Tole looked suspiciously at the unsheathed blades of the two guards and then relaxed a little when he saw that they were clean.

"He sat upright in bed, clutched his chest and said, 'my heart' and then he died."

Morwenna went to the king's side. "Let me look at him. I have seen many men die." The chamberlains stepped back as the witch passed. The fear in their eyes amused the murderess as she placed her head next to the king's mouth. She stood and placed her hands on his chest. "Your father is dead. I fear his heart has burst. You are now the king, your majesty." As she stood she managed to, clumsily knock the amphora to the floor where it shattered. No one would drink the poisoned wine and create suspicion. "Sorry, King Tole. Your father was a good king and I am clumsy."

Morwenna had been very clever. The King of the Selgovae had to be chosen by the peers of the land. It was not inevitable that Tole would become king. Morwenna needed him as king for that would guarantee that the Selgovae would fight Rome. She watched as the two chamberlains dropped to their knees and said, "Your majesty."

Radha entered the room, her face suitably distraught followed by the Steward and others who had been close by and heard the commotion.

The Steward took it all in, the King, obviously dead, the lack of blood and the two chamberlains kneeling. He dropped to his knee, as did the others as he said, "The king is dead, long live the king." Morwenna smiled in triumph as did Radha, their smiles hidden by their hands as they feigned tears.

When Radha finally reached Traprain Law, their arrival had been heralded by scouts and the King had lined the route to the oppidum with his army and his people. The King was besotted with Radha and had sorely missed her whilst she had been away. Her two letters had been read and re-read until he knew their contents by heart. Now that she had returned he vowed never to let her leave his sight again. His hill fort was far to the north of the land of the Romans both remote and safe from a sudden revenge raid from an enemy still smarting from a major defeat. Had his wife's settlement of Tamburgh not been raided by the Roman barbarians, he doubted that he would ever have ventured so far south with his army but that raid had guaranteed his enmity. It had also created, in the King's mind, a hatred for Aindreas of the Selgovae. During his wife's absence he would have destroyed the traitor but for her letter which urged caution and restraint until she returned with ideas gleaned from Morwenna. He trusted his wife, he knew that many other men did not, but Lugubelenus did for he knew that she had a brain and mind as sharp as a keenly honed blade.

As he watched the entourage wend its way between lines of cheering crowds he resisted the urge to gallop down and sweep her in his arms. He was a young king but he had a wise head on his shoulders and knew that he had to maintain the dignity of the crown at all times. When she finally reached the gate she dismounted and she ran to him, kneeling before him to kiss his hand. "My husband I am sorry that I have tarried so long away from my heart's desire. Please forgive me."

Lugubelenus raised her up and, embracing her, kissed her long and hard. The roar from the people showed their approbation. When she stepped back she gestured with her hand. "And this is our honoured guest Morwenna, Queen of the Brigantes."

"Welcome Queen to my humble settlement."

"Thank you, mighty destroyer of Romans. I look forward to our discussions and plans."

Had Lugubelenus been any other king then he might have been a little put out by the thought of a discussion with a woman, albeit a queen, but he had learned in his short time as king that listening to the widest number of views usually resulted in the greatest success. "And I, you, come let us go to the quarters I have prepared. Your men can sleep in my guard's quarters, the hall of the warriors. It is a large hall and they will be close to you."

Morwenna noticed the contrast between the reception of the Selgovae and that of the Votadini; it was the difference in confidence between the two rulers. Lugubelenus trusted his men and his people and the results could be seen in the warm welcome they received. As the King led his Queen towards their chambers Morwenna followed close enough to listen in to their conversation. "How many will be attending the conclave, my husband?"

"All who were invited." He had a wry smile on his face. "Who would refuse free hospitality in the coldest time of the year?"

Radha stopped and turned to halt all but Morwenna. "We would be alone for a while. We shall see you all at the feast." Once they had passed the gateway and the guards Radha, a sly smiling dancing on her face said, "You will need to set a place for another for Tole will be attending."

"Tole?" The name was familiar to Lugubelenus but he could not place it or the man.

"Yes, King Tole, the new king of the Selgovae son of the dead betrayer of hopes, Aindreas."

The King was a man without guile and his face betrayed his raw emotion. "A Selgovae! Under my roof never!"

Morwenna slipped her arm into that of the king so that he was flanked by both women. "It was his father Aindreas who betrayed you. Not his son and not his people. They resented the dishonour and Aindreas is now dead."

"Dead? How?"

The two women shared a knowing look and Radha leaned up to kiss her husband. "His heart."

The King looked dubious, "But…"

"Best you not ask husband, let us just say that we have had our revenge." She leaned up and kissed him gently.

As they entered the fortress Wolf and Quintus reflected on the change in their fortunes. They had been accepted by Morwenna's men although shunned by the Votadini. It mattered little to the two deserters. They were fed and they were safe for the moment, at least. They were phlegmatic about their situation. Things could only get better and they both awaited their summons from Morwenna when their fate would be decided.

Livius was pleased with the new recruits. They were well trained, disciplined, and so far had shown their loyalty for the entire world to see. All the patrols had yielded little sound intelligence and the reason was obvious to the Decurion Princeps who knew that was because it was harvest time and warriors were too busy bringing in crops to be interested in raiding. He was just grateful that they had not done so in the summer before his men were trained. He and Cassius had also discussed the possibility of longer forays into the land of the Votadini to see what they could discover. The ways of the Explorate were difficult to forget and both men knew that they could easily discover more information by donning disguises and visiting settlements. When the nights began to grow colder he called a meeting of the decurions. He and Cassius had already planned their strategy and were both in agreement.

"Gentlemen you have done well so far but now it is time to build on that success. I have sent a message to the Prefect at Coriosopitum and he has agreed that we can winter there. There is an old cavalry fort south of the river which we can refortify. We have put upon Marcus Arvina enough." The Prefect was in the corner and he shook his head in disagreement. He would miss the lively troopers and their officers but it would be good to get back to the normal routine. "We leave tomorrow and we will begin a different strategy. Myself and those turmae commanded by an Explorate will venture into Votadini territory to discover what they intend. Decurion Spartianus and the new decurions will patrol the south bank of the Tinea to control any incursions."

The newer decurions looked dismayed. It sounded as though the Decurion Princeps had put them under the command of the hated Spartianus. They fidgeted and looked as though they were going to object until they caught the subtle shake of the head from Cassius.

Spartianus, for his part, was surprised and delighted. Although his cronies were spread amongst the other turmae he had begun to bully and coerce a couple of the younger recruits and was busy building up allies again. Who knew, he might even subvert some of the other officers.

"Any questions?"

The quartermaster coughed. "When do we leave sir? It's just that I have wagons and mules to load and…"

Appius Sabinus was a fussy, though efficient officer and Livius knew he could be trusted. "You will follow whenever you are ready. Turmae twelve will escort you. The rest of us will leave," he paused dramatically, "now!"

Dere Street was less safe now than before the demise of the Ninth. Coriosopitum was isolated and close to Votadini warbands. Its position on the north side of the river meant that it protruded into what Lugubelenus considered Votadini land. The Camp Prefect had been delighted to have reinforcements just south of him for it meant he had double the number of men to defend the vital crossing of the Tinea. Apart from the Explorates none of them had been this far north before and, although it looked similar to the land they had patrolled for the last few months, it had more hills, long undulating climbs with blind summits and more places to ambush the unwary. All of them were nervous and all of them delighted to crest the ridge and look down upon the frontier fort and the stone bridge.

Livius turned to Cassius. I can see that the new fort is further east than the old one."

"Aye, and it looks as though the defences have been improved."

Every time Livius looked on the site he admired Agricola even more. It had been the general who had seen what a perfect site it was. It was close to the Tinea close to the juncture of the two tributaries of that important waterway. There was a flat area which gently rose to its front and the river protecting the rear. "It's as safe as anywhere Cassius but we are now at the most northerly fort in the Empire."

"A sobering thought."

Livius and Cassius left their men to begin work on the camp while they went to pay their respects to Gnaeus Turpius, the Camp Prefect. Like Arvina he had known some of them from Marcus' Horse days when he had been a young optio and was glad that veterans commanded this new ala. "Glad to see you, boys. We feel a little isolated up here."

The sentries all had a haggard, hunted look about them which both Livius and Cassius had noticed. It contrasted with the relaxed appearance of the garrison stationed at Morbium. "Are things difficult here then?"

"We don't patrol any more. The last six we sent out either never returned or were attacked just north of the fort. Even staying on the road we are attacked."

"Which explains the lack of intelligence then? "The Prefect spread his arms and shrugged as though to say that was impossible. "You have heard nothing?"

"The occasional visitor tells of the king building a new fortress on the rock at Din Eidyn and there have been supplies heading through the gates to his oppidum. He has many guests coming, that is certain." Although the Votadini and Rome were not friends the Roman artery was still the main and most efficient means of moving goods from the south to the barbarians in the north. They might resent Rome but they liked Rome's goods.

"They don't usually attack in winter do they?"

"They aren't that kind of supplies they are more in the nature of hospitality goods; blankets, amphorae of wine, that sort of thing. The traders further south must be making a fortune. Besides, they captured so many arms from the Ninth that they don't need to import weapons for the foreseeable future."

"Well Prefect we don't want to upset the locals but we are going to probe the region. We need to find out what they are up to for the new Emperor Hadrian wants a complete assessment of the security risks on the frontier."

"Well, I can tell him in one word, high! Any time they want to they can come straight through here. There are crossing points further upstream they could use and with just one cohort here and the other forts equally thinly garrisoned well... they destroyed the Ninth didn't they?"

Livius could see that morale was an issue. "I think the Ninth were badly led by an incompetent legate. Would you have taken the Ninth into those forests?"

"I wouldn't have taken my lot in there, never mind close order infantry. You are right but don't be fooled, this King is not like the other barbarians; he considers, thinks and plans and his wife is shrewd too."

"Radha isn't it?"

Something in Livius' voice alerted the prefect, "Yes, have you heard something?"

"We have news that a high born group of Votadini women travelled south and have returned north with Morwenna."

126

"Shit! That is all we need, the fucking Witch Queen up here again! If you don't mind I will keep that from my lads. They are a superstitious lot anyway and some of them remember the last time she came and what she did."

"We will get back to our camp. I intend to have half the ala patrolling the south bank of the Tinea. The rest of us will be working further north, in Votadini country."

"Good luck to you then and watch your bollocks. The bodies we found had neither bollocks nor dicks nor noses. The Allfather alone knows what they use them for."

As they walked with the Prefect down the slope towards the bridge Livius nodded at the walls and buildings. "I see you have beefed up the defences then?"

"Yes but every time we try to put more stones in to make the walls higher some bugger attacks us and the work is slow. The men have one eye on the forests and don't build as well as they should. It's why I am so grateful to you and your boys. We can leave the patrolling to you and it just makes us a little more secure. I'd like deeper ditches and higher walls before the snow falls. Once it is winter here you just hunker down and try to survive."

"I know. When my quartermaster arrives I will have to give him the thorny problem of getting some fodder here." They were just crossing the river as he said this and he stopped making Cassius and the prefect look at him.

"Are you all right sir."

"I am an idiot Cassius, an idiot. All the rivers flow to the sea! Simple enough eh?"

Bemused by the enigmatic Decurion Princeps the camp Prefect returned to the fort while Cassius tried to get inside the complex mind that was Livius.

Gwynfor and his men were becoming bored. They had sat at the river crossing for over a week and the only people they had seen using the bridge were tribesman. Not even a merchant had ventured across, much to the chagrin of those waiting, who would have relieved them of their goods and money. Gwynfor was wondering just how long he had to wait when Idris ran up the trail. "A Roman cavalry patrol thirty of them."

Gwynfor was disappointed. Thirty was too many for them to take without either losing too many men or risking discovery. They would have to follow and see if the Romans made a mistake, in Gwynfor's experience that was unlikely but one never knew.

Spartianus was enjoying his freedom. This was the third day they had patrolled and there was no one either to criticise or watch and he ruled his turma as he had done the ala with insults, threats and bullying. He had found two candidates to join his coterie, Querelus and Suetonious. Both were new men but not young men and it had not taken much persuasion for them to accept his offer of advancement in return for their support. Leaving the rest of the turma he took his two potential allies north for a reconnaissance he told the others, but in reality for a conference. Once they had crossed the primitive bridge he had them dismount.

"Now I know that you are committed to my cause and will help me to regain the ala. What I need to know is who else might join us?"

Suetonius was the bolder of the two. "The trouble is, sir, that most of the lads like their officers, especially the Decurion Princeps. And they all think the sun shines out of the arses of the two sergeants."

Querelus was a little more devious. "Of course if any of the lads got into trouble and were punished then they might turn against the bosses."

"I like your thinking. Let's try to work out how to do that."

Gwynfor and his men had closed to within thirty paces of the trio. While two of his men watched with bows strung, Gwynfor led the others on foot to below the bridge. He gestured for three of them to climb up one side whilst he and the others climbed the other. They were stealthy but the sides of the bridge were bare and that was where they could be seen. It was just one man's bad fortune to slip on the slippery muddy bank just as he was going to pull himself up on to the bridge. Aelius reacted the quickest and slashed down instinctively with his sword. Although the blade missed his target the two archers fired at the same time and Suetonius received an arrow in the leg. The three Romans quickly mounted their horses and fled across the bridge. The rest of the turma had heard the noise and were armed and ready to support their comrades. Cursing his luck Gwynfor led his men back to their horses.

"I have had enough of this. You remain here while I ride to Traprain Law and speak with the Queen. It is a waste us being here. We need more men if we are to ambush successfully."

As he rode northeast the others began to take apart their erstwhile leader. "He just doesn't want to live in a field."

"He always wants to be near Morwenna."

"I would rather have Idwal now he is a good leader, not a piss pot like Gwynfor."

Aelius and the patrol bandaged Suetonius and then rode back as swiftly as they could. He had wondered if he ought to head for Vindolanda which was slightly nearer than Corio but the thought of more barbarians waiting for them convinced him to head back to his own fort. Metellus was back in camp, having had the shortest and least successful patrol. "Did you catch a look at them? Were they Votadini, Selgovae, Brigante or that bunch we saw with Morwenna?"

"We just got out of there as quickly as we could. If we had stayed then we might all have been killed. Is that what you want?" Part of Spartianus' anger was that he knew, as an officer that Metellus was right and another part was frustration that he had been nearly killed in an inconsequential little skirmish.

Metellus sighed, had it been any other decurion he would at least have had a description. One of the turma stepped forward. "I saved this sir. I don't know if it is any help." He brought out the arrow which had struck Suetonius.

"Good lad. This is perfect. "He examined the arrow from every angle. "It isn't Votadini, Selgovae and it isn't Brigante. It is definitely not Roman. It is one of Morwenna's men's which makes me wonder why they were there." He turned to the turma. "Thanks, lads and this is a good lesson, thankfully not fatal. You need to keep your wits about you up here. We are on the frontier. Beyond that river, everyone is an enemy which is why we try to keep you south of the river." Metellus glared at Spartianus who stomped off with Querelus. To no-one, in particular, Metellus said, "Now I wonder what those three were doing north of the river? "

Chapter 14

Livius and his patrol had headed north up the Roman road. It was not in the pristine state that the legion building it had intended for the undergrowth had grown in closer to the sides making it less safe and more prone to attack. He had chosen this route for himself as it was the most dangerous. The others were spread like fingers in the forests, heading west and east. The road steadily rose until, about two miles from Coriosopitum, he found himself looking down on an enormous swale which was like a dry river valley running east to west. He halted the patrol and turned to the troopers behind him. "You two split up and make sure there is no one in the forests on either side. You two," he ordered the next two. "Keep your eyes peeled ahead of us. I have a bit of drawing to do." The rest of the turma edged forward to watch their leader as he took out a wax tablet from his saddlebag and began to use a stylus to draw the view ahead.

One of the braver ones nudged his horse forward and ventured, "Never seen that done before sir. Do all the decurions do that?"

The others backed their horses away, especially the ones who had served with Spartianus. That sort of comment would result in a beating. Livius smiled. "No, just the ones who were Explorates but it is a good habit. Keep your eyes open," he said to the turma at large, "and always try to remember what you see. Never be afraid to tell an officer if you have seen something of interest. It could save someone's life. And now we can venture a little further," he whistled twice, a signal he had taught his turma straight away, and the scouts returned. "Anything?" They shook their heads. "We are now in enemy territory. If we have to return to the fort then we do so at full speed. Clear?"

They all chorused, "Sir, yes sir!" and Livius led his first patrol into the enemy's lair. He took them north-west and found the land largely devoid of people. In the distance, he could see a few farmsteads with small herds of cattle. He avoided those. After a couple of miles, he saw that the land rose steeply and when he reached the top he saw that it dropped quite steeply, preventing further movement north. He took out his wax tablet and sketched again.

Later that night Livius sat in his tent with the other, as he called them, Explorate Decurions discussing the events of the day and what they had discovered on their patrols. "So," said Livius, "we have a patrol attacked over here by an indeterminate number of warriors, probably Morwenna's. There is no other sign of any barbarian force within ten miles of this fort." He looked around, "That it?"

He noticed that Macro was squirming a little, "Well not entirely sir." Marcus looked equally embarrassed. "I changed into civilian clothes and visited one of the villages. I pretended I was on my way south to visit Brigante relatives." Livius had to smile to himself. Macro was a born Explorate. He could see him now heading south through the settlement to make it look as though he had passed through much Votadini territory already to allay any suspicions they might have. "They were all going on about how the cowardly king of the Selgovae, Aindreas, had died and his son was the new king. They seemed really happy about that."

"We saw him flee the battle didn't we when the Ninth were almost beaten?" Macro and Marcus nodded. "I think if they hadn't we might have all been massacred. It is no wonder that the Votadini aren't happy."

"There's more sir. They have a meeting planned for the Yule up at Traprain Law and every tribal leader is attending."

"And Morwenna is there." They all took in Livius' words. It was the final piece of the jigsaw. "Well thank you all, especially Macro who doesn't yet understand that he is now in the army and no longer an Explorate. Cassius if you could stay, I have a report to write."

When they were alone Cassius said, "I assume this is a report for the Senator?"

"Yes, I need to give him my assessment on the Governor and on the situation here. That meeting at Traprain Law is just the sort of job we would have taken on when we were Explorates you know. A shame we haven't any available at the moment." Cassius was busy rearranging the chairs and did not see the glint in his commander's eye. Livius coughed and went on, "I have some ideas about the limes the Emperor wants to build. I took a drawing today."

"You know who we could use don't you?"

Livius scratched his head with the stylus as he thought. "Can't say that I do."

"The new clerk, Julius Longinus. He can't know about the code and the message but he is a writer and he could draw a map for you couldn't he? All of us could give him the information the patrols collect. If it is on paper it is easier to look at and take it in. "

"Good idea. Tell him tomorrow!"

"With pleasure! Hen's scratching indeed."

Livius wondered how long it would be before Cassius had his revenge, a mild form, but revenge nonetheless. "I also have some things

I would like the senator to acquire for us. Perhaps we'll see old Hercules sooner rather than later eh?"

Cassius had given up trying to work out what Livius meant. He seemed to be working at a different level to the rest of them. Livius was indeed thinking on a different level for his time with Julius and the Emperor had shown him the importance of small actions. All of his life had seemed to prepare him for this point, the training with Marcus Maximunius, the imprisonment, the service with the ala and the experience of encountering the witch, Morwenna, the training and life as an Explorate and, finally, the hunting of his brother and the treasure, all of that had made him what he was now. He no longer thought of the plans for the next day or even the next week; he was thinking further ahead, to the day when the Emperor would come to build his *limes* in Northern Britannia. He was not just thinking of the ala next week, but in a year when, perhaps, it would be Cassius who would be in charge and now he was planning his letters to the Senator which would set in motion events which, he hoped, would secure the frontier, at least for the next generation if not beyond.

Gwynfor made good time covering the seventy miles to the Votadini capital. Morwenna did not know why he had deserted his post but she was willing to give him the benefit of the doubt. Radha had pressed her husband into building a roundhouse for Morwenna. This suited both of them for it was a place safe from men who might eavesdrop and a place of privacy for intimacy. It was just outside of the ramparts but well protected in the unlikely event that they were attacked. Morwenna took the warrior into her new home.

"We waited for over two weeks and only one patrol came, they were Roman cavalry. We tried to capture one but there were thirty of them. We either need more men or a better strategy. This is just a waste of time."

Morwenna did not answer immediately. She was thinking. She went to the door and said to her guard, "Go and fetch the Roman deserters." She returned to Gwynfor. "I left you with a simple task and you deserted your post."

"But it was a waste!"

"I decide what is a waste and what is not." Her eyes flashed the anger which the words did not and he felt himself begin to quail before her. She lifted not a finger but he felt as though he had been struck.

"No! Please! Forgive me. I will not let you down again." When he was on his knees, almost sobbing, she relented and gently stroked his hair, as though he were a puppy she had chastised and was now petting.

"I know you will not so for the next time you do, you will die." She went to her seat which was next to the table. Radha had ensured that the seat looked magnificent. One of the Votadini woodworkers had been preparing the seat as a gift for the King of the Novontae but now Morwenna sat upon it, a queen on her throne, raised above the others and regal. The guard called from the door and Morwenna called, "Send them in."

Wolf and Quintus had not been hurt or treated badly whilst with the barbarians. Quintus' leg had healed and he now only had a slight limp. Both men were less neat and tidy as they had discarded those parts of their uniform which encumbered them and replaced others which had worn out. They had been wondering when their fate would be decided. Neither knew why they had been left alive but as the alternative was to risk crucifixion at the hands of the Romans, they awaited their fate patiently. When they had spoken on the long journey north they had deduced that they were being kept alive and kept alive for a purpose. Both had agreed that whatever task came their way they would carry it out. Having tried murder there was little that would be beyond their particular pale.

"My warrior here saw some Romans near the Tinea. There were thirty of them and they were cavalry. Do you know who they are, who commands and where they are stationed?"

Eagerly the answers poured out, they were both pleased that they could satisfy this ferocious woman who terrified grown men like the red-faced warrior crouching at her feet. "They are probably our ala. We are the only regiment of horse in the north. The First Sallustian Wing of Pannonians. The Decurion Princeps is Livius Lucullus Sallustius."

"So Livius still lives. Interesting. Carry on."

"They were stationed at Morbium but if you saw them near the Tinea either they have moved or they have built a temporary camp. When we served with them there were only two hundred and fifty and they were awaiting new recruits."

"Good," she turned to Gwynfor and raised him to his feet by placing her hand under his chin and lifting. "Do you see Gwynfor. These men want to please me and they are holding nothing back. They are desperate to tell me all. I have seen their thoughts and know they speak the truth. Now let us try the same with you."

"I will do anything your majesty, please give me another chance." The two deserters were taking all of this in. If this warrior could be so intimidated and afraid then they would do well to obey all orders.

"Could you identify any of the troopers Gwynfor?"

"There was an officer and two men."

"You said thirty!"

"Yes, majesty but only three crossed the river."

"Describe the officer."

"He was a little taller than him," he pointed to Wolf, "he had dark hair and a beard. He had angry eyes."

Quintus looked quickly at Wolf who said, "Aelius!"

"You know the man?"

"It sounds like our friend, certainly it doesn't sound like any of the others. He was our Decurion and he was the one who sent us to kill Sallustius. He is no friend of your enemies."

"And would he help us?"

"If he thought you would get rid of Sallustius then the answer would be yes."

"Good I have an idea how we can use you. First, you are, of course, committed to helping me are you not?"

It was more of a command than a question but both men were more than willing to serve. Wolf's agile brain had worked out how Morwenna would use Aelius to destroy the ala. He had no regrets about consigning his old comrades to death. His business was his life. "Yes Majesty," they both said as they knelt before her.

"Good, then take them to Idwal, Gwynfor, and have them join my guards. I want them equipped as the others. Then I want the three of you to return to the Tinea, find this Aelius and find out what Sallustius intends. We will do nothing until spring by which time we should have a complete picture of their intentions." She went to her bag and took out a small pouch of coins. "Give him this as a sign of our good faith and promise him more the day that we kill this Livius Lucullus Sallustius. When you are ready then return to me. Gwynfor I will have other warriors to accompany you."

Morwenna slipped silently from their hut and made her way to the main hall and the royal quarters. Unlike every other visitor, Morwenna went where she pleased. The King had acquiesced to his wife's request that Morwenna be treated as a sister rather than a visitor. The King did not understand this relationship between the women but, in all things, he trusted his wife and when he reflected upon it he thought that it was no different to that of a warrior and his blood sworn. As she crossed the open area before the steps to the hall she saw the King and some of his lords set to go hunting. She smiled; while his people slaved to get in the crops before the winter the King was able to take advantage of the clement weather and autumnal foliage to go hunting. She swept up the steps, through the hall and into the rooms of the Queen.

"I have a request sister."

"Speak and it is done."

"We may have a way to insinuate ourselves into the Roman cavalry who are now on your borders. I believe we may be able to gain a spy in their midst."

"That is wonderful news." Her brow furrowed, "Cavalry? I had not heard of Roman horsemen on the frontier."

"The men we left at the bridge saw them. The deserters we discovered came from that cavalry. I will send them to join my men and see if they can persuade one of their comrades to spy. The hairy one, Wolf, seems to think that one of their officers is a plum ripe for the picking."

"What do you require of me sister?"

"A small group of your warriors. My men do not know the land and will waste time becoming lost. With your men, they would be able to speed their way around the land of the Votadini."

Radha was quick-witted and she went into the hall and shouted, "Send Angus to me." She turned to Morwenna. "He is one of my loyal bodyguards and his land was close to the Tinea. He hates the Romans for the ponytailed barbarians killed his sister and father. He can be totally trusted."

When Angus arrived Morwenna was impressed for he was a powerfully built warrior but what made her take greater notice was the anger and hatred which were etched into his face and eyes. She doubted that he would ever smile. She was fey and could not only see into the minds of others but sense their feelings. Even had Radha not told her of his grief she would have sensed it. "Angus, choose five men and accompany the Roman deserters and the Queen's warrior Gwynfor." He reacted with an angry snort when the Roman deserters were named. "Angus, the deserters are important to us and should not be harmed. You are going to the Tinea to recruit a spy in the Roman camp. You will guide our friends by the safest and most secret paths."

He bowed, "I will do as you wish my lady."

When he had gone Morwenna kissed Radha lightly on the lips. "You are right he is an angry man." She held the Queen at arm's length, "We have been apart for too long. Come to my quarters tonight, it is time we spoke."

Radha's eyes lit up with excitement. "The King will celebrate the hunt tonight and I will be able to leave him."

"Good for we have much to plan, and even more to do."

Angus made it quite clear to Wolf and Quintus that he hated them and having no time for Romans either as soldiers or deserters he made it clear that he was only helping them at his Queen's request. Gwynfor had grinned at the men's discomfort for he was not keen on dishonourable warriors who changed sides either. Although Quintus was afraid of the two men Wolf had shrugged it off. He did not need to be liked and Angus had better watch out that he did not get a blade in the back; others who had crossed this killer had found that to their permanent cost. Now that they were armed once more Wolf had regained some of his confidence. He had watched how the warriors worked and knew that he could inveigle his way to a position of power; they were full of noble ideals such as honour and blood oaths. They were fools! Wolf would gain the attention of one of the two Queens whom he recognised immediately as holding the real power. He relished the thought of having power over Aelius Spartianus who had used Wolf and the others as a tool in the past. The balance of power had shifted for Wolf knew, unlike the men he travelled with, including Quintus, that if the decurion refused their offer he would die and Wolf would find someone else, probably The Fist to cooperate with them. The Decurion Princeps was too open and honest a leader to keep secrets from his men and it did not need an officer to divulge the secrets of the ala. The simple fact is there would be no secrets.

When they rejoined the men at the bridge they discovered that no more patrols had visited the bridge. Wolf had scorned, "That is because you attacked them. I know Spartianus. He would run a mile to avoid a fight he thought he might lose. We will have to find him."

Angus and Gwynfor did not like this deserter giving them what amounted to orders. Gwynfor chose to reassert his authority. "You are here to communicate with your friends not make decisions."

"Really? And what the hell are we going to do then? Sit here and wait while a tree grows up our arses hoping that he returns. Doesn't bother me but I think your Queen might not like that." Wolf spoke with confidence having seen the humiliation suffered at the Queen's hands by Gwynfor and he knew that he had struck home when he saw the Manavian warrior's eyes flicker in pain and anger.

Turning to Angus the warrior asked, "Where would the Romans base their cavalry? Somewhere close to here?"

Angus thought for a moment, his face hardening as he remembered the day the ponytailed killers came from that fort to kill his family. "There is but one place. The fort on the Tinea, the one they call Coriosopitum."

Wolf nodded, "Coriosopitum. Yeah, I have heard of that. It is the first fort on the Stanegate."

Gwynfor suddenly felt like he was the only one without any knowledge and he was being made to look foolish in front of his men. "What is this Stanegate?"

"It is the road which joins Corio to the fort on the other coast Luguvalium. The Romans use it as a way of moving swiftly along the frontier. It runs along the valley of the Tinea."

Gwynfor chewed his fingers nervously as he debated what to do. He hated to admit it but the Roman was right, waiting here would not achieve their ends but would Morwenna regard this as a dereliction of duty? He looked at the mocking look on Wolf's face; the man remembered his treatment in Morwenna's hut. When the time came he would end the hairy one's life. "Let us go to this Corio then. Lead on Angus. This is your country; you will know it better than we."

"We will follow the ridge." He gestured to the forested crest of the hills which led east. "It is but a couple of hour's travel."

The land rose and fell but Angus was as familiar with this part of the world as with his own hand. They travelled invisibly, the tracks almost indiscernible until Angus took the path when they became as obvious as the Stanegate which sliced through the land below them. The river cut through the valley beyond the Roman road and Gwynfor was glad that Angus was with them for he would have crossed the bridge and that would have put them firmly in Roman territory.

Suddenly Angus held up his hand and they halted. They dismounted and, leaving the horses with the bulk of the men, Angus led Gwynfor and the two deserters through the forest. They were no longer on the path and this was almost virgin woodland. Tall pines fought for light and it was a dark and foreboding path that they trod. Angus led them down the hill, twisting and turning but always heading south. His hand came up and they halted silently waiting; the forest was becoming lighter. He edged forwards and then gestured for them to join him one by one. When they reached the edge of the trees they were at the edge of a narrow stream but on the other side the land had been cleared and there, less than half a mile away, was the fort of Coriosopitum. Wolf could see the Batavian sentries on the gates and towers. He could almost make out their facial features they were so close.

Gwynfor led them back into the forest. "Well done Angus, this is perfect." He turned to the two deserters. "One of you will have to be here at all times for you know whom we seek. The rest of us will camp in the forest. Angus, you had better find us somewhere close but where we cannot be seen from the road." Wolf glanced to the side to see the road rising up towards the ridge in a perfect line from the isolated

Roman outpost. "As soon as one of you sees your friend we will follow then and then it will be up to you two to make contact."

Wolf stroked his chin. "They will have a fort somewhere else. They won't be sharing with the Batavians." The two barbarians looked at him questioningly, "The garrison in the fort. It would be handy to know where they are."

Angus nodded. That made sense to him. "When we have made camp I will find this horse fort."

"It will be within a half-mile of this one. I would guess it will be south, probably near to the river and the bridge which I assume is down there. I will come with you, who knows I may see him then."

Angus nodded, "They have a bridge and there are towers at each end but the river is not wide here, a man can swim across on his horse."

An hour later and the scouting party had settled down to wait. Quintus was on duty first, Angus and Wolf had gone to find the camp and Gwynfor's men had gone hunting. This time they would be prepared for a long wait. They intended to eat better than on the last stakeout.

Angus and Wolf rode along the ridge above the Stanegate. They were well hidden by the trees and yet could observe anyone using the military road. They had gone barely half a mile when Wolf halted the Votadini. "I can see it." He pointed to the south of the river where the newly turned earth and wooden stakes stood out, clearly marking a new fort. Behind it could be seen a column of men and horses heading east, obviously a turma on patrol. "That's it, that is the cavalry fort."

Angus looked at the column of men. "Where would you say they were heading?"

"Probably towards the coast, I believe it is not far away."

"Let us return then to the others."

"Listen, Angus, I know you do not like me or my kind but believe me I am on your side and I want Morwenna's plan to succeed." Angus snorted and spat, he was not interested in the witch Queen but Radha and the eviction of the Romans was a different matter. Undeterred by the enmity Wolf carried on. "Gwynfor's plan isn't good enough. We are just waiting. Who knows Spartianus may be confined to the fort, wounded, heading east, we just don't know where he might be. If you can get me closer to the fort then I will have a better chance of making contact and we can be out of here sooner."

Angus looked suspiciously at Wolf. He did not trust any Romans, especially those who had changed sides but the quicker he could return to his Queen the better. "I can get you there Roman but if you are intending to betray us and rejoin your comrades, know this; I would cut out your heart even as you lived if you did so."

Wolf shook his head. "You do not know the Roman army do you, Angus?" The tribesman shook his head in disdain as though he did not need to know them. "They have discipline and Quintus and I have broken two cardinal rules. We tried to kill a superior officer, that counts as mutiny and we deserted. Now I am not exactly sure which punishment they would choose but the options are crucifixion, put me on a cross, break my arms and legs and leave me there to die or perhaps the quicker one, where I am beaten to death by the rest of my trooper comrades. Now I have to be honest with you, none of those deaths would be a good one but having my heart cut out would guarantee me the quickest way out so let us just say that I am not going to betray you. You can come with me, in fact, I want you to, because I want to make contact and get out of there as quickly as I can, believe me, I feel as you do, I want to be as far away from here as I can be."

Angus looked carefully at Wolf, he knew he was a devious man but in this, he could see no deception and Angus felt he was a good judge of men. He still did not trust the Roman deserter but he would not betray them here. "We will tell Gwynfor what we intend." He pointed upstream. "The river splits and there is an island in the middle. It is shallow enough now, before the snow and the rains for a man to ride across. Then we can ride to the south and approach from that direction along the Roman Road. They will be less vigilant there."

"Good plan. Let's do it."

Wolf was smiling to himself as they approached the island. Gwynfor had not been happy about the Votadini's usurpation of his authority but when he had been knocked flat by a punch which would have rocked even The Fist, they had left. Wolf had noted that Gwynfor's men appeared to have no love for their leader as none had offered to help him as he lay bleeding on the ground at least one tooth missing from his bloody mouth. He stored that information up for a later time. It was late afternoon by the time they had quickly traversed the stone-lined road. Now showing its age, it was in need of repair and Wolf knew from that sign of slackness that the Batavians were stretched and ripe for the plucking. They had waded across the river, having first ensured that there were no patrols coming down the Stanegate. Once in the tree line on the south of the road, they could see the two forts almost one above the other. The Batavians could be seen in the ditches around the upper fort and on the walls improving the defences. "They are worried about your lot," he pointed to Angus, "they are busy improving the defences."

Angus looked disdainfully at the Romans. "When we come we will not be stopped by a few ditches."

Wolf knew that the barbarian was right but he also knew that they would lose many warriors doing so. For before they could reach the ditches they would have been decimated by the deadly artillery, the scorpions. Reaching the eastern side of the road they tied their mounts to a tree and made their way through the scrubby hedgerow. It was open land with a few bushes and small trees dotted around. They crawled from each bush and tree to the next point of concealment. Wolf's only worry was a patrol coming from the south which might detect them but all the traffic had appeared to be north, east and west of the fort. One snippet of information gleaned by the sharp-eyed deserter was that he had not recognised any of the decurions in the three patrols they had seen south of the Tinea. He didn't know why but he would find out when they made contact.

Once they were less than fifty paces from the ditch Wolf halted them. He spoke quietly to Angus, their dull covered cloaks blending in with the earth to provide good cover. "We'll get as close to the gate as we can and I will look to see if I recognise any of the sentries. If I do I'll risk a conversation."

Angus shook his head. "If you are captured then it is all up with us."

"No it isn't, you still have Quintus and unless it is one of the newer officers they probably won't turn me in. I am not stupid, I will wait until I see someone I recognise who might be amenable."

"We could be here forever."

"No, we won't. They change the guards every four hours, especially at night. I am sure that I will spot someone in that time." He shrugged, "Just one night in the cold eh Angus? We'll head back to the horses in the morning before the sun is up if I don't recognise anyone." Reluctantly Angus agreed. They settled down to wait. Wolf was curious, the gate was still open and yet it was close to sundown when it was normally closed. He was speculating on the reason why when he heard the clatter of hooves from the west. They pressed themselves down hard into the cold ground. The last patrol from the west was coming in and they rode for the road to turn at right angles and enter the southern gate, the Porta Decumana. The road passed within a few paces of their hiding place. Yet Angus had chosen their sanctuary well for there was a scrubby bramble which had sprung up and had not, as yet, been removed, its blackberries still adorning it and the leaves afforded cover whilst still allowing them to spy beyond.

As the turma turned on to the road, Wolf desperately sought out a friendly face. Each one was a newcomer, from the decurion and signifier all the way through the ranks. He thought the Allfather had deserted them until he saw one figure hanging back from the rest as though wishing to detach him and his horse from the rest of the turma. He immediately recognised the unmistakable figure of The Fist, probably his oldest friend. He was fifteen paces from the last man and Wolf heard the decurion shout, "Come on you lazy bastard. I have my eye on you. Three of your mates deserted; let's not make it four eh?"

Wolf heard his friend mutter, "Fuck you."

As his horse clattered on the road next to them Wolf called, "Fist!" The Fist glanced down in surprise at the source of the call. He saw Wolf hold his finger to his lips and The Fist gave a subtle nod and galloped on. As they entered the gates, they were closed behind them and Wolf was suddenly aware of the darkness around them.

"Can you trust that one?"

"Believe me he is the nearest thing I have to a brother. I can trust him. The question is how will he make contact? I know he will but how?"

The answer came an hour after the darkness had deepened. The gate suddenly opened and they heard a conversation between the officer on duty and The Fist. "I know you are a dozy lump but how in the Allfather's name could you misplace your cloak?"

"It was when the decurion told me to hurry up I was so keen to catch up that I didn't notice it fall. It will just be on the road."

"Well if the Votadini are out there they are welcome to your balls. Knock on the gate when you return." He laughed, "If you return. I would buy a new one rather than risk being captured."

There was a flash of light from with the fort and then darkness as the gates were slammed shut. They could both hear The Fist's caligae on the stones of the road and could hear his mutterings. "It has to be here somewhere I know."

"Psst!"

The Fist halted near to the bush and began to scratch his head and then he walked around the bush as though looking for the lost cloak. "I thought you would be long gone, Wolfie, or dead. You got a friend there?"

"Aye, a Votadini." He saw the hand go to the dagger and said quietly, "A friend and he will be a friend to both of us. Listen we haven't got much time. Is the decurion still around?"

"Yes. Not happy but he is still around. Why?"

"Tell him if he wants to make a little money and get back at the Decurion Princeps he should meet me tomorrow north of the Batavian fort at...."

"Can't do that, he is confined to the south of the river. It's only Sallustius' pets who go north."

"Right well then meet us at the island west of here towards sunset. Think he can manage that?"

"Should be able to. He has a couple of men in his turma who will help." He suddenly bent down and took his cloak from under his mail, "Ah there it is." He said loudly enough for those in the fort to hear. "I am tempted to come with you and do a runner. I fucking hate this army!"

"Better you stay there for a while. I will explain to Aelius."

"Be safe Wolfie, I miss your hairy little face." He tramped back to the fort waving the cloak above his head for the sentries to see. They heard him bang on the door and then saw the light as it was opened and he was readmitted to the fort.

"So, what do you say, Angus? Do you trust me now?"

The hint of a crease of almost a smile appeared on the Votadini face. "A little more Roman but we shall see. Let us just say I prefer your company now to the sour-faced Gwynfor."

"Steady on big fella, I am not that sort."

Chapter 15

The next morning began as any other in the fort. The sentries were changed; since moving from Morbium Livius had used one turma each day to be on duty and guard the fort. This close to the enemy it was not safe to spread the Batavian infantry's duties. They would be the first point of an attack. He and the Explorate decurions left just after dawn to begin their daily, and as yet fairly fruitless, patrols to try to discover the state of the frontier's security.

Cassius was the duty decurion, having had six consecutive days of patrol. His troopers would, apart from performing their sentry duties be able to mend and repair broken equipment and just have some quiet time. Cassius and Livius were well aware of the need for such time. It kept troopers sharp; if they had been further from danger he would have allowed them to go out hunting but here it was just too dangerous. They were living in a war zone. He checked the gates and walls to ensure that half of his turma were at their posts. They were a sound enough group of men. The one trooper he had had from Spartianus' crew had learned to join in with the others after his face had met the fists of his comrades when he slept through one shift. Now Cassius knew that they would change duties without any monitoring from him. He decided he would see how Julius was getting on with the map. As he was crossing the parade ground he heard the strident voice of Drusus, Decurion of the twelfth turma. He had only recently been promoted; one of the older members of the ala, Livius had recognised in him qualities of leadership which would help some of the younger decurions to emulate.

Cassius shook his head in dismay. It was The Fist and they had thought that they were actually winning with the malcontents. "Now then, I let it go last night, losing your cloak, having the gate opened, being a general pain in the Imperial arse. I even overlooked the fact that you lagged behind the rest but this." He spread his hands in an exasperated manner.

Cassius could see Spurius and Aelius preparing to leave with their turmae but watching how the newly promoted decurion dealt with The Fist. Cassius decided to take a hand and help the decurion out. "What is it Drusus?"

"Nothing sir." Cassius looked at him patiently for a few seconds and the Decurion sighed and continued. "It is this man sir. He reckons he is sick but the capsarius can find nothing wrong with him. "He glared at the huge brute of a man. "I think he is malingering sir."

The Fist affected a look of outraged indignation. "I am not! I have a gut ache something chronic."

Septimus was just passing on his way to the kitchen area. "Well don't blame my food, tosspot, no-one else is suffering!"

Cassius could see this degenerating into farce. "The decurion is right. It is your turn to patrol so deal with it."

Cassius did not see the look flicked at Spartianus but suddenly the decurion dismounted and said. "If I can be of help decurion. I know this man and he has always had a funny gut. With the decurion's permission, I will take him to my tent and give him a draught of my special medicine. I guarantee that it will cure him." Drusus looked at them suspiciously and then at Cassius, who nodded, equally perplexed at this sudden display of concern.

"Interesting; that is strange. I have never known Spartianus to be helpful. Keep your eye on the situation Drusus. Let me know if you need me, I will be in the Principia with the clerk."

"I'll handle it sir, but thank you."

In the tent, Aelius said quickly, "Come on man, out with it. I know you want to tell me something but what is the urgency?"

"It's Wolfie sir. He's back and he's with the Votadini."

Spartianus was taken aback. "You've seen him?"

"Last night. He said for you to meet him today at the island in the river west of the fort before sunset. He has money, lots of money, and an offer to help get rid of Sallustius. Do you know the island he spoke of?"

"Yes, I passed it the other day. What do you make of the offer?" Aelius was tempted but he knew that barbarians sometimes used tricks like this to capture prisoners. Still, it was Wolf and he was loyal...

"He had a big Votadini with him but he seemed genuine enough."

"What about Quintus?"

"I didn't have time to ask." He paused. "You are going then?"

"I can't see what I have to lose. It's not like they are working with Sallustius is it? That is the enemy. Now you go and keep your nose clean today. Don't give them the chance to be suspicious. This may be the chance we have waited for."

Drusus looked at them suspiciously as they came out. The Fist sprang like a newborn lamb on to the back of his horse saying, "Ready sir!"

Drusus peered at Aelius' innocent face, he knew them of old, "You must let me have a taste of that special medicine. Never seen anything work as fast in my life."

"Old family secret! Just for my special friends."

144

From the office, Cassius watched as the patrols left and wondered just what was going on. He would have to mention it Livius when he returned. If it wasn't the Votadini, it was the enemy within. He turned to look at the map. "It's coming on nicely Julius."

"Huh. It would come on better if I had some actual measurements. You decurions are all a little vague."

"I am sure the Decurion Princeps would be happy to let you accompany us with your measure."

"No, thank you, adjutant. This is dangerous enough for me. Besides I am using mathematics and the measurements I do know to fill in the gaps."

"How do you mean?" Cassius was genuinely interested.

"We know the width of the road and the length of the road, by using a groma we can calculate the heights and if you decurions relate every height to the ridge at the end of the road from Corio then we have a rough approximation."

Cassius was impressed. "Good. I will tell the decurions at the briefing and you should have more accurate information from now on."

Wolf had chosen their meeting place well for there was a small stand of trees which hid them from casual view. He was certain that they would not be betrayed but they had a good escape route if it was needed. Wolf liked to get out of trouble as fast as he entered it. Gwynfor was the only one who was unhappy as the four of them waited for Aelius to appear. "It is too risky waiting here all afternoon!"

"We have explained you dozy sheep shagger that we have to be here out of sight when the patrol comes. We saw them all leave this morning and that is why. It is safe."

Angus laughed at Gwynfor's pouting. His face still showed the marks of Angus' punch and there was a gap where a tooth had been lost. Gwynfor was losing the little credibility he had. "But how do we know he will come?"

"He will come," Quintus spoke confidently. He for one would be much happier when Aelius was with them. Somehow the officer seemed to make things happen.

"How do you know? You weren't even there!"

Quintus smiled an enigmatic smile. "I know Aelius Spartianus and I know that the lure of money will draw him like a moth to a flame."

That had been two hours ago and they had all taken a turn at watching. Hearing the hooves on the Stanegate Quintus awoke them. "Someone coming."

All of them gripped a weapon. Although three of them believed it would work all of them knew that they were in danger of being captured by one of the other patrols crisscrossing the valley. Wolf hissed, "It's them. I can see Aelius."

They watched as Aelius reined in his horse and dismounted to look at its hoof. He stood to say something to the men and then twenty-nine troopers rode slowly east leaving Aelius with two men on the other bank. Aelius left his own horse with one of the two men, mounted the trooper's horse and then waded across the river. As he climbed the bank he said, "Wolf! You there?" The four of them all had swords pointing at Spartianus' throat as he dismounted. "What's this I thought I was invited? Not very friendly is it?"

"You were supposed to come" hissed Angus, "alone!" He gestured with his sword at the two men peering at the island.

"Don't worry, they are trusted men. It would have looked strange if I had waited here by myself in enemy country. Someone said something about money and revenge?" He smiled as Wolf threw the bag of gold to him which he easily and deftly caught. Aelius opened it, tested one coin with his teeth and put it in his pouch. "And there will be more?"

Gwynfor had had enough of others stealing his thunder and he stepped forward. "There will be more if you come up with the goods."

"The goods?"

"Yes, information. What is the cavalry doing? What is happening behind the lines?"

"I can do that but how does that help me with Sallustius?"

Wolf had a sly look on his face. "I have an idea; how about the Decurion Princeps being ambushed, along with his little band of brothers eh? Then you would be in charge again."

"That sounds like a better idea. Right well, here it is so far. The old Explorates are leading their men deep into Votadini territory to find out what the defences are. The Batavians are building up their defences and the new Emperor is coming with more soldiers. There is talk of a new legion coming to replace the Ninth."

Gwynfor looked at Angus and then Wolf. To Aelius, he said, "When?"

"Won't be this year. Too late in the season. Probably next year is a more likely option. The Emperor will be travelling from the East and that takes time. He has concluded his peace there and then he will need to go to Rome. Since the Decurion Princeps met the Emperor the little toadies around him talk of nothing else."

Wolf stepped forward, "Do you know where the Decurion Princeps takes his patrols? We could take him out sooner rather than later."

Spartianus almost spat his answer out, "No he doesn't tell us that. His dogsbody, Cassius, allocates us minions our patrols along the river. The rest leave the fort and then we find out when they return where they have actually been."

"We can still do something." He turned to the two barbarians. "If Morwenna gives us enough men we can wait at our camp and ambush them as they leave the fort."

"That could work. You had better go and catch your men."

"How will I contact you again?"

Angus looked around and he saw the old remains of a tree which had been struck by lightning and was now a hollowed blackened stump. "Leave a piece of red cloth here if you want to talk and we'll meet the following evening about this time. If we need to talk to you it will be a dead crow we hang from the top."

Quintus looked at him in amazement, "A crow! Where, in the name of the Allfather, are you going to get a crow?"

In answer, Angus took one from his saddlebags. Wolf just said, "I am not even going to ask!"

The first biting snows of winter had fallen on the oppidum at Traprain Law when the group of scouts returned. Morwenna had seen their approach and she and Radha greeted them at her quarters just outside the wall. Wolf noticed that there were even more huts proliferating outside the walls as more and more kings, princes and chiefs arrived for the conclave. The cold that was on the ground had made travelling easier but all knew that, when the snow fell in earnest, travel would become much more difficult. The last wagons were pulling up the slope from the road leading to the sea and the little fishing port where the barrels of meats and wines had finally finished arriving. The King and his Steward were busy allocating quarters. Although normally a task for the Steward alone only the King could hope to know who were allies and who were potential enemies. If Morwenna's conclave were to work then it had to be a harmonious meeting with only one outcome, an alliance against Rome.

Morwenna and Radha were therefore left alone to question the four men. Morwenna gauged the mood the moment they walked through the door and she knew, instinctively, that Gwynfor had not done all that she requested. She and Radha sat on the throne on the raised dais, each one slumped at each side of the enormous seat. The four men looked at each other, not knowing who should speak first.

Morwenna looked directly and intensely into each man's eyes and she saw that only Gwynfor looked down. It was then that she knew and then that she made her decision. "Gwynfor, begin and answer me simply. Were you successful?"

Breathing a sigh of relief he answered in a torrent of words, "Yes your majesty. We met with the officer and he agreed to aid us. He gave us the information we requested."

Morwenna gave an imperceptible nod to Radha who continued, "And Angus, were there any problems or did you find the decurion easily."

Angus glanced contemptuously at Gwynfor. "We would have been sat scratching our arses still if he had had his way. The Wolf and I hid near the fort and made contact."

"Wolf?"

"Yes, majesty. We contacted one of my old comrades who arranged for the Decurion to meet us the next day. All went well."

"Excellent. "Morwenna and Radha rose as one and went to an amphora of wine. They poured out six beakers and took them over to the men, carefully giving each man a particular beaker. "You have all done well and I am pleased with all of you. Wolf and Quintus, you have passed the test and I will instruct Idwal that you are now my men and should be given the honour of blood brothers. Angus you have shown yourself to be resourceful and your Queen is rightly proud of you." Morwenna paused at Gwynfor and holding her goblet in her left hand, ran the nails of her right hand gently around the face of the warrior, tracing the outline of the bruise inflicted by Angus. "And you Gwynfor you have brought the matter to a satisfactory conclusion but you appear to have been injured," she said it softly and sweetly, much as a mother would with a small child. "How did that happen?" When he shot an angry glance at Angus and said nothing she continued. "Ah, I see. Angus, may I see your right hand?" He proudly held out his right hand the knuckles red and scraped where they had struck Gwynfor. "And when you hit Gwynfor, were his men present?"

"They were."

"Gwynfor did your men not defend you when you were assaulted?" He shook his head. "How sad; it is said that when a leader is not defended by his men then he is no longer a leader. Do you believe that Gwynfor or are you a leader still?"

Wolf and Quintus were watching the Queen, mesmerized, for she was like a cat playing with a wounded mouse. In a small voice, he said, "Yes I am still the leader."

Laughing Morwenna said, "Good! I am pleased for I should hate to lose you. And now raise your beakers and join in the toast, 'Death to the Romans'." The other four all drank deeply but Gwynfor hesitated, the beaker hovering close to his mouth. "What? Will you not drink? Ah, of course, you believe it is poisoned. Do you think I have poisoned you Gwynfor?"

"No your majesty," he said half-heartedly.

"I cannot have you thinking that. Let us exchange beakers and I will drink from yours and then if you are correct I will fall in a writhing heap, dead at your feet." Her laughing tone made it seem like a silly joke and she threw off the contents of the beaker in one motion. Suddenly she looked as though she was choking and they all held their breath, then she laughed. "Sorry, Gwynfor I couldn't resist a small joke. Death to the Romans!"

He finally raised his beaker and, with a weak foolish smile on his face drank the contents of the beaker, "Death to the Romans."

The Queen reached forward and took the beaker from his grasp, "Ah Gwynfor. I did warn you. I said the next time you let me down you would die. And you did let me down. Were it not for others we would not have a spy in the Roman camp. Farewell."

They all watched in grim horror as his eyes began to bulge and a green froth erupted from his mouth. His body spasmed and he grabbed his stomach as though someone had put a brand in there. A silent scream tried to come out of his mouth as he fell, writhing, to the floor. They watched with morbid fascination as blood began to run down his nose and a red stain appeared on his breeks. Finally, his body shook and, with his bowels and bladder emptying, he died.

"Get rid of this body on the dung heap, clean it up and then tell me all that the Romans are up to."

It was noon by the time the body and the mess had been cleared and the reports were given. "So let me get this clear whilst you still have it fresh in your minds. It will be next year at the earliest before the Romans can come north. The cavalry is probing deep in enemy territory but this devious Decurion Princeps is not letting others know where. And finally, they are building up the defences of the forts." The three of them nodded. The information did not sound that useful. "Good. I want you to send a message to your spy, this Aelius, and tell him to begin small acts of sabotage."

Wolf raised his hand, feeling like a small child. "The problem is your majesty that we did that when the new commander came and now he has the saboteurs watched carefully all the time."

"This Livius is efficient but annoying. Would that we had his like here." She added, almost to herself, " In that case have him mark the Decurion's horse's hooves with three parallel lines and we can watch for him. When there is snow on the ground or mud he should be easy to track. Tomorrow I want Angus and Quintus to go with Idwal with a column of my men. Wolf, go with them and contact your friend. Bring the latest intelligence back to me. Quintus can speak to this spy for us. We need to stop the supplies to the fort and I want you to raid the road south of the fort."

Radha intervened and spoke against Morwenna for the first time. "I think that you need your men close to you to ensure that you are seen as powerful. Better if Angus takes our men as they know the country and we will have men to spare."

Morwenna looked appreciatively at Radha. The Queen was correct and it was a good plan. "You are right my Queen." To the three waiting men she said, "You may go." When they had gone she turned to Radha. "We will need to speak with your husband before the conclave. We must be able to have a plan which will succeed for this is our best chance before the Romans have reinforced and brought over more troops."

Livius held back the Explorate patrols until the others had left the fort. Julius Longinus stood at the rear patiently waiting. It was Macro and Marcus' turma's turn for duty and Livius wanted them to be able to speak securely. He looked at the small group of highly trusted men. He could trust others but they had not the skills for the task he intended. It was also a difficult task to command and he had wrestled for a week with its correctness. "We have found out little about the plans of the tribes on the borders during our patrols and that is making us blind. I cannot believe that we will receive reinforcements before the end of next year, at the earliest and that has left me with a difficult decision. I need to ask for volunteers to go into Traprain Law and spy on the conclave and its outcomes."

He could see the eager looks on their faces and he held up his hand. "Firstly anyone whom Morwenna knows by sight cannot go for that would jeopardise the mission. That rules Cassius and me out. Secondly, we only need a couple of you to go otherwise it would leave us shorthanded and thirdly we need to hide the destination of the mission from all of the men as, I am afraid, we cannot trust everyone. So," he took a deep breath, "volunteers."

As he had expected all of them stepped forward. Smiling he turned to Cassius. "It is as we thought. They are as willing as we believed. This is a serious and dangerous mission and Cassius and I have thought long and hard about the best two for the mission. All of you could have done the job but two of you have the best chance of success, Macro and Metellus."

Marcus looked crestfallen. The pain on his face suggested that he had been struck by his commander. "Sir? Why not Macro and me, we work together well and we think alike." He turned to Metellus. "No offence Metellus."

Metellus spread his hands to show that none was taken and Livius answered. "Macro was chosen because he looks like a Caledonii with his red hair. He could move around the camp and not be noticed. Metellus will not be going into the camp itself. He will be the contact outside, just as we did when we were Explorates, working in pairs. I have chosen Metellus, Marcus because he is the cleverest and most creative thinker amongst you all. The scouts will be operating over eighty miles behind enemy lines and, in Aquitania, it was the quick thinking of Rufius and Metellus which saved not only me but also the mission. It could easily have been Rufius but his skills as a tracker and archer will not be needed. What will be needed is a quick and devious mind, and that means Metellus. In addition, his fair hair would make him look like one of the northern people."

Metellus feigned offence, "Well that is a backhanded compliment if ever I heard one."

"Now as to the details. Julius."

The clerk stepped forward with the map of the region. He unrolled it and spread it on the table placing four beakers, one at each corner. "The safest route will be along the coast. Dere Street will be watched and those travelling along it will be under suspicion. The coast will take longer but also has the advantage that the sea air will make it less likely that there is snow to hinder you." He shivered. "Why the Parcae thought to send me so far from the sun I shall never know. I must have done misdeeds in my childhood."

"Julius!"

"Yes sir, where was I? Ah yes. The coast. It also means that you will not be approaching Traprain Law from the south. You will carry on along the coast until you come to here," he pointed to a spot not far from the coast, "Din Eidyn, it is a mighty rock and the site of a new oppidum. If you come from that direction then it will appear that you have travelled from the north and are, therefore, unlikely to be spies." He leaned back and folded his arms.

Metellus looked at the map and Livius smiled. Macro just wanted the mission but the older, wiser Metellus was already planning. "Firstly what is our escape route?"

Julius looked at Livius who nodded. The clerk had been involved at every stage of the planning process. "If all goes well then back the way you came, west to Din Eidyn and then back down the coast."

151

"What if we need to leave in a hurry?"

Julius coughed, "Ah. This is the part of the plan which is less satisfactory. There is a small port here, just north of the oppidum. It is about six miles away as near as I can calculate from the basic maps I have," he pointed to a spot on the map. "The Decurion Princeps and the adjutant think you can steal or hire a boat." The look on his face told them all that he thought that was unlikely.

Metellus nodded, "That is fine with us," he glanced at Macro who nodded, "two escape routes are always handy."

"But how will you get a boat?" Julius was intrigued and perplexed. How could they expect to do that, there may not even be a boat!

"While Macro is in the oppidum I will be securing that escape route should we need it and scouting out the best way to attack this oppidum."

"Now as to the rest of the subterfuge. Marcus will take the two turmae south along with Metellus and Macro, ostensibly to get more horses from Morbium. "He looked at the sergeant. You will, in fact, go to Morbium and collect some winter feed which we ordered two weeks ago."

"That is wonderful! My brother gets to have an adventure and I get to bring hay up a road." He glared at Livius. "Sir you owe me a mission!"

Laughing Livius said, "You shall have it."

"I realise my young friend here is excited but what is our cover up at the oppidum?"

Cassius leaned forward, "A good question. You have travelled from the western isles from the lands of the Epidii tribe. The Epidii are very reclusive apparently. We are hoping that they do not send anyone and this is the one part of the plan which is the weakest for if there are Epidii there...."

Metellus looked closely at the map. "The Epidii live where?" Julius stabbed a bony, inky finger at a group of islands off to the west. "If they live on a number of islands then there will be different clans. We will just have to be creative and think on our feet. If we just turn up as though we were invited and join a group entering then no-one may ask us. The plan is just to get in but now that I know where the Epidii live I can plan."

Livius looked at Marcus and said gently, "Now you see Marcus why I chose Metellus. You and Macro are a good team but with Metellus, we are more likely to have both of you back here alive." Marcus could see the wisdom in Livius' words but it did not make the pill any easier to swallow.

Chapter 16

Aelius Spartianus was delighted when he saw the two turmae head south toward Morbium for it meant that three of his enemies were leaving and it also meant that it would be easier for his new allies to bring an end to Livius' command, sooner rather than later. He smiled and joked around the fort surprising all the old hands and showing the newer recruits what a good officer he was. Everyone had noted the change in him since he had helped Drusus. Cassius was suspicious but Livius was more generous. "You can only go battering your head against a wall for so long before you realise that it is pointless. Splitting him from his friends and not picking on him seem to have helped. Why last night he even took my horse to the stable for me to rub it down."

"Now that is suspicious!"

"Give it a week or so Cassius, you'll see, he has changed." Neither of them knew that the wily decurion had used the time to mark Livius' horse's hoof.

Aelius saw the two officers talking and knew it was him they were talking about. He and The Fist were standing at the water trough waiting to water their mounts and were able to talk albeit quietly. "Look at them there. They think they have won."

"I'll be glad when we can stop being so pleasant. I just want to punch someone."

"That time will come. Now, remember if you see a red cloth in the tree on the island tell me. It will look suspicious if I visit it every day."

"Won't it look suspicious if I keep going there? "

"No, you just say you thought you saw some movement. If you find the cloth you say that it caught your attention and if it isn't there you say you are mistaken. You know how the new decurions like you to be keen and keep your eyes open. Trust me you will not be punished."

On the road south, Marco and Metellus waited until the road dipped below the skyline before turning east and riding away from the turmae. Metellus had turned to his turma and said, "Right lads obey the sergeant as you would me and no-one speaks of this."

They chorused a, "Sir." Livius had also chosen these turmae as they had none of Spartianus' men in their ranks. All of them would have followed Metellus to Hades and back; to follow this order was easy.

Macro and Livius dismounted taking off their auxiliary uniforms and weapons. They took, from their spare horse, the clothes they had worn as Explorates, the dull coloured breeks and tunic, the leather jacket and the fur hats. They slung bows across their backs and slid their swords in their scabbards. With their blankets over their saddles, they were as ready as they could be. Macro turned and grinned at Marcus, "Perhaps I should have asked father for The Sword of Cartimandua eh brother?"

"That would have marked you as an enemy as soon as shouting, '*I am a Roman*' from the top of their highest tower!"

"May the Allfather be with you!" Marcus and Macro clasped arms and Metellus knew it would be hard for them over the next couple of weeks. They had never been separated before and this would not please either.

"Come on Macro, we have a river to cross." Metellus looked at the two boys knowing they were the sons he would have chosen had he had a choice.

They rode northeastwards. There was no other bridge east of that at Coriosopitum but Metellus knew of a wide curve in the river which, at low tide, could be crossed without swimming. Once across the mighty Tinea, the other rivers they would have to pass were less daunting. Metellus understood that the great danger was discovery before they reached the coast north of Traprain Law. Close to the conclave, they would be legitimate but travelling from Roman territory would be suspicious.

Macro broke the silence as they rode north of the Tinea, the damp breeks drying only slowly in the chill wind. "Metellus are you worried?"

"Worried?"

"Yes, I mean you have done this before have you not?"

"So have you. You too were an Explorate."

"That was different. The rest of our men were close by and we were never more than a day's ride from help. You were an ocean away from help when you and Livius were in Aquitania."

Metellus realised that the young man was right. "I suppose we were, but we never thought about it. This is more dangerous by far, for we are not in Roman Aquitania but the barbarian north. There we only had to fear a few traitors to fear, whilst here, every man is an enemy. But, if it is any consolation, we will only be two days away from friends. We will camp tonight close to the oppidum which is near to the islands of seals."

"Isn't that dangerous to be so close to the Votadini and their warriors?"

"Any further west and we will be close to the road and we need to avoid that. I have planned this out thoughtfully with Livius and Julius."

Macro laughed, "The old clerk? What does he know of war?"

"Nothing but he knows much about strategy and he is not old, he just looks old. We deduced, or rather Julius deduced, that if those in the oppidum were supporters of the king then they would have sent their best warriors and leaders to the conclave. There will probably be only old men and women. Besides the route close to the coast is the easiest to negotiate, less rises and falls for our mounts which will have a hard journey. We will make good time and tomorrow we will be close to Traprain Law."

They passed by the oppidum after dusk and could see a few lights burning. The cliffs rose to their right and, a mile from the settlement, they found a hollow sheltered from the sea with a stand of scrubby, windblown bushes to hide them. They did not risk a fire and ate dried venison, apples and washed it down with watered wine. It had been Julius who had recommended the wine which had surprised everyone. He had explained his thinking as though to children, "The closer you are to the sea the worse the quality of water. Bad water makes you ill. The wine will make the water cleaner and, if you are wounded or injured then watered wine will clean the wound far more effectively than mere water."

As they drank the heavily watered wine, they were pleased at his suggestion. If nothing else it would help them to sleep for Metellus was not looking forward to a night on the ground after the weeks he had enjoyed in a bed. They rolled themselves in their blankets and fell immediately to sleep.

The five brigands who had watched them pass by the oppidum had seen a golden opportunity. Two men and three horses would make them twice as rich as they were. They had eyed the swords and relished the thought of wielding such weapons. Once they had killed the travellers they would argue amongst themselves about the ownership. They had waited until the conversation stopped before surrounding the camp. The five potential killers were fifty paces away and the moon shone brightly, revealing their faces. The only problem was that they could not see their prey through the thick bushes and leaves; they knew where they were but could not actually see their victims. Occasionally, they managed to see the horses move but that was all that they could observe. They were patient, for they had all night and the five of them moved very slowly forward. Suddenly one of the horses whinnied and they froze but there was no movement from within the camp and they moved gingerly towards their goal.

As soon as his horse whinnied Metellus was awake. He saw Macro's eyes flash white as he too woke. Metellus gestured twice with his right hand and Macro rolled to his right notching an arrow into the bow kept by his side as he did so. Metellus rolled to his left, pulling his sword from its scabbard, and as Macro had done ruffling the blanket to look like a body with the fur hat at the top. The men approaching them were not warriors, nor were they experienced in fighting at night, for their white faces shone in the moonlight like a torch lit in the darkest night. Metellus crouched at the roots of a blackthorn tree, its barbed branches protecting his back. He noted with some satisfaction that he could not see Macro. Neither man needed any more instructions. The double hand gesture had given all the command that Macro needed. They now had to wait.

The five men edged their way closer to their intended prey until they came to the trees. Metellus almost smiled as he sensed their dilemma; they had to get through the trees without making a noise. Metellus had chosen this particular camp because there was only one way in and one way out. When they had worked out their strategy they came slowly in. Metellus marked the first man through for he was the boldest. They looked to be a sorry bunch and Metellus idly wondered who they were; there would be time for that soon enough. As the last man entered, Metellus leapt forward, his sword aimed at the bold one's neck. Macro's arrow took the rearmost man as Metellus' opponent silently died. With a backhand sweep, the second man was despatched, the fourth man receiving an arrow in the back as he tried to flee. In normal circumstances, Metellus would have allowed the last man to live but their mission could not afford such sentiment and Metellus finished him quickly. They had been poorly prepared opponents.

Silently they dragged the bodies out of the camp to view them better in the moonlight. They were Votadini and they saw the clan marks and amulets. However, they were so ill-armed and equipped that Metellus could only suppose that they were outcasts or outlaws. "Find one who is your size Macro and take his clothes. They may come in handy. Take their daggers and their amulets, in fact, anything you think we can use."

Macro nodded. It was distasteful stripping a dead body covered in blood and gore but, as they had discovered before, sometimes it was the only way. None of them had anything else which identified them as Votadini although one did have a pendant in his pouch along with a couple of coins. "Take the coins as well, they are not Roman and may well help the deception later on. Once they had taken all that they could, they carried the bodies one by one and hurled them over the cliffs into the sea. The tide was coming in and the two bodies that landed on the rocks would be washed out soon.

The next day they headed swiftly up the coast. They were doubtful that the men they had killed would be missed but it didn't do to take chances. They had both donned some of the Votadini clothes, both were wearing the Votadini daggers and Metellus had the pendant beneath his tunic. The icy wind blew from the northeast, driving tiny droplets of salt water into their faces, crusting their beards, or at least the early stages of the beards. Drizzle turned to sleet and washed off the salt but soaked them making them feel more tired than they were. It served a purpose as it was such a filthy day that there would be few people out on the coastal path.

They came above a small fishing port with a fortified wall and oppidum. "Julius is good. He knew that this place existed but not its name. Apparently, this was mapped by the Classis Britannica during Agricola's invasion but no-one thought to find its name."

"Thank you for the lesson teacher but how does that help us?"

Metellus pointed to the west. "Because, young Sergeant Macro, that hill which you can see there, is Traprain Law and we are almost at our destination. We need to skirt this town, cross the road, which will be busy and make for the coast. If we get to the road we can wait until night."

The road followed the valley of the small river which ran into the sea under the walls of the hill fort. There was still much traffic making its way along the road for the conclave which would begin in a few days' time. There was nothing for the two Explorates to do but wait until nightfall. The risk of going through and being seen at dusk was too great. They camped close to the beach of the Bodotrian estuary and Metellus relaxed a little. "That is the first hard part finished. If we play our parts well then we will find the next hard part will be getting close to Traprain Law."

Macro looked over nervously at Metellus. "I am not becoming frightened or getting cold feet but did Livius think through the plan of getting into the fort?"

"I know what you mean. They normally have tight security, hand over weapons, only the chiefs and bodyguards allowed through but I think that is why Livius sent me and not Marcus. I will need to come up with a plan once we have scouted Traprain Law. That will probably be tomorrow at about noon."

"The other worry I have is that we do not speak the local dialect. I have a few words of Votadini but I would have no idea what someone from the islands sounded like."

"I wouldn't worry about that. There will be so many different dialects that they will all use the common tongue, the ones the Brigante use and that is second nature to you. If anyone tries a dialect you do not actually understand then just say you don't understand or ask them to talk slower."

Once they saw the enormous rock that was the new oppidum of Din Eidyn, Metellus led them south. They had had a morning without a single traveller who crossed their path, the weather was that bad. Metellus also knew that most visitors would have arrived before they had for the conclave was but two days away and any visitor would want to maximise the hospitality. Once on the road south, they could see that it was well travelled from the ruts and heavy hoof prints.

The sharp-eyed Macro suddenly murmured. "People up ahead."

"Keep going at the same speed, don't slow down. It will look suspicious." Metellus began to put his machine-like brain into action. He saw that it was a large group of about thirty travellers. The ones at the rear were obviously servants or slaves and had the pack animals. At the sides were six outriders, guards and in the middle was a carriage with the important people. He deduced that there would be outriders at the front too. The carriage marked the people as either a king or an important chief along with his wife. Metellus frowned; it was unusual to take your wife to a conclave such as this.

Someone saw them and two heavily armed riders rode back to speak with them. Both men had spears, armour and good helmets. Metellus could see that they were experienced warriors by their battle amulets and scars on their faces. "Our master Burdach, King of the Dumnonii wishes to know your business."

Mentally Metellus took a deep breath. "We are travelling to the conclave called at Traprain Law by Lugubelenus, the King of the Votadini."

Metellus noted with relief that the tips of the spears dropped and the men relaxed. They turned their horses to ride alongside the two Romans. "We too go there."

One of them leaned over to Macro and said, "I will be glad to get into the warmth of a fire for this cold soaks through to your bones."

"You are late arriving. It was better weather last week."

The guard ignored the obvious question which was to ask why they had left it so late but Metellus had such an easy way about him that men spoke easily to him. "And we would have left last week but we were waiting for one of the Chiefs from the Epidii, Curach, who wished to accompany us but we received a message saying that he was delayed and would not be attending."

Metellus reacted quickest to the news. "The Allfather is mighty is he not?"

"Yes but..."

"We are from the Epidii. We are related to Curach through his wife's sister and we were visiting the chief when he sent the message." He grinned at Macro, "My young cousin and I thought it would be a great opportunity to visit the mainland and see other chiefs." He looked conspiratorially at the guard, "And sup all the ale and food that such a conclave entails. The Allfather has indeed looked after us."

The guard looked suspiciously at Metellus. "Then why did you not say so when I said we were from the King of the Dumnonii?"

Metellus shrugged innocently, "We did not know. The Chief did not tell us that we were meeting anyone. He just said he couldn't make the trip because his legs were playing up in the cold and we asked if we could go in his stead."

The guard relaxed. "Aye, he is an old man and old men suffer in the cold. I will go and tell my lord." Leaving the other guard with them he trotted off. Metellus risked a glance at Macro on the other side and winked. He had been deadly serious; the Allfather was looking after them. When the guard returned, he asked if they would join the royal party.

As they trotted between the guards Metellus wondered if they should have dressed in a better way. He had confidence that Macro would remember their story. Their main problem now was talking about the place where they lived for surely the king would ask those sorts of questions.

When they reached the carriage, they could see that it was nothing more than a box between two horses carrying the queen, a rather overweight and red-faced woman. Riding on her right was the king a greybeard, who like his wife, obviously enjoyed good food. They were, however, both jolly folk who greeted Metellus and Macro like long lost relatives. "I knew Old Curach wouldna let me down. The leg was it?"

"Aye," Metellus picked up on the burr and accent straight away, "he wasna very happy aboot missing the grand food and drinks."

The king looked conspiratorially at Metellus. "Saved us a wee fortune this has. We're looking forward to his hospitality aren't we, my dear?"

"Aye, and you look as though a good meal wouldna go amiss nor your wee brother there." Metellus did not try to correct the Queen, it all added to the story. He noticed that Macro was riding next to a pretty girl; no Metellus looked again, a young woman. The queen saw his glance. "Aye, and the other reason we are happy is that wee Morag is now a woman and with no son and heir, we hoped that she might meet one." She looked Metellus in the eye and said bluntly, "Have you a title? Money?"

"No, we are the poor relatives from Dun Eibhinn."

"Dun Eibhinn? It is no wonder you have no money, for it is a pitifully poor place."

"Aye, but we like it."

The king nodded wisely, "Aye well if a man disna love his own home it is a poor thing. No offence er..." He gestured for Metellus to close with him.

"Darach and that is Aodh."

"Well Darach no offence but your wee brother is a bonnie looking lad but he hasna neither enough money nor a title to be courting yon lassie so give him the word eh?"

Metellus smiled, "I will do and thank you for your honesty sir."

"Ach we are almost family, now tell me more about this poor little isle of yours."

By the time they reached the encampment which surrounded Traprain Law Metellus and Macro were part of the Dumnonii royal party and the king included him as one of theirs whenever they had to pass through security. Finally, they reached the gate where the Steward and the King awaited them. "Good to see you Burdach. We thought you might never get here."

The King winked at Metellus, "Aye a few wee problems. This is kin from the Epidii, Darach and Aodh."

Lugubelenus came over to embrace Metellus. "You cannot know how glad I am that some of the younger folk from the isles are here. We need your support too. How is old Curach then? Still suffering from the cold?"

"Yes your majesty, it is his legs."

"The Allfather curses all of us with some ailment."

"Aye and it gets worse when you get older," Burdach rubbed his hands together. "I hope you havna put us in a tent Lugubelenus."

"You know me better than that. You and your daughter are close to the main hall, "he chuckled," and the fire. I am afraid, Darach, that you and your kin will be in a tent but rest assured we will give you all the passwords and you will be eating in the great hall. My Steward will accompany you."

Metellus and Macro both bowed, "Your majesty is too kind. We brought our own blankets and would have been happy enough to sleep in a field."

As the two kings walked away Lugubelenus said, "What a polite and thoughtful young man. Are there many like him in the isles?"

"No, he is one of my better-behaved kin from the wee poor land of Dun Eibhinn."

Macro and Metellus thanked the Steward for his kindness as they were shown to the leather tent provided for them. As they laid out their gear Macro suddenly said, "Well of all the cheek."

"What?"

"This tent, it is one of the Ninth's, look you can see the markings."

As Metellus examined it he replied, "Well it is no wonder he can house them all."

"By the way Metellus…"

"Darach," he pointed to his ears and then at the outside.

"Sorry, Darach but Livius was right."

"About what?"

"About you coming and not Marcus. Marcus would never have been so quick thinking back there. Perhaps Rufius would have been a better companion."

"Don't put yourself down. We only need one world-class liar in this team. Find anything out about the bonnie lassie?"

"Just that she wants to shag my brains out! She was so hot I was getting a little worried."

"Well keep it in your pants, my young friend, the king told me to warn you off. You are too poor and you don't have a title."

"Thank the Allfather for that. How do we play it tonight?"

"Let's put our horses in the stabling area. We don't know when we might have to leave in a hurry and then we'll try out the passwords the Steward gave us and wander in the compound. Let's stay together and pick up as much information as we can. They think you are my brother so let's play you as the shy little boy just away from the islands."

"Why?"

"They will feel sorry for you and are more likely to let slip something important."

The guards gave them a quick scrutiny but, having recently seen them talking to their king they did not see them as a threat and they gave the correct passwords. Inside the compound, they could see that new huts had been built for the nobility who had arrived. There was fresh straw on the ground to soak up the melting snow and tendrils of smoke rose from every hut. The main hall was in the centre and raised to be higher than the other buildings and even the wall. Only the four towers at each corner were taller.

"Keep your eyes peeled and we will share the intelligence tonight." There were guards at the open doors of the main hall and they scrutinised the two men more closely but as they had the passwords they were admitted. Inside, the roaring fire gave instant heat and light. There were many nobles gathered around and, for a moment, the two of them felt slightly intimidated. It was one thing to wander into a tavern in a strange place but here… they were out of their depth. Fortunately, they heard a booming shout, "Darach. Over here, boys."

As they walked over to the King, they saw that he was sitting at a long table with others of a similar age and they all had foaming horns of ale in their hands. "These are two distant kin from Dun Eibhinn." He paused and then looked at each of them in the face. "You wouldna have heard of it as it is a piss poor little island that no-one wants to fight for." They all laughed and the King looked at Metellus, "No offence laddie."

"And none taken, uncle," Metellus deliberately used the affectionate title given to friends of the family to further the deception and the King did not seem to mind. It raised their status with the other nobles. "In fact, it is why my wee brother and I are here. If we are going to start knocking a few Roman heads about we might either get some money or a wee bit of land?" He winked at Burdach, "It'll stop us stealing our neighbour's land eh?"

Macro thought that Metellus had gone too far for there was a brief moment of silence before they all laughed. "Oh, I do like the laddies from the islands. Nary a coin between them but witty as."

Lugubelenus wandered over, "I can see that this is the table to be at. I love to see my lords enjoying themselves."

"It's wee Darach here. He's ready to take on the Roman army and get some treasure for himself."

For a moment the king became serious, "Romans? It is only one idea."

Metellus was saved by another king, Luarch of the Novontae, who said, "A bloody good idea. Save you, Darach here, coming to steal my gold or his wee brother from stealing my daughter." Macro blushed. "Oh aye, laddie, we all heard how you stole Morag's heart. We'll have to watch our women folk around a good looking laddie like you."

Metellus and Macro performed their Explorate trick of appearing to drink as much as any, appear to be as drunk as any of the others but remaining stone-cold sober. The looks between then showed when they had gathered information and when they had gleaned something valuable. They watched and they learned. The Great Hall filled up as more and more people arrived. Finally, everyone stood in silence as the King of the Votadini strode in, now attired in a magnificent suit of mail armour, glistening like gold. He was followed by his wife Radha who seemed to float above the room like a pixie or fairy. Every man fell in love with her in an instant. Eventually, after a silence which seemed to ache in to a lifetime. Morwenna walked in. Macro had never seen her before but he had never seen aught so beautiful and he was entranced instantly. Metellus felt a shiver across his soul and Morwenna, well Morwenna stopped as though she had walked into a stone wall, there was a silence and even Radha looked around in confusion. Morwenna's face showed, for the first time, indecision and confusion. Somewhere in this room was her child!

Angus pushed his men on. He wished it were Wolf and not Quintus with him for he trusted the hairy Roman. They had rushed through the night and crossed the river by the island they used to communicate. Quintus left a red cloth and the column headed south leaving Quintus too. Angus was no fool; he did not intend to go too far south for, when he attacked any column trying to supply the forts, he would need to get his ill-gotten gains back to Votadini country as swiftly as possible. He waited but three miles south of Corio; he needed to go no further. It was better to let the Romans do all the work and they would be relaxed within touching distance of their fort. He could destroy them, take their supplies and be back in his own land within an hour. He had all the time in the world. If the Romans did not send supplies then the garrison would die, starving in the freezing northern winter. What he did not know was that the garrison had supplies for a year and the cavalry could find enough grass for their horses to survive for a few more weeks, but most importantly, Livius had put in place a course of action which would negate all of Morwenna's plans.

Chapter 17

"Sir,"

"Yes, sentry?" Livius was patient with the new recruits, especially when standing a watch. He had told them to report first and not to worry about getting the officer's attention. He sighed, it was early morning and that was when the sentries would become most jittery. "Now come on Marius, I have already told you, the report first it could be important."

"Yes sir, it's just that, well there's a ship." He pointed downstream where there was indeed a ship sailing towards the two forts. Livius could hear the consternation in the Batavian fort and he heard the buccina sounding which woke up the ala too.

He smiled. "No son, that isn't just a ship that is hope with an attitude. It is my old friend Hercules and '*The Swan*'." There was no jetty but the ship could not get beyond the bridge anyway. Livius shouted, "Tie up on this bank."

He saw the gnarled old seaman wave and heard his voice across birdsong as dawn broke. "I thought you would have had a man to catch the rope Livius."

"Give me a moment and I will oblige. Open the gate!"

Cassius had heard the buccina and raced to the walls to see why the alarm had been sounded. He met Livius as the gate opened. "It is Hercules, Cassius, we have our supplies."

As the two men walked to the river bank Cassius asked, "And Marcus? Will he be bringing back more?"

Livius shook his head, "No I arranged for this delivery from Eboracum to be certain we were supplied. Besides we needed the deception to enable Macro and Metellus to evade observation."

"Let's see if you can still catch, horseman" Hercules tossed the rope easily and Livius caught it, not necessarily in a seamanlike manner but caught none the less. "Tie it to the stump of that tree." When the forts had been built the banks had been cleared to provide a good field of fire. The resultant stumps made perfect mooring points.

As soon as the ramp was down Hercules stomped down to greet Livius. They embraced, "The Senator sends his best wishes and..."

Suddenly Livius heard feet racing along the deck and a voice shouted, "Livius!"

"Furax! What in the Allfather's name are you doing here?"

Hercules sniffed, "The boy was becoming bored at home and he yearned to see you again. I think he wore the senator down."

"Whatever the reason, it is good to see you. Bring your men ashore and we will feed them. My men can help to unload later."

Hercules looked sceptical as he ordered his men ashore. "Roman army rations? I think I would rather chew tree bark."

"Wait until you have tasted Septimus' cooking and then judge." He looked around for Furax and smiled as he saw the boy exploring the country which looked so different from the city of Rome in which he had grown up. "Come on Furax, food first and then we can explore."

Cassius had left quickly to warn Septimus of the extra guests. "They are friends Septimus so come up with something a little special eh?"

Septimus spread his arms. "You want special, tell me the night before, not just before the guests arrive!"

"Come on Septimus, you have something tucked away, I know you."

Grinning, the cook said, "I suppose I might. Right lads let's get to it."

While the crew went into the eating area Livius filled the time with a quick tour of the fort with Hercules and Furax. "It is only a small fort but we built it in a couple of days. The men are busy building up the defences which is where the supplies you brought will help." Just then a turma clattered through the gate to begin the day's patrol, the Decurion, Spartianus, saluting and smiling at Livius. Livius could not help but notice the huge change in attitude of not only Spartianus but all his followers. "That is one of the daily patrols. They will be heading upstream towards Vindolanda, the next fort."

By the time they had seen the whole of the fort, they were all ready for food. They heard the clatter of a ladle on a pan. "Come and get it."

"Are you hungry Furax?"

"Starving Livius."

Hercules shook his head, "Don't get excited son, it will probably be porridge and thin porridge at that."

When they walked in Livius laughed out loud as Hercules' jaw dropped. Septimus had cooked a huge platter of eggs and chopped wild mushrooms into the mixture seasoned it with olive oil and surrounded it with borage. Next to it was another platter with steaming slices of wild boar meat. Cooked the previous day the wild meat had been thinly sliced and then fried and finally, there were steaming loaves fresh from the bread oven. Furax looked accusingly at Hercules who shrugged and murmured, "Of course I could be wrong."

Aelius wondered about the ship. He had seen it before, in Eboracum and wondered what it meant. It had taken him by surprise for he had not seen a ship since leaving Eboracum, especially not at this time of year. The coast of Britannia was renowned for its winter storms. He saw the dead crow and headed his men across the river. He turned to his chosen man, "Head downstream for a mile and look for tracks then return here." He gave no explanation to his men; he did not need to for he was decurion. He dismounted and feigned looking at his horse's rear hoof. As the turma trotted out of sight he heard his name called and looked up to see a grinning Quintus emerge from the trees.

"Where's Wolf?"

"Oh, he is the blue-eyed boy of the witch now. But at the moment he has the shits and I am here waiting for a message and then I am going to join the big bugger you met last time. He is just down the road waiting to ambush the next supply train. Wolf will take your latest intelligence back to the Queen."

"Excellent, the Queen should be pleased for I have exceedingly good news, Metellus, Macro and Marcus took two turmae south to Morbium a couple of days ago. They were headed to the fort to pick up supplies. We are short of feed so they should be travelling slowly with heavy wagons and civilian drivers. I think they will be here in the next day or two. What will you do after you have captured the supplies?"

Quintus pointed north. "Cross here and head back home."

Aelius noted the use of the word home and realised how quickly his former comrade had gone native. "I will make sure that I am assigned this patrol then and I will keep my lads occupied. If you go now you can head south before the patrol returns. I will take them to Vindolanda."

"Right."

"Oh and Quintus?"

"Yes sir?"

"Don't forget to tell the Queen that I require payment for these services.

"So you arranged this, weeks ago?"

Hercules sat back, full for the first time since leaving Rome for he had had a difficult voyage. "Yes, the Senator sent for and arranged a cargo of feed and other goods to be loaded aboard '*The Swan*'. We also took on trade goods for Eboracum. There were some supplies at Eboracum about to be sent to you by road but when they saw the Senator's letter they loaded them aboard us. We called there first and then headed up here. We have already made a profit on the voyage before we are paid by you."

Livius laughed. "You old pirate. I am sure that the Senator paid for the goods."

"Hercules shrugged, "Worth a try though. "He looked at Livius. "He also sent you a message."

"If you come with me to my quarters then I will read it. Rufius, can you look after Furax? Cassius, get the men and we'll start to unload."

By the time Aelius returned from his patrol the last of the supplies had been unloaded and were being ferried by the tired troopers. He was perplexed. Why had the Decurion Princeps sent the two turmae to Morbium when he had supplies coming by sea? He could see that the granary tents were full and the fodder already safely covered by canvas. What were the turmae doing? He wondered if it was a trap, a devious plot of the commander but that would mean that he knew he had a spy and Aelius had seen no sign of that. He hated not knowing and he did not know what was going on. He determined to find out. He would play the happy soldier and engage his peers in conversation; with luck one of them would give an inkling as to what was going on.

Once in the Principia Hercules handed over the packet containing the message. Livius took out a wax tablet and wrote out the key words and then began to transcribe. It took him some time but Hercules was quite happy watching and drinking the ale which had been thrust into his hand. When he had finished he looked up at the old man. "Do you know what it contains?"

"You mean the actual words? No. Do I know what is going on? Then, yes I do."

"How?"

"I took many of the messages between the Senator and Capreae and I keep my ears open. So yes, I know that the Emperor's enemies were all executed and I know that the war in the east has ended and many senators are less than happy with the Emperor's first couple of years in office and yes, I have heard that there is trouble on the Germania borders."

He took a long drink of his ale and wiped his mouth with the back of his hand. Livius shook his head and then looked at the paper. "So, apart from one item of news, you could have given me the report eh?"

"Better from the Senator though? Well now that we have unloaded the cargo my task here is complete. We'll spend the night here if you don't mind and then back to Rome and warmer climes. I don't know how you survive up here. I have never been so cold in all my life."

"That is why it is called winter but I want you to delay your departure by a few days. Can you do that?"

Hercules sighed and then chuckled. "That Senator must have known you were going to ask me something like that. He said, before I left, that I was to place myself at your disposal."

"You never told me that."

"I never lied. I just wanted to get back but to answer your question I can stay here as long as you like only don't make it too long eh there's a mate. I have some amphorae of wine I could throw your way in return for the swiftest departure possible."

"We'll see. Right. Julius!"

The clerk must have been within listening distance for he appeared almost immediately. "Yes Decurion Princeps?"

"Quarters for the..."

"Already arranged; follow me, er Hercules is it? What a strange name how did you..." The two men went off together like two old friends.

"Cassius! I have news from the senator." After he had told him the main points he added, "But there is more that Hercules did not know. The Governor omitted to mention any problems in the borders and, in particular, about the presence of Morwenna. It did not sit well with either Attianus or the Emperor. I believe that we may well have a new Governor ere long. And we have the use of '*The Swan*'."

"You still intend to put the plan in place."

"Yes."

"It is risky. "

"But in all likelihood, it is the only way that Metellus and Macro can complete their mission. So have you identified the ten best bowmen?"

"Yes and I think they will work well as a team under us." Cassius looked expectantly at Livius.

"It is not us Cassius. I told you that. I will take Rufius and you will command here in my stead."

"Why cannot you command and let me go?"

"Because Cassius, I will be putting '*The Swan*' and Hercules in danger. Julius Demetrius is allowing me to use the ship out of our friendship. I cannot in all conscience let you put yourself in danger whilst I wait here besides, I need you to keep an eye on Spartianus."

"He has behaved himself lately."

"And does that not strike you as suspicious?"

Cassius knew that Livius was right. It seemed totally out of character for the truculent Decurion Spartianus. The fact that his men, his cronies, had also changed their spots was equally remarkable. He had been tempted to tell Livius before now but he thought that the

Decurion Princeps might think him petty and vindictive. He had had the other men watched by their decurions and so far none had deviated from their duties. But Spartianus was an officer and it was difficult to monitor him. "Yes, I am suspicious. I do not believe that this leopard can change his spots."

"Is there none in his turma who can spy on him?"

Cassius did not like the idea of setting men to spy on others besides which it could be dangerous but if it meant getting to the truth and finding out what was at the heart of this sea change then so be it. "There is one of the older troopers, Scipio Aurelius, he is a loner and does not seem to like being in the turma. He has been disciplined by Spartianus on a number of occasions. He has asked for a transfer. I will have a talk to him later this evening and see what I can discover."

"Good and, just as a precaution, can you make his turma the duty turma the day that I leave and your turma can have the duty along the road."

The next day, Metellus and Macro were the focus of attention of other chiefs who were keen to hear what this new pair of warriors had to say. Their polite nature, the way that they listened and appeared interested in all that was said, made them the most popular pair in the camp. They found themselves and their ideas sought out by kings who had travelled far and were undecided about their course of action. As they were the waverers amongst the tribes Lugubelenus took it upon himself to sit and listen to their conversations. He did not want these two callow youths to be the reason that some of his potential allies did not join him. He too found that the one called Darach was a considered and well-spoken man and his ideas were sound. He had worried that he was a firebrand who would rush into some headstrong action and precipitate a war. He found, to his delight that he was of the same mind as himself. After their noontime meal, King Lugubelenus took him to one side. Macro and Morag had gone for a walk in the snow and Metellus worried that the old king, her father, would become alienated if the young warrior took advantage of his virginal child, However, he knew that getting the information was his most important task, it was more important than their own lives and so he went with the king to a private chamber.

"You seem sensible and, I believe, trustworthy. The fact that your people have not been involved in the politics of the mainland bodes well for us and gives you an interesting perspective. If we could manage to persuade all the tribes to rid this land of Romans then this conclave would be a success. How would we manage that with such a hotchpotch of tribes most of whom were fighting each other last week and will be again as soon as they depart?"

Metellus was on the horns of a dilemma. He was being asked to come up with the plan which he would take back to the Decurion Princeps. He thought quickly, that was why he had been chosen. He stared into the fire and the king did not hurry him, in fact, he thought that this was a sign that Darach was giving it deep thought. He was, but for different reasons than the king thought. What was the worst scenario? An attack on Corio was the most disastrous for that led directly to the main road south and into the heart of Britannia. Eboracum would fall in an instant for there was no Ninth to defend it this time. He had to persuade the king to split his forces.

"Well your majesty, I suspect you have thought of this yourself already, but if I were to attack with such a variety of tribes then I would split them up. Put those tribes who work well together and have no history of feuds in the same army. Then I would strike at three places on the frontier, Coriosopitum, Vindolanda and Luguvalium. Even if the Romans had a reserve force, which my uncle tells me they have not," that was a lie but he was sure that the king would not verify the facts, "then they could not reinforce all three places. Once you were through their three major forts then the rest of the province would be at your mercy and you would be able to use the tribe's differences to your advantage."

"And I could use two other kings as leaders to placate their feelings of obeisance from following a younger king. That is a masterstroke! You have a mind for strategy. Would you not consider joining me?"

"I would be honoured to do so but I am sure that you had come to the same conclusion."

"No Darach, I had some of those ideas floating around in my head but talking to you has made them clearer." He leaned over confidentially, "The Queen usually listens to my ideas and straightens them out but this Morwenna appears to hold her attention."

Secretly Metellus was pleased because both he and Macro were keen to avoid running into her. Metellus more so than Macro, for the boy still did not know that the witch queen was his mother. "I am sure that her attention will soon return to you oh king and I am pleased that I have been of some service."

Macro and Morag were walking in the woods. Macro was torn; half of him enjoyed the flirtatious pleasure he got from Morag but he also disliked the fact that he was not doing his job. He had not recovered from the stare of Morwenna that first night. He and Metellus had gone out of their way to avoid her presence. He felt Morag's fingers intertwine with his. "If your father sees us…"

"Wisht! Are you a man or a wee mousie. He is not here and besides, you are not the first laddie I have walked with." She giggled, "And kissed."

"Look Morag, I think you are the loveliest girl I have ever seen but…"

"Girl! Am I not a woman? She put her hands beneath her ample breasts and pushed them towards Macro. Had he not known that he would have offended her he would have burst out laughing.

"Look, you are a bonnie lassie and I would like to kiss you but we need to find the time and the place." He pointed to the walls of the oppidum which had many sentries staring out. This is too busy."

"Well, when then?"

"Tonight after supper, I will meet you by the horses. I have to feed them tonight."

"All right but you had better be there."

Morwenna and Radha lay in each other's arms. For the first time since she had met her, Radha felt that Morwenna had needed the comfort more than she. The Red Witch had been out of sorts since that first dinner. Radha did not mind, it made her feel more important and more needed. Her life was as good as it could be and she could only see it getting better.

Morwenna was troubled. There was a presence, a spirit that had come into the hall and she had tried to divine it but had failed. Someone was hiding from her and she needed to know who it was. The problem she had had was that there were just too many people in the room and she could not isolate the spirit which emanated those vibrations. She decided that at the feast later that night, she would visit each table in an attempt to isolate where the power was.

Suddenly there was a shout from outside. "It is Tole the King of the Selgovae." There was an enormous noise from outside, the clanging of metal on metal and the cheers of people. He had finally arrived, the last of the kings. The delay had been deliberate; it had been Morwenna's decision in order to increase the impact he would have.

She leapt to her feet. "We must greet him. He is the final part of our plan. With him, on our side, the conclave will choose war and the Roman rule in Britannia will end."

Although she smiled and hugged Morwenna, Radha could not help but be a little disappointed. Tole would now have her affections and she would no longer be the vital part of the Red Witch's needs. Her world

171

suddenly seemed a little emptier and lacking some of the colour it had had.

Metellus and Lugubelenus heard the noise and Metellus noticed the irritated look on the king's face. It told him that this alliance with the Selgovae was not a marriage made in heaven and he stored that piece of intelligence away for future use. "I suppose we will have to greet the new King and his entourage."

When they emerged on to the steps of the hall they saw Tole and his fifty bodyguards in gleaming helmets and with shining swords. The king was irritated that the men at the gate had allowed the entry of so many armed men but he knew that it would be churlish to mention it and he had to ignore it, for the moment. "Welcome King of the Selgovae."

Tole hopped from his horse and bowed to the king. "Thank you for the invitation oh mighty king for it gives my people the chance to redeem themselves and regain the honour they lost so ignominiously when they deserted you allowing you to defeat the Romans single-handedly."

The deliberate obeisance had been carefully scripted by Morwenna and, as she and Radha watched from the side, she saw that it had worked. Lugubelenus picked up the youth and embraced him. "From this day forth we will fight together as allies and together we will drive the Romans to the sea."

Metellus caught sight of Macro and Morag slipping in through the front gate and breathed a sigh of relief that everyone's attention was on the embracing kings. Things were going well. They would be able to leave in the morning once he was certain that the king had taken the plan to heart. Now that Tole was present, he was sure that they would begin the conclave and he hoped that it would come to a rapid conclusion.

Chapter 18

Marcus was angry after he had spoken with the Prefect at Morbium. The apologetic commander had told the young decurion that a message had reached them that their fodder and other supplies were being taken by sea to Coriosopitum. Although angry, Marcus was experienced enough to know that this was none of the Prefect's doing. He declined the offer of beds and took his two turmae south-west towards his family home. He turned to Sextus Lepidus, his chosen man, who had looked questioningly at the popular decurion when he made the surprise decision. "We'll be able to get back, quickly enough in one day, if we leave in the morning and my parents will give us better rations than the well-meaning Prefect."

The idea cheered up all of the men in the turmae. They had all heard many stories of the legendary Marcus' Horse and Marcus' father, Gaius, who was the last surviving member of that famous ala. He was also said to be the guardian of the Sword of Cartimandua, the famous symbol of the Brigante people. All cavalrymen had affection not to say adulation for swords and the stories of this one, first wielded by the Decurion Princeps, Ulpius Felix, had been told and retold in the barracks. They were superstitious troopers and, secretly, they all wanted to touch the sword as though some of its legends and magic might rub off on them.

The original farmstead had been built upon and enlarged ever since it had been first constructed. Gaius had had his wife and children kidnapped once and now a ditch and a fortified wall surrounded the extensive property. It was a smaller version of Morbium and the locals knew to seek refuge there when the barbarians raided. He was now a highly successful farmer, although as he admitted to any who asked, he did not know how. His men, who tended his animals and land, were now numbered in their tens and acted as a local defence force in times of need for the frontier was still a dangerous place and raiders from both north and south of the farm plundered isolated settlements.

As they clattered up the cobbled road, leading to the farm, their standard and their uniforms clearly marked them as Roman and the gates were opened. Marcus' elder brother Decius greeted him and embraced him in a bear hug. Marcus was not a small man but Decius dwarfed him. He was rounder and taller than Marcus and obviously enjoyed the good life on the farm. When he was finally deposited upon the ground Marcus patted Decius' belly. "You aren't expecting my nephew are you brother?"

Decius roared with laughter, "No but my young wife is. You must see her soon, for her time is almost upon her."

"I cannot wait." He gestured at the cavalrymen behind him. "I hope you don't mind but I brought the turmae."

"No, that is not a problem. Father will be pleased to see you and them." He shouted over his shoulder, "Gaelwyn!" Marcus started at the name and then realised it was not his old uncle, the great scout who had recently died but his much younger cousin. "Take these men to the barn and stable their mounts. Get one of the house slaves to bring food and drink."

The column trotted off and Marcus turned to his brother, "How is father?"

"Surprisingly well for a man who is over sixty years old. Everyone comments about his youthful looks. They are convinced we have the fountain of eternal youth on the farm for mother is also as youthful as ever. Come they will be in the house."

Gaius had just become greyer as he had aged. There were few lines on his face, which was still as open and honest as it had always been. Ailis had less grey but the years of captivity with the Caledonii had left their mark in the lines of old pain upon her face. Their faces lit with joy when they beheld their son and they embraced him tightly, the tears pouring uncontrollably down Ailis' cheeks. When he eventually prised himself away and sat before the fire, a beaker of home-brewed ale in his hand, they began the torrent of questions. The flood was halted when Ailis asked of Macro and Marcus' face darkened.

Although Macro was the son of Macro and Morwenna he had been abandoned when a few months old and Ailis regarded him as a son, every bit as much as Marcus and Decius. They in turn called him brother, which he was. "He is well is he not? You would not hide it from me?"

Marcus smiled, realising that his own anger at not being selected for the mission had clouded his thoughts. "No, he is fine and in good health. He is just on a patrol." Marcus hesitated. Should he break security and tell them of his brother's mission?

His father saw his hesitation. "Do not break your bond, my son." He put his hand on his wife's arm. "We knew that when they joined the Explorates they would be doing difficult things. Be proud wife that our sons make the frontier safe for us." The wise old campaigner moved the conversation to safer subjects. "How is Livius? Now Decurion Princeps I hear?"

"More than that father, he is a close confidante of the new Emperor and will be Prefect soon. The Emperor made him a member of the

174

equestrian class; a great honour for a Briton. He is enjoying the role and he is a good commander." Marcus suddenly felt guilty about praising someone who had been his father's junior.

"He was always a good man and I liked him. I am pleased that he is doing well."

"And he met the new Emperor Hadrian when the old Emperor died. He and Julius Demetrius met him in Surrentum."

"I knew the lad would do well but hobnobbing with Emperors! And it is good to know that Julius has done well." He smiled fondly at the memory. "I remember when he first came to the ala, so shy and serious."

Decius piped up. "Didn't his father have you flogged?"

Wincing still at the scars on his back he said, "Aye but he was not like his son. Julius was, is, a good man. And you son? What of you?"

"I am the horse master, a sergeant and I command, with Macro, a turma. He too is a sergeant and the weapons trainer."

"Just like his father eh? That was brave of Livius to promote him in a new ala. Did the older members of the ala not resent it?"

"There were a handful but when Macro defeated their biggest bully in a training bout they were won around." He smiled at his parents. "You know Macro, everyone likes him."

"Just like his dad."

Ailis asked the question which had been on all their minds. "And the frontier? Are we in danger?" With the prospect of becoming a grandmother and remembering the slave raid which had taken her and her children north, it was a fear constantly in Ailis' mind.

He shook his head. "It is not good. There are but three cohorts on the border, and our ala. Little enough to stop raids but the tribes are gathering in the land of the Votadini and," he paused, wondering if he ought to mention the name, "Morwenna has returned. She is at the conclave."

Ailis' hand went to her mouth. "I thought we had finished with her."

Gaius' face darkened and his eyes narrowed. "That snake needs scotching. She has been responsible for more death and destruction than ever her mother was."

Ailis put her arms around her husband, holding him tightly. "It was a dark day when Marcus had her crucified. Perhaps her daughter would not have demanded so much revenge had she been spared."

"No my wife, there is evil in the world and Fainch and Morwenna are both evidence of that evil." He shook himself. "Come let us not talk of such dark things when the nights are long. Your men will be hungry and we are being poor hosts."

Decius stood, "I had the slaves feed them but you are right. I will go and tell the cook to cook the deer I killed yesterday. It could have been hung a little longer but…"

"The men are just grateful for the roof over their head and now, where is my pregnant sister in law? I would like to see her and see if her bump is bigger than my brother's."

Later that night, they lit a huge fire outside the barn and the family, household and turmae shared the sweet puddings made by the cook from the damaged fruit which would not last until spring and aqua vitae. The ale flowed and they sang the songs of the ala; Gaius reliving his youth, his eyes moistening as he remembered dead comrades. Sextus said, in the lull between songs and tales. "I am of Brigante stock and I would dearly like to see the sword." There was a silence as the young trooper had posed the question lurking on everyone's mind. The drink had loosened his tongue and as silence descended he began to regret his impetuosity.

Gaius smiled. "Go Decius, bring it forth. These comrades of our sons deserve to see it."

When Decius brought it out in its plain scabbard there was hushed reverence as though a holy relic was being paraded. Gaius held the sheathed sword in his hand and then, looking at Marcus' proud face nodded to him and said. "You are a warrior now and I am just a farmer. Draw the blade, my son."

The jewelled hilt glistened and glittered in the sparkling firelight and it seemed that time had stood still as the blade was slipped from its scabbard. It seemed to Gaius that the voices of the dead who had followed the blade whooshed and whooped their own approbation as the shining steel emerged. The eyes of the troopers told Gaius all that he needed to know about the men and boys who followed his son, they were warriors and they respected the legend of the sword.

Marcus stood and, impulsively, raised the blade to the bright stars above the farm, "The Sword of Cartimandua, the sword of my ancestors!"

Ailis and Gaius felt the hairs on their necks prickle as the turmae rose as a man, took out their swords and yelled, "The Sword of Cartimandua."

Sextus came over and asked shyly. "May I touch the blade?" Marcus and Gaius looked at each other and nodded. First Sextus and then every man laid his hands on the blade. Each one closed his eyes as he did so, intoning a silent prayer on this most magical of swords.

Marcus returned it to its sheath and sat with the sword across his knees. One trooper asked, "It is said that when the sword went into battle the ala always won. Is that true?"

Gaius had heard the legend many times. He thought for a moment. "There were but a handful of us who wielded the weapon, the mighty Ulpius, Marcus Maximunius and myself. I can honestly tell you that we never lost a battle whilst we wielded the blade and the ala survived." He looked intently at the young men who were hanging on to his every word. "Not all the men in the ala survived many of those battles, for the ala was always in the forefront of the defence of the frontier and many times it seemed that the ala and the sword were Rome's only defence but we endured and the stories of Marcus' Horse and the Sword of Cartimandua are all true."

The men turned, bright-eyed to each other to tell the tales they had heard of the mighty ala. Gaius heard one trooper say, "Would that the sword were with our ala for then we too would be undefeated."

Gaius looked at the way his son held the sword, like a proud father with his firstborn child. He thought too of Ulpius Felix who had relinquished the sword into Marcus' care as he lay dying, of Marcus who passed it to Gaius married to the last of the Brigante royal family and knew that he had been selfish in holding on to the sword. He knew that the sword had a power which made its bearer fight better but it also meant that the bearer was in greater danger as every opponent tried to capture the sword and in killing its bearer gain the honour. He glanced over at Ailis. '*She must be fey*,' he thought for he knew that she read his mind. A half-smile appeared on her face, although her eyes were moist and sad and she nodded. Gaius returned the nod. He stood and gently took the sword from Marcus who looked crestfallen. Ailis laid her hand on her son's shoulder as Gaius raised the sword above his head. "The time has come to pass the sword on to the next generation. I hereby give the sword to my warrior son," he caught the eye of Decius who smiled and nodded, "Marcus, knowing that he will carry the sword with honour and defend this land of Brigante and Roman, his two peoples."

He handed the sword back to Marcus who unsheathed it again, this time as the owner. Sextus came forward and knelt before Marcus; it was impulsive but something in the moment made him do it. He had been told, by his Brigante father, of the sword and its meaning for his people. "My lord I swear allegiance to you and would be as your bondsman, your oath brother."

Before Marcus could react, one by one every trooper came to make the pledge. Marcus looked around in confusion. Even Gaius was unsure of what should happen next. Old Gaelwyn the scout would have known but he was long dead. Ailis knew and she stood next to her son, whispering in his ear, "You accept their oath and tell them you will lead them as a father and you give them the father's oath of protection."

Swallowing quickly to enable him to get the words out at such an emotional moment his voice seemed unnaturally loud in the still night with the dying fire crackling at their feet. "I accept your oath my oath brothers and I swear, on the Sword of Cartimandua, that I will be as a father to you and give you the protection of my sword and my life."

The next morning the turmae, despite the late-night drinking were up bright and early, eager to ride back to the fort and proud of their actions the previous night. Marcus sat a little higher on his horse as he waited for them to assemble behind him. Decius and his wife waved at him and he shouted over. "It will be a boy and I expect a Marcus, not a Macro."

Decius laughed and shouted back, "It could be a Gaius of course."

Nodding his approval he yelled back, "Better still!" He leaned down to grasp his father's arm, his mother looking up with tearful eyes. "Thank you for the sword father. I will look after it."

"It will look after you but remember my son its magic does not mean you are invincible. Do not seek combat for the sake of it. The sword will make you a wiser and better leader, it did make me." He looked up, "May the Allfather watch over you and Macro, wherever he may be."

"I will look after him I promise when he returns."

As they rode away Ailis couldn't help but get a shiver down her spine. Gaius said, "Is it the cold?"

"No, I fear something bad has happened, either that or someone is walking over my grave."

The conclave did indeed begin. Macro and Metellus placed themselves well away from the firelight and the eyes of Morwenna on the raised dais. Metellus had explained to Macro that they would leave in the morning. "Thank the Allfather for that. Morag intended to meet with me tonight in the stables and I feared it would end with her father after my blood."

"No my young friend you must still go to meet her otherwise she will come looking for you and I would have us leave this night. Once we know the outcome and the feast begins then you go to the stables, if I know Morag then she will follow you. I will get our weapons from the hut and meet you at our mounts. We should be able to make the coast within the hour and, once there, either take a ship or head south."

"Sounds good to me."

Now as they listened to the conclave they heard the words of Darach spoken by the King. They obviously impressed all, for Tole and the other kings nodded as he made each powerful point. Even Morwenna looked to approve and Radha sat with eyes once more adoring her man. Lugubelenus noticed and it pleased him, he had begun to worry that he was losing his queen. He had been concerned by the fact that she had distanced herself from him. His world was, once again, the perfect sphere. With his new adviser, Darach, and his wife, once again by his side, who knew what heights they could scale; they had defeated the Ninth now there were only auxiliaries to face them. The whole of the Northern half of Britannia was behind him. The only major tribe, not present was the Brigante and, with the Queen of the Brigante with him then they would soon follow once they crossed the Dunum.

The King held up his hands to silence the cheering, of the animated audience. "Friends, fellow Kings, Chiefs can I formerly ask that you confirm the conclave and its decisions. We will invade Roman Britannia in the spring, attacking their three major forts at the same time!" The cheer and the roar even took the two Romans by surprise. "And further that the three columns will be led by myself, King Tole of the Selgovae, and King Burdach of the Dumnonii?"

There was an equally loud, drunken cheer. Metellus, soberly, reflected that they could have voted his horse as a general and they would have accepted it. He kept his eyes on the Queen Morwenna. She had looked self-satisfied throughout. She had the look of a snake which had just polished off a satisfying meal and was enjoying the digestion. Metellus wondered how long Lugubelenus would survive if the attack was successful? Looking at the young King Tole of the Selgovae, he could see someone who would not be willing to be subservient to a king, not many years his senior. When he made his report to Livius it would be a positive report. Things looked grim and dark but there was hope. Having attended the conclave he knew that the alliances were fragile and old enmities could be exploited. He remembered reading how Agricola had saved many men's lives through effective hostage-taking and diplomacy. That could work again. All he had to do was to return to Livius and make his report. Metellus looked at Macro their faces alight with the joy of knowing that they had the plan of the King of the Votadini. It would still not be easy but, by moving cohorts from Morbium and the other forts in the hinterland they could plug the gap at Coriosopitum. The troops from further south could be marched north to help stem the tide of this barbarian invasion.

He spoke quietly to Macro. "Time to make good our escape. You fetch the horses and I will fetch the weapons. We have done all that was asked of us and now we can return to safety"

Wolf was exhausted after his long ride north. Having the shits had helped neither his disposition nor his comfort. He had persevered, as he knew that it was important information. If the supplies from the south could be stopped then the fort would be ripe for attacking sooner rather than later. He eased himself in the saddle as he saw the lights of the oppidum in the distance. Within an hour he would be safely ensconced in the fort, he could make his report and then get drunk!

Macro slipped silently towards their horses in the stables. He gave the correct password to the guards and entered. He found their horses and gave each one a handful of grain. They would need all their energy to escape this frozen fort deep in their enemy's heartland. He slipped the saddles on to the two horses and tied the third by a short halter. It was unlikely that they would need it for supplies but he knew from past experience that a horse could go lame and they would need a spare. He wondered what plan Metellus had to get them out of the stable area. He realised that he had come to rely on Metellus totally. If he were left alone to make these decisions what would he do? He came to the only conclusion he could; slit the sentry's throat.

He suddenly heard a conversation at the guard post. Had Metellus arrived? When Morag slipped in he knew that he would have to think quickly. "Morag you are early!"

She rushed up and, embracing him, kissed him full on the lips. "I saw you slip away and knew that you were making the time for us to be together." She suddenly saw the horses in his hands. "Where are you going?"

For the first time, Macro had to react and think creatively. "The reason I slipped away was that Darach received a message. Our father is sick and we must return to our home in the islands. He has gone to collect our traps and then we can return home." Macro was rather pleased with himself. The story sounded plausible and explained why Metellus was not there with them.

"Oh, my love I am sorry. This is a disaster! When will I see you again?"

"We are but an island away and do not forget with your father at the wars I will be able to see you more easily."

She squealed with delight and kissed him again. There was a noise behind him and Macro was certain that it would be Metellus. He looked into Morag's eyes and said, passionately, "I will see you again soon my love!"

Suddenly he heard a snarling and familiar voice, "Roman dog! A spy!" Wolf's sword was out in an instant. Macro's arms were still around Morag and the sentry and his companion came in looking confused. Wolf snarled at them. "This is a Roman. He is a sergeant in the auxiliary cavalry. Raise the alarm!"

The sentry began hollering and banging on his shield and Macro just hoped that Metellus had made good his escape for he was now surrounded by a sea of spears and soon he would face Morwenna, the Red Witch. When that happened, the young man knew that he was in for a world of pain. He would never return home now and he would end his days tortured in this barbaric outpost of the civilised world.

Chapter 19

Angus was pleased with his ambush. He and Quintus had arranged their fifty men into two groups. Over the last few days, he had come to trust the wily Quintus who told him how the Roman cavalry worked. They had discussed how the two turmae would escort the wagons with their supplies. "They will split their men to ensure that each wagon has at least six men around it. Their prime objective will be to protect the supplies and that is their weakness. One party attacks the head and the other the rear. They should be able to deal with the men there as they will outnumber them. That will leave little pockets of men to sweep up."

Angus had liked the plan and he had taken the head of the column whilst Quintus the rear. Quintus had estimated that the column would be almost two hundred paces long and they hid accordingly. The key would be to attack as soon as the column passed the respective warriors. They had no way of knowing how long the column would take to reach them but they were patient. The men would be tired when they did arrive and would be easy meat for men who had been resting for three days. Once they had stolen the supplies they could return home; as Quintus had said, by destroying two turmae they were making a serious dent in the forces Rome could array against them.

Quintus was enjoying his new role as a leader. For years he had followed the likes of Wolf, The Fist and Aelius; he had lived in their shadows, following orders. Now he was respected and listened to. It was a position he enjoyed; who knew he might become a valued chief. The entire plan had been his and Angus had respected it. He knew that it would be a hard fight, fifty barbarians against almost sixty troopers but he knew the way the ala worked. They would be tired and distracted by the wagons and the Votadini had the element of surprise. Many of the troopers in the two turmae were recruits, and they would run. Quintus remembered his first action, much less daunting than this one, and he had almost wet himself and fled. Had a decurion not been behind him he would have done so. These recruits had nothing to fight for and they were led by two young men. The only warrior with experience was Metellus and Angus knew to take him out first, then the rest would fall. The hardest part was the waiting. Angus was hidden two hundred paces up the road and the forest seemed very dark and very threatening. Suddenly his scout ran up. "They are coming."

"Good. Run and tell Angus that they approach. The rest of you hide in the forest until we see the backmarkers." They could smell the horses before they could see them. The trees made it hard to make out details and Quintus hoped that Angus would have no difficulty in identifying Metellus. His slingers were ready as were his three archers. If they could have good strikes then they would soon outnumber his former comrades. Quintus became aware that he had not heard wagons; perhaps they had brought mules. He held his hand up to hold his men and slithered forward to get a better view. To his horror, there were neither wagons nor mules. The turmae were in a solid column in lines of four and he could see that the rearmost ranks were almost level with his ambush. He froze on the icy ground and the column had passed. He had to do something. He crabbed his way back and signalled his men to attack. He hoped that the front of the column had reached Angus or he, and his band, could be in serious trouble.

Quintus had shown his lack of military strategy. His archers and slingers were to the left of the path and the ala had their shields slung on their left side. As the three arrows and ten stones clattered against shields and helmets only one trooper was stunned and fell to the ground. Sextus was the rearmost trooper and he yelled, "Ambush!"

At the front Marcus heard the shout and immediately halted the column, each man readied himself for whatever onslaught would appear. Angus had no option and he had to launch his attack. "Sound the buccina!" Marcus had no way of knowing how many men were attacking and any help from the fort would be welcome.

Angus had not made Quintus' error and some of his missiles found targets, the troopers crashing to the ground struck by arrows and lead stones. Angus, desperately, sought out the Metellus he had been told was the leader. He could not see him but he suddenly had to defend himself as a young warrior hurled himself at him yelling, "Cartimandua!" In his hand was a sword which seemed too large to be borne by one man.

With terrifying speed, the columns of four formed into a cunei, a wedge behind the leader, an arrow of blades which was aimed at the heart of the attackers and Angus saw sixteen men with spears pointed directly at him. He watched in horror as the two men next to him plunged to the ground with javelins sticking from their bodies. The scything sword cut down another two. The Votadini had made the mistake of fighting on foot to enable them to be more accurate with their missiles. It was to prove their undoing as Angus' command were ruthlessly slaughtered by oath brothers desperately protecting their leader. Angus stood bravely ready to face his enemies and determined to take as many with him to the Allfather, as he could. He watched the young warrior with the mighty sword make straight for him and he hefted his war axe above his head. He would kill this young fool at any rate. Warriors always worry about their left, even when they don't have a shield and Angus was no exception. The huge barbarian watched as the horse was aimed at his left side and he anticipated the strike swinging his axe in a long and deadly arc. Marcus smiled to himself, his enemy had made a cardinal error and with a twitch of his knees, his responsive horse jinked to Angus' right, the Votadini axe hitting fresh air. Marcus struck the Sword of Cartimandua where the body joins the head and both were separated by the razor-sharp blade.

At the rear, Quintus had taken fewer casualties, as Sextus had not managed to form his men into an organised body. "Turn! Turn and face them. The sergeant has the front. Protect yourselves."

The delay allowed some of the Votadini to realise that discretion was the better part of valour and to begin to slink off. It happened just as Sextus saw Quintus. "Traitor! Deserter!"

It was too much for Quintus who took to his heels and raced through the slippery forest to his horse. The rest of his remaining men followed their erstwhile leader as he fled the field. Mounting his horse Quintus was horrified to hear an answering buccina from the valley where the forts were. The ala had been alerted and a turma sent out. He knew he had to cross the river as soon as he could and he kicked his horse north-west towards the message island which was his only escape route. He was in a race against his pursuers and the prize was life. As he crested the rise he risked a glance behind him and saw the mounts of the armoured troopers struggling up the slope after him. Others were finishing off his men but he cared not. He was on the downhill section and they would not catch him for he had no armour and he had a fine mount. As he cleared the trees he could see the fort and he saw two columns of riders leave, one headed up the road whilst the other seemed drawn to him and headed to cut him off. He kicked hard; if he were recaptured then he would be crucified, he had to win the race to the island. His hopes rose when he saw the column spread out in an attempt to cut him off. They were struggling to keep up their speed so close to the river which was muddy and cloying, sucking the hooves into the river bank. Soon there were only two riders who were close enough to him and Quintus tucked his head low to maximise the speed of his escape. He looked ahead and saw the island less than half a mile away. Once on the other side, he would lose them easily in the deep and dark forests. Risking a glance under his arm he saw that there was but one rider pursuing him, a decurion. He hoped it was not Rufius or Cassius for he feared both men. He hoped it was a newly promoted man who might fear the old bully. As he struck the water he looked over his shoulder and saw, to his relief that it was Aelius Spartianus, he was saved; he would live. That momentary relaxation cost him his life as Aelius' javelin struck his unprotected and unarmoured back. He crashed into the water; his lifeblood seeping into the Tinea.

Lying there, his life slipping away in the icy waters of the river, Quintus looked up at his old friend and muttered, "Why?"

"Couldn't risk you being caught and giving me away. At least you weren't crucified." The ironic smile showed Quintus just what his former leader thought of him. The last sight the deserter had was the rest of the turma riding to join their decurion and patting him on the back.

When the last of the raiders had been killed Marcus ordered recall and the troopers, tired but exulted, rode up to form lines along the body littered road. They had fought in their first encounter and they had won. Every face, including the wounded, was beaming with pleasure as Marcus rode down the ranks to count them. Sextus, a gash across his face, rode down the other side and Marcus approached his chosen man. "I make it five troopers dead."

"Me too sir and about ten with a wound of some kind." He self consciously touched the open wound and looked down at the blood on his hand.

"You did well Sextus."

The chosen man shook his head angrily. "No, I did not sir. I didn't react quickly enough. Poor Marius and Decius might have been alive if I hadn't frozen. We need to train for those situations."

"In which case, it is my fault as the man responsible for training you. This was your first action and I am proud of you, "he raised his voice, "I am proud of all of you. Our first action and we won."

The turmae smiled at each other and then Sextus shouted, "Oath brothers of the sword ha!"

The rest of the turmae took it up as Cassius and his turma arrived. The adjutant was smiling despite the dead bodies. "Oath brothers eh? I haven't heard that in a long time." He could see that they were embarrassed and changed the subject. "Well done Marcus you and your young recruits performed well. I believe the last one died over there. Let us get back to the fort and you can get your wounded seen to." He gestured to his chosen man, "Appius take them all back."

The two friends waited on the ride while the three turmae trotted back to the fort. Cassius waited until they were out of earshot and then said, "They knew you were coming. This was a well-planned ambush. "

"You are right sir. Had we had wagons then we would have been cut to pieces."

"Either we have not patrolled well enough or we have a traitor." Cassius led them back to the fort. "We will be short-handed for a while, Livius took Rufius and a turma in '*The Swan*'; they are sailing to be close to Traprain Law in case Macro and Metellus need some help."

Marcus shook his head. "I doubt that they are two of the most resourceful men I have met. They are probably on their way home even as we speak."

Cassius could see Aelius Spartianus waiting for them at the bridge. "I wonder what he wants? Probably a pat on the back for doing his duty."

Aelius was, however, in a humble mood. "Well done sergeant you did well." He pointed at the backs of the turmae entering the fort. "Your men were singing your praises, how you took their leader's head with a backstroke. Good sword work indeed."

Marcus replied modestly, "I didn't have time to think. The training took over."

"Did you catch the one who tried to make it to the river?"

"Yes sir, he is dead." Aelius paused dramatically, "It was Quintus sir, the deserter."

"Now what, in the Allfather's name, was he doing with the Votadini? I don't like this, gentlemen. Officer's call when we return."

Marcus checked in the hospital to ensure that his men were being treated. He had to pull rank on Sextus and tell the capsarius to see to him first. "Can't have a potential officer dying of such a wound. Have the men use the Batavians baths in half turma, Sextus. They have earned it." The bathhouse was outside the Batavian fort and close to the river. The Prefect had been quite happy for them to use it as it fostered good rapport between the two forces and the Prefect knew that in any attack from the north then Coriosopitum would be the frontline. This had changed from being a war zone to a battle zone.

In his office Cassius summoned Julius. He had grown fond of the fussy clerk and enjoyed using him as a sounding board despite the barbed comments he received when he made a gaffe. "You keep your ear to the ground and you do not miss too much Julius. Do we have a spy or were we sloppy with our patrols?"

The clerk sat down and picked up his pointer. As he made a point he identified it on the map. "Let us look at this logically. Any barbarian coming south either has to cross close to Vindolanda, the bridge here or at the shallows near to the island upstream. Now let us rule out this road and Vindolanda for they would have to pass the fort to get to the bridge and the ground there does not suit horses. That leaves the island. Now we have sent a patrol to that island every day and they have not reported any sign of a barbarian war band." He leaned back as though he had explained the problem away.

"I'm sorry. I don't understand you are saying it is impossible for them to have crossed the river."

Exasperated the clerk leaned forwards. "No, I am saying that they must have crossed by the island and so why did the patrol not spot their tracks?"

"Ah. And which of the turma...."

"It was the same turma each day."

"What? I thought I gave orders for them to be rotated."

"And so you did but Decurion Aelius Spartianus did deals with the other decurion to swap duties. I believe that they fear him somewhat. He is somewhat of a bully." Julius Longinus could not understand the concept, it was so illogical.

"Which means that he is a spy."

"He could be but you would need proof. He could be incompetent or lazy and it is some other man who is the spy or spies."

"So how do we find out? Torture?"

"Barbaric! Roman soldiers! Are you not born with a brain! We use our brains and set a trap. "Realising that he would have to fill in all the gaps the clerk went on. "You tell him something and no-one else, you tell him a lie and then, when that information is revealed you have him."

"So what is the lie?"

"I haven't thought of it yet. He is a clever and devious man; we will need to be subtle. I will come up with something by tomorrow in the meantime...."

"I know in the meantime don't trust him."

"Well thank goodness you worked that one out. My intelligence must be rubbing off on you."

"It is a good job I hate paperwork or you would be on a charge. Send the officers and sergeants in."

When they all trooped in Cassius saw just how much they had grown in the past months. "Firstly well done for today. It was our first action and you all acquitted yourselves well. Now until the Decurion Princeps and the other three officers return we will be shorthanded. I believe we can use this to our advantage. I have spoken with the Prefect and he agrees that we need to increase the security at the river. His men and ours are going to dig two double ditches on either side of the bridge and erect two gates, one on each end of the bridge. We will make it hard for any enemy to attack the two forts. In addition, we will have three patrols each day. They will be rotated. I have heard of some officers having informal arrangements." He was pleased that the decurions all looked at Spartianus who affected an innocent and injured look. "This will cease as of now! One of the patrols will travel up the road to the high ridge which looks north. One patrol will head west to Vindolanda and the third will head east to the sea. That means we will have eight turmae to build with one on duty. Any questions?"

"Not really a question sir but isn't it all a bit pointless. I mean it isn't as though the barbarians will attack in winter."

"Well Aelius I might have agreed with you had not a warband of fifty attempted to massacre two turmae of your comrades. Any other questions? "Every man looked at Aelius as though he had the plague. "Then dismissed."

The ten troopers chosen by Livius had been delighted to be chosen for this mission but now, as they pitched and tossed in the icy mare Germania they began to regret their joy. Few still had the contents of their stomachs much to the joy of Hercules who loved it when landsmen went to sea for the first time. He clutched, in his hand, the chart given to him by Julius Longinus. Livius was constantly amazed at what the clerk had in his trunk. All that he had said when asked was that he liked to be prepared for all eventualities. Now as they passed, well to seaward the place marked as seal islands Hercules stabbed a finger at the chart. "It seems the fleet drew these up but they didn't bother to put ashore. It looks to me like the only port south of the Bodotria is here."

Livius looked at it and compared it with the map Julius had drawn for him. "That looks like the best place then. It is just six miles from Traprain Law. The road passes through it, or near enough to it and then heads south so our two lads would be coming back down this road."

Rufius peered over his commander's shoulder. "I thought Metellus was supposed to get a ship himself?"

"I know but it struck me that was asking a little much. It is a long enough shot that they have got inside the conclave and gathered the intelligence, it is a little much to expect their luck to last to here and acquiring a boat. Besides," he said grinning, "I fancied an ocean voyage."

Hercules sniffed, "You go for an ocean voyage in the Mare Nostrum not here on the edge of the world."

"Don't worry, you won't drop off, the fleet sailed all the way around Britannia, it is an island."

"Aye, but they never went any further north or west did they? No. This is far enough north for me. Now there are a couple of problems of which you ought to be aware. Firstly if there are any big boats in the harbour we could find ourselves outmatched. Secondly, if it is a small harbour we might not fit and we might be forced to have to lie out to sea."

"If there is a bigger ship then we will take it."

"Take it! I can see that you have never fought at sea."

Rufius grinned, "Actually we have. We fought with the Classis Britannica against German pirates and we fought against deserters in Aquitania."

"As for the size of the harbour then yes, by all means, lie off the shore and await a signal. You must be safe otherwise none of us escapes." Livius and Rufius had anticipated all the problems which Hercules could throw at them.

"Well as long as that is understood. Let's get on with this because the port is just around that next headland."

Just then Furax came running along the deck. Hercules roared at him. "You never run at sea, you can slip. How many times do I have to tell you!"

"Oh, I am fine. This is much better than the seas at home. It is more exciting the way the deck goes up and down, it is like being on a horse."

"It is a pity there was no one at the fort to look after you, I can do without your ridiculous good humour."

Livius smiled at Hercules, "Now you know you don't mean that. You love the boy as much as Julius does."

"Bah! Soldiers, what do they know?" But as he stomped off to return Furax below decks Livius noticed the twinkle in his eye.

Metellus had just emerged from their hut with their weapons when he saw Macro being marched off at spear point. '*Wolf, you traitorous bastard. You will die by my hand for this.*' The silent oath and the grim look on his face were the only signs that Metellus gave of the disaster which had befallen them. They had discussed the possibility as they had ridden north and agreed that the survivor would leave the other. Metellus smiled to himself, as though that was going to happen. He could not leave the young boy to the privations, not only of the barbarians but the cruel witch who was his mother. There was an irony in that she was the high priestess of the cult of the Mother and yet she had not a maternal bone in her body.

He knew that he was now a hunted man. They had both been in each other's company and everyone in the camp knew that, besides, with Wolf in the picture he could no longer hide; Wolf knew who he was. He had to secure the means to ride to the coast, that much was obvious. He suddenly realised that the men marching with Macro were the stable sentries. They had left the stables unguarded. He raced to the stables and found their horses ready to go. They had been so close to making good their escape. Suddenly he heard a whimper from one of the stalls and he quickly drew his blade.

"Please don't hurt me, sir."

It was Morag. "You saw what happened."

"Yes, Darach. They said he was a Roman. Is he, and are you one as well?"

There was little point in a lie and, besides, Metellus thought the girl had been hurt enough. "We are. We are Roman cavalrymen."

Morag looked up at the man who was an enemy but had a kind face and thoughtful manners. The one, who had taken her love away, had had a cruel face and was evil looking. "I don't care. I still love him. He was kind and he was funny and unlike every other man and boy I know he didn't smell like a week old pole-cat!"

Metellus spied a tiny glimmer of hope. The question was could he, in all conscience, put the innocent young girl in harm's way? The reality was that he knew she was expendable. He and Macro had to return to the fort or the frontier might be lost and he could not leave the young sergeant alone. If he could he would take her with them, it might slow them up but they had three mounts; on a horse, he would bet the two of them against any. He shook his head to clear the indecision, solve each problem as it came, that was the key. He was sure that Ailis would look after her. "Then will you help us?"

"How, I am but a girl?"

In answer, Metellus slipped her a pugeo. "First, could you find where they have taken him then meet me at the gatehouse in an hour? Can you do that?" Suddenly, looking like the little girl she was and not the woman she pretended to be she nodded eagerly and ran off. Metellus vaulted on to the back of the horses and led them at a fast trot out of the camp down the road towards the coast, so close he could almost smell the salt. The track twisted down the hillside and then headed due east. At the bottom of the hill, he found a stand of trees, struggling in the poor and rocky soil. Leaving Macro's weapons there he tied the horses to the tree. With any luck, the stable sentries would think he had left and they would search for him away from the oppidum. He made his way quickly back up the hill but scrambled up the steeper slopes to avoid the path. It was fortunate that he had for he suddenly saw torches and heard voices. "There were definitely two horses saddled and they have gone along with a packhorse. If we hadn't taken the prisoner to the Queen then we would have been able to stop him."

He saw Lugubelenus and the sentries with six of his warriors appear. The King scanned the road heading east. "He cannot get far. You six men, ride to the port and see if he has tried to board a ship. I will send more men to Dun Eibhinn and in the morning I will take the rest of my guards south. We will have this spy and I will cut out his heart."

Metellus watched the six horses gallop away. So far so good, they were looking further afield than the hill fort. He could move around the camp knowing that they were looking elsewhere for him. He quickly scrambled the last few feet to the summit and then ran across the open ground to the gate. There he found Morag crying. "He is in the Queen's hut," she pointed to the roundhouse just outside the walls. There were three men standing guard outside, including Wolf.

"Who is in there with him?"

"The Queen Radha and the Witch."

"We can do nothing until they leave. When they do leave I want you to take a jug of water in. Say you were sent by the Queen to give it to the prisoner and if you get the chance slip the knife to him but," he put his hand on her arm. "Do not take any chances. If you cannot help him just leave the water."

She looked at him bravely, "I will do as you ask," then she became a little tearful, "but not if the witch is nearby. I am afeard of her."

"Good, because so am I. You are right to be afraid for she is an evil and cruel woman. Now go and get a jug of water and wait here."

"Where will you be?"

"I will get closer and see if I can overhear what they are saying."

As he closed on the hut he heard Morwenna's voice, "Wolf, get yourself in here." Metellus studied the land carefully. There were other huts close by and he could hide nearby and watch. Once the witch and the Queen left, and he hoped they would, then the sentries would die and they would escape if Macro was still alive and that was the pain nagging at Metellus' insides. He knew how cruel and evil the witch could be. If she had begun to torture her son would he be able to travel? It would be cruel to rescue him and then find he could not escape. Metellus took a deep breath; he was just making problems which did not, as yet, exist, take each step one at a time and try to solve each problem as they came.

When Wolf entered the hut, Macro was secured by four ropes to four of the central posts in the roundhouse. His leather jerkin had been removed and his tunic ripped open. His eyes showed anger and hate, not fear and he stared at the witch with the red hair, the witch who seemed so familiar and yet how could that be for he had never seen her before

191

this night? She had a sly leering smile which made her normally pretty face seem, somehow, ugly. Radha was just mesmerized. They were now in foreign territory; she had fought in battles but only killed in battle and never in cold blood. It looked like the Queen was going to use torture and she wondered how she could do that. The boy seemed suddenly so young and there was something about him which sparked a memory.

"So, Wolf. This is a Roman?"

"Aye," he spat a gob of phlegm at Macro which landed on his chest.

"Now Wolf, he is a guest. Behave. Who is he? He seems a little young to be a spy."

"Don't be fooled, my Queen. This boy is a sergeant and he was an Explorate, a Roman spy." He looked at Radha. "He fought against you with the Ninth and gained fame as one of the lads with the eagle."

Radha suddenly looked at Macro as though for the first time. "Now it comes back. There were two of them at the end when we had them surrounded and they fought like heroes. I can believe it, my sister, he may look young but this is a warrior. He is tougher than he looks."

Morwenna went to the fire and took a piece of burning wood from it. "So a spy and a hero." She blew on the brand to enrage it. "And, according to the Queen, tough. How tough I wonder?" She put the burning brand on the gob of phlegm which sizzled and steamed and then pushed it on to sear Macro's flesh. Radha wrinkled her nose at the smell of hair and skin burning but Macro never uttered a sound, he just stared at his torturer with pure hatred in his eyes.

"See I told you, tough."

"What do you think he was doing here Wolf? Trying to kill someone or to spy on us?"

"He could do both. He defeated the best fighter I knew, a friend of mine back in the ala. His father had been a great fighter too. They have the same name but I think that he was here to find out what was going on."

"And where is your companion?"

"He wasn't alone?" Wolf looked over in surprise.

Morwenna suddenly realised that Wolf had never met Metellus. "He had a companion, called him his brother."

"He does have a brother, about the same age and equally good with a sword."

"No, this one was older with a little grey at his temples."

"Metellus!"

192

"You traitor, Wolf, you will die for this." Although weak from the pain Macro hurled the words with all the venom he could.

In answer, Wolf punched the helpless trooper in the ribs enjoying the noise as two of the young man's ribs snapped and broke. "If Metellus is here then I had better look for him. He is a dangerous bastard."

When Wolf left to seek out the other spy Morwenna took Macro's left hand in hers and began to stroke it tenderly, it seemed incongruous to Radha. "So you are a warrior. I knew a warrior once, he is now dead and I am glad although sad that I did not have the opportunity to watch him die." The Red Witch was looking carefully at the young red-haired sergeant and a memory was sparked. "Warriors need their hands do they not? I wonder if they need their fingernails." She took her knife and, very carefully, slit the skin on his left hand just where the nail met the thumb. The cut opened like a ripe, fresh fig, red and raw. She then took a pair of pliers and began to slowly pull the nail out of its, now severed, bed. She pulled as slowly as possible to make sure the pain would be excruciating. Although tears of pain trickled down his cheeks, Macro made not a sound. His hatred for the witch and Wolf drove the pain to the dim recesses of his consciousness. Radha could feel the bile rising in her throat but she was hypnotised by the cruelty of her mentor. Although there was little blood Morwenna took a burning brand and sealed the wound shut. "Wouldn't want you getting an infection now, would we? We need you to last as long as possible before you die."

Radha looked at Macro and felt admiration for him. Even though he had fought against her she remembered the courage of those who had fought for the eagle. Here too, he was showing more courage than many men she had known. She wanted Morwenna to stop but she knew she would not and she knew that her mentor would think less of her if she did so. "I don't think he is going to talk."

"Neither do I but it is a long time since I was able to enjoy myself like this. Sergeant, I think you could at least tell me your name. That way when you die we can record it and your courage will be remembered. Would you not like to die with your true name and not the lie that you gave us when you lived here as a spy?"

Macro could see no harm in telling her that simple fact, reflecting he realised that he would be proud to, as it would afford him the same glorious death as his father. "I am Sergeant Decius Macro Culleo, the son of the greatest warrior in Marcus' Horse, Decurion Macro Culleo."

Morwenna laughed a blood-curdling laugh which almost made the guards outside rush in and which caused Metellus to shiver as he heard it. "Oh Radha, the Mother was watching over us this night for this…

this thing is the child I never wanted, the child I abandoned and hoped was dead, this is my son." She leaned over and kissed him hard on the lips. "I am your mother and I am going to enjoy your death!"

Chapter 20

As *'The Swan'* came around the headland Livius could see that the harbour entrance would be a little tight for the ship to negotiate safely. Hercules shook his head. "We could be trapped in there and they could block us in with a fishing boat. I will land you on the seaward side of the stone breakwater. You will have to signal me when you want me to come in for you."

Livius knew that the captain was right, "Rufius get the men and be ready to get over the side as soon as we are within jumping distance of that wall."

Rufius looked down at Livius' legs, "You up to a jump sir? I mean I know you are better than you were but…"

"Thank you for your concern, Rufius, but I will be safe enough."

Hercules barked orders out as he tried to get the ship as close as possible. He had to time it perfectly or he could be dashed against the rocks and their escape plan ended before it had begun. "Get the foresail down! Put the spare sail and ropes over the side, I don't want the rocks to hole us." To Livius, he shouted, "I will barely touch and then I will have to head out to sea. You will all have to jump at the same time."

"Rufius get the men along the side and be ready to jump on my command." He could see the selected men with bows and shields slung over their backs. They were encumbered but Livius had no way of knowing how many Votadini and other enemies they would have to face.

"Get the oars unshipped and be ready to push us off. Ready Livius?" Livius waved and the captain pushed the tiller hard over. The back surge from the breakwater held the boat up enough for it to almost kiss the rocks and Hercules shouted, "Now!"

The twelve men all leapt the eight feet or so to the rocky breakwater. Miraculously only one slipped into the water, his caligae not finding any purchase on the weed-covered rocks but his companions on either side pulled him up to safety and Livius watched as *'The Swan'* slowly turned to move slowly away from the shore.

Rufius and two men had raced down the breakwater as soon as their feet touched the rocks. The sharp-eyed scout could see the small oppidum on the opposite side of the harbour but he had no way of knowing if they kept a night watch. There was nothing which he could do about that eventuality anyway. At the end of the breakwater, he and his two scouts formed a defensive arc and scanned the few huts ahead. They appeared to be in darkness, their owners probably asleep. Rufius had worried that the shouted commands would have alerted the inhabitants but all he could hear was the sound of the sea breaking relentlessly on the rocks. They appeared to have landed successfully and he felt Livius tap him on the shoulder and point to the gap where the river flowed into the harbour and they could see a primitive wooden bridge. Rufius led his men at a jog and crossed over the bridge, spying the track which emerged from the gloom in the west. By the time Livius had joined them Rufius had sent his two scouts to the road where they guarded the entrance of the small port.

Livius led the troopers along the track to join the scouts and Rufius saw that he was limping. When they stopped at the road, three hundred paces from the nearest house Rufius knelt down and examined the bleeding scar on Livius' leg. Livius shrugged, "It's not so bad."

In answer, Rufius took out the bandage from his pouch and the herbs. He rubbed the herbs he had brought with him, on to the leg and then tied the bandage tightly. "You won't be going far with that sir."

"None of us will Livius. We will wait here until we see our boys."

"Suppose they have gone or they are delayed. We cannot expect that we have come at exactly the right time."

"No, but we can hide up there in the woods." He pointed to the tree-lined hills. "Besides Julius and I worked out how long it would take them to get here and how long it might take to get the information. The earliest would have been tonight." He pointed back to the harbour. "No fishing boats! If Metellus and Macro were here they would be waiting for a boat. No, we are on time, I hope." He peered up the track as though willing the two troopers to appear. "Rufius send your scouts about a mile up the road. They will give us warning of any movement, friendly or otherwise and then send two to keep watch on the settlement. The fact that the boats are at sea bodes well for it means there are unlikely to be many men in the town."

Wolf reappeared at the hut. "Your majesties. King Lugubelenus has summoned you to the main hall."

"Has he found the other warrior?"

"No Queen Radha, but they have discovered three horses are missing. He has escaped. The King wants a council."

"Has he summoned all the kings?"

"No majesty, just King Tole and yourselves."

Morwenna was reluctant to leave off her task of torturing her son but she needed to be with the two kings whose plans she was directing. She could control both men, one through her own charms and one through Radha; besides there would be time to continue her torture later and at her leisure. She found that she wanted this more than she knew. She had hated Macro and had wanted to kill him. She had hated her child and wanted him dead. Now she had the chance to do both at the same time; to pay back her dead husband and to kill their son who bore the same name. The delay would only increase the boy's pain as the two wounds he had suffered began to throb and pulse as the blood flowed again to the damaged parts. Yes, this was the Mother's doing, she was aiding Morwenna to exact the maximum revenge on those men she loathed. "Guard him well but, Wolf, inflict no more pain, that pleasure is reserved for me."

Wolf felt the full force of the green eyes and the latent power of the witch queen and he nodded. He watched as the two Queens swept out of the hut. As the door closed he noticed a slight lightening of the skies. Within a few hours, it would be dawn and they could begin to search for the missing Metellus.

As soon as he saw the two queens return to the main compound Metellus strung his bow. Now was his chance. He hoped that Morag would create a distraction but he could not count on it. He was just glad that Wolf was inside for it left him only two men, outside, to deal with. He could take one with an arrow and then cover the thirty paces to the second and use his sword to despatch him. He pulled the bow back and chose the man furthest away. At this range, he would have no possibility of missing and he could choose his target to within an uncia. He chose the throat, he wanted silence. He was just about to release when he saw Morag approach with a jug of water.

"The Queen sent me." The two guards looked at each other in indecision. "Queen Radha will not be pleased if her commands are not obeyed."

'*Good girl*', thought Metellus as they opened the door for her. When the two guards faced outwards again Metellus released and, slinging his bow with one hand, drew his sword with the other. The arrow struck the guard in the neck, a look of surprised horror on his face as he fell, dead. The second guard panicked and looked for the archer, turning to look in Metellus' direction the sword sliced swiftly into his throat, silently ending his life as his arterial blood gurgled through the ripped opening.

Inside Wolf turned to look at the girl. "What are you doing in here?"

Bravely Morag stood up to Wolf. "The Queen sent me."

"You lying little bitch." He threw the jug to the floor where it shattered and then he backhanded her across the face. Drawing his knife

197

he grinned evilly. "It has been a long time since I had a woman, even a scrawny little bitch like you; I am going to enjoy this."

"Leave her alone you sick bastard." Macro struggled against the bonds, ignoring the pain which pulsed through his body from his wounds. On the floor, Morag tried to edge her way away from this evil-looking man.

"It's a good job the Queen said not to harm you or I would have your bollocks on the floor now."

Metellus opened the door and the movement caught Wolf's eye. He whirled around, the dagger flying from his hand before he saw who it was. Although Metellus avoided the blade he was forced to move to the side allowing Wolf the opportunity to draw his own blade. "Metellus! I am going to enjoy this and when I take your head to the King I will be rewarded handsomely. Maybe even become a general, how about that for a trooper?"

Metellus stabbed forward with his sword. "Make sure you have beaten me first, traitor."

Wolf easily deflected the blade and pulling his dagger from his belt attacked with two weapons. Wolf was younger and smaller; in the confines of the hut, he had the advantage. Macro struggled against his ropes as he tried to free himself and help his friend. Morag struggled to her feet and, taking the pugeo from beneath her shift she started to saw through the ropes which bound Macro. Wolf sensed the movement behind him and he slashed, blindly, with his own dagger making Morag duck in fear. The opening was all that Metellus needed and he thrust his blade forward with his sword aiming at Wolf's throat. The deserter desperately tried to deflect the blade but he only managed to push it towards his left arm where the point stabbed into the muscle at the top of his arm. Involuntarily Wolf dropped the weapon and then countered at Metellus' head. Metellus dropped and thrust upwards at Wolf's unprotected stomach. As his sword entered Metellus twisted; he could not afford to continue the fight, they needed to escape. Wolf had the shocked look of surprise that comes from someone who underestimated his opponent. He had always thought Metellus to be a gentle and thoughtful man and would have been easily dispatched, as he tried to push his entrails back into the gaping wound, he tried to question Metellus but, instead, he fell into a dying heap.

Metellus had no time for congratulations and he used his sword to sever the last two ropes. Metellus and Morag looked in horror at the raw wounds on Macro's body. The young sergeant just gave a painful grin. "It's not so bad; you want to see the other fellow."

They both helped him to his unsteady feet. "Can you walk?"

"Yes, they hadn't got to them yet."

Metellus turned to Morag. "Thank you. You can stay here. No one knows you helped us."

Morag looked at Macro and said in a determined voice, "I have no home here. I will come with you. Even if you do not want me."

Macro looked indecisive and Metellus cursed mentally. That was all that he needed, a lover's quarrel. He had no time to waste and Morag could at least help Macro. "Right. You can come with us, at least until we get to the horses. We have to get down the summit to the mounts." He took them outside and was horrified to see that the sky was even lighter than it had been. He took the cloaks, bloodied though they were, from the dead sentries and their spears. "Here put these on and hold the spears. We walk through the camp as though we are guards. Walk slowly and keep the cloaks above your heads."

It was the longest walk of any of their lives. In the oppidum, they could hear the sound of men being called to arms and torches flickering. Groups of soldiers were marching across the camp looking, to Metellus' relief, just like them. No-one appeared to pay them any attention. They passed through the camp of the retainers who were now being awoken as the news of the flight of the prisoner spread. Metellus only hoped that no-one would notice the two dead guards before they had reached their horses. As they walked down the winding path from the oppidum, Metellus wondered how he would deal with the six riders sent to the port. Macro was in no position to help him. One problem at a time ran through his mind. He had to get to the horses first and then he could plan for his next problem.

"The Allfather watches over us today Macro," Metellus said as he heard the welcoming whinny of their mounts. He had worried that they had either been spotted or worse, escaped, for afoot they stood no chance. "Morag do you ride?"

In answer, she sprang on to the back of one of the saddled horses. "I'll take that as a yes. Macro, get on the other saddle horse and I will ride the spare." He helped Macro on to the horse. He saw his young companion as he caught first his wounded chest on the saddle and then his thumb on the reins. "You are doing well Macro. Just hang on and leave the thinking and the fighting to me."

As Metellus mounted Macro said. "What is the plan?"

"Try to get a boat from the port but," he added, "there are six warriors waiting for us."

As Metellus led them down the road Macro, riding behind Morag, asked, "Why not ride across country?"

Suddenly from the camp came a huge roar. "I think they have discovered the bodies of the sentries so that will not be an option. It is the port or nothing. We cannot outrun the barbarians for long."

Livius looked behind at the slowly lightening sky. "I think, Rufius, that we may have to hide soon. He pointed out to sea where on the horizon were little spots of white."

"The fishing fleet."

"Aye. I wonder what they will make of '*The Swan*'."

"At least Hercules has arms for his crew. They may be able to help."

Just then the two scouts came rushing down the track. "Riders, six of them."

The second scout added, "And they are not our men."

Livius quickly ordered. "Riders coming on horses. Ambush!"

The well-trained men took positions on either side of the road, their bows aimed at some point in the middle of the track and ahead of them. They heard and smelled the horses before they saw them. They all had to hide in whatever cover there was to avoid being silhouetted in the lightening sky. Rufius was at the front to the ambush with Livius closest to the port. The six warriors had not raced along the track from the hill fort. They had taken their time to watch for places their fugitive might have left the road. They were convinced that he had not preceded them as there were no tracks on the frosty trail. They were the first to travel that way. Their leader looked ahead to the watchtower on the headland. "We'll wait up there. If he does come down the trail we will see him easily."

They were the last words he spoke as two arrows thudded into his unprotected chest. Rufius' arrow took out the rearmost man and the other four soon fell to the arrows of the Romans. "Get rid of the bodies. Rufius mount up three men and ride up the trail. See if you can get within a mile of the oppidum. If these six were hunting Metellus then we might have missed him. Don't hang around." Rufius chose his men and trotted up the trail which was now a little clearer. The Decurion Princeps began to wonder had he underestimated his men. They might have escaped already and he would have put his men in jeopardy for nothing.

Livius turned to one of the troopers. "Go down to the breakwater, avoid being seen by the fishing boats and signal '*The Swan*'. I think we may need to leave in a hurry." It was not going to plan. He had heard the warrior's words and felt his heart sinking. He had said 'he' and not 'them'. Only one had survived but which one? With a sickening feeling in the pit of his stomach, he could not say which one he wanted to be found.

Metellus heard the noise of the horses in the distance. He estimated they had just over a mile start but just ahead were six warriors who were trying to close the door on his escape. He strung an arrow to his bow. If he saw them he would have no time to think; he would just have to react. He glanced over his shoulder, Morag could ride and was easily coping with the fast pace he had set. Metellus had decided that there was little point in saving their horses. They had to reach the port before their pursuers. Suddenly he saw movement ahead and heard hooves. He pulled his horse up and then aimed his bow. He saw the rider no more than thirty paces to his front and he began to release the arrow. Just as his fingers let go of the arrow he recognised Rufius and his left hand jerked the bow to the left.

Rufius felt the arrow sing over his shoulder and then he too recognised Metellus. "A nice way to greet a friend."

"No time for niceties, we have the whole of the barbarian horde on our tails."

"Livius is up ahead, we have '*The Swan*'. We'll cover your back." The troopers spread out in an arc, their bows at the ready.

Livius looked up and thanked the Allfather when he saw Metellus, Macro and a strange girl arrive. He had no time for questions. He just pointed to the sea. "Get down to the port and get aboard '*The Swan*'." He pointed to a trooper. "You take them. Where is Rufius?"

"Waiting for our pursuers. I'll wait here with you. Macro is wounded."

Livius slapped the rump of Macro's Horse. "Go! Go!" He glanced at Metellus who had turned his horse to face the road and notched an arrow. "Get the information?"

"Yes but they know I am a spy so it may be useless." He shrugged. "I'll explain if we get out of this."

Rufius' sharp eyes picked out the first scouts who were hurtling down the road. They had a chance. The pursuers were so keen to get their hands on their prey that they had thrown caution to the wind. Rufius said, out of the side of his mouth. "They must all die. I'll take the last man."

There were six men and they found themselves facing a volley of arrows which took four out of the saddle immediately. Rufius took out his sword and spitted a fifth and the last man fell to three arrows. "Right lads back to the Decurion Princeps. That should slow them."

The six dead men were Selgovae and when Tole and Lugubelenus arrived they halted their men. "Spread out. They are here and these men were ambushed." Tole took charge and Lugubelenus showed his displeasure with a grimace.

One of the scouts shouted, "They were killed by Roman arrows."

"Then there are more. Move but be very cautious. They may have another ambush set up."

'*The Swan*' was edging its way into the breakwater. Hercules kept glancing over his shoulder at the fishing fleet which was getting ever closer. So far they were just curious but once they saw the Romans on the jetty then anything could happen. "Furax! Get the weapons on the deck and put them at regular intervals along the side. We may have a fight on our hands."

Furax trotted off happily and Hercules shook his head. To the young boy, this was all an exciting game but if there was a fight then it would be a deadly game in which his young life might be suddenly ended. He saw to his relief at least six people at the breakwater. He looked again; one of them looked to be a girl!

Livius and Metellus were glad to see Rufius. "They are right behind us."

Livius turned to his men as the bell in the watchtower began to toll its alarm. "That's it, they know we are here. Double riders and back to the ship." There were five horses and seven of them so two horses carried two troopers but it made their route back to the boat that much quicker. As they reached the breakwater they saw that Macro and the others were perched on the end awaiting '*The Swan*' which was tacking around to enable a swift getaway. The fishing fleet, alerted by the Roman uniforms and tolling bell were now heading for the ship.

"Shit! That's all we needed."

"Well Rufius, at least we have a fighting chance." Smacking the horse's rumps to send them away the seven men ran as quickly as they could over the slippery, weed-covered breakwater. Their horses ran straight back the way they had come, heading for their stables six miles away. They delayed Tole and Lugubelenus as they negotiated their way around the frightened mounts.

Morag looked in terror at the foaming water between her and '*The Swan*'. Macro too was worried but he found that his fear subsided as he gave Morag instructions. Aboard the ship, they could see a cheerful-looking boy who yelled, "Jump! We will catch you."

The sailor next to Furax grinned at the boy's confidence. "Come on, the lad is right, we'll catch you!

"Go on Morag. I'll be right behind you." Over his shoulder, Macro saw the rest of the troopers arrive and, close behind over a hundred warriors. Closing her eyes the brave Morag leapt and felt her body being lifted carefully over the side. Macro jumped the moment he saw her being pulled over but his damaged left hand hit the side of the ship the pain from his wound made him pull back and, suddenly, he was hanging by one arm above the sharp teeth of the rocky breakwater. Before he could plunge to his death he found himself hauled up by the grinning sailors.

"You'll have to take lessons from the young lady sir."

The rest of the troopers flung themselves at the side as arrows from their pursuers clattered on to the rocky breakwater. Hercules saw that the last man, Rufius was aboard and he yelled, "Push us off with the oars!"

The oars, which were stacked by the weapons, were grabbed by sailors and troopers alike and their combined effort pushed their bow so that it was facing out to sea. The arrows from the shore were now hitting the deck. "Get your bows and fire back!" The eleven bows used by superb archers cleared the end of the breakwater and a mound of bodies marked their demise.

Hercules shouted above the cheering crew. "I'd do something about the fishing boats first before I'd start celebrating."

Ahead of them, the fleet had spread out in an arc to prevent their escape. Livius shouted, "Troopers to the bow." In his mind, he knew that he could not slaughter the fishermen who were just bystanders in this but he needed to escape. "Shoot over the heads of the helmsmen. Don't kill them. Just make them turn." Rufius looked at him as though to say why? In answer, Livius shouted, "They are not soldiers just scare them."

They were the best ten archers in the ala and they used it as target practice. Once the arrows began to remove hats and thud into the rudders the less brave began to edge their boats away from this potentially deadly foe. Hercules saw the gap and felt the wind pick up from the north-west. "Hoist the mainsail!" As soon as the wind caught the massive mainsail '*The Swan*' leapt forward like a deer, knocking two boats out of the way. Where they had been in imminent danger of being trapped suddenly, they were heading south into a brightening sky. They had escaped.

Chapter 21

Cassius smiled as Aelius Spartianus strolled casually and confidently into the Principia. "Ah good of you to join me Aelius. I have a delicate matter to discuss with you." He lowered his voice implying that he was going to share some secret with him. "As you know the Decurion Princeps is away from the fort at this moment and the men are wondering why. I can tell you that he is on a delicate and secret mission. He has been to Eboracum to bring up reinforcements to repel this potential invasion from the north. He only has Rufius and Metellus with him. I am worried now that as with Marcus, he may be ambushed along the road. I would like you to take your turma and ride south to the Dunum and wait for him there. He will not have the reinforcements yet for they have a long way to come and travelling alone he will be vulnerable. I know that he would not have asked for this help but I will feel easier if you are there to protect him."

"Of course sir, I am honoured that you think of me. Reinforcements?" Spartianus' mind was rapidly working out how to get this message to his spymaster quickly. He couldn't resist a slight smile creeping on to this face. He would be rewarded and the Decurion Princeps killed in one fell swoop.

"Yes, apparently a legion has been sent for. Don't know which one yet but that is good news eh Aelius?"

"The best I have heard in a while. Should I take extra rations in case we have to wait for him?"

"Good idea."

"I'll go and tell the men. We should be able to leave in a couple of hours."

"Very well."

After he had gone Julius popped his head around the door. "Did he bite?"

"I think so but we will know when Decurion Gracchus reports."

It was some hours later that Cassius heard the unmistakable sound of the turma leaving the fort to head south. A short time later Drusus came in clutching a red cloth. "So he went to the island."

"Just like you said sir, he went to the hollow tree and put the cloth where it could be seen. He looked north of the river and shouted 'Wolf' for a few minutes and then came back to the fort."

"Good you have done well. Mount up your turma and we will go and arrest this traitor."

'*The Swan*' was making good progress south. The capsarius trooper was with Morag and Furax tending to Macro's wounds. Furax appeared to have a morbid fascination with them whilst Morag was tearful. Livius stood apart, with Metellus and Rufius, at the stern where Hercules was pretending disinterest. "Before we get to Macro and the girl, what of the plans?"

Metellus sighed, for he felt that they had let Livius and the ala down. "I don't know sir. I may have failed in the mission. It was all going so well. They thought we were leaders from the islands and the King of the Votadini, Lugubelenus, he actually heeded and appreciated my advice. They were planning an all-out attack on Coriosopitum which I knew would be a disaster for the fort and the frontier." He looked back at the coast, disappearing behind them and gestured, "They have every tribe on their side. The only one not there was the Brigante but as Morwenna is their Queen, well they may join anyway."

"So what did you suggest?"

"Three attacks on our main forts." He shrugged. "He thought it was a good idea. There is still distrust especially between the Selgovae and the Votadini. He liked the idea of splitting his forces. I thought we had a better chance of defeating them bit by bit rather than all of them attacking just us and the Batavians. Perhaps I was wrong."

"No I think that you were right but why do you think it has failed?"

"They know who we are. Wolf was in the camp and he recognised Macro. Morwenna got her hands on him."

The three of them looked at the sergeant who was being bandaged. "Does he know?"

"That Morwenna is his mother? He does now. She didn't seem to know him at first but the second she did it seemed to make her worse than ever. She began to torture him. It was she who pulled out his nail and burned him. It was horrible to watch. She is not a woman; she is some fell beast from Hades."

Rufius pointed at Morag. "And the girl?"

"She fell for Macro and a good thing too. She is the daughter of the King of the Dumnonii and without her, we wouldn't have escaped so easily. I gave her the chance to stay but she wanted to leave." He shrugged apologetically. "Perhaps you were wrong to send me sir. Seems like I made a couple of bad decisions."

Livius put his arm around the decurion's shoulders. "I can't see that. You were right to bring the girl; in fact, we can work it to our advantage."

Metellus and Rufius looked at Livius, "How?"

"When Agricola came north he didn't always fight his enemies. Sometimes he bribed them and sometimes he took hostages. Does her father know she came of her own free will?"

"Well no."

"In that case, we send a message to the Dumnonii that she is a hostage against his behaviour. Perhaps it will stop him joining with the enemy."

Metellus thought back to the fat old king and realised that Livius was right. "I think that would work and the old man has a lot of influence. He might start others to question the war."

"As for the plan; it was as good a plan as any. I can send messages to the other two forts and they can prepare to resist an invasion. We can get more troops from the south, bring up the Morbium garrison. We now know that they will attack and we know where."

"But sir if they know it was me they may revert to their original plan and attack Coriosopitum."

"The same thing applies. We improve the defences and use troops from further south. Now that '*The Swan*' has made it up the Tinea we can use the Classis Britannica to support us."

"If the Governor will allow it."

Livius hated the fact that his men did not know as much as him. The Classis Britannica would receive their orders not from the Governor but from the Emperor. "Don't worry about that. I can be persuasive."

"Sir about Macro… His mother said some fairly disgusting things to him. He will need someone to talk to him. I could but… well sir you have known him longer."

"You are quite right and I should have thought of it. Get some rest and I will go and talk with him." As Metellus and Rufius made to go Livius restrained Metellus' arm, "It was not you Metellus, it was the Parcae that allowed Wolf to return when he did. You were about to escape. Who knows what the Allfather and the Parcae intend. Perhaps he wanted Macro to know who his mother is." He shrugged his shoulders. "We are but tools in their hands Metellus."

Macro tried to rise as Livius approached. "No, don't get up. Furax, could you take Morag here and show her where the galley is. I am sure that Macro could do with some food inside him." She looked at him sceptically and Livius continued, "Go on. I want to talk to Macro."

"Now don't you tire him out. I won't be long." She glared at him accusingly. The capsarius hid the grin and went to deal with the other minor wounds incurred in the skirmish.

The Last Frontier

Macro sat holding his damaged thumb in his right hand. He appeared to be studying it as though to work out the effect it would have on his weapon skills. "You have had a rough few days. I wouldn't worry about the thumb, the nail will grow back."

"Oh, I am not worried, sir. And I am all right."

Livius held Macro's chin in his hand so that he had to look him in the eye. "Now young Macro, I have known you since you were a child. I commanded you in the Explorates and I know you as well as any man. You are not all right and bottling it up inside will not help you."

"Did you know sir?"

Livius had been dreading the question. "About your mother?" Macro nodded. "We all did, everyone that is, apart from Decius and Marcus."

He looked accusingly at Livius. "Then why didn't you tell me? Why didn't someone tell me?"

"Would it have done any good? Every time someone mentioned your mother would you have been able to take the comments? Would you have been able to do your duty knowing that your mother was an enemy?"

"But I know now don't I?"

"Yes, but you also know how she feels about you and that is different. If Gaius and Ailis had told you that you were hated and abandoned would you have believed them?"

He said weakly, "If they had told me that Morwenna was my...."

"Macro?"

"Probably not." His eyes filled with tears and looked pleadingly at the Decurion Princeps. "Why did she hate my father?"

"That goes back to her mother. Your father and the ala put her to death and she swore revenge on all of them. From what I can gather she hates most men. I heard a rumour that she has buried her children who were male and she only raises girls."

"Then how did I survive?"

"I don't know. I think the Allfather was watching over you." Furax and Morag reappeared. "I will leave you now to think about what I have said. If we have done you wrong then I apologise for all of us but Gaius and Ailis, they have been good parents to you have they not, even though you are not their trueborn son?"

His eyes shone in anger, "Of course! The best and I will kill anyone who says otherwise!"

"Then think on that Macro and thank the Allfather for providing you with two such caring people."

207

Morwenna was incandescent with rage when Tole and Lugubelenus returned empty handed. "You have let them slip away! You have failed to stop the Romans becoming aware of our plans! Are all men such fools?"

Radha unconsciously began to move away from Morwenna. She had never seen her like this, her face suffused with anger, where was her peace and calm now? Suddenly her beautiful features were criss-crossed with angry lines and Radha wondered had she really known Morwenna.

Lugubelenus and Tole were equally angry. Women did not chastise kings! If she had not been the Red Witch then both of them would have already put her in her place but she was the high priestess of her order and both men bit their tongues and took the abuse. Lugubelenus vowed he would speak with his wife for he no longer wanted Morwenna as an ally; it was more trouble than it was worth. He reflected that he did not need her; he now had his allies. The conclave, whilst not his idea, had worked and the tribes were, largely, allied.

Tole for his part knew that he could do without the Queen. It had been interesting to have an older experienced woman and she certainly knew her way around his body but there were many women to be had and he was young and puissant; he could do without her. He secretly knew that she had killed his father and for that he was grateful but now that he had the power he would use it. King Lugubelenus had played into his hands by giving him command of the army which would attack Luguvalium and that would be his springboard to greater glory and conquest. Perhaps one day he would become High King.

Morwenna looked at them both and pitied them. They would invade Roman Britannia, she knew that, but they would not listen to her. She would return to her island with her warriors. Now she knew that her son lived she had another purpose; she and her daughters would work to end his life. "You may attempt to invade Britannia but they know you are coming. You could not even catch a wounded man, a girl and one warrior so how will you defeat the Roman army. You were lucky the first time Lugubelenus," the king bridled at the lack of title but suffered the humiliation, "you had your Queen with you. Let us see how you manage without her. Come Radha we will return to Manavia."

She turned to leave the Great Hall but Radha moved next to her husband. "Thank you, sister, for all that you have taught me. I truly believe that we will become better rulers thanks to you. Thank you for the peace and calm you have brought to my angry soul."

The irony was not lost on Morwenna whose green eyes flashed hatred for them all. For the first time, her sexual powers were waning;

she had been rejected by a man and a woman. "And I thought you and I could have achieved such greatness! Stay here with the fool of a man and you will achieve nought. Idwal!"

The great door slammed and echoed as Queen Morwenna summoned her men and rode furiously back to her island fortress. The three of them looked at each other. Radha used the moment to her advantage. It was time for her to regain her rightful place as Lugubelenus' confidante. "She is correct in one respect."

Lugubelenus had recovered his dignity. "How is that, my love?"

"The Romans know two plans, you will either follow the Roman spy's advice and attack on three fronts or you will attack Coriosopitum. Either way, they can prepare. We will no longer have the element of surprise."

"Are you saying we put off the invasion? The longer we do so the more chance they have to prepare."

"No, I am saying let us discuss with the other kings and chiefs on our best course of action."

Tole shook his head. He could see a way to increase his power and influence. "None came up with any ideas before and I believe their confidence in us will be shaken if we ask them a second time for advice and counsel. Perhaps there is a third way."

They looked at the young warrior who looked to be a muscle-bound warrior and nought else. "Go on. Explain."

"What if we attacked two fortresses, Coriosopitum and Luguvalium, at the same time. The Romans would still be expecting you to attack Vindolanda and the smaller forts. They would not commit their reserves and those forts would be waiting for an attack which would not materialise. With each of us having a larger army then victory would be assured and the forts in the centre would be isolated. I could push to join you at Eboracum and together drive south before they have time to react."

Lugubelenus could see much merit in the plan but he was also wise enough to see the ulterior motive. Tole would have an army as big as his. He looked again at the young man. He could become a threat in the future but Lugubelenus was confident enough in his own ability as a leader to believe that, if the young man tried to wrest power from him, he could defeat him. "I like your plan. Together we will put it to the conclave tonight at the true start of Yule."

Livius was almost sad that the voyage had ended. They had entered the estuary of the Tinea and, under a shortened foresail were tacking back and forth to travel the few miles to Coriosopitum. Livius and his two decurions took the opportunity to examine the banks of both sides of the estuary. The found a place, just before a large bend in the river where another bridge could be built, at some time in the future and that one would be easier to defend. It would all go into the next missive to Julius Demetrius.

"You would have to build a fort at either end and it would prevent ships sailing to Coriosopitum."

"When I was in Surrentum the Emperor said he was looking for a border which could be defended. Perhaps the Tinea is that border."

"To be truthful, I have seen nothing further north that is in any way worth dying for."

"Did you see any reason, closer to the Votadini capital, which might be worth defending? That surely must be important to them if they placed their capital there."

Metellus thought about it and Livius smiled. His decurion always gave weighty thought to any question and his answers were usually illuminating. Rufius, always impatient, tapped his fingers on the ship's side. "If you looked at the people we met and spoke to, they were poor. Even the nobles lacked clothes of quality. We thought that we would look like ordinary folk in our Explorate gear but we fitted in with the best families in our ragged, worn travelling clothes. They do not use fine beakers and platters, even at the King's table and Septimus produces far better food."

"What exactly are you saying?"

"Rufius do not be impatient and listen to Metellus. He has answered me. If the richest in the land are poorer than we, then what could we gain from taking over such a desolate country? Why just down the coast from here there are more valuable materials to be had with the holy black stones that Hercules is taking back to Rome. Now those mines are worth hanging on to. The lime mines at Morbium and the stone quarries, they are worth hanging on to. Further north? I think I agree with Metellus. It isn't worth dying for."

Rufius did not look convinced. Metellus said slowly, "Rufius, they use turf to burn on their fires! Not wood but turf."

Furax sat watching the river slide by; he had left Morag and Macro as they did not seem to be in a talkative mood. Hercules might moan but he would always listen to and answer Furax's interminable questions. "I like '*The Swan*'."

"Well that is very good of you I am sure. "

"Can I sail with you again?"

"When you are older and learn not to race along my deck."

"You mean I can? I will ask the senator when we return because he owns me."

Hercules looked at the boy. "He does not own you and he would be offended that you thought so."

"But I thought that..."

"Well you thought wrong. Do you think you are treated like a slave?"

"Well no but I thought that was because the Senator was a kind master."

"He is but he is your guardian. He is looking after you, keeping you safe until you can look after yourself."

"Will I need a trade then."

"Well yes, every man needs a trade or else he is worthless, a slave."

The young boy who had lived on the streets of the Lupanar and grown up too quickly looked off at the bluffs on either side and eventually said, "The whore masters are rich. I shall be a whore master."

"You don't set your sights very high do you? There are better trades than that. More honest trades than letting girls and boys be used like that."

His young face wrinkled at the memories. "You are right. They were sad and that is not fair." He considered again and then, looking slyly at Hercules said, "I have it. I shall be a sailor."

Snorting but with a smile on his face Hercules said, "I will be glad when I deliver you back to your guardian."

Morag was feeling sad and unhappy. Macro didn't seem interested in her any more. She knew that Morwenna had done something to him but she could make his life so much better. She wondered if the witch had put a spell on him, preventing him from returning her affection; she would have to ask someone but then it dawned on her, she had taken herself away from her family and she had no-one now. She had been a fool. Suddenly her family didn't seem as bad as when she had run away. She began to cry, the tears flooding down her face.

Rufius went to comfort her but Metellus restrained him. "No, old friend, let us see if tears from another can heal Macro." Rufius looked at Metellus as though he was speaking a foreign language. But then most times Metellus confused him.

"Don't cry Morag. It will be all right," Macro put his good arm around her shoulder.

She looked at him, her young eyes were suddenly old. "Why? You do not love me. You used me to get out of the camp and now I have left my family and I am alone and I hate myself."

Macro looked over to Metellus, his eyes pleading for help but Metellus shrugged and pointed his hand at Macro. "Look, Morag, my mother and my father, well not Morwenna obviously, but the parents who raised me are the best and most kind people in the world. They will give you a home and look after you and my father would help you to get back home in the spring."

She sniffed back her tears. "Where do they live? "

"Half a day south of here. They have a lovely farm with horses and it is beautiful."

"I like horses. My father promised me one when I married."

"I will give you one as soon as we reach the farm."

She threw her arms around him and hugged him. Rufius looked at Metellus and shook his head. "Sometimes I think that you are a witch or at the very least descended from one. How do you do it?"

Metellus said, seriously, "Don't even say that in jest Rufius. I have had enough of witches to last a lifetime. And as for my skill? I watch people and I listen. You ought to try it some time."

The bridge at Coriosopitum hove into view. "The tide is turning Livius and I will need all the daylight I can get to return to the sea. This will be a quick turnaround."

Clasping his arm Livius said, "Thank you old friend and thank the senator. You have those letters for him?"

"Aye, including the one you wrote this morning."

As soon as the gangplank was down Macro and Morag left first, shouting their goodbyes, Morag was excited once more. The troopers left next exchanging banter with the sailors. Finally, the three decurions took their leave. "Next time you come to see us Furax, we will show you the country properly."

Very seriously he shouted, holding tightly on to Hercules, "Next time I come I shall be a sailor." Although he lifted his eyes to the skies, Livius could tell that Hercules would indeed make the street urchin into a sailor. Hercules was as good as his word and, using oars as fenders they turned the ship around and unfurled fully the foresail to disappear around the bend in the river. *The Swan'* was gone in a flash.

As they walked through the gate Livius noticed that Cassius was waiting for him. "Good to see that you are all safe and I can see from the girl that there is a story."

"Ah yes, Morag. Get Julius to look after her. I think she might be intimidated by the rest of us and get the Greek doctor from the Batavian fort to have a look at Macro. The capsarius did a good job but he fell foul of Morwenna."

Cassius showed the shock on his face, "His mother?" Livius nodded. "He knows?"

"He knows."

"Sentry, go to the Batavian fort and ask for the Greek doctor. Metellus, good to see you, can you take the girl to Julius Longinus?"

"Will do. Come along Morag. You will see Macro later."

"I still can't get used to his new name."

"That is his real name."

Cassius shook his head in disbelief at the strange conversation. "Come to the Principia sir we can talk quietly there." He looked over his shoulder. "I assume Hercules has the letters."

"He does."

Once in the Principia Cassius just came out with it. "We have a spy in the camp. Aelius Spartianus."

Livius leaned back in his seat. "Are you sure? I know neither of us likes him but a spy?"

"You are too honest for your own good sir although I suppose being accused of treason when you were innocent would colour your judgement. No, we have evidence." Cassius explained about the trap which had been set and the evidence they had gathered.

"Any corroboration?"

"Two of his turma admitted that he met with people on the island but they didn't know why."

"Hm less guilty than the decurion but they are also guilty none the less. Now, this is difficult territory for me. I have never had to deal with such a serious case before."

"And me which is why I asked Julius for the options. If this is a dereliction of duty putting his colleagues at risk he would be beaten to death by the ala. If this is treason then he would be put into a bag of snakes and thrown into the river."

"That's it?"

"According to Julius, yes and he is normally right."

"I take it we have no snakes?"

"No snakes sir," although a serious matter Cassius could not help but smile.

"I am not sure I want the bastinado for him. But I don't want a crucifixion either and strangulation is normally reserved for leaders and generals so I guess it will have to be the bastinado. First things first let's get the sentencing out of the way." He went out to the sentry. "Officer's call," The buccina sounded. "I won't order a man to beat someone to death we will ask for volunteers."

"And if there are too many?" Livius looked horrified. "He is not a popular man."

"Then we draw names."

The officers all came in to the small office wondering what it portended. Those who had not been in '***The Swan'*** had a slight idea but the others were in the dark.

"This is a formal meeting and I will try to be brief. We are going to pass sentence upon a traitor, Aelius Spartianus. Adjutant, could you fetch him?" The decurions looked uncomfortable. Most were new and none, including Metellus and Cassius, had ever had to sentence a fellow officer, even one as nasty as Spartianus.

When he was brought in, hands bound behind his back, he had a wild and savage look in his eyes. "You have no..."

Cassius roared, "Silence! You will be told when you can speak. This is a courtesy which you do not deserve but your commanding officer is a compassionate and caring man." Aelius snorted but wisely kept his counsel. "You are charged with treason. You did conspire with deserters and the enemies of Rome to bring death to your fellow troopers and to endanger the state. Have you anything to say?"

Arrogance returned to Spartianus. "You have no proof."

Cassius smiled a mirthless thin-lipped smile. "We have the testimony of your turma that you deviated from your patrol route several times to leave and pick up items from the island upstream. We have testimony from two of your confederates, who will be punished later, that you met with two deserters, Wolf and Quintus and passed on information. We have evidence from a fellow decurion that you attempted to leave a message for your paymaster in order to ambush the Decurion Princeps. Now, have you anything to say?" His face became ashen as it drained of blood. He slowly shook his head, he seemed incapable of speech.

Livius stood and said to the decurions. "How do you find your fellow officer guilty or not guilty? Left hand for not guilty and right hand for guilty." Slowly every hand that was raised was right. "Decurion Spartianus I sentence you to death by the bastinado." The decurion slumped to the floor in a dazed heap.

The next day, before breakfast, the twenty men selected from the two hundred who had volunteered were assembled with cudgels and sticks they had acquired themselves. The two members of Spartianus' turma who had helped him were strapped to wheels awaiting their flogging and The Fist was trying to make himself as small as possible.

How he had evaded the punishment he had no idea but he thanked Aelius' loyalty and silence in his prayers to the Allfather. The deposed decurion was brought out, his eyes angrily scanning those who were to kill him. As he was tied to a stake in the middle of the parade ground his eyes sought out The Fist and when he found him his eyes bored into those of his confederate. He mouthed the words, 'Kill them all' and waited until the thug nodded. He looked up at Livius. "When you come to Hades watch for me for I shall be waiting."

Cassius nodded and the twenty men went silently to work breaking his legs, his feet, his arms, his knees. His cries screamed over the fort like a flock of angry seagulls. His ribs were shattered and they started on the head. The screams suddenly ceased. Within a few moments, all that was left was a bloody pile of skin and broken bones. The two men waiting for their flogging suddenly looked heavenward to thank the Allfather for sparing them that.

"A warning to others. The punishment for treason or dereliction of duty is death. Death to all traitors." The whole fort echoed the shout and across the river, the Batavians wondered what their comrades in the nearby fort were doing.

Epilogue

The Emperor sat with Julius and Attianus in his private quarters, finally relaxing after his long and exhausting journey from the east. He had shed his stained travelling clothes and the three of them had shared the baths and were now enjoying iced white wine in the cool of the evening. "It is these little pleasures one misses. Clean clothes, pleasant company and chilled wine."

"The east is secure then?" Attianus showed the pressure of running the Empire in Hadrian's absence. He was relieved that the weight had been taken from his shoulders.

"As secure as it will ever be Attianus. I know that there will be many who say I gave away all of Trajan's gains but we were being bled dry there in the dusty and empty desert and I have secured the trade routes as well as creating buffer zones defended by new allies. No, the east is secure for now. We can now build up the finances to help us with the frontier in Germania. I intend to go there once I have sorted out the Senate."

"Good luck there then sir. I would rather face a horde of barbarians than those backstabbing, work-shy wasters." Julius had learned the hard way that life on the frontier did not prepare you for the dirty world of politics.

"So Julius you do not have a high opinion of your peers?"

"I think I spent too long with warriors who were real men, honest, loyal and Roman to the core, even though they were born in the provinces."

"Good Julius because I have another job for you. I have recalled Bradua and the new governor of Britannia is Quintus Pompeius Falco. A sound man and he will make a good Governor."

Julius nodded, "A good man."

"He has my instructions but I would like you to go with him and prepare the work for building *limes* across Britannia. Livius has done a good job already and he has some good ideas. Once I have sorted Germania out then I will join you. You can take the Sixth. They are a good legion. Base them at Eboracum and use vexillations from all of the legions and the Classis Britannica to survey the area. I want camps building along the border to house the legions and I want Livius to keep it safe with his cavalry. If the tribes do come south I want legionaries to face them as well as the auxiliaries. Now, are you up to it? I know you are no longer a young man."

216

The Last Frontier

Julius smiled for since he had met up with Livius in Rome he felt younger and more invigorated than he had for years. "I would be honoured and I thank you for the trust you have in me."

"No Julius the events in Rome and Britannia have shown me that those who can be trusted should be given complete trust."

Even though it was the depths of winter Livius had given permission for Marcus and his turma to escort Morag and Macro to the farm. Marcus had made Macro much happier and, as Metellus had pointed out, Morag seemed as keen on Marcus as she had once been on Macro. Marcus, for his part, was flattered that such a pretty girl took an interest in him. As they approached the farm she turned nervously to Macro. "I can still have that horse?"

Laughing Macro said, "When the weather is better I will have Cato take you to his stud and you can choose your own."

"Who is Cato?"

Marcus looked at Macro, "Let us say he is just another one of the extended family of Marcus' Horse."

Under his breath, Macro said back to Marcus, "Which is getting bigger by the day."

The guards had seen them approach and Gaius, Ailis and Decius were there to greet them. Ailis went straight to Macro and hugged him tightly. She held up his injured thumb, now healed and kissed it. Embarrassed he pulled himself away. "Mother, father this is Morag Princess of the Dumnonii and we would like her to be our guest."

Ailis embraced the girl. "Of course." Livius had sent a messenger as soon as they had landed and the fact that she was really a hostage made clear to Gaius and Ailis. Livius knew that the bird would be in a cage but it would be a large and gilded cage and she would not know.

Marcus looked at his father who glanced down at the sword hanging from his hip. "We heard about the use you put the sword to. I am glad that you listened to my words."

"I always listen to your words and speaking of words, where is your wife, good Decius, and my nephew, Marcus?"

Macro snorted, "You mean nephew Macro."

"You are both wrong. My son Gaius Ulpius Aurelius is being nursed by his mother but I will take you to pay your respects."

Across the seas in Manavia Morwenna and her daughters were gathered around a fire and a pot. Morwenna looked older than she had but she was now focussed on a new mission. They held a small doll with a sword and a shield. "Now Mother, help us destroy this man." In their hands they had sharp needles. The pain, now symbolic, would become real and Morwenna was determined that Macro and the bitch who had fled with him would suffer such torments as nightmares are made of.

The End

List of characters and places in the novel

Those names in italics are fictional

Ailis-Gaius' wife
Anchorat-Morwenna's acolyte
Angus-Votadini bodyguard
Appius Sabinus-Quartermaster
aureus (plural aurei)-A gold coin worth 25 denarii
bairns-children
breeks-Brigante trousers
Brynna-daughter of Morwenna
Burdach-King of the Dumnonii
Capreae-Capri
capsarius-medical orderly
Caronwyn-daughter of Morwenna
Coriosopitum-Corbridge
Danum-Doncaster
Derventio-Malton
Deva-Chester
Din Eidyn-Edinburgh
dominus-The master of a house
Drusus Graccus-Decurion
Dumnonii-A tribe from the west lowlands of Scotland
Dunum Fluvius-River Tees
Eboracum-York
Eilwen-daughter of Morwenna
First Spear-The senior centurion
Gaius Metellus Aurelius-Ex- Decurion Marcus' Horse
Gaius Saturninus -Regular Roman Decurion
Glanibanta-Ambleside
Gnaeus Turpius-Camp Prefect Corio
groma-surveying equipment
Gwynfor-One of Morwenna's chiefs
Idwal-One of Morwenna's chiefs
Julius Demetrius-Senator
Julius Longinus -ala clerk
limes-Roman frontier defences
Livius Lucullus Sallustius-Sallustius' nephew

Luguvalium -Carlisle
Lupanar-The red light district
Maban-Morwenna's acolyte
Macro-Son of Macro
Mamucium -Manchester
Manavia-Isle of Man
Marcus Appius Bradua -Governor of Britannia
Marcus Aurelius Maximunius-Former ala commander
Marius Arvina-Camp Prefect Morbium.
Mediobogdum-Hardknott Fort
Mona-Anglesey
Morbium-Piercebridge
Morwenna-Fainch's daughter
Neapolis-Naples
oppidum-hill fort
Parcae-Roman Fates
phalerae-Roman award for bravery
Porta Decumana-The rear gate of a fort or camp
Scipius Porcius-Prefect at Eboracum
Seteia Fluvius-River Mersey
Surrentum-Sorrento
Taus-River Solway
Tava-River Tay
Tinea-River Tyne
Tole-Son of the King of the Selgovae
Trajan-Emperor of Rome
Traprain Law-Capital of the Votadini
uncia-Roman inch
Vedra-River Wear
vicus (plural-vici)-the settlement outside a fort
Vindomora- Ebchester, County Durham
Vinovia- Binchester, County Durham
Viroconium -Wroxeter

Historical note

Lucius Quietus was a real senator who was arrested and executed along with four other senators after Hadrian became Emperor. It was on the orders of his guardian Attianus who was ruling Rome in Hadrian's absence. The real reason may have been that they opposed Hadrian and questioned the legitimacy of his rule but I have created the fiction that he was plotting to become Emperor himself. Hadrian became Emperor in 117 and then went to Britannia in 122. As work had begun on the wall already I have used the device of Livius as his agent to do so.

Trajan did die in Selinus, later called Trajanopolis, of edema (dropsy). His wife confirmed that Hadrian was to be his successor but some of Hadrian's opponents said that this was after Trajan's death and was not sanctioned by him. It was also said that Hadrian had left Selinus already. The Empress may have done as Hadrian's enemies said but I cannot believe that the Emperor would have kept Hadrian so close if he did not wish him to continue his work in making the Empire safe. Hadrian's first acts as Emperor were to pull Rome out of Mesopotamia and make Armenia a Roman client state of Parthia.

The *limes* were the defences erected by Trajan and Hadrian along the border with Germania. They were made of wood and turf. Hadrian's Wall was a more substantial stone structure which was intended to mark the beginning of the Roman Empire rather than its extremity. It was originally covered in plaster and painted white. It would have stood out quite clearly in the green open spaces of northern Britannia and been a symbol of Rome's power rather than a sign of its weakness.

There was a unit around the wall at the time the book is set. It was the 2nd Sabinian Wing of Pannonians named after one of their officers, Sabinus. I have merely substituted Livius Sallustius as the officer after whom the ala was named. Marcus Appius Bradua was appointed by Trajan but only spent a short time in Britannia. As soon as Hadrian returned from the east he was recalled and replaced. History does not give us a reason.

The punishments inflicted were as stated. It does beg the question what did they do if they didn't have snakes? Perhaps they were more common in the past. The bastinado also seems a fairly brutal punishment but as the men's lives had been put at risk, perhaps not too extreme.

Above all this is a work of fiction. The only writing we have is from the Roman side either Tacitus who, as Agricola's son in law, was a little biased or Aelius Spartianus the biographer of Hadrian writing two hundred years after the events in the book. Even the evidence for the Romans in Britain is sketchy, a few inscriptions on walls and tombs. The truth is, apart from the legions we are not certain who did what and when- as a writer this suits me! If I have offended anyone I am sorry for the offence but not the story.

Griff Hosker July 2012

Other books by Griff Hosker

If you enjoyed reading this book, then why not read another one by the author?

Ancient History

The Sword of Cartimandua Series
(Germania and Britannia 50 A.D. – 128 A.D.)
Ulpius Felix- Roman Warrior (prequel)
The Sword of Cartimandua
The Horse Warriors
Invasion Caledonia
Roman Retreat
Revolt of the Red Witch
Druid's Gold
Trajan's Hunters
The Last Frontier
Hero of Rome
Roman Hawk
Roman Treachery
Roman Wall
Roman Courage

The Wolf Warrior series
(Britain in the late 6th Century)
Saxon Dawn
Saxon Revenge
Saxon England
Saxon Blood
Saxon Slayer
Saxon Slaughter
Saxon Bane
Saxon Fall: Rise of the Warlord
Saxon Throne
Saxon Sword

Medieval History

The Dragon Heart Series

The Last Frontier

Viking Slave
Viking Warrior
Viking Jarl
Viking Kingdom
Viking Wolf
Viking War
Viking Sword
Viking Wrath
Viking Raid
Viking Legend
Viking Vengeance
Viking Dragon
Viking Treasure
Viking Enemy
Viking Witch
Viking Blood
Viking Weregeld
Viking Storm
Viking Warband
Viking Shadow
Viking Legacy
Viking Clan
Viking Bravery

The Norman Genesis Series
Hrolf the Viking
Horseman
The Battle for a Home
Revenge of the Franks
The Land of the Northmen
Ragnvald Hrolfsson
Brothers in Blood
Lord of Rouen
Drekar in the Seine
Duke of Normandy
The Duke and the King

New World Series
Blood on the Blade
Across the Seas
The Savage Wilderness
The Bear and the Wolf

The Last Frontier

The Vengeance Trail

The Reconquista Chronicles
Castilian Knight
El Campeador
The Lord of Valencia

The Aelfraed Series
(Britain and Byzantium 1050 A.D. - 1085 A.D.)
Housecarl
Outlaw
Varangian

**The Anarchy Series England
1120-1180**
English Knight
Knight of the Empress
Northern Knight
Baron of the North
Earl
King Henry's Champion
The King is Dead
Warlord of the North
Enemy at the Gate
The Fallen Crown
Warlord's War
Kingmaker
Henry II
Crusader
The Welsh Marches
Irish War
Poisonous Plots
The Princes' Revolt
Earl Marshal

**Border Knight
1182-1300**
Sword for Hire
Return of the Knight
Baron's War
Magna Carta
225

The Last Frontier
Welsh Wars
Henry III
The Bloody Border
Baron's Crusade
Sentinel of the North
War in the West

Sir John Hawkwood Series
France and Italy 1339- 1387
Crécy: The Age of the Archer

Lord Edward's Archer
Lord Edward's Archer
King in Waiting
An Archer's Crusade (November 2020)

Struggle for a Crown
1360- 1485
Blood on the Crown
To Murder A King
The Throne
King Henry IV
The Road to Agincourt
St Crispin's Day

Tales from the Sword

Modern History

The Napoleonic Horseman Series
Chasseur à Cheval
Napoleon's Guard
British Light Dragoon
Soldier Spy
1808: The Road to Coruña
Talavera
The Lines of Torres Vedras
Bloody Badajoz
The Road to France

The Lucky Jack American Civil War series

The Last Frontier

Rebel Raiders
Confederate Rangers
The Road to Gettysburg

The British Ace Series
1914
1915 Fokker Scourge
1916 Angels over the Somme
1917 Eagles Fall
1918 We will remember them
From Arctic Snow to Desert Sand
Wings over Persia

Combined Operations series
1940-1945
Commando
Raider
Behind Enemy Lines
Dieppe
Toehold in Europe
Sword Beach
Breakout
The Battle for Antwerp
King Tiger
Beyond the Rhine
Korea
Korean Winter

Other Books
Great Granny's Ghost (Aimed at 9-14-year-old young people)

For more information on all of the books then please visit the author's web site at www.griffhosker.com where there is a link to contact him or visit his Facebook page: GriffHosker at Sword Books

Printed in Great Britain
by Amazon

59686485R00137